ROBYN CARR

A FAMILY AFFAIR

mira™

ISBN-13: 978-0-7783-3380-7

A Family Affair

For questions and comments about the quality of this book, please contact us at CustomerService@Harlequin.com.

Mira
22 Adelaide St. West, 41st Floor
Toronto, Ontario M5H 4E3, Canada
www.Harlequin.com

Printed in U.S.A.

Recycling programs for this product may not exist in your area.

Praise for the novels of Robyn Carr

"Brimming with insight, tender sensuality, sympathetic characters, and family anxiety, this story blends painful realities with healing love in a strong, uplifting tale that will lure both women's fiction and romance fans."

—*Library Journal*, starred review,
on *The View from Alameda Island*

"This is well-crafted women's fiction, where the emotional journey is paramount, and the satisfying focus on Lauren's innermost feelings and thoughts does not disappoint."

—*BookTrib* on *The View from Alameda Island*

"This novel of sisters and secrets has a pleasant setting, a leisurely pace, and a sweet story line for Krista that will please fans of Carr's Virgin River series. Themes of responsibility, forgiveness, and the agony and ecstasy of female relatives will appeal to readers of Debbie Macomber and Susan Wiggs."

—*Booklist* on *The Summer That Made Us*

"The summer flies by as old wounds are healed, new alliances are formed, and lives are changed forever... With strong relationship dynamics, juicy secrets, and a heartwarming ending, it's a blissful beach read."

—*Kirkus Reviews* on *The Summer That Made Us*

"A satisfying reinvention story that handles painful issues with a light and uplifting touch."

—*Kirkus Reviews* on *The Life She Wants*

"Insightfully realized central figures, a strong supporting cast, family issues, and uncommon emotional complexity make this uplifting story a heart-grabber that won't let readers go until the very end.... A rewarding (happy) story that will appeal across the board and might require a hanky or two."

—*Library Journal*, starred review, on *What We Find*

Also by ROBYN CARR

Sullivan's Crossing

THE COUNTRY GUESTHOUSE
THE BEST OF US
THE FAMILY GATHERING
ANY DAY NOW
WHAT WE FIND

Thunder Point

WILDEST DREAMS
A NEW HOPE
ONE WISH
THE HOMECOMING
THE PROMISE
THE CHANCE
THE HERO
THE NEWCOMER
THE WANDERER

Virgin River

RETURN TO VIRGIN RIVER
MY KIND OF CHRISTMAS
SUNRISE POINT
REDWOOD BEND
HIDDEN SUMMIT
BRING ME HOME
  FOR CHRISTMAS
HARVEST MOON
WILD MAN CREEK
PROMISE CANYON
MOONLIGHT ROAD

ANGEL'S PEAK
FORBIDDEN FALLS
PARADISE VALLEY
TEMPTATION RIDGE
SECOND CHANCE PASS
A VIRGIN RIVER CHRISTMAS
WHISPERING ROCK
SHELTER MOUNTAIN
VIRGIN RIVER

Grace Valley

DEEP IN THE VALLEY
JUST OVER THE MOUNTAIN
DOWN BY THE RIVER

Novels

SUNRISE ON HALF MOON BAY
THE VIEW FROM ALAMEDA
  ISLAND
THE SUMMER THAT MADE US
THE LIFE SHE WANTS
FOUR FRIENDS
A SUMMER IN SONOMA
NEVER TOO LATE
SWEPT AWAY (formerly titled
  RUNAWAY MISTRESS)
BLUE SKIES
THE WEDDING PARTY
THE HOUSE ON
  OLIVE STREET

Look for Robyn Carr's next novel,
The Friendship Table
available soon from MIRA.

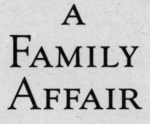

A
FAMILY
AFFAIR

ONE

Anna McNichol gently grasped her mother's bent, arthritic hands. "I don't know what I'm going to do," she said. "I will be alone forever."

Blanche was eighty-five and in assisted living but she was on the facility's wait list for their full care because her health was slipping and Anna knew memory care was just around the corner.

"You have me, though I'm not much use anymore, and you have your children, though they're your children and you're supposed to clear the way for them, not the other way around. I think at the end of the day, we're all alone, aren't we? We all have to stand on our own no matter how many people surround us. I guess you'll have to be strong. Like you have always had to be."

"Weren't you ever scared?" Anna asked Blanche.

"I was always scared," Blanche said. "But what are you gonna do? Quit? What good does that do?"

"I'm not sure how to go forward from here," Anna said.

"And yet go forward you will," Blanche said. "Because there's really no choice about it."

The truth hit her at her husband's funeral. That's when Anna became suddenly and painfully aware of that thing she'd been missing, that reality. When she saw the pregnant woman with one of the assistants from her husband's office she knew. All she was lacking were the facts.

The woman looked so young, not yet thirty. Maybe thirty-five if she was very young looking for her age. She was poised and distant, not mingling. There was a radiance about her, that motherly glow. The assistant, whose name Anna did not remember, escorted the woman. Anna watched as they greeted a few people, made a couple of introductions and then they stayed back.

Could it be or was Anna imagining things? She was filled with guilty doubt—of course she was being reactive.

But no, she was sure. That woman was carrying her husband's child. The temptation to go to her and introduce herself and ask her how she had known Chad was strong, but just then Jessie, her oldest daughter, touched her arm and said, "We're supposed to be over here." And Anna had nodded and followed her.

Anna and Chad had been going through one of their serious rough patches. She thought it was about the fourth noteworthy one in thirty-five years and she had insisted on counseling. Of course *she* had. Chad was a psychologist. He counseled people for a living and he knew all the tricks. According to what she knew from friends and what Chad had told her, that number of marital disruptions over several decades barely surpassed interesting. Few marriages even lasted that long these days. She knew only too well that marriage was a rocky road and it had nothing to do with how smart or simple, how successful or religious, you were. She also knew, from personal experience, that just because you were an expert in relationships, it didn't necessarily give you an edge on keeping your own marriage healthy. So, they'd been struggling, had been seeing a counselor, dealing with Chad's overall discontent, something vague and filmy. He wasn't happy. He was feeling unfulfilled. He was bored and his life lacked excitement. He was seeking something *more*.

Fitting, then, that he died while white-water rafting. Bet that was exciting.

It was as if Chad was having a giant midlife crisis, a tad late for a man of sixty-two. He kept asking, *Is this all there is?* Ninety-eight percent of the population would give an arm and a leg to live as they did. But since Chad was often melodramatic and moody, she let it slide. Is this all there is, indeed? Perfect health, great and successful work, good retirement savings, strong family ties, quality friends? *Yes, Chad, this is it. Why isn't that enough for you?*

As Anna had come to realize, this is what a man does when he's attracted to another woman. Act like you've been suffering. Suddenly find your life and your marriage are severely lacking. It's not your fault and you must have been unhappy for years and years, so the obvious solution is to move on. Get yourself something new. Wait, correction—your wife must have failed somehow and now you should find another, better woman. God forbid you honor your commitment and stay with a woman you find slightly less than perfect! The number of times in her life she had heard it said of the unfaithful husband that there must have been something missing at home; it all made her want to throw up. And now she was here to honor the great man's wonderful life.

During the service, Anna turned around a couple of times to see if the pregnant woman was emotional. Remarkably, she didn't seem to be. She appeared serene. Maybe that wasn't Chad's baby swelling her middle. Maybe she was a client? The assistant with her…what *was* her name? She was older and kept leaning toward the younger woman's ear, whispering.

"What are you looking at?" Jessie asked. "Don't stare!"

"Sorry. You're right. I'm just so tired."

Tired from spending days putting together a video montage from old photos for Chad's celebration of life, making funeral arrangements, selecting an urn for his ashes, making phone calls, choosing a dress, hiring a caterer, so many details. And on top of all that, not sleeping. But she'd done it, compiled their memories, the very best ones, and did what she did best: she made him look like a god. Like the perfect husband and father. Which he was not, but let's not speak ill of the dead.

Unless his pregnant girlfriend came to the funeral. That was a good enough reason.

A firm hand pressed down on her shoulder and she turned to look up into the dark eyes of Joe, her friend for over thirty years. Chad's friend first, then their friend, then couple friends, until Joe and Arlene divorced. Never just her friend, though she'd always loved him as much as Chad had. He was a great guy. She hugged him, holding on extra long. "How are you doing?" he asked.

"I'm okay," she said, longing to talk with him for an hour or six. "This is more grueling than it looks. Emotionally taxing."

"I can imagine."

Just then all of her children surrounded them. Joe hugged Jessie, who, at thirty-one, was a beautiful woman; then twenty-eight-year-old Mike, who was the image of his handsome father. Joe then turned to lovely Bess, short for Elizabeth, the baby at twenty-four. He didn't hug Bess because she didn't like being touched without warning. After a moment passed, Bess opened her arms to him and everyone nearby visibly relaxed.

There was a little small talk—sorry for your loss, call on me for anything, if there's any way I can help, if there's anything you need—all that sort of thing. For Joe these were not empty offers. Anna knew he would deliver if needed.

Chad had been widely loved and why not? He was great fun, smart, funny, had a tongue smooth as silk and always knew the right thing to say. Anna was equally well loved and respected. As a couple they were popular and often envied—they were attractive, successful, entertaining and stable. In fact, if their circle of friends had any idea what shit they'd been going through lately, they'd be shocked. But they were careful to keep their issues to themselves.

Joe was one of the few men who was on par with Chad personality wise, equally successful. He was a devoted friend. Chad had gone to high school with Joe; they'd played ball together and stayed friends through college, though their paths had diverged. Chad taught and then got his master's in counseling followed by a PhD; Joe got his PhD and taught history and some theology at Stanford. The men only saw each other a few times a year but both always said it was as if no time had passed. They could still laugh like boys. Anna saw Joe less often than Chad did but with her the feeling was the same.

The celebration of life was not held in a funeral parlor or church but rather in a fancy clubhouse in an upscale Mill Valley community. It was furnished with comfortable sofas, chairs, small round accent tables, thick carpet and carefully chosen art. Its primary purpose was for hosting parties. Residents in the community could rent it for events, which Anna had done. There was a huge viewing screen upon which the pictures of Chad's life played, a hundred and fifty of them, carefully and lovingly chosen by Anna with a little help from the kids. Every picture had Chad in it, starting from old childhood prints she'd inherited from Chad's mother years ago. She'd glance up to see one of him in a high school football uniform looking the worse for wear with a big grin on his dirty face; she caught a huge blowup of their wedding picture; there was one soon after of him with baby Jessie asleep on his chest. There were many pictures of Chad alone, a few of Chad and Anna, one of a young Anna gazing lovingly up into Chad's face, several family groupings. The focus was Chad, his life, his accomplishments, his achievements, his happiness, a few of the important people in his life. Chad, Chad, Chad. Just like before he died.

Things had been tense lately, but she remembered those younger years fondly because, although it hadn't been easy, they had been deeply in love. They met through what can only be described as fate, as destiny. In fact, their meeting was a legendary family story. Anna had been in San Francisco, shopping on her lunch hour down at Fisherman's Wharf. Shopping but not buying, which was typical for her as she had been and still was very frugal. She loved the sea lions, enjoyed watching tourists, sometimes found bargains at Pier 1, enjoyed the occasional meal on the pier.

On that day, something strange happened. She heard a panicked cry rise from the crowd of tourists on the pier, saw a food truck trundling across the pier without a driver, picking up speed. A man in work clothes and an apron was chasing the truck. She only had seconds to take it in. It seemed the food truck, its awning out and moving fast, was headed toward a group of people. Right before her eyes the truck knocked a man off the pier before the truck was stopped by a barricade. The man, completely unaware, flew off the dock and into the water below, startling a large number of fat sea lions who had been sunning themselves nearby.

The sea lions scrambled into the water and the man

was flailing around in a panic. Someone yelled, "He can't swim!" Hardly giving it a thought, Anna dropped her purse, kicked off her shoes and jumped off the pier, swimming to the man. Getting to him was no challenge; she practically landed on top of him. But he was hysterical and splashing, kicking and sputtering. "You're okay, come on," she said, grabbing his shirt by the collar. But he fought harder and sank, nearly pulling her under with him.

She slapped him in the face and that startled him enough he could let himself be rescued. She slid her arm around his neck and began pulling him to the dock where a couple of men seemed to be standing by to pull him in.

There was a lot of commotion, not to mention honking noises from sea lions. Anna was shivering in her wet clothes and all she could think at the time was how was she going to locate a change of clothes for her afternoon at work. Then there were emergency vehicles and a handsome young police officer draped a blanket around her shoulders and took a report. The near drowning victim was taken away in an ambulance and Anna was given a ride to her apartment by the cute policeman. She was delighted and surprised when the police officer called her a week later. She almost hyperventilated in hope that he'd ask her out.

"The man you pulled out of the water has been in touch. He wants your name," the officer said.

"He isn't going to sue me, is he?" she asked.

"I don't think so," he said with a laugh. "He seems very grateful. He won't have any trouble tracking you down but I said I'd ask. He probably wants to thank you."

The man's name was Chad. He was finishing up his PhD at Berkeley while she was working in a law office in the Bay Area. She was twenty-three and he was twenty-seven and she was not prepared for how handsome he was and of course much better put together than when he was dragged out of the water.

He took her to dinner and, as she recalled, their first date was almost like an interview. He wanted to know everything about her and was utterly amazed to learn she'd had a job as a lifeguard in a community pool for exactly one summer when she was a teenager and yet jumped in to save him with total confidence. They fell in love almost instantly. The first time they made love, he asked her to marry him. She didn't say yes right away, but they knew from the start they were made for each other. What they didn't know was how many fights they'd have. Very few big fights but many small ones; she thought of them as bickering. They fought about what was on the pizza; a scrape on the side of the car that was not her fault, not even remotely; what kind of vacation they should have and where they should go. As Anna recalled, they always went where Chad wanted to go. They fought about what movie to see, where to eat, what was grumbled under his or her breath.

They fought seriously about his affair. That was in the distant past but it took a long time to get over. Years. But when they finally pledged to stay married, to do their best to make it good, they fell into bed and had the best sex of their lives. And they had Elizabeth.

That experience was how she knew that all the excuses for this current marital rift, no matter what he called it, was probably about another woman and not them growing apart or having divergent needs. He wouldn't admit it and she had no proof, but she had better than average instincts. She believed he'd gotten all excited at the prospect of falling in love and was rewriting their history to make that acceptable. He was looking for an excuse that would make it reasonable to step outside the bonds of marriage. She could feel it; he'd been involved with someone else.

Or maybe she hoped that was the problem because another possibility was more impossible for her to fix. He had seemed very angry with Anna, and she had watched that anger slowly build for the last three years. Ever since Anna had been selected to fill a vacancy on the Superior Court bench. He had sneeringly addressed her as *your honor* several times. Chad, she suspected, was jealous.

There was also the fact that Anna disagreed with him on political issues. He complained she didn't show enough respect for his opinion. She complained that he didn't listen to what she was saying, acted secretively. He didn't think she was trying hard enough to be attractive; she'd put on a little weight and he said that showed she didn't care. They'd lost their sexual edge and hardly ever had sex anymore. She couldn't do or say anything right. At least the kids were no longer living at home. Anna and Chad had been at odds for about six months.

"Admit it, we have little in common anymore," was one of the last things he said before leaving on his trip.

"Over thirty years, three children and quite a lot of history," she had replied. "Not much, I suppose."

So he booked a trip he said would help him clear his head. "When I get back, we should have a serious talk about our future," he said. "We might have a lot of past but that doesn't mean we have to be stuck in it. I'd like to sort out a few things."

People kept streaming into the large room, many of whom Anna didn't know. She was acutely aware that some would be clients of his, people who would never see him outside of the office except for an occasion like this. In fact, some of his clients might find themselves in a crisis, having their counselor die suddenly.

There would be a program, of course. While the pictures were rotating on the big screen, there was soft music playing. The bar was open but the food wouldn't be brought out until after the speaking was done. They all agreed it should be brief and not open to those who hadn't been asked to speak. Get it over with, Anna had said, and then people will either stay, eat and mingle or bolt, as is their preference.

"Ladies and gentlemen, if you'd take just a moment to freshen your drinks or grab a cup, we'll be toasting our departed friend one more time after a brief tribute from his family," Joe said. "Find yourselves a comfortable place to sit. I believe I received the honor of opening this program by virtue of the fact that, other than Chad's siblings, I've known him the longest. I first encountered him in the eighth grade and while months and sometimes years separated us, we've managed to keep up with each other ever since. It's been such a privilege to call myself his friend."

Anna glanced over at Max Carmichael, the doctor who was the director of the counseling practice where Chad had worked for twenty years. Max not only offered to preside over a testimonial, he had clearly expected to be the one to do so. But the truth was Chad had hated him.

It was going to be Anna and the kids and Joe. Each one of them was going to tackle an important aspect of Chad's character, deliver a short summary of love and devotion. Of course they couldn't decide who did what without almost coming to blows, and at the same time Jessie was the only one who actually wanted to speak. Poor Mike was really hurting and it showed; he was Chad's only son and they were very close. And little Bess, his baby, was shattered. The subjects to choose from were fought over like two dogs and one bone. Bess didn't have a dog in that fight; she had made up her mind on what she wanted to say.

I'll do integrity, Jessie had said.

I thought I'd get that one, based on his coaching and sports training with me, Mike argued.

Well, if I can't have integrity, then I should get loyalty, Jessie said.

And so on.

Anna was thinking that after six months of adversarial marriage counseling, she had begun to question her husband's integrity, his failed honesty and lack of loyalty, so she just ignored the squabbling. She was going to talk about how nonjudgmental and open-minded

Chad was, how much he was able to help his clients with his tolerance. She was being the bigger person because in truth she was furious with him. After all, she had begged him not to go on the damn rafting trip he was not qualified to take on. At the time of her begging she had wondered if it was really a rafting trip or rather a lovers' getaway.

Instinctively she looked around the room for the pregnant woman. She didn't see her anywhere.

Jessie delivered her testimony dry-eyed and powerful, sure of herself. She spoke of his integrity, though that had not been her assignment. Mike, not so dry-eyed, did the same but added loyalty and talked about how Chad had been a great leader and how much people depended on him. Elizabeth, soft-spoken but clear-eyed, opined on the way Chad could accept people even when they were very different from him. And she should know—she had a mild form of autism and Chad had been her champion, pushing her into therapy that helped her function better and learn acceptable socialization, which probably saved her life. It was the one area in which Anna had been jealous of him. As a mother, she had always wished to be the one to save Bess from the stresses of Asperger's syndrome.

Finally Anna spoke of his commitment to those he loved.

She was fifty-seven and at no time in her life had she felt old and alone. Until now. Her husband wasn't coming back. Not even the dissatisfied Chad who didn't know what he wanted or what it would take to make him feel fulfilled; not even the worst parts of Chad were coming back.

Anna ended her short tribute by inviting her guests to stay as long as they liked, to eat and drink and laugh, as that would do Chad honor. Joe returned to the podium to propose a toast to Chad and a life well lived.

Finally, Anna could relax somewhat. She could visit with her guests, have another glass of wine. She didn't have to take care of anyone now; her elderly mother, Blanche, had not attended and was still safe at the assisted living facility. Chad's brother, Scott, his wife, and Chad's sister, Janet, and her husband were all heading straight to the airport by limo in about an hour.

"Almost over," said the raspy voice of Phoebe in her ear. Phoebe had been one of her closest friends since college and was now her clerk of court. Phoebe had arranged the catering for the celebration of life. "Would you like me to come over after this?"

"You don't have to," Anna said. "I'm not fragile. And I really need to get some sleep."

"Okay," Phoebe said. "I'll give you a call later to check in so just turn off your phone if you're resting. How about the kids?"

They had rushed to her side, each for different reasons. Elizabeth had needed her comfort in the confusion of her father's death, Mike needed someone to commiserate with and Jessie needed someone to acknowledge that it was all about her. Jessie was most like her father but not quite as charming. "I'm hoping they're ready to go back to their homes, but of course I'll leave that to them. Bess has already fled to the comfort of her apartment where no one will upset her routine and I think I might need to be alone."

"Then I will be nearby just in case you change your mind about that," Phoebe said.

There was a large gathering for the celebration of life. Chad's colleagues and hers had come and there was no cross-pollination among them. There were longtime friends and neighbors and friends of the kids. They all seemed to want to stay forever and she wasn't sure how long they actually did because, after four hours, she said a few farewells and went home. She was the bereaved widow and was allowed to do this. For once in her life she didn't worry about playing the perfect hostess.

She went home, Jessie in tow, and put on her jeans and a bulky sweatshirt. She put clean white socks on her feet while Jessie packed up her overnight bag.

"Are you sure you're all right to be alone?" Jessie asked.

"I think I need to be," Anna said. "No offense and I appreciate all your support, but I'm worn out and done with this extravaganza. I need a little quiet time to re-group. Phoebe might come by later, though I told her I wanted some alone time."

Mike came by the house and asked, for probably the third time, if she was sure she should be alone. "Are you sure *you* should be?" she asked.

"I'm okay," he said. "And I haven't seen Jenn in three days except at the funeral. Or whatever that was."

"Celebration of—"

"Yeah, yeah, I know what it was." He kissed her cheek. "Call me if you need me."

"Thanks, Mike. You're a good son."

She'd been home about an hour when the doorbell rang and she took a deep breath, hoping it wasn't going to be anyone high-maintenance. It was Joe.

"I should have called," he said. "Before I drive all the way back to Menlo Park I wanted to be sure you're all right."

"I'm all right," she said. And because it was Joe, she said, "Would you like to come in for a while? Maybe have a coffee before your drive?"

"If you're sure," he said. "It's normal not to know exactly what you want right now."

"Oh, I know exactly what I want," she said, holding the door wider. "I want to know *why*!"

Anastasia Blanchette Fallon was raised by her single mother, Blanche Fallon. She used to tell people she was named for Blanche DuBois from *A Streetcar Named Desire*, but the play was actually written several years after Blanche was born. Anna's mother was fierce, independent, stubborn and a little rough around the edges. She had worked in every imaginable job but mostly as a waitress and, when Anna was older, a bartender, as well. She usually had two jobs since there was no husband or father or family to help them. And now Anna looked after her mother. Blanche was plagued by varicose veins, arthritis and out-of-whack discs in her back, reflective of a life of hard work on her feet.

When Anna was young Blanche used to say, "You want to have legs like mine? No? Then study."

Although her mother's legs were appalling to her,

that wasn't her motivation as much as fearing she'd get pregnant, be abandoned with a child and live a life of grueling hard work and long hours. She realized early that education was her best way out of that kind of life. She studied hard, but it became a lifelong quest to not become her mother.

Anna actually admired her mother very much—Blanche was fearless, feisty and unfailingly loyal. But Anna wanted more for herself. Security, for one thing. Enduring love. An above-average existence, for another. She and Blanche had managed on a very low income and Anna was determined that her adult years would be more comfortable than her mother's had been, especially if there were children. It was that goal that kept her from getting mixed up with the wrong guy. In fact, it kept her from getting involved with any guy! Her dating experience became a never-ending battle when she wouldn't have sex. But damn it, she wasn't about to do what her mother did and be trapped for want of an orgasm!

And that is how Chad McNichol won the lottery—he had everything she was looking for in a mate and she fell for him. Even though she was twenty-three, she presented him with her virginity and he thought he'd taken a trip to the moon. On the spot he wanted to marry her. Urgently. Desperately. And she wanted to marry him just as badly. He was well educated, came from a good family, had no big debt and had a good reputation. Plus, he seemed kind. There were quite a few ex-girlfriends and even one former fiancée in his past but he was twenty-seven. And handsome. What else should one expect? There were no ex-wives or police records, a positive sign.

They planned their lives so everything would work out perfectly. Anna had a good job as a legal secretary in a successful firm of criminal lawyers and Chad was a counselor in a small mental health clinic in San Francisco while he was finishing his doctorate in clinical psychology. They had a fairy-tale wedding, then a baby girl and three years later a baby boy. Anna was deliriously happy despite the fact that she worked through two pregnancies and took a three-month leave for each baby. But when Mike was a new baby, she almost got divorced. She caught her perfect husband in an affair with a woman whose identity she never learned. He wouldn't tell her who it was but admitted he'd been involved. He deeply regretted it, swore it was over and wasn't inclined to end their marriage on account of it. Especially since they had two small children.

Oddly, Blanche and Chad's family joined forces to urge them to work it out, a challenge not for the faint of heart. They limped along for a few years, always on the brink of separating. In all honesty, if Chad hadn't been so determined they stay together and try to make it work for the sake of their children, Anna would have thrown in the towel. How could she ever trust him again? How could she ever feel adored again? She hated him so mightily she wanted to kill him.

Instead, she took the LSAT and applied to law school while he was working and the kids were small. She was determined she would not be left a penniless divorcée with no prospects. It was hell, law school while mothering, but she did it. Against all odds. Nothing can motivate a young mother like the fear of being left penniless with a family to raise.

Then it was the boost her achievement gave her ego and brought her up to the finish line, to a place of confidence where she could either leave him or give him another chance. She decided he'd been good and faithful for a few years and had earned another chance so she let herself fall in love with him all over again, and along came Bess.

There were a few times after that reconnection that she doubted him, wondered if maybe he was sliding away from her, but she dismissed her doubts. Chad had always needed a lot of attention, but he responded well to adoration, so she obliged. He also needed to give a lot, so if she fussed over him, he would kiss her shoulder while she brushed her teeth, pat her ass while she rinsed the dishes, lay his head in her lap while they watched TV. She told him he was like a Labrador puppy, always looking for approval and a good petting. A few sweet words and he worshipped her again. That was the balance they struck for the rest of their marriage until recently.

"With Chad, it was never enough," Anna said to Joe. "Did you know we were in counseling?"

Joe sipped his coffee. "I hadn't talked to Chad in quite a while," he said. "That didn't come up. But it wouldn't surprise me. Chad, being a counselor, had people in therapy at any excuse. I think it was a favorite pastime of his."

"This time he was talking of being unfulfilled. He

was depressed, not sleeping well and said he was in a crisis because he wasn't ready to get old. Telling him it was just a state of mind didn't work."

"I'm sorry," Joe said. "I didn't know."

"That's what the rafting trip was about. It was about living life to the fullest, having adventure and excitement before it was too late. Frankly, I thought that was ridiculous and I'd be more likely to believe it was an affair. I suppose it was not, since he died. Rafting. Sort of."

"Sort of?"

"The coroner said it was a heart attack followed by drowning. I'm told it isn't uncommon. Especially for men who wanted to prove something, like that they weren't getting too old."

"He was sixty-two," Joe said. "In good health and great shape."

"Not great enough shape," she said. "He always needed a lot of reinforcement. There was a young pregnant woman at the service. She looked about thirty. She didn't seem to know anyone."

Anna just waited, silent.

"Surely not," Joe said.

"Would he have told you? If he was having an affair?" she asked.

"I don't know," Joe said. "He didn't, if that's what you're asking. He shared a few sensitive things he described as confidential but they had a lot to do with work. He thought we had some of that in common. Therefore…"

"You wouldn't tell me?" she asked. "Even now?"

"I wouldn't break a confidence, even though Chad isn't with us now. An oath is an oath, don't you think? I'd keep a confidence of yours past death."

She just stared at him for a moment. She sipped her coffee. "How bloody admirable."

"Why don't you tell me what you think has happened," Joe suggested.

"His malaise and complaints began about a year after I took the bench," she said. "Chad has never been comfortable with my success. It made him needy. And I should admit—there comes a point when I just can't endure it and turn into a bitch."

Joe merely smiled. "And the young woman?"

"I don't know why she'd be there unless she had an important connection to Chad. And I may never know what that is," she said.

"Chad had his issues, as we all do, but I never knew him to chase young women."

"He was a crazy flirt!" Anna protested.

"Flirt, yes, but that's not the same as an affair. And with a young woman? I don't know, Anna. It's possible, but I don't know... I can honestly say, without breaking a confidence, I knew nothing of a situation like that. I have no advice. I'd help if I could."

"I've been too busy to even go through his desk. I checked his text messages, but I didn't have time to do a thorough look. The kids were here and we were so busy with arrangements."

"Are you sure you want to know?" he asked.

"Yes," she said. "Absolutely. Because he put me through a lot the last six months with all his discontent and frustration that life just wasn't enough for him and then he *died*. Leaving me to wonder if I'd failed. If it was somehow my fault."

"No! Anna, no! Listen," he said, setting his cup on the coffee table even as he scooted to the edge of the sofa, leaning toward her. "Everyone is in charge of their own happiness. Responsible for their own coping. Happiness is largely a choice. And everyone goes through periods of discontent, but they work through it or make major changes. But unless you're abusing someone it is not your fault. And I know you weren't abusing Chad."

"The opposite," she said. "We had a system. All he needed was to have his way. Since he hardly ever needed me to trade off attention to my kids or my career for his happiness, it was easy. If that was what we had to do to make the marriage last, to make it work, it was easy. I'm a good sport. And then there's the fact that when Chad is happy the very sun shines brighter." She took a sip of her coffee. "I kind of hated him for that." Then she smiled and said, "The widow should not be drinking coffee."

"Wanna do shots?" he asked, grinning.

TWO

Anna's kids responded very differently to the loss of their father, but then they were very different kids. Jessie was brilliant and beautiful and very high-maintenance. Anna and Jessie got along well about half the time. The other half was often a struggle. Anna liked to think Jessie got that touch of narcissism from Chad but she hadn't seemed to inherit Chad's charm. Chad might have been all about Chad but he used his gifts well; he had charisma and magnetism. He knew how to win people over. That was very important in counseling. He gained the trust of his clientele immediately. Jessie, an internist, was often praised as a wonderful doctor who went the extra mile for her patients. But with her family, she was a lot of work.

Unsurprisingly, she was angry about her father's death. "You should never have let him do that trip," she had scolded Anna.

"What makes you think I could have stopped him?" Anna had returned.

So, Jessie was not so secretly blaming Anna for Chad's selfishness and death. She hadn't come right out and said so, but it was there.

Mike, middle child and only boy, was an angel. He was all charm with very little self-centeredness. Where Jessie was often hard on Anna, Mike was soft on her. He seemed to think he should try to take care of her now. Anna appreciated his love for her to the point of tears. Mike and Chad also had a great, close, affectionate and mutually supportive father-son relationship, but Anna and Mike had a very special bond. He was her protector and defender. He had no partner yet, rather a parade of beautiful and smart young women who wanted that job. He'd been dating Jenn, a lovely young woman, for a few months now and Anna hoped, as she had before, that it would last. One day soon he would commit, and Anna knew that while he would always love her devotedly, his passions would move to a wife who would step into the role of first female. Mike was a high school health teacher and part-time coach who wanted to be a full-time coach. And the sudden death of his father had left him in a puddle of tears—he was such a tender, vulnerable soul.

Bess was a brilliant loner who carried the weight of Asperger's. Emotionally, she struggled. Her emotions were sometimes flat and at least minimal. She reacted pragmatically to her father's death and seemed astonished by emotions she didn't normally feel. Her tears of grief seemed to confuse her and her response was typical anxiety. Fortunately, she was willing to take antianxiety medication for such situations and appeared calm and even-tempered in the aftermath of Chad's death. But Anna was at a loss as to how to act and what to expect. Bess was severely introverted, didn't want to be touched, formed very few relationships. As a toddler, she didn't want to be fed; she grabbed at the spoon so she could feed herself. She operated on sheer logic. She didn't seem to need anyone. Anna constantly worried about Bess's loneliness, for no one could communicate with her as Chad could.

Anna brought a crystal decanter to the living room and placed it on the cocktail table. She pulled two shot glasses from her pockets. She went back to the kitchen for two tall glasses of water. Then she sat beside Joe and poured. "Tequila," she said. They clinked glasses and tossed them back. Anna wheezed and coughed; Joe smiled.

"He left behind a lot of unfinished business," Anna said.

"Doesn't everyone when they die?" Joe asked. "When is it okay to go?"

"When you're one hundred and five and there's no possibility you'll be needed for anything else or that you have any explaining to do. There is something to be said for having your affairs in order. Chad didn't."

"If you don't mind me asking…"

"Something was going on with him, something to make him inexplicably unhappy. Yet he never worked through it. He left many questions." She lifted the delicate decanter and poured them each another shot.

"Remember when you were expecting Jessie? He was

overwhelmed. Kind of quiet and sweet and pitiful, he was so happy. So vulnerable."

She didn't answer. "Remember when I decided to go to law school?" she said. "Mike hadn't been potty-trained yet, Jessie was in preschool, I had to quit my job, money was a terrible problem, childcare was nearly impossible, and I went, anyway. He was furious with me."

"Why did you go to law school?" he asked. "I mean, besides the fact that you're brilliant and ambitious."

"I don't think I was those things," she said. "It was after Chad's affair and I was afraid that I was going to be abandoned. I had something to prove. To myself and to him. He accused me of being selfish, of not putting the needs of the family first. Said the man who stepped out on his pregnant wife! Where had he put the needs of the family when he had an affair? Remember?"

"How could I forget? In fact, if we had had cell phones back then, I might never have known. I called your house phone, asked if Chad was around, and you blurted it out, that you didn't have any idea where he was because you caught him in an affair. You accused him, laid out your proof, and he admitted it."

"Did you ever find out who it was?" she asked him.

Joe shook his head. "I admit, I didn't ask."

Not for the first time, Anna wondered how men did that. Decided not to ask, decided not to wonder.

Twenty-eight years ago, when Mike was a baby and Anna was exhausted, Chad had developed a pattern of not being where he said he would be, running late all the time, getting strange phone calls that he tried to pawn off as clients, perfume on his shirt, just the most obvious stuff in the world. She needled him constantly until he admitted he'd met someone, a colleague, he said, that he'd had a brief fling with and regretted it and it was over. It would never happen again, unless Anna kept harassing him. She couldn't stop, though. Then he said, "Fine, do you want a divorce? Because I won't fight you on it."

They were overwhelmed by bills and debt, could barely make the mortgage payments, which was why Anna kept working. She was afraid to leave him or let him go. Her worst nightmare seemed to be coming true, becoming an impoverished single mother like her own mother had been. It was a dark and painful time, betrayed and isolated as she was, when out of the blue Joe called and asked for Chad and on the brink of despair she asked him if he knew. She sobbed and dumped it all on Joe and Joe encouraged her to try to patch things together for the sake of their children.

"And I decided right then and there I was going to have to build something for myself and my kids that was a little more substantial than being a legal secretary, because if he cheated once, he'd cheat again. I was never aware of another affair, however."

"Ah, so you might suspect, but…" Joe said.

"All the signs were there. After all these years. After I sucked it up and did everything I could to make it work."

"It was a long time ago, Anna. A lot of water over the dam. It was probably just a midlife crisis."

"He was sixty-two! How the hell long was he expecting to live?"

Joe lifted his glass. "Much longer than he did. It took a lot of strength for you to get over it and make a good life, a good marriage."

She just stared at him as if he was insane. "What makes you think I got over it? I never got over it. I've been looking over my shoulder for almost thirty years!" She sipped her drink carefully. She didn't want to scorch her throat again.

Joe threw his back.

"Arlene and I couldn't hold it together," Joe said of his ex-wife. "Do you ever hear from her?"

"Never," Anna said. "Do you?"

"A little," he said. "It's about the kids or the grand-kids and is mostly confined to texts or the occasional email. Arlene and I were not meant to be. The divorce, though painful, was destiny. We got off to a bad start. I have two great kids and a couple of beautiful grand-daughters. But I thought you and Chad invented mar-riage. In spite of all you'd been through."

"Because I'm a good sport, that's why," she said. "And because everything I ever said about him, about us, made him look like a king. Or at least a benevo-lent despot."

And in a way it was true. For years she acted as if it didn't hurt her that he'd stepped out, found another woman and cheated. She knew exactly what it took to make him feel loved and special and she delivered, whether she felt it was irrelevant. She let it go that he was bad at remembering special occasions, that her feel-ings were less important than his.

"It seemed you loved him very much," Joe said.

"Of course I loved him, but that wasn't the reason I put so much energy into trying to make a decent marriage. It was my commitment. I didn't expect that he'd never grow old, never get sick, never have issues. I didn't take for granted that we'd be in love every day. Hell, there were days I hated him and I assumed he had those days, too—isn't it inevitable? I stayed, anyway. It was Chad who was the part-timer. When it started to get challenging for him, he was always weighing the advantages of leaving. I, on the other hand, never saw any advantage in leaving. Until his latest depression. It was the last straw for me. He had everything and yet he complained. He was ungrateful. He kept saying something was missing, as though it was my job to figure out what that was and deliver it." She shook her head. "But if he had come home in a better frame of mind... We were usually distracted by discussions of our competing schedules, some major repair or purchase we had to talk about, or if one of the kids had a problem."

"Amazing how easy it can be to not talk about it, isn't it?" Joe said.

"Thirty years of practice will do that for you," she said.

"And yet, you never considered a life on your own terms?"

After a quiet moment, she said, "Because I did love him. I did. But—"

Anna's phone chimed with a text. *Are you okay?* Phoebe was asking.

Perfectly fine, thanks, Anna answered.

Good. If you don't need me, I'm staying home. Headache. If you need me, call.

Go to bed, I'm fine. Talk to you tomorrow.

She took a breath. "No one knows this but Phoebe.
And now you. His last struggle with unhappiness co-
incided with my appointment to the bench. That had
become a pattern. If I had something to be proud of, he
became very needy. I was planning to suggest we live
separate lives. I thought it was time he figure out how
to be happy on his own."

"Whoa!" Joe said, shocked. "After all these years?"

"I love what I do," she said. "I've worked so hard to
get to this place. I'm only fifty-seven. And I'm tired
of always focusing on Chad's happiness. I thought it
was my turn…" A solitary tear ran down her cheek. "I
guess it is now."

Anna and Joe talked into the night. They got past
Chad's discontent and Anna's confusion about it and
covered all those years when their kids were young,
when they all got together for backyard barbecues or
day trips to the lake and one trip to Disneyland that
was a near disaster when Anna and Chad briefly lost
Bess and finally found her with a princess. She told
him about when Chad was helping Mike coach and
how proud she was of both of them. "I wanted to kick
him in the ass, but I didn't want him to die," she said,
another large tear spilling over. "Sorry, tequila tears."

"You should go to bed," he said. "And I need to borrow a couch."

"Nonsense. I have two guest rooms. Would you like to borrow a pair of Chad's pajamas?"

He made a face. "You will never see me in your husband's pajamas. I'll rough it."

"Take Mike's room. Mike put fresh sheets on the bed before he left and there's shaving stuff and new toothbrushes in the bathroom. I'll get the coffee ready, so if you get up first, just flip it on."

"Thanks, Anna. It would be stupid of me to try to drive back to Menlo Park."

"I wouldn't sleep at all, thinking of you doing that. I'll sleep a lot better knowing you're tucked away for the night." She started to leave the room, then turned back. "In all these years, this is a first. I don't believe you've ever stayed the night before."

"Not that I recall. I promise not to make a habit of it."

Jessie had had a lump in her burning throat all day and she was relieved to get home to her town house in Sausalito so she could let go and drain the emotions. Everyone expected her to be strong and she hadn't let them down but she didn't feel strong. She could act strong but sometimes it was so hard it made her just appear mean and cranky. She wasn't sure what was harder on her—her father's death or the fact that Jason hadn't even called her to see if she was all right. She had called him, told him about her dad, told him what arrangements were being made and invited him to the celebration of life. He said he might have to work but he'd try. They had lived together for two years; he'd gotten close to her family! They broke up a year ago but it felt like only yesterday in her mind.

He had not come. He hadn't sent flowers. And she was alone. So alone. Her brother had his girlfriend, Bess would prefer to be alone, her mother was exhausted and her grandmother barely knew what day it was and was safer with the ladies at the assisted living home. Jessie had no one. It had been a long time since she'd even had a really close girlfriend.

She threw herself on her bed and sobbed.

Successful medical doctors were not supposed to cry. So she thought; so she'd been told. She wanted to call Jason, but she didn't want to hear his voice mail, and of everyone in her life he was the one who most wanted her to "roll with it." He thought she was high-maintenance, always riled up about something.

Her poor father. She had no idea why he was so rest-less lately but she blamed her mother. Anna should have found a way to get to the bottom of whatever problem was troubling her dad; what if he was sick and keeping the fact private, suffering in silence? Anna should never have let him go on that stupid rafting trip!

Her cell phone chirped and she looked at the screen on the phone. Her heart nearly sang. It was Jason! She had longed for him the past few days; she'd left him a couple of messages and he texted his replies, but this was him!

"Hello," she said thickly.

"Jess, how you doing?"

"I'm having a really hard time," she said. "You didn't even come to the celebration of life!"

"I'm sorry, Jess. We had an emergency. I was at the hospital until just a little while ago."

"What kind of emergency?"

"Femur and lots of other things. Car accident."

"Were you on call?"

"I was on call until noon, but the injury came in right as I was getting ready to leave so I handled it. It was pretty complicated and I wasn't the only surgeon there. More than one of us was needed—head, spleen and femur. It was bad."

"You could have at least called!"

"I'm calling you now!"

"You could have sent flowers or something."

"I was going to come but I had an emergency!"

"I really needed you!"

"Jess! Stop or I'll just hang up! You're doing it again!"

She didn't know why this happened to her, why she got so angry and defensive and caustic when all she wanted in the world was Jason's soft, sweet voice, the one he used to calm patients and soothe their families. Better would be his arms around her, comforting her. She just wanted everything to be all right. She wanted to feel safe and protected and given a guarantee that nothing would fall apart.

"Sorry," she said. "I'm just having such a hard time."

"Listen, you should think about talking to someone. Sometimes you push people away. You have this damn short fuse and sometimes there's no explanation for it. I told you I had to work. I'm sorry I couldn't be there for you but we broke up. Remember? And why did we break up? Because I can't deal with your temper. No one can ever do enough."

"I said I was sorry! You'd think you could afford me a little extra patience since my *father* just died!"

There was silence. A long moment that stretched out. "I'm so sorry for your loss, Jessie. Find some support. I'll check on you in a few weeks."

"A few *weeks*? Can't you even say, *If there's anything I can do*...? Because I can think of about twenty things you could actually *do*! A *few weeks*? Where is the love, Jason? You could at least—"

But he was gone. She'd done it again. Some devil inside of her caused her to lash out and drive away any offer of affection. She always felt a little hungry, as if the portion she was fed was just not enough. If she had dinner with a friend, she'd want to go clubbing afterward, then maybe stop off for a nightcap, then make plans for the next night or at least the next weekend. Because it was never enough.

And now her dad, her hero, was gone and she didn't know how she'd live without him. His love, his praise, sustained her. Her mother constantly let her down by being busy all the time. You'd think that Jessie, being one of three internists in a San Francisco office, would understand being busy, but then she didn't have a husband and three children as well as a demanding job. Besides, Mike and Bess took up a lot of Anna's attention and Jessie often felt left out. If she was honest, even if Anna gave Jessie all her attention, it might not be enough.

So she cried and cried. Why didn't Jason come back

to her, to love her and be devoted to her. She'd been so happy.

But had she? She couldn't remember any longer. It seemed she'd been very happy but too briefly. Maybe she should talk to someone. And say what? That no one loved her? It was too bleak to even think about.

Anna thought the most difficult and grievous part of getting her life back on track was probably going through her husband's personal belongings and letting them go. That, she thought, would dredge up feelings of loss and saying a painful goodbye, but through the whole process she was as dry as a bone. She dreaded the paperwork of becoming the single adult in a formerly coupled household—the death certificates mailed to everyone from the insurance carrier to the Department of Motor Vehicles, having the house put in her name alone and closing bank accounts.

She couldn't have been more wrong. All of that took her a couple of weeks and the first of May was on the horizon. The worst part came as a complete surprise. Her attorney informed her, "The will you have in your possession is not Chad's most recent will."

"What?" she said, sure she had misheard him.

"Chad updated his will a few months ago and made a couple of changes."

"Without saying anything to me?" she asked, gobsmacked.

"His changes don't affect you monetarily."

"Then what did he change?"

"I'd rather we do this in the office," he said.

"Larry, come on! You've been our lawyer for thirty years! Spit it out!"

"He added a recipient but nothing you held jointly is affected in any way."

"Who?"

"Anonymous for the time being, until said recipient chooses to reveal their identity."

"A mistress!" she blurted.

"Not a mistress," Larry said without missing a beat.

"He went behind my back and named some secret recipient? How could he do that?"

"He could leave his share of the estate to a house for homeless cats if he wanted to. As I said, this will not affect what you inherit, and in all fairness, you could have done the same thing. In fact, now that you're a widow and on your own, you can do anything you want with your inheritance."

"Then what does it affect?"

"The half of retirement funds and savings that go to the kids. Instead of being divided into thirds, it will now be divided into fourths."

When they were younger, when the kids were younger, everything was left to the surviving spouse or, in the event Anna and Chad perished at the same time, the totality of the estate was to go to the kids. When the kids were all over twenty-one, they divided it differently. They left the bulk of their joint holdings to each other but divided half of their individual retirement funds, 401(k)s and such, among the kids. Anna did not have to worry about money. She worried about the identity of that anonymous recipient.

Like a jet engine was lodged firmly in her posterior, she began tearing through Chad's personal things. They each maintained their own checking accounts and retirement accounts, but she had access to both and didn't see anything suspicious. They had decided, years ago, to each name their estate attorney as the executor and administrator of the will. When they'd done that, the kids were still in school and didn't want anything that complicated and time-consuming to fall on their shoulders, plus they'd been close friends with Larry Merton for many years now and trusted him implicitly.

She went through every pocket, every section of every wallet, the briefcase he couldn't part with after many years, his sporting equipment and backpack, even his fold-up tent. The only thing she didn't have access to was his work laptop, which went to a colleague who would take over his counseling cases. What information about his clients might be contained therein was sensitive and confidential.

Would he have left thousands of dollars to a client?

The will would be settled quickly; there would be no probate as everything was tied in a nice legal bow but for that one outstanding item—the unknown identity of one recipient. She was not usually left at a complete loss, but this time she certainly was. She would have to tell the kids, but she wasn't sure how.

"You don't have to tell them anything," Larry said. "All that's necessary is that you inform them that their father left them a portion of his estate in an irrevocable trust. I'll draw up the papers, give you the amounts, and they can either get their own legal representation or

I'll help them transfer the money into their savings or checking or investment accounts. It's generous but not big enough to trigger an inheritance tax. I'm also not obligated to tell them how much has been left to you nor am I obligated to tell them that there's an irrevocable trust, nor in what amount, nor who the trustee is. As a courtesy and with Chad's permission, I will tell you the trustee is a lawyer who has been commissioned to keep his client's identity secret. And that's all I can say."

Anna had practiced law for twenty years before being called to the bench and even though her specialty was criminal defense and not estate law, she knew Larry was speaking the truth and giving her the facts. The gathering of the family for the reading of the will was not the law; it was often convenient and it made a great motion picture scene. In fact, Larry would invite Anna and the children to his office to sort out the details. It was not necessary for them to even know there was a fourth recipient but Chad had, in the event of his untimely death, agreed that Anna should know, if they were still married at the time.

"I'm surprised by the wording," Anna said. "Right before leaving on his trip, I told him we should discuss separation when he got back. I haven't mentioned that to the kids. And apparently he changed his will before I brought up separation."

"He mentioned there was a bit of a kerfuffle between you," Larry said.

"Kerfuffle?" she barked out, laughing.

"Look, you and Chad logged on...what? Thirty-five years? There had to be at least once every five years you thought you were down for the count, yet worked things out and put it back together. If Chad hadn't died, this might have gone the same. I'm sorry, Anna. And yet, doesn't this represent a typical marriage? A few ups and downs, a few close calls? How many perfect unions are you aware of?"

She gave a huff of laughter. "That's your explanation? Or is that an excuse?"

"I'm just saying, of all the possibilities, this is hardly the worst case I'm aware of."

"Do you know who it is?"

"I do not," he said. "I told him how to put together an anonymous recipient."

"Did you *ask* him?"

"Yes, and he said, 'Then it wouldn't be anonymous, would it?' I was given the impression that it's the choice of the heir. This doesn't necessarily mean he has done something underhanded. It could be a charity. Or some otherwise needy individual."

"Unless you consider the fact that he's kept a secret from his wife, who also contributed to those retirement accounts this unknown person is receiving. And that it cuts into what my children receive. I expected better than this from you, Larry. If you can't be more honest with me, you should at least have tried to talk him out of this course of action. What if I sue?"

"Please don't do that, Anna. Remember, it's his money to do with as he pleases. He was of sound mind when he made up this final will, which isn't very different from the last will. Maybe he owed a debt and didn't want the family to know. Maybe it is a house for homeless cats. Let it be. And for your information, I did try to talk him out of taking this action."

"Oh?" she asked, lifting a brow. "Now why did you do that? Because today you're championing his actions."

"Because secrets fester," Larry said. "And I told him that it's been my experience that nothing good comes from secrets."

"You got that right."

It took roughly ten days to get the financials together and that was all. Chad had only been gone a few weeks and the late-April sun was warming the air and bringing out new blossoms, giving a feeling of renewal to the land. The accountant and the fiduciary who managed Anna and Chad's retirement and investment funds were working with the estate attorney to calculate the sums so they could move the money around and the inheritances could be paid out. Anna had already signed her documents approving the transfer of funds and now there would be similar paperwork for her kids. They would have to identify the means by which they would receive their funds.

Jessie had established an account for her retirement, savings and investing. Mike said he didn't have enough money to worry about such an account, and Bess said she was ready to do so and wondered if Anna's financial planner would take her on. They learned they each had an equal percentage that was just over a couple hundred thousand and of course they were very grateful and thrilled, but certainly would rather have their father.

"We last discussed this a couple of years ago after

Bess graduated and what your father and I were concerned about was how difficult it might be for you to get into a home of your own. Of course, what you choose to do with the money is entirely up to you, but your dad wanted to make sure you could buy a home if you wanted to. But we never considered the possibility of your father's untimely death. We were thinking by your late thirties... And I'm well aware you all have issues other than houses." Jess, for example, had some medical school debt, Mike had been living on a shoestring and had maxed a charge card and Bess...? Bess had started law school. The cost was staggering and she was managing on scholarships.

Anna had expected this meeting to turn into a circus but it was calm, quiet and somewhat melancholy. The only one who showed a threat of tears was Mike. He was so lost without his dad.

Larry explained what would happen. "Your father had a list of items he had special homes for, just a few. His car to his brother, his collection of antique books to his sister, his golf clubs and sporting gear to his son, his other book collection to his daughters and everything else to be dealt with by Anna."

"If there's something of your father's you want, just let me know. Take your time and think it over. I packed up his clothing but I haven't delivered it to a shelter yet. I just can't imagine you wanting any of his clothes, but if there's anything..." Anna said.

"Am I reading this right?" Jessie asked, holding up a page from the will. "You have sixty percent and we each have ten percent?"

"I guess that's right."

"There seems to be ten percent missing. Where is it?"

Larry cleared his throat. "Ten percent is to be paid to an irrevocable trust and the trustee is an attorney. I don't know the recipient and your father didn't name one. Just the trustee. It could be anyone or anything. It could be an undisclosed charity. It could be someone in need your father wanted to help. I honestly have no idea. This sort of thing isn't that unusual."

"Oh? Is it a secret?" Jessie asked.

"I suppose you could see it that way. Or it could be your father wanted to take a small amount out of his estate for some cause he supported..."

"But it's not small," Jessie said. "It's over two hundred thousand dollars! Mom?" she said, looking at Anna. "Do you know?"

"I don't," Anna said. "I admit, I'm curious. But it wouldn't surprise me if there was a client or needy family he knew about that he wanted to remember in the event of his death. His untimely death."

"Why would he keep it a secret?"

"I have no idea," Larry said. "He said it was a pet project that he wanted to remain confidential, then he added that he wasn't planning to die and so it would likely become irrelevant. I took that to mean he'd probably donate money before the next revision of his will."

"We often did that at the end of the year," Anna said. "Depending on how the taxes were looking, we might make a charitable donation to help out as well as bring our taxes down, but he didn't talk to me about this trust, either."

"Maybe we should contest this will, if only to learn where the money is going. It's a lot of money," Jessie said.

"It won't change the percentage you're getting," Larry said. "And there would be legal fees. Sometimes it's easier and cheaper to let the departed have their way. It is his money to disperse as he will."

"I realize that," Jessie said. "But that ten percent stands out like a pimple on a nose and I'd like to know what my father's intentions were and, if possible, why."

"Why don't I write a letter to the trustee, explain your questions and confusion and see what the response is. Before you consider dragging this out in a lawsuit, which will certainly deplete your funds."

"I don't care what he wanted to do with his money," Mike said. "It was his money."

"If Jessie wants to sue Daddy's estate, she's on her own. I won't go along with that," Bess said.

"Don't you want to know this part of Daddy's life that was secret?"

"People are allowed to have secrets," Mike said. "I can live with that. We know he wasn't a bad person."

"Mom?" Jessie asked, looking for support.

Anna took a breath. "I'm completely blindsided by this and I don't know what to do. Part of me thinks this might be something I don't want to know, another part wonders what the hell was going on. I'm conflicted."

"You must have suspected something," Jessie said. "You were always in his business."

Bess gasped, Mike grunted in disapproval. Anna sat silent. And Jessie cried. "I'm sorry. I didn't mean it in a bad way, but you two always communicated everything and I don't understand what was up with him. Why he decided he had to go rafting on one of the most dangerous rivers in the country! And leave a part of his estate to an unknown person! We should all want to know."

"It's not that unusual," Larry said, interrupting the tirade. "I have a client who disagreed with his wife politically—they both have large portions of their individual estates willed to the political party of their choice, the only way they had of getting even. I know of a man who has bequeathed part of his estate to a horse, ensuring said animal will be pampered into old age, though that's not confidential. Another client is bequeathing money to a person who helped him out of a huge gambling debt and no one, absolutely no one, knew he had a gambling problem, including his family. Whatever or whomever this small portion will go to, it's probably something Chad thought would create a problem or argument if disclosed. It's not something he wanted to share and I didn't press him because it's his money and his decision. He didn't need my approval. And he didn't need yours. Pursuing it could create more trouble than it deserves.

"Consider this," Larry went on. "Let's proceed with the will and disposition we have and think about the unknown factors. Give yourselves some time to think about it and discuss it. We can deal with it in a month or two."

Anna nodded gravely but what she really believed, at that moment, was that in a month or two his young pregnant mistress would have spent all of the money.

THREE

Jessie went to the hospital after leaving the lawyer's office because she knew exactly how to function on the job when clearly she did not know how to function in emotionally charged personal situations. She had come down hard on her mother and siblings when all she had really wanted was to understand what the hell had been going on with her father. And she wanted someone to put their arms around her, hold her, tell her everything would be all right.

She pulled into a reserved parking spot. There were three patients to check on, none of them critical. She could easily have passed on this errand. In fact, given her circumstances of grieving the death of a close family member, she had colleagues checking on her patients and they would continue as long as she needed them to.

She grabbed her bag, pressed the door lock and exited the car before realizing she was without her purse. The car was still running.

So much for her powerful memory and excellent coping skills. She hadn't turned off the Lexus, the key fob was in her purse, the doors were locked. Her phone was also in her purse. In the running car. She leaned against the car in equal parts exhaustion and frustration. She cradled her head in her crossed arms and just moaned, trying to figure out what to do.

It was probably only a minute. Then she felt a hand on her back.

"Jessie?" a male voice asked.

She looked up into the eyes of Patrick Monahan, a neurosurgeon with privileges at the hospital. Her luck was not holding out. Just what she needed was to look completely stupid in front of a colleague. All she could utter was, "Um…"

"What's wrong?"

"I, ah, didn't turn off my car, and my purse, phone and keys are locked inside."

He pulled out his phone. "I bet you have a service we can call. If you tell them the license plate number they can unlock the car remotely."

"Yes. You're right but… I can't remember. Shit, I should've read the manual."

"I'll call Lexus." He dialed up the number and she wondered…

"Do you have a Lexus?" she asked.

"No. Tesla. I searched it. Here," he said, passing her the phone.

She explained her situation and they suggested a few vehicle services; she recognized one and Lexus connected her. She gave them her name, cell phone number, license plate number—and within a minute, pop.

The door was unlocked. "Is there anything more I can do for you, ma'am?"

"Thank you, I'll be fine now."

She handed the phone back. "And thank you. I was a little rattled today. My father passed away recently and I just met with my family about the will. It was emotional. Distracting."

"I believe I heard something about your father," he said. "A rafting accident?"

"Yes. I have no idea why he was doing that. He never had before."

"I'm so sorry for your loss, Jessie."

"Thank you. Well. I thought I'd check on a few—"

"Anything urgent?" he asked.

"No, but I thought I'd—"

"Grab your purse, lock your car safely. Come with me and let's go get a taco. You've had a rough few days or weeks. A little social escape is a good idea."

"Surely you're too busy to—"

"Actually, I'm kind of hungry and there's this great place nearby, a hole in the wall. We can eat outside. Great food."

"I'm really not all that—"

"If you're not very hungry, pick at some nachos and have a beer. Then go home. I recognize the syndrome— you go to work because you don't know what else to do and you don't want to just hang out alone at home where there's nothing to do. Doctors tend to do that. But maybe you'll decide to talk about it. If not, that's all right. The tacos are great."

She had no idea why he was doing this. It's not as

though they had a relationship other than he was a physician at the same hospital.

"I've never ridden in a Tesla before," she said, strapping in.

"It's a complete indulgence," he said. "I couldn't justify it in a million years. I don't need it and I'm not rich. But for some reason just having it makes me feel younger and slightly more reckless, something I can't afford to be in my real life." It roared to life under her and she tipped her head back and laughed.

The spring air was so fresh and light; it was finally warming up and the flowers were popping out everywhere. In other parts of the country it had probably grown green and lush weeks ago, but in the Bay Area spring was a little more sluggish because of the cool ocean breezes and the clouds. It was a lazy sun but when it shone, like now, it was brilliant.

"I love this car," she said, caressing the dashboard. "Maybe it's time I had a new car. A fancy toy."

He pulled into a strip mall not far from the hospital, right in front of a restaurant with a sidewalk dining area surrounded by a wrought-iron fence and pots of geraniums. "Good. My favorite table is empty."

"Do you come here a lot?" she asked.

"Pretty often. I live alone and hardly ever cook. I go out or pick something up most of the time."

"You're single? I guess I didn't know that."

"Divorced for a few years. Doctors are horrible people to be married to, I'm told."

There was a pause as they got out of the car and walked to the café. "My favorite table is here," he said, grasping her elbow and steering her toward a table at the corner of the patio. They could be out of the way of the servers and other diners and have a good view of the sidewalk for people watching. "Since you're not hungry, can I order for us?"

"Of course," she said. Then she began to wonder about the propriety of splitting or picking up the check because right away she felt a little odd. Even though she didn't report to Patrick Monahan, he was a well-known neurosurgeon with a strong reputation at the hospital.

She liked him. He was pleasant and professional on the job; he was serious and focused. He treated people with respect, from the intern to the visiting specialist. She had never anticipated spending this kind of one-on-one time with him.

"Are you a beer girl or would you rather something else?"

"Wine," she said. "Chardonnay."

He ordered a beer and a chardonnay.

"Aren't you going back to work?" she asked.

He shook his head. "I'm not seeing patients today. I'm not even on call except that I'm always on call. I wanted to pick up some charts from my office. And you're not really seeing patients, are you? Just looking for something to do in which you feel competent. A death in the family can throw us off and we always go back to the place we feel like we know what we're doing."

"You know this how?" she asked.

"Been there," he said. And before he could say any more, the waitress returned with their drinks and waited for him to order. He asked for a small plate of loaded nachos, four soft tacos and a Mexican pizza.

She assumed he must be starving and didn't expect her to help him much.

"Do you want to tell me about your father?"

She didn't hesitate. "He was wonderful. He was a counselor, a psychologist. He helped so many people. And he was a devoted family man. I have a brother and a sister and he was completely there for us all the time. Something was going on with him lately. He was restless and searching, as if he hadn't done what he wanted with his life. That's what the white-water rafting was about—adding some adventure to his life."

"How did your mom take that?"

"She was mad at him for not being satisfied with all they had managed to achieve. She called him an ungrateful man-child. They were going to marriage counseling, and rather than being worried about him, my mother was pissed."

"But you were worried?" he asked.

"I was a little bit pissed, too," she admitted. "He wasn't himself lately."

"People get off-kilter sometimes," Patrick said. "Although I'm sure you were greatly affected by his mood, I'm also pretty sure it had nothing to do with you."

"That's what he said," she muttered.

"His death was an accident, I assume?"

"Sort of," she said. "He got in trouble in the kayak, flipped over and, in the struggle, had a fatal heart attack. They tried to revive him, but…" She sipped her wine. "It should not have happened. He was in great shape. He worked out. He had regular checkups. He never had problems with his health. I watched him for symptoms of— His health never concerned me. He was only sixty-two. It made no sense!"

"He hadn't been rafting before? Or steep climbing or running or similar strenuous exercise?"

She shook her head. "He went to the gym," she said. "He had a bike he rarely rode. He played golf and some tennis, but it was recreational stuff, not endurance stuff."

"But that rafting trip...?"

"Was extreme," she said. "He joined a group that was going down one of the most dangerous rivers in the country. I don't know what he was thinking. He wasn't trained for that, he wasn't prepared. I've since learned that it's not uncommon for people, men especially, to sign up for a risky and thrilling adventure or sport in a psychological quest to prove their youth isn't slipping away."

"Jessie, there's a very good chance you're never going to know what he was thinking," Patrick said. "Tell me what it was like growing up with him."

She described their first house, the one she remembered from her earliest days before Bess came along. It was like a dollhouse and her parents walked with her to preschool and then kindergarten and first grade. Her mother was very busy back then, when she was small. Anna was working and in school, while her father filled in with the kids, helping with homework and such. What she remembered best about those years was that Mommy was always too busy and Chad seemed to be able to find plenty of extra time. And once Mommy wasn't too busy, along came Bess and, soon after, the district attorney's office.

"Your mother was very successful, I take it," Patrick said.

Their food was delivered and they began to feed off the three large plates, while talking.

"She is very successful, but not in a showy way. I mean, she's not in politics in the city or among the society rich. In fact, not rich, that I know of. But after several years in the DA's office she went to a private firm that specializes in criminal cases because she is first and foremost a litigator.

"She likes being in the courtroom," Jessie said. "She often said the only person who could out-argue her was my father. That's probably because he was a psychologist and could read people. Fast."

"A power couple," he said.

"Yes," she said in a breath. "Yes, I guess they were."

"The only problem with being half a power couple is not knowing which half you are. The top half or the bottom half."

She thought about that for a moment. She wasn't sure who had the power in her family. Her mother was the one to fear; she didn't take any shit and she smelled a lie a mile away. But her father, Dr. McNichol, was the one people fussed over. He was active in city politics, charities, community affairs, that sort of thing.

"Do you have siblings?" she asked.

"I had a brother," he said. "He was killed in an accident when he was twenty-two, hit when he was changing a tire. It screwed up my parents and probably me, but I was in medical school and couldn't indulge even grief because of how consuming medical school is. I vowed never to be that kind of administrator, the kind who knows nothing about my staff and abuses them that way. I hope I've kept my vow."

"I think you have a good reputation," she said. "I mean, I hear only good things."

He laughed, maybe slightly embarrassed by the compliment. "I love hearing about your family. They sound so breathtakingly normal. My father left me on the little merry-go-round in front of the grocery store when I was four. He went home. I had begged and begged and begged to ride the pony. He was trying to remember everything he promised to get, gave me some quarters and forgot me. By the time he got back to the store, the police had been called. These days he'd have been locked up or Child Protective Services would have been called. Back then, they told him to pay closer attention and gave me to him."

"How times have changed," she said. "I'm almost afraid to have children."

He lifted a brow in curiosity and grabbed another nacho. "And who might you have these children with?"

Rather than getting all emotional over the thought of Jason, she simply smiled and said, "There is no candidate at the moment."

"Astonishing," he said. "Having a hard time narrowing it down?" he asked with a sly smile.

"No," she laughed. "I'm not seeing anyone right now. I broke up with a guy about a year ago and thought it best to go solo for a while. You know, get to know me. Me alone."

"Doctors are busy," he said. "We neglect ourselves sometimes."

"And make terrible partners," she tossed out, repeating what he said earlier.

"So says an ex-wife. Who, by the way, was also a doctor. If you ask me, she was the difficult one. No one asks me, however."

She laughed and asked him what his schedule was like and whether he had any time for hobbies or special interests. It turned out he loved sailing and fishing and biking through the countryside; that his schedule was usually packed but he made time for relaxation and exercise. He loved being outside when the weather was good. Jessie admitted she should do more of that. She'd been thinking about getting a dog. "I think maybe I'm alone too much. My favorite pastimes are reading, watching movies, going to art galleries, that sort of thing."

He liked movies, too, and they compared a long list of favorites.

Before she knew it they had talked about so many things it was growing late in the afternoon and they'd each had a second drink plus a couple of coffees. For someone who hadn't been hungry, she'd put a major dent in the food. "Look at the time," she said. "I've taken up your whole afternoon!"

"I didn't have any plans," he said. "I enjoyed myself. I hope you're feeling a little better."

"I am. I still have some things to figure out. My father left a small legacy. Some retirement funds and a few personal items and one mystery beneficiary who is anonymous. None of us has any idea who or what it could be." She explained the division of the will. "We're all guessing. I think maybe a client of his, a person he was counseling who could use a break. My brother thinks a scholarship for a young athlete. My sister doesn't care and my mother won't discuss it, she's so angry. But my mother swears she doesn't have any idea. I think she has an idea and I bet she thinks it's another woman or something and it couldn't be—my dad would never... If you haven't guessed, my mother and I can be like oil and water. I think the big thing we're all struggling with is whether to pursue finding out the who and why of this anonymous beneficiary or leave it alone and regard it as our dad's final wishes."

"As he obviously wanted," Patrick said.

"It's hard, though," she said. "No matter who or what, that means my dad had some kind of secret life, one that he wouldn't share with his family. If it's a needy person or charity or something like that, no one in the family would fight it. Not if that's what he wanted."

"I take it there's no letter or video or explanation?" Patrick asked.

"Nothing. He didn't even tell his lawyer. And the lawyer is an old friend, a guy Dad used to play golf with sometimes. He changed his will behind my mom's back, secretly, and didn't even tell Larry, who had to carry out his wishes."

"Maybe you should have a family meeting," Patrick suggested. "Just so you're all on the same page."

"I think I'll save that as a last resort," Jessie said. "I seldom agree with my mother, brother and sister. And they never agree with me."

About a half hour later they were pulling into the parking lot at the hospital.

"Thank you for rescuing me and for treating me to such a nice afternoon," Jessie said. "It was really nice of you. And I had a great time. Even though I talked your ear off about my dad and my family, it put me in such a better state of mind."

"It was a pleasure. I'm leaving the day after tomorrow for a conference in New York. I'll be back the end of the week."

"Have a great time," she said.

He went around the car and opened the door for her. He put out a hand to help her. "When I get back, if it's all right, I'd like to call you."

"Oh, thank you, but I'm sure I'll be fine now..."

He smiled lazily and she realized how handsome he was. "When I call I'd like to ask you out to dinner. Something nicer than a taco stand. You have several days to think about what your answer will be."

"A...date?"

"A date. If you're interested. I enjoyed the day and I think an evening out would be nice."

She was speechless. Her mouth hung open. Her eyes were probably as large as hubcaps.

"Forty-five," he answered to her unasked question. "And no, I'm not involved with anyone. I'm going to go to my office and get my files. Think about it."

"Yes," she said.

"I'll talk to you at the end of the week."

"I mean, yes, I'd like that," she said.

He smiled. "Good. Talk to you later, then."

It was part of Anna's routine to visit with Blanche every week. Sometimes twice if her workweek wasn't jammed. Anna and her mother were very close; after all, it had been just the two of them all of Anna's life. She talked to Blanche almost every day and made it a point to run her errands and visit her mother on the weekend.

Anna always brought a bouquet and maybe a book. On this Saturday she brought flowers and cookies even though Blanche wasn't supposed to have cookies. She was prediabetic and watching her sugar levels. She kissed her mother's papery cheek and hugged her close. Then she found a vase for her flowers.

It was always a relief to see Blanche. Blanche still had her nails manicured even if her fingers weren't perfectly straight and kept her hair colored bright red. It was teased and fluffy. She had her lipstick on, though she wasn't planning an outing. It was her habit. In fact, she was much flashier when she was younger and had toned it down quite a bit.

"Let me look at you," Blanche said. Blanche held Anna's upper arms and looked at her face. "I expected you to look better by now. More rested at least. How do you feel?"

"Okay," Anna said. "Having someone die is a lot of work."

"I'll try to go quietly," Blanche said.

"Try not to die, that would be better. How are *you* feeling?"

"Ach, just cranky. Have you talked to his family?" Blanche asked.

"I called his sister and she talked about herself for a while and how much she misses Chad, though I can't remember the last time she actually saw him. I think they spoke on the phone maybe five times a year."

"They put on a big show for weddings, funerals and graduations but the rest of the time were invisible."

Anna sat on the edge of Blanche's bed while Blanche sat in her leather chair with her feet up. Blanche reached out an old hand and touched Anna's cheek. "Are you sleeping?"

"I'm sleeping okay but all day long I'm distracted and it's hard to concentrate on work. I'm checking on the kids frequently, though I think they're getting comfort from their friends. They check on me a lot. I have a bunch of calls every evening. More than I want or need."

"Some people just won't go away after they die, if you know what I mean."

"Please, Mom. Don't start in on Chad..."

"I was trying not to speak ill of the dead but I'm very annoyed by Chad. At the end there he wasn't exactly good to you. He had a great life and a good wife and what did he do? He complained! The bugger."

"But we're not going to go there now, are we? Because he's dead and I've been remembering some of the good years. And there were good years. Many. And he was good to you."

"When it suited him," Blanche said. "He was uppity."

"He wasn't uppity. He was very accomplished, had a thriving practice, was active in the city and community, helped a lot of people… Tell me how your visit with the doctor was? Is your blood pressure okay?"

The look on Blanche's face was one of shocked surprise, which she immediately shook off, probably embarrassed by not remembering that she saw the doctor just a couple of days ago. Her doctor visited her at the home; he saw a lot of his patients at the assisted living center.

"Everything is fine," Blanche said.

Anna would make a point of asking the supervisor before leaving.

Ten years ago, when Blanche lived in her own little house and managed her own life, Anna would have told her about the will, about the pregnant woman she still suspected had some connection to Chad. They had been able to talk about anything. But in the last few years Blanche proved unable to keep a confidence and sometimes she'd mix up the order of events.

"I talked to Jessie just the other day," Blanche said. "She was going on about something at work, something about being at her office for twelve hours straight or something. And tell Mike to come by sometime, will you? I haven't seen that boy in months."

It hadn't been months. They were all together the day of the celebration of life for Chad, and Mike had driven Blanche home to her little efficiency apartment before all the guests arrived because large crowds tended to bring out the worst in her. But rather than remind her,

Anna just said, "I'll tell him. Have you heard from Bess?"

"I think she called last week. She still hasn't heard about law school, has she?"

She'd been in law school for a year, but Blanche clearly didn't remember that.

"All is well. Did you play mah-jongg this week? Or bridge?"

Blanche immediately launched into some of the same stories she told regularly. Her friend Joyce was having trouble with her son; he was threatening to take over her finances because she'd made a few small mistakes in her budget. She was certain that Karen was stealing food again; she thought that mean old woman stole everyone's food, and since none of them locked their doors and all of them slept like the dead, it was easy enough to do. "The ambulance came for Mr. Wilson, took him away, and he's been gone a long time. I don't think he's coming back." And Clarice was flirting with all the men. "She's disgusting," Blanche added. "What that wrinkled old woman wants with a man at this late date, I'll never know."

They chatted for about an hour, and Anna made them a pot of tea; Blanche couldn't have coffee or soft drinks anymore. Anna heard all the latest on the assisted living population and then began to make her way out. She kissed her mother's cheek again and Blanche said, "If you have time this week, will you check on Mrs. Rothage? I worry about her. I think she's very lonely."

It brought Anna up short. When Blanche had her own little house in Oakland, Mrs. Rothage was her neighbor. It had been years since Mrs. Rothage went to the nursing home. She had been dead for three years. But she said, "Sure. I'll let you know."

It broke her heart. Blanche was declining. She would not have to report back on Blanche's former next-door neighbor; Blanche would probably forget.

Anna's life suddenly flashed before her eyes. Wife, mother, widow and then she would become her mother. She had a sudden and desperate yearning to make the next years count.

Then she remembered that's what Chad had been talking about. Except he had never once said he'd like to live to the fullest with *her*.

FOUR

Anna had a great deal to get accomplished on her errand day. Before visiting with her mother she stopped by the dry cleaner, the watch repair, the hairdresser and the nail salon. After seeing Blanche she went by the grocery store and made a quick trip to Target for odds and ends for the house. When she turned down her street she saw Mike's big SUV parked in front of her house. The garage door was open and her big trash cans were sitting on the driveway.

He was cleaning out the garage.

She pulled into the driveway and got out. "Mike, what are you doing?" she called out to him.

He leaned the broom against the wall. "When I was here last week I noticed the garage probably hadn't been cleaned up in a while."

"Like a year," she said with a laugh. She grabbed her dry cleaning. "I should've called someone. I have help, you know. It's just a matter of getting it on the schedule. Bob Stone said to call him with anything I need. I did manage to get the landscaper to clean up the yard and flower beds and gutters."

"How's the pool look?" he asked, joining her at the car and helping himself to grocery bags.

"I'll get the pool cleaner to drain and acid-wash it, but it's not in bad shape. Not really. But…"

"But the patio furniture is pretty dirty," he said, toting four bags into the house. She noticed he wiped his feet before going in. When they got to the kitchen, he got busy emptying the grocery sacks. "I was planning on doing a little work in the backyard tomorrow so I'll power-wash the patio and furniture."

"I don't want you to spend your whole weekend working over here," she said.

"I'll be done by noon tomorrow. It's no big deal. I want to be sure everything is done. Everything Dad would've done."

She chuckled to herself. Chad probably would have instructed her to hire someone to do it because he'd rather play golf. "Are you going out tonight?"

"I don't have any plans yet, but it's early," he said.

"Would you like to stay for dinner? As you can see, I've been to the grocery store."

He lifted a head of romaine off the counter and shook it at her with a grin. "I've been cleaning the garage. I'll need protein. Or something."

"I can put together something hearty that you'll like. And I can rustle up a beer. No pressure. I don't have any plans, so if you want to stay, I'll cook. And if you don't, that's perfectly all right."

"I have a couple of hours left in the garage," he said.

"I really appreciate it, Mike. Especially you just doing it without asking."

He ducked his head a little shyly and grabbed a bottled water to take with him to the garage.

Anna didn't consider herself a great cook but she was certainly adequate and had managed to feed her family all the years they were growing up, even if sometimes that meant a casserole was left in the refrigerator for them to heat up.

There was spaghetti and meatballs in the freezer and one of Mike's favorites was spaghetti casserole. She defrosted it, then added cheddar and mushrooms and black olives to the casserole. Then she showered and cleaned up the kitchen and great room. She put out place mats, napkins and utensils; they usually didn't bother with a lot of fuss. She and Chad had eaten on TV trays for the last several years unless they had one or all of the kids join them. She found herself breathless with excitement for a couple of uninterrupted hours with her son.

When he was finally done in the garage, the casserole, along with garlic bread and a salad, using some of that romaine, was almost ready to serve. Mike went to his old room to wash up and came back wearing a clean T-shirt he'd found somewhere amid the stuff he'd left behind. Anna was so happy to see him she put her arms around him and he embraced her.

Her cheek against his firm chest felt so good. It was then that she realized how much she missed touching. This was going to be yet another adjustment she'd have to conquer, being alone now.

"You doing okay, Mom?" he asked sweetly.

"I'm getting by pretty well," she said. "There are a hundred adjustments. A hundred. I'm trying to figure out how to be the only person on the team—the cleaner, the bill payer, the investor, the worker, the shopper, the stocker of supplies, the list maker and the person who has to get things crossed off that list. Sometimes my head spins. I forget things—I guess I'm just distracted. And of course I miss talking to your dad."

Tears began to gather in Mike's eyes.

"Have you lost weight?" he asked.

"Let's sit and eat," she said. "Tell me about school. Tell me about Jenn."

He piled spaghetti on his plate. "Your weight?" he asked again.

"I think I have, but it's just the confusion and having no appetite and for some reason without your dad around I don't know what will taste good. So I have a bite of this, a bite of that, and then I lose interest." In the eight weeks since Chad had died she'd lost twenty-two pounds. "You know what Grandma said? She said I could spare it."

"How is Grandma?" he asked.

"The same. Cranky and more forgetful by the day. But they know at the senior center and she'll be moving over to the full-care facility soon. And to memory care as soon as there is room. Mike, tell me about you. How are you getting along?"

"I'm doing fine," he said, scooping food into his mouth. "I have trouble with the idea that he'll never be around again."

"I forget that sometimes and start to text him…" she said.

"I know!" he said. "It makes me feel a little crazy!"

"It's perfectly normal," she said. "I've heard people talk about it going on for years. I've even shouted down the hall for him, getting his name half out before I realize… It's strange."

"Are you okay with this will business? The ten percent to the unknown person or thing?"

"I'm not sure *okay* would be the best word," she said. "I want to know who, what and why, but then I always have those questions about everything. When you get down to it, it was part of my job to want to know, as a defense attorney and as a mother." She added a laugh so he would know she was taking the light side on this subject. "How about you? Are you okay with it?"

He chewed, swallowed and took a drink of beer. "I'm okay with it."

It gave her pause. "You really are?"

He shrugged. "It's his decision. His business. His money. If he didn't want it questioned… Yeah, I don't care."

"You truly don't care or you can decide you don't care because you think that's what your father wanted?"

"What's the difference?" he asked.

"There's a huge difference," she said, believing it to be accurate with every word. "You can have absolutely no interest to the point that if you found out the details, you might actually forget them because they're that unimportant. Or you can make an emotional decision not to pursue the answers out of respect for someone else's request. In this case, your father's."

He put down his fork. "God, you sound exactly like Jenn."

"In what way?" Anna asked.

"In the way that she thinks it's very weird that I can not care about something she finds so care-worthy and she doesn't get it. Maybe that's a girl thing. Ya think?"

Anna recalled there was a party once, a backyard thing. Just four or five couples. Three of the women had read a book in their book club about a woman who found a sealed envelope in her attic. It was in a box full of records—taxes, receipts, house records, legal correspondence. On the outside of the envelope it said, *To be read by my wife in the event of my death.* But he wasn't dead.

Everyone at the party weighed in on whether they would read what was in the envelope. What if it was written by a woman for her husband, would the men read it? To the last one the women said they would tear open that envelope and read the contents immediately. Likewise, none of the men wanted to know what was inside, not even Chad.

Chad said, "There's nothing in there I need to see."

One of their best friends said, "That couldn't be good news."

She told Mike the story. "Would you open the envelope?" she asked him.

"No way," Mike said. "It was sealed for a reason. Would you?"

"In less than a second," Anna said.

"Then it is a girl thing," he pronounced.

She laughed. "How is Jenn?" she asked. They'd been dating about six months and she was certain Jenn was very fond of Mike. She thought maybe this was the one.

"She's fine," he said, filling his mouth again. After a couple of moments he said, "I don't think things will go long-term with us."

"Really?" she said, shocked. "I guess I thought it was getting serious."

"Jenn is great. And I care about her, I do. But… I'm just not there yet. Something is missing. I don't see myself and Jenn being anything like you and Dad were."

Probably a good thing, she thought dismally.

"I'll know I'm with the right woman when I can see us being as good a married couple, as good as parents, as you and Dad."

She twisted spaghetti around her fork but didn't bring it to her mouth. "I'm not sure we were that great at either," she said. "You might be idealizing us a little. Maybe because of missing your dad so much."

"I know you had your issues sometimes, but you were a great couple and great parents."

Of course neither of them had ever mentioned the affair to the kids. Anna had told herself that if they had divorced and she had to explain one day when the kids were old enough to understand, she probably would have told them. But they put things back together and explaining was moot. If it didn't do anything positive, there was no point. She wondered how Mike would react if she told him now about their latest struggles and the fact that she was planning to suggest they separate and were perhaps heading for divorce. Would it break his heart even more? Or would it help him understand that relationships are never easy?

"Do you suppose that has something to do with you not being curious about your father's anonymous recipient?"

Mike shrugged. "I guess it could. I want to respect his wishes and his privacy. And also, what will it change? Will it make me happier? Sadder? Why open that envelope? The girls, though. They want to know. They think they have a right to know."

Anna was a little surprised. "Even Bess?"

"She doesn't stir things up much, but yeah—even Bess. Though you know Bess will do just about anything to avoid confrontation. But eventually Jessie is going to push you to try to find out."

"I doubt that will do any good," Anna said.

"Can't you contest or something?" Mike asked.

"Sure, if I want to build a case that I deserve that ten percent, which I don't. But even if I won the ten percent I might never learn the identity of the anonymous recipient."

"But you do want to know?" he asked.

"Here's where I am on that," Anna said. "I thought your dad and I didn't have secrets. Not important ones. I knew his passwords, his bank card code. I even made his doctor appointments. It galls me that he had such a big secret. Maybe a secret life of some kind. I'm equally pissed that he died."

"Maybe he was sick," Mike said. "Ever think of that?"

She shook her head. "Your father was a strong and brave man in many ways, but not with his health. He couldn't endure a hangnail without complaining. Remember how we used to laugh at the 'man cold'? That was the main reason I didn't want him to go on that rafting trip. He sprained almost everything on his body on the last long-distance bike ride he took and swore to never do anything like that again. You know how we met. He fell off the pier and nearly drowned in the San Francisco Bay! But he wouldn't be stopped on the rafting trip. It was mysteriously important to him."

Mike sopped up some sauce with his bread, chewing thoughtfully. "I guess he was kind of a candy-ass."

"Sometimes," she agreed. "Emotionally and psychologically he was a brick. The things he had to hear in therapy sessions were sometimes stunningly terrible, things that would make a meeker man sleepless for a year. That was his true gift. Not to mention the number of people he helped."

"Like I said, Jessie is eventually going to push you to try to find out the identity of the person getting the money," he said.

"But not you," she said. It was not a question.

"Not me," he said. "You were his wife. I think he should have always been honest with you and you with him. You probably have a right to know. But he should be able to have a private life from his children. If that's what he wanted and needed."

She rested her chin on raised folded hands. "I think that's just an extension of refusing to open that sealed envelope. You're afraid of what might be inside."

"No," he said. "No."

"Yes," she said. "What if there's something inside that causes you to lose respect for your father? What if you don't admire him as much? Missing him and grieving him is hard enough, why add another dimension to that?"

"I guess," he said with a shrug.

"What we all have to get through this process is the reality that none of us is perfect and it's okay, even admirable, to love an imperfect soul deeply. Right now, snatched from us, he appears perfect. Remember that old saying—the good die young? It should be the young die good. Live long enough and there's plenty of time to screw up. At the end of the day, we are all human. And imperfect." She paused, thinking about that long-ago affair she'd never told her children about. "We all have secrets."

Michael pushed his plate away. "Remember that pot you found in my backpack? That I said was Matt's?"

"Yes," she said, remembering it clearly.

"It was mine," he said.

"I know," she said, laughing.

Anna loved Mike best. That was the thing a mother was never supposed to say, so she kept it her shameful secret. But they sat in the great room after spaghetti casserole and talked until eleven and it was a bit like coming home. She tried to ignore the fact that Mike was like Chad in his sensitivity, his perceptiveness. His empathy. He asked her pertinent questions: *Did you feel he understood you? Do you miss him or the idea of him?*

And Michael said profound things. *He was really just a goofball who liked playing with kids, that's where we bonded. In his own way he was charismatic and knew how to make people follow him—not only was that his gift, it was the thing most important to him. I think what he really wanted was to be most popular.* Anna thought that was entirely true.

That was it, of course. Chad knew how to make people follow him, lean on him, need him—her, Joe, a mistress some time ago, clients, perhaps other women along the way. Chad was their guru.

She was filled with her son's spirit all the next day. Mike came back to finish chores around her house, but while he let her make him a sandwich, they didn't share a meal or sit up late talking. He had plans and off he went.

The next day was Monday and because her colleagues were still giving her plenty of support and covering for her quite a bit, Anna took a long lunch despite the fact that the cases were piling up in her office. For the first time in her memory she was having trouble staying focused. Instead of working, she dwelled on her grown children, starting with Mike. She grabbed a sandwich and sat on a bench in a small park near her office and thought about her son.

He was a gift. A joy. He made her feel she'd mastered motherhood; he was that wonderful.

Jessie was hard on her, often critical and difficult to please. Jessie filled her with nervousness because Anna was always afraid of saying the wrong thing and being the victim of Jessie's sudden and impossible anger. Jessie, like her brother and sister, was very attractive and smart. All three kids had dark hair and amazing blue eyes, like Chad's, and had excelled in school. Yet they were as different as night and day.

Bess, the reward for putting a fractured marriage back together, was an enigma. She was solitary, introverted, brilliant in school, even skipping a grade, but she didn't always play well with other children. Three seemed to be her limit and then only if the spirit moved her. Crowds, even a normal-size classroom, made her anxious. She never seemed to be lonely when her older brother and sister ignored her; she was independent and self-oriented but she could be convinced to share nicely. She was absolutely no trouble at all and there might lie a problem—she didn't seem to need anyone. No one. There were times she seemed withdrawn but it would turn out she was only entertaining herself with a book or experiment. One of Anna's friends asked if it was possible she was on the spectrum, but by the time the question came they had already concluded she might be, and she was high-functioning and a happy child. Bess was incredibly literal. *You said I wasn't to go out but you didn't say out of what, so I didn't go out of the yard but I did go out of the house because, frankly, I was feeling stuffed inside.* That was when she was eight.

Anna had immediately done some research and her brilliant conclusion was that it was probable Bess was mildly autistic and she watched for problems associated with the disorder. But Bess was content and rarely frustrated. She was perhaps a little odd sometimes, compared to other children, but she was also brilliant with an amazing memory and—

Anna's mind skidded to a halt right there as she recognized a woman, the young woman from the memorial service. She was pushing a stroller across the grass. In the weeks since Chad's death, she had given birth.

She found a spot not too far from Anna, parked the stroller and pulled out a blanket. She settled herself on the ground beside her baby. She was so beautiful, sitting on the blanket in her slim jeans and sandals, her blondish hair pulled back in a ponytail.

Anna rewrapped what was left of her sandwich and put it in her purse. She found herself walking toward the young woman and baby, unsure what she would do or say when she got to them.

"What a beautiful baby," Anna said, and meant it. "How old is she? I assume she's a little girl, given the amount of pink all around her."

"Thank you. Yes, this is Gina. She's six weeks."

Anna took a deep breath and looked skyward as if enjoying the summer warmth. So, she had given birth not long after Chad's death.

The park wasn't large by San Francisco standards and was up on a hill with a partial view of the bridge. There was a bike path at the bottom of the hill and some wonderful Victorian-style townhomes.

"You picked a beautiful day to introduce her to the park," Anna said. She dropped one knee to the ground in a semicrouch. "I promise not to get too close."

"Thank you."

"She has the most amazing rosy complexion, doesn't she? And that beautiful dark hair."

"My husband is dark. He's Indian."

"I am that," said a male voice. Anna started to rise and a very handsome man said, "No, stay where you are and continue to admire my daughter." He held a take-out cup toward her while he handed one to his wife. "It's coffee, black with cream and too much sugar."

"Oh, I couldn't! I've invaded your family time long enough!"

"Stay," the young woman said.

"Stay," said the man. Then, looking at his wife, he said, "I apologize, there was a call while I was in the coffee shop and I must step away and return it. I won't be long, I promise. I'll just return the call and walk back to the shop at the same time and get another coffee. If you're all right?"

"Perfect," she said. "Take your time."

He leaned down and kissed the top of her head. She reached up and clasped his hand. There was such love between them that Anna knew she'd been wrong about her suspicions. Then off he strode, leaving the baby and mother to Anna and she couldn't imagine this young woman ever being unfaithful.

"Your husband is a very kind and trusting man," Anna said.

"Nikit is good to the soles of his feet. And I don't think you mean us any harm," she said, adding a lovely smile.

"Is this your first baby?" Anna asked.

"She is, and it all happened much faster than either

of us expected. We got married, talked about starting a family and zip! Here she was. And everything about it was fast!"

They talked for a while about children and families. This charming young woman, Amy, was a nurse practitioner. Her husband a doctor. They met at work. It was a first marriage for both of them but they had quite a lot to overcome since Nikit's family had promised him to another Indian woman, even though Nikit had warned them he wouldn't cooperate.

"I'm pretty sure my mother-in-law still resents my intrusion," Amy said.

"You appear to be very secure in your husband's devotion," Anna said.

The baby started to fuss and Amy picked her up. "I'm secure. Tell me about your family."

"I am recently widowed," Anna said, even though she was certain she recognized Amy from the memorial service. "I have three grown children." And she described them in their most admirable light. Jessie, the doctor; Mike, the teacher and coach; Bess, the law student. All such a comfort to her now.

She noticed Nikit just across the way, gazing out in the direction of the Golden Gate Bridge, his back to them and his cell phone to his ear, his coffee in the other hand. He turned once, looked at them and merely lifted his chin to indicate he saw them. He smiled briefly and Amy waved.

They talked for a while about childbirth; it seemed to go with the territory when talking with a new mother.

Then they talked briefly about Anna's job, since her office was not far from this park.

"Which I should get back to," she said, getting to her feet. "Do you live around here?" she asked.

"We live on Alameda Island. Nikit works in the city and I will go back to work when the baby is a bit older. This is a lovely respite, this baby break. We used to come into the city regularly before we were married. Working in the city, you must spend a lot of time here."

"I'm usually completely wrapped up in work," Anna said. "I don't think I've taken the time to enjoy it in years. When I was younger and worked in the city, I spent a lot more time appreciating it. I should do this more often."

"You should," Amy said.

"I enjoyed our visit," Anna said. "Thank you for being so friendly. Have a wonderful day." Then she turned and began to walk away. Abruptly, she turned back toward Amy. "I apologize," she said. "My name is Anna."

Amy smiled up at her. "I know who you are, Mrs. McNichol."

Anna gasped in surprise, then sank again to her knees, once again that feeling of knowing in her heart that something was happening, yet not knowing what. "Who was my husband to you?" she asked directly.

Amy bit her lower lip for just a moment. "He was my father," she said.

FIVE

"How old are you?" Anna asked Amy.

"Twenty-eight," she said. "I haven't known about my biological father for very long. Just a few years. I imagine you have questions and I don't know whether I can answer them but I can't do it today. That's probably for the best. Take your time and think about what you want to know and let's get together for a talk."

"Did he know about you?" she asked.

Amy nodded. "Yes. He contributed to my welfare and education. Apparently he sometimes watched from afar—a high school concert or my graduation. I met him for the first time when I was a teenager but I was told he was an old friend of the family. I found out the whole story when my mother was in the last stages of cancer. I didn't get in touch until after she had passed away and I only did it because… Well, it was unfinished business. Nikit and I have a real thing about making sure we don't leave things unfinished in our pasts."

"Did your mother marry? Have other children?"

She reached into her diaper bag and pulled out a card. "On the back is my cell phone number. Think and digest, then call me and let's set up a time to get together. Maybe you can take an afternoon and come to the house? It's easier for me to be at home with the baby."

"Do you know my husband was married with children when— Although I didn't know about you, I knew there had been a relationship."

"I'm sorry if you were hurt," she said. Nikit had returned and was beside her again as if he could sense her need. He crouched down, sitting on one heel, his hands on her shoulders so it looked as though he quite literally had her back. "If there's anything specific I can tell you, I will. Just think about it and give me a call. Or if you'd rather not…"

"I'll call," Anna said. "I promise. So…you lost a father…"

"Mrs. McNichol, I never really knew my father," she said. "I knew about him, that's all. And I knew that you and your children didn't know about me. I communicated with him not very long ago and I'm so glad I did."

"Why now, Amy? After all these years?"

"Because, for better or for worse, living a lie is toxic. Living with the truth can be difficult and require strength but living with secrets is unhealthy at best. My mother had so many secrets and she didn't have to. I could never have stopped loving her even with the truth. Lies and secrets are just a mistake from the start. Maybe deadly."

Anna thought about that and wondered what the real

difference was between keeping secrets and being private. Shouldn't everyone be entitled to a private life? But lies? Lies, she had to admit, led to no good.

Anna had a jury selection in a battery case scheduled for the afternoon and so had to spend at least a couple of hours in the office, though she was distracted. She took some small comfort in the fact that Chad probably had not had an ongoing affair for years and years if Amy had never even been aware of him. She needed many more details to better understand the situation. Like, what was that business of him supporting her welfare and education?

She thought it must be Amy who was the mysterious recipient of the ten percent.

The DA and defense attorney were hard at it, selecting jurors; the defendant was also a victim. She had killed her abusive husband, claiming self-defense. This was a case that fell into Anna's area of specialty; she was a well-known advocate for women in abuse situations and the first order of business, she knew, would be the DA asking her to recuse herself. Since she didn't know the defendant or the victim she would refuse. This was the kind of case that got her blood moving.

But today she was struggling to stay focused. In spite of that, they got their jury empaneled and scheduled a court date. Although there were calls to return and lawyers who wanted a few minutes, she asked her clerk to handle the details.

She then spent about two hours on the internet researching and found dozens of references to similar situations to her own, in crimes, court cases, tell-all memoirs, articles and bios.

That she was thinking about her marriage and her husband, and the fact that Chad seemed to have lived an entirely secret life, one that included an unknown woman and a child, had disrupted her even more than his death.

She'd thought their relationship, despite its occasional troubles, was cocooned within their family, involving only them and the children—perhaps, on the fringes, their parents. Yes, she knew there had been an affair because Chad admitted it, but what he didn't admit was it had been so much more than that. He had a second family, whether he had seen them or not. Just because Amy said she hadn't known her father didn't mean Chad hadn't been involved. In fact, might he have been involved with Amy's mother? Could there have been others? Just how many liaisons might there have been over the years?

Was he ever planning to tell her the whole story?

She missed the Mill Valley exit and found herself driving toward Bodega Bay and before long she was standing on the cliffs high above the ocean. It was light much later in these days of summer. She did a mental inventory of all those intimates who might wonder at her whereabouts. She had spoken to her mother before lunch, texted with Jessie earlier this afternoon. She had seen Mike on the weekend and Bess rarely checked in. She just watched the ocean for a while. Then she got back in her car, drove for over an hour and found herself standing at Joe's front door. It was dusk.

"Anna!" he said, shocked.

"You were his best friend," she said. "You knew he had an affair. Did you know he had a daughter from that affair?"

"What?" he asked, clearly shocked.

Suddenly her eyes welled with tears. She'd done very little crying since Chad died, which was not to say she hadn't been grieving. She'd been grieving deep in her soul and now even more so as she questioned what her marriage had been made of, after all.

"I'm sorry I didn't even call," she said softly. "I didn't know where else to go."

"You can always come here," he said. "Come in. Let's talk…"

"Are you sure it's okay?"

"It's always okay. Are you just coming from work?"

"I left work hours ago," she said with a heavy sigh. "I can barely even remember where I've been. Driving. I went to the coast north of the city. Then here."

"Here," he said, cupping her elbow in his hand. "Come in. Can I get you a drink? A glass of wine or something?"

"I'm not doing shots with you again," she said with an abbreviated laugh, letting him guide her into his house.

"I don't even have tequila," he said, leading her past the small living room and dining room to the back of the town house. This was clearly where he lived, in the back of the house. The kitchen was clean, though there were dishes in the sink. His laptop and a stack of folders sat on the dining table. The small family room was cluttered; a pair of sweatpants and T-shirt were tossed over the back of a chair, shoes lay where they'd been kicked off, a briefcase sat on the breakfast bar and appeared to be emptied of papers. He had to clear a pile of papers and books from one end of the sectional. "Maid's day off," he muttered. "Come and sit here," he said, indicating the cleared space.

She decided against commenting that it looked as though he lived like a college student.

She took her seat and he brought her a glass of wine. Then he darted around the small space to gather up his clothes and shoes and take them away. She didn't stop him. He was on a mission to make sense of his mess. Maybe it had something to do with how he wanted her to see him. They'd never actually spent any time alone together while Chad was alive. He quickly put his books on the shelf and straightened the stack of papers and folders, closed the laptop and the briefcase and fetched himself a glass of wine. He looked so young, rushing around in his jeans and polo and loafers without socks; it was hard to put him at sixty-three. But then sixty-three was younger these days than it had been.

He returned and sat on the ottoman so closely their knees were nearly touching. His brow crinkled in a slight frown as he reached for her hand. "What's this about a child?"

"It's been a very hectic few weeks," she said.

"Sounds like it," he said.

"There was the business with the will when we learned Chad had left ten percent to an undisclosed party. I kept it to myself that I suspected a mistress.

Turns out I was wrong about that. I took my lunch to the park by my office today and ran into the young woman I had seen at Chad's service—a woman I had never met. We spoke just briefly today. She told me she is his daughter and has just given birth to his granddaughter. And I never knew this was going on. Of course."

"Has he known about this all along?" Joe asked.

"The details are still a little murky, but she said she met him when she was a teenager but thought he was a family friend. She learned more about him later and she contacted him recently. She said she knew I'd have questions and she'd meet with me later, after I've had time to gather my thoughts and decide what I want to ask. She did say he's contributed to her welfare and education."

"But they had no relationship?" he asked.

"Apparently not much of one," Anna said. "I don't know about her mother. I don't know if he had two families. Joe, did you know any of this?"

He shook his head. "No, and I never suspected he was keeping any secrets."

"He never said anything that made you wonder if his relationship with the woman was ongoing? If there was more to it than a fling? Or even an affair?"

He put his wine on the side table and took her hand. "Listen, here's how it went. In anger, you ratted him out, told me you'd caught him in an affair and you were leaving him. A lot of excuses and arguing and jockeying for position followed, and while you two stayed together, it was rocky. And then it seemed to smooth out. I didn't dare ask if you'd forgiven him because all

I cared about was that you two weren't living in misery. I cared about you both. And besides, I was going through my own thing then."

"Were you? Was that when you were going through your divorce?"

"Prelude to divorce," he said. He took a sip from his wineglass and hung his head. "We were all so young and thought we were so old. I was just over thirty and had two kids and I remember thinking I was wasting my life by staying in such a toxic relationship. I was very sympathetic to you and Chad but my situation was so much sloppier."

"It was?" she asked. "Forgive me, I don't even remember. Just that you were divorced about the same time we were contemplating…"

He took yet another deep breath. "It was a mess. Lots of abuse and neglect, several affairs or flings… Whatever they were, they certainly counted as cheating. Arlene was unstable, her whole family was unstable. I followed suit and mimicked all the instability. We lived in chaos for about five years. My mother left my father at home and moved in to make sure the kids were being taken care of. It was unhinged and crazy. And in the midst of that, you and Chad seemed to pull it together and I found myself leaning on him." He sat up a little straighter. "I'm sorry, Anna. I made that all about me."

"What was going on with you and Arlene?" she asked, almost grateful to take the focus off her.

His dark eyes were glassy. "Everything. Our romance was tempestuous and burned hot, our early marriage was a painful roller coaster. We married poorly and divorced even worse. Couples fight about things like possessions and custody, that's a given, but our divorce was so filled with lies and delusions and obsession for control on both sides it's a miracle we survived. In anger she even stole my car and torched it. She spent a few days in jail for that, but only a few days and then got community service. It was horrendous and went on for years."

"I wasn't even aware…"

"Because you were fighting your own battle. It seemed like no time at all passed when you were put back together and you were in law school, then pregnant. I don't know how you pulled it off."

"It was more than the marriage. More than his affair. I didn't realize it for a few years, but it was so much more personal. You know that I was raised by a single mother," she said. "It was a good life, but there were times we didn't have enough. There were times we were broke and times my mother was scared. Sometimes she brought food home from the restaurant where she worked. She might've taken it off patrons' plates. She was a waitress and worked so hard and pushed me to go to school, to plan on a future that wouldn't be as hard. Every year older I got, in spite of debt and struggle, the closer I believed I was getting to not feeling that any second I'd be hungry and homeless. We were never completely without a roof over our heads, but there were some close calls, like sleeping on a friend's sofa while waiting for an apartment to be available. But I got through school, I worked and helped my mother, we paid off a lot of debt. Then I met Chad and fell in love." She swallowed hard. "It was a defendant who said to me, 'We're all just one man away from being cleaning ladies or waitresses.'"

Chad came from an entirely different kind of family, a stable, upper-middle-class family. His parents funded his undergrad education; he went to good schools and they lived in an upper-class neighborhood. She thought the rest of her life would be safe and secure; she thought she was building the kind of family she had always longed for. The kind of family he had come from. Then his mother had said, "If you don't put your marriage to my son back together so he can be with his children, don't expect any help from me!"

She had worked and supported him while he finished his PhD; he worked part-time while he finished his degree, which set him up for a long and distinguished career as a therapist. At the time it had been all she had ever dreamed of—a spouse who was kind and helped people. A husband with a strong moral compass. There was nothing more she longed for.

"Michael was a baby when I learned of Chad's affair…"

"How?" Joe asked.

"I suspected because of odd phone calls, because Chad was gone or missing at odd times, and I did the unthinkable thing—I snooped through his personal papers and confronted him. Chad admitted he was seeing a woman. It turned out to be one of the clients of the counseling institute where he was working. It was the first time I felt my future and the future of my children was threatened and I lost it. I was so angry and hurt I wanted to kill him. It was right during that time I was on maternity leave and I planned to go back to work. And suddenly we were talking divorce."

"But you didn't even separate," Joe said.

"We couldn't afford to," she said. "We were getting a lot of pressure from my mother and Chad's parents to get counseling, to try to work it out for the sake of the kids, but that wasn't what did it. It was the advice of a partner in the law firm where I worked. He was a man in his fifties, a former cop and married for the third time himself. He said, 'You will never be happy, married or single, as long as you cling to this fantasy that some man will rescue you and make you safe and secure. Make *yourself* safe and secure. It's the only way you'll really feel that way. It's the only way you can really protect your children. In the end you will see that no matter who you're married to, you are responsible for your own happiness or security, two things no one can give you.'"

She fought that advice for a while. She wanted to believe the right man would do the trick. If only she could find a man who had that strength of commitment, one who could be trusted, one who wouldn't stray. One who didn't have a weak character.

"I began to study for the LSAT right away. I got a lot of help and support from the partners in the firm. I had mentors there, and even though they didn't know all the details of my personal life, they encouraged me to build my confidence and independence and form a strong career in law. As months turned into years, I did get stronger and more determined. Everything evolved from that point. I kept working as much as possible—the firm had work I could do part-time while I was in school. I helped with depositions, filings, document prep and research. In retrospect, I don't know how I made it."

It was during law school combined with her job in the law office that she stumbled upon her specialty and cases that involved domestic violence. After law school during her time in the district attorney's office, she prosecuted batterers, and later, in private practice, she spent as much time as possible helping the victims of battery domestic. Defending women who had been accused of assault when they relied on self-defense to save their or their children's lives was her specialty. She had become a well-known advocate for battered women.

"And then there was Bess after you put your marriage back together," Joe said.

"Not exactly," she said. "Not that simply. There hadn't been much affection between us for a few years. But Chad did spend as much time as possible helping with the kids and the house. First of all, his schedule was not as demanding as mine, and second, he seemed to genuinely want to save the marriage. I still ask myself why. I never had the impression it was love. I never had the sense I was chosen. More to the point, I never had the sense he'd forsaken all others.

"Bess was a surprise. I might have been exhausted and needy. I might have decided I didn't have any fight left in me. Most likely I decided I didn't care anymore. Bess was a lucky accident. Not only did she focus me, I was stronger and I could accept the life I had as better than most. It was, you know. It was better than most people get. But after Chad stepped outside our marriage, I was no longer in love with him. I liked him. I knew exactly how to get along with him and make the most of what we had. I think I grew to love him again, I'm not entirely sure. It was all about the five of us, holding our family together because there's strength in numbers."

"You seemed to be in love," Joe said.

"I never trusted him again. I also never looked too closely at what he was doing or how he spent his time, afraid of what I might find. I might have found out about his daughter sooner if I had."

"If I hadn't been so busy with my own marital problems I might've noticed," he said. "But I didn't."

"The great irony is, he did exactly what my biological father did. My mother had a fling with a married man and he stayed with his family. I never knew him. I mean, I knew who he was later on, after I was married. I don't know how his marriage and family turned out but he didn't help out like Chad apparently did. Isn't that weird? The same set of circumstances?"

"You stayed a long time for a woman who had no trust and very little love."

"While I might not have looked too closely, Chad was a good partner. Until just lately. As I told you, a few months before the accident he started to complain of not being happy enough. He said his life was unfulfilling. He was missing something. I was furious, hearing that! After I'd made the commitment to stay despite the imperfections, he had a nerve! That's why I suspected an affair." She laughed hollowly. "When I saw her at the service, I thought his pregnant daughter might've been his mistress."

"And he was a good father, in spite of his shortcomings," Joe said.

"His children loved him very much," she said. "I suppose I have to tell them…"

"Do you?" he asked.

"I don't know," she said. "God knows I don't want to."

"Why? Are you worried about how it's going to make them see their father?"

"No. I'm worried about how it's going to make them see me."

Anna and Joe talked for a long time, through at least three glasses of wine each and some Thai takeout. Anna told him she had always seen her life and her marriage as fairly simple. It wasn't perfect by any means, but compared to the relationships some of her clients struggled with, hers was uncomplicated by comparison. She knew Chad well; she knew exactly what she could trust. And she knew exactly what she didn't want to know.

She didn't want to know just how unfaithful he had been because that would inevitably lead to just how little he valued their relationship. Their marriage. Before Bess was conceived, while they were still knocking around the idea of divorce, Chad continued to praise her, but he didn't tell her he loved her. She would ask him from time to time and he would answer, "Of course I love you, Anna. I will always love you. You're the mother of my children."

She had been asking herself for more than twenty years if that was a compliment or more the lesser of evils.

Joe's expression changed slightly when she said that. "What?" she asked. "Why did you suddenly look uncomfortable?"

"I don't know," he said. "What a bastard," he said. "You were the wronged party and he didn't do much to make you feel vindicated."

"From that time on I always suspected I was just one of many. He might not have been sleeping with many women, I'll never really know. But you know Chad. He was a flirt and a man who thrived on the attention he got from women."

"That much is true," Joe said. "Who among us hasn't been guilty of that? You don't have to answer, but did you take a lover?"

She just shook her head. "I took a career."

And no ordinary career. She became a popular talk show guest and experienced expert witness. Eventually, she was appointed to a superior court justice position. Her honor.

Chad became quite well-known in the city, having done a great deal to support charities. And Anna became well-known for her position as a judge whose verdicts were thoughtful and fair.

It was after ten when Anna reclined on the couch and nodded off. She was vaguely aware of Joe covering her with a throw, which she pulled around herself as she yielded to sleep. In the early predawn, the house dark but for a stove light in the kitchen, she rose, found her sweater and purse and set about leaving. After a visit to the bathroom, she went to the kitchen and began scribbling a note on the notepad that listed eggs, bread, mayo and laundry detergent.

"You're leaving?" Joe asked from the shadows.

She jumped. "Oh! Did I wake you?"

"Not really. I heard you moving around. You're leaving?"

"I thought I'd go home, curl up in my own bed."

"You can stay. You can have my bed if that would be more comfortable."

"Thanks, but I think I'd rather find my own bed. And I've taken enough of your time and sympathy."

"I didn't mind, you know. Any time you need me..." He gently grabbed her shoulders. "Are you all right to drive?"

"Sure. It's been hours since I've had alcohol."

"Will you text me when you're home safely?"

"Okay. It's a long drive, you know."

"I know. I'd appreciate the text. And I'd like to say, when this storm passes, remember that it's all right for you to be happy. To think of yourself sometimes instead of putting everyone else first. That's what you've been doing, I know. This next stage, this can be yours."

"Thanks, Joe," she said. "No one has ever said that to me before."

SIX

Jessie McNichol was a beautiful woman, so the only person surprised that Dr. Patrick Monahan was attracted to her was Jessie. People often told her she was beautiful but Jessie thought of herself as vulnerable and naive. She fell in love quickly, totally and frequently. And, usually, tragically. She had tallied up a string of heartbreaks a mile long, starting with Ryan Siverhorn in the sixth grade.

Patrick Monahan was sexy and enormously accomplished in his field. Even though he'd been single for years, she had never heard any hospital gossip about him dating or being involved but she instinctively knew she would be the envy of every woman who knew, maybe even the married ones. And for the ninety-secondth time, she thought, *Maybe this is it*. She was not the least troubled by their age difference.

He phoned her as he said he would, and even though it was very late when he called, they chatted for an hour. He sent her a text in the morning saying he very much enjoyed their chat. He wasn't due any time off for a few days after returning to town, but he called and their talks grew more personal and entertaining. It took exactly two days for her to begin to look forward to his calls and she learned so much about him. For one thing, he was so kind and tender. He asked repeatedly how she was doing with missing her father, something she needed to be asked. She really needed someone besides her mother to care. And he told her what sorts of things made him happy. Good fiction lit him up; he looked forward to having a great story to read and hated to see it end too soon, but of course he read too fast—a by-product of medical school. He loved live music, as did she. And movies. They began a list of books, concerts and movies they wanted to see together.

And about five calls into their new relationship, she asked him what happiness meant to him. He said, "Successful surgeries, good sailing weather, minimal conflict in the neurosurgery department and it always feels good to be madly in love." He seemed to add that as an afterthought.

She was in a fever of longing.

Finally the night of their dinner out arrived. They were going to a nice restaurant in the city and would walk around San Francisco after. She lived a quick commute to the city while he lived in the city so they arranged to meet. He waited outside the restaurant, and when she approached him, he smiled and stood stockstill, just staring at her. His eyes glittered. "My God, you're beautiful."

She smiled back and said, "So are you."

He slid an arm around her waist and pulled her toward him, giving her cheek a kiss. "Thank you for going out with me."

And Jessie thought, *Are you kidding me right now?*

Here he was the most attractive, smartest, most successful doctor she knew and he was thanking her? She was just a thirty-one-year-old internist with a string of failed relationships in her past, and yet he was thanking her?

That fast, she was a goner.

He took her to an exquisite seafood restaurant in Union Square. It was elegant, dimly lit with plenty of dark corners and fancy specialty drinks. Other diners in the room would immediately know they weren't married because of how intently they talked and talked. They entertained each other for a while with med school and internship tales.

They walked around the city after dinner, confessing to each other that it was such a nice change from last year when COVID had been raging and the streets and sidewalks were barren. Now there were more people about, though most restaurants had kept their occupancy lower than capacity. About half the people out and about still wore their masks in public, including Patrick and Jessie, especially in crowded places, though they had both received the vaccine and the virus was now so low in numbers it was no longer required. They talked a little about what a dark time that had been, especially for people in medicine. "For a while I was so lonely I answered the spam calls," she told him, making him laugh, and he pulled her close for a squeeze.

"My house isn't far from here," he said. "I cleaned up before coming to get you just in case you'd accept my invitation for a nightcap. Or, if you're not comfortable with that, I'd be happy to take you home."

"Not comfortable? I know where you work," she said with a laugh.

"I'm pretty harmless," he assured her.

Nonetheless, she did a little math. They'd been talking on the phone for a week and change; she knew he was close to his mother and knew her name. He'd lost his father to a brain aneurism when he was young, which could account for his specialty. So he said, not her assumption.

"I bet you're not, but I'd like to have a nightcap, and you can feel free to join me. I'll be happy to Uber home."

They took a cab to a Victorian atop a steep hill, a large home divided into three apartments. His was classically male, decorated in dark wood, off-white and tan paint, brown and beige furniture, a long curved sectional, a marble fireplace and a very impressive window seat from which there was a view of the city. She was drawn to that window seat and with a long, *Ooh*, she sat there and was captivated by the view.

"How about a brandy?" he asked.

"That sounds perfect. This is beautiful. How long have you lived here?"

"Just a few years," he said. He kept talking from the kitchen. "One of the doctors I knew was renting it out right about the time I was looking for something and we came to an agreement in an hour. The closeness to the hospital and city—it was an easy decision. When he decided to sell, I was ready to buy."

"I love it," she said.

He returned with a brandy and sat down beside her. "What's your schedule this week?"

"Monday through Thursday I have clinic and on Saturday I'm on call for the practice. You?"

"I'll be working all week between clinic and surgery. But I'm not working tomorrow. Do you have any interest in going out on my boat? The weather is supposed to be perfect."

"I'd love it. Aside from a ferry or party boat, I've never been sailing. I have no real experience."

"But you're willing to learn?"

"Absolutely, but I don't want to be a lame sailor! Are you sure I wouldn't be any trouble to take along?"

He grinned at that, shaking his head. His hand wandered to her shoulder and he gently massaged her. "It could be wonderful. We can just sail around the bay with all the other weekend sailors."

She had already started to fantasize about sailing, pulling ropes and setting rudders and learning all the rigging moves. Then his hand was on her elbow, then stroking her arm. He moved close and his lips slowly touched her cheek. Then her neck. Then her lips. He took the brandy from her hand, put it aside and kissed her again. He investigated her mouth with his tongue and then took possession. His arms went around her, hers went around him, and their lips were locked together for a long, delicious kiss. Minutes, by her estimate. Several times his lips slid to her neck and he moved her long, dark hair away and inhaled her scent.

While he was busy kissing her, she was deciding what to do. Let him touch? She wanted to be touched. Desperately. It had been a long time. His caresses roved around a bit, sliding to her butt, her thighs, her knees. Then he whispered against her lips. "We could get more comfortable…"

This was what she had longed for since that day in the hospital parking lot, to have someone as smart and handsome and accomplished as Patrick want her. But she didn't want to seem too eager. "On our first date?"

"Not really, though, is it? How many hours have we logged on the phone? We know almost everything about each other."

"True. But…"

"It's entirely up to you."

He treated her to a little more kissing and caressing and when his hand slid deftly over her butt and under it she sighed and said, "Yes."

He took her hand and led her down the hall to his bedroom. They passed a couple of rooms that she took no real notice of but what she did notice was how the hardwood floors shone and how immaculate the walls and floorboards were, as though freshly painted. And then the main suite—large king-size bed, dark wood chests, large-screen TV on the wall. She couldn't help but wonder if he had tidied up in anticipation of bringing her to bed or if he was naturally so neat. Nothing was out of place, no clothes tossed over the furniture.

She glanced into the large closet and everything was hanging in perfect rows.

He put his arms around her from behind, circled her waist, pulled her hair away from her neck and kissed her there. He pulled her against him and she could feel it behind her, his erection. She moaned in equal parts desire and excitement.

He slowly undid the buttons on the back of her sundress and with deftness he slid it over her shoulders and let it drop to the floor, pooling around her ankles, leaving her in a bra and panties, so she turned in his embrace and put her arms around his neck. "Perfect," he said in a coarse whisper. "You're beautiful."

But she thought he was the beautiful one. His eyes had darkened to little circles of coal and she began to unbutton his shirt, one button at a time, until she got to his waist and then she undid the belt and button and zipper.

He took her lips again in a passionate kiss, and while his tongue played, he slipped his long, soft fingers into her panties and stroked her there in the dark and secret part of her body and she nearly screamed with pleasure. Then she dropped back onto his bed and he kicked off his pants and threw off his shirt as he lay down beside her. They were instantly in each other's arms, straining together, grinding hungrily.

"I don't think I can wait," she whispered.

Her panties disappeared that fast and he pressed into her. "I don't want you to wait," he said. Then he turned her onto her side, pulled down his boxers, made her bra disappear and entered her from behind. She wasn't so sure about that move until he fondled her breast with one hand, gently pinching a nipple, and sliding the other hand down to that special place that filled her with crazy erotic energy and nearly drove her out of her mind. He filled her, pumped his hips, sucked on her neck, rubbed her between her legs and she was gone.

This had never happened to her before. Orgasms were generally difficult to achieve and she was suddenly exploding. He was pumping and rubbing and groaning and she was ready to faint from satisfaction. He gave her a few more hard, deep thrusts and let it go.

And Jessie just about collapsed. A long sigh came out of her and she pressed her butt harder against him.

"Whoa," he said.

"Oh my God," she said.

"Yeah, that was perfect," he agreed. "Quick, but perfect. We can slow it down next time."

"Next time," she repeated. "Good." She snuggled into his arms, his breath soft and warm against her neck. She was far too weak to walk downstairs to catch an Uber. She couldn't move. His hands were so soft and he caressed her from her knees to her shoulders and it was heaven. Every once in a while he would stroke that soft, supple, dark place and it would send a jolt through her. And she would say, "Oh. Patrick…"

"Right here…"

"I can't move…"

"Don't move," he said. "Stay right here." He tightened his arms around her.

Eventually she rolled over, facing him, meeting his lips.

"I think that was the best sex I've ever had," she said.

He chuckled. "Worth the investment of all that phone time?"

"Oh God, yes," she said. She looked into his eyes. With the heat of the moment past, his eyes lightened to that beautiful greenish blue she remembered. "You're an amazing lover."

He brushed the hair back over her ear. "That's very sweet. You're quite amazing, as well."

She laughed softly. "No one has ever said that to me. If you're not very careful, I could fall in love with you."

He laughed a little and pulled her close. "Then I'll be very careful…"

She smiled. "Not interested in love?" she asked.

"It's a little soon," he said. "We have plenty of time to get to know each other."

She mentally chewed on that. She tried to say nothing, but in her typical way she couldn't let it go. "Let's see," she mused aloud without looking into his eyes. "We know each other well enough for amazing sex, but love is out of the question?"

"Don't do that, sweetheart. Love is just premature, that's all."

She gave that a moment to sink in. She wished she hadn't said it first. She wished she'd put off sex, even if it really was the best sex ever. "I'm sorry," she whispered.

"You don't have to be sorry, Jessie. You just have to be patient."

"If I'd been patient, we'd be wearing clothes now. But we're not."

He sat up in bed, bracing on an elbow, and looked

down at her. "We'd better have an honest conversation. I'm fond of you. I like you. I enjoy you. I desire you. You stimulate me in a lot of ways, intellectually and emotionally and sexually. I'm not in love with you, but there's potential for that if things between us continue in this direction. I want you to ask yourself, right now, do you want that? Because you seem to be in a hurry for something. And I'm enjoying the now of us."

"Maybe I should go?"

"You can if you want to. I'm not taking hostages. Or you can stay. It's entirely up to you. But let's not argue about the future of a relationship that started minutes ago."

Jessie gritted her teeth and forced herself to be quiet when she actually felt like she had a lot to say, and none of it productive. Frankly, she was scared and didn't know what to do because she didn't understand why she was never quite satisfied, why she could never seem to get enough. She'd ruined more than one relationship this very way. The secret only she knew—if he had said he loved her, she'd then want to know when could they discuss their future.

Jason was right, she drove people away. She had no idea why.

She ended up staying the night with Patrick and in the morning he made them a delicious breakfast. Then he drove her home to get the proper clothes for sailing. She offered to take her own car to the marina but he said he'd be more than happy to drive her and take her home. "It will be early today because I'm in surgery tomorrow and that means I have homework tonight."

"Of course," she said.

She worked on not asking for more all day and it was torture. She thought it was a successful day all around—the sun was out and Jessie didn't push for more. But by the time Patrick dropped her off she had a splitting headache.

I have a problem, she admitted to herself.

Anna checked in with Larry and told him about meeting Amy before she set up a visit. "Just remember, we don't know who the anonymous benefactor is so don't ask her about the will. If it's not meant for her, she may decide to sue his estate to claim her share."

"Huh," Anna said. "Thanks. I hadn't thought about that. If she is indeed his daughter, she could be entitled."

Anna drove from her home in Mill Valley to Alameda, which was just south of the city and, following the directions on her GPS, found a darling little house in an established neighborhood within walking distance of the middle of town. When Amy let her in it was as much like a dollhouse inside as it was on the outside.

"This is so pretty," Anna said, complimenting the decorating.

"A lot of redecoration and even remodeling had to be done, but now we have a new, modern kitchen and screened-in porch. Would you like something to drink? The weather is so nice we can take it outside."

"A diet soda would be nice. Can I help you?"

"Yes, just sit with Gina on the porch while I get our drinks," Amy said. Then she led the way to a charming and cozy porch decorated with indoor/outdoor weath-

erproof furniture—a sofa, two love seats, two chairs
with ottomans at one end and a table that could seat six
at the other. There were accent tables, as well, making
it a perfect place for entertaining, but right now taking center stage was little Gina in her swing, sleeping.

Anna's heart softened, for the baby was beautiful
and so precious. What would her children think? Say?
Would they be angry? Jealous? How could they be,
once they saw her?

Anna was back with a couple of tall, iced drinks
and that's when she realized that, although Amy didn't
have the same hair color, she definitely resembled her
children, especially around the eyes. Her kids all had
dark brown hair and blue eyes while Amy was a blue-
eyed blonde, which was more natural. She had someone else's smile and her face was more round than oval.
But now that she knew, Anna could easily see she was
Chad's daughter.

"Have you decided where you'd like me to begin?"

"I want you to tell me anything you're comfortable
with telling," Anna said. "As you might guess, I'm
mostly curious about your mother."

"Well, I started asking about my father when I was
very young and the only facts she was willing to share
were that he was a good person, a very kind man, but
he was not a part of our lives and wasn't interested in
being a part of our lives. But Bill was interested. Bill is
my stepfather. He married my mother when I was five
and they had two children of their own—Stephanie
and David. They're twenty and twenty-two now. I did

a lot of babysitting. David is in grad school and Steph is still in college.

"When I was twenty-one my mother told me her story. She had fallen in love with a married man. She said she didn't do it knowingly. And they weren't involved for very long before he explained that one of the reasons he didn't see her often was because he was married with children and by that time she knew she was pregnant. He had told her he traveled for work and was out of town all the time but eventually he admitted he'd made that up. So, they didn't see each other after that. Her decision to have me anyway was strictly her decision. She promised she never begged him to leave his wife and family, nor did she ask for any help."

"You said he contributed to your welfare," Anna reminded her.

"Not at first, but later. My mother said he checked in with her occasionally, asking how I was getting along, asking how my mother was getting along, if there was anything either of us was doing without. He contributed to my welfare, though there was never a set amount either monthly or annually. My mother said she had been determined from the moment she found out I was coming that she would be a good single mother."

"But how? What did she do?"

"She was a nurse," Amy said. "Probably why I'm a nurse practitioner."

"And she had a good marriage, in the end?" Anna asked.

Amy took a deep breath. "My mother and Bill were married for seventeen years. Bill had a drinking problem but he's been sober since they separated. They divorced amicably. He's still a part of the family, and when my mother was sick and then in hospice care, Bill was very much a part of our lives."

"How old were you when she passed away?" Anna asked.

"I was twenty-two," Amy said. "I had barely graduated. It was after that that I contacted my father. I wanted to let him know. We got together twice—we had two very long lunches to catch up. It would be fair to say we never had a real relationship. But he contributed to my college education."

"Even your graduation and wedding…?"

"My mother said he attended my graduation but didn't sit with the family and he wasn't invited to my wedding. My mother had passed by then and it was Bill who walked me down the aisle. I did see my father one more time—to tell him he was going to be a grandfather. After twenty-eight years of knowing he was my father, it was that thing that rattled him. He actually cried. That was the first and only time we ever talked about the fact that I have siblings who don't know I exist. That was the first time I had a whiff of regret from him. The first and only time he seemed to be sorry."

"About those siblings," Anna ventured. "Do you want to know them?"

"That's really irrelevant, isn't it? Do they want to know me?"

"I have no idea," she said. "After all, I just learned about you and my husband is dead! I knew there had been an affair…"

"According to my mother, not much of one. But it only takes a moment to make a baby. When did you find out?"

"It was spring. I had a new baby."

"Oh, how terrible," Amy said, then instinctively reached for her baby, lifting her out of her swing and holding her close.

"Of course I didn't know there was a child. I thought there was only another woman and that was difficult in itself."

"Did he confess?" Amy asked.

Anna shook her head. "I accused him of seeing another woman, of having an affair. I was relentless and eventually he admitted there had been."

"But you didn't leave him," Amy said. It was not a question.

"I stayed. I didn't really have the means to support two small children, work, take care of a house and family… And he said he didn't want a divorce. He wanted to be forgiven. It was a very long time before I could. Your mother must have had an equally difficult time."

"I don't remember it being hard, but I was so young. We lived with my grandparents and I was spoiled, an only grandchild. I actually had a very good life. I always felt something was missing but I can't say I suffered. I didn't ever suffer, not even later, when I was older. I just wanted to know why our family was different."

"I grew up in a different family, too," Anna said. "Mine was like yours. I never knew my father and he died before I ever had a chance. He didn't help my mother and there were no grandparents. And now I'm a lawyer who specializes in the needs of women and children who are abandoned. I should rephrase, I'm a judge. Of course I'm a lawyer who became a judge. I should be a little pleased that Chad offered support. It was the responsible thing to do." She laughed and shook her head. "Amazing the way things come full circle."

"Will you tell your children?" Amy asked.

"I'll have to tell them," Anna said. "They have a right to know they have a sister."

"How do you think they'll take it?" she asked, and Anna couldn't help but notice she shuddered slightly.

"I have absolutely no idea," she said.

They talked for another two hours, going over the details of their lives and families. At one point Amy brought out a photo album and showed Anna pictures of her mother, stepfather, grandparents, half siblings, holiday photos, graduations and such. "I don't know if I'm relieved or jealous—your mother was so beautiful."

"But you're beautiful, Anna," she said.

"No one thinks of me as beautiful," Anna scoffed.

"I bet everyone does."

"No," she said with a laugh. "No, my husband once told me he thought I was the most capable woman he knew. You know how I met him? Wait till I tell you…"

Anna went to see Blanche in the assisted living residence, though it was not her regularly scheduled visit. She was thinking about Amy and her family and Chad. She liked Amy quite a lot. She was acutely aware that under different circumstances, she might hate her. But she was a fully mature woman with a baby. Her mother was dead and she had no extended family, really, except her stepfather. And it was no small matter that Chad was also dead. And this all was something that happened in the long ago.

Blanche was all dressed up, though she was sitting in her comfy chair with her feet up.

"Well, hello," Anna said. "You're looking very nice today."

"We had entertainment today," Blanche said. "It was good—some school choir acting out some scenes from a musical. I can't remember which one. But an hour of dangling my feet and my ankles are as big as my butt."

Anna laughed but she thought, with a surge of relief, Oh good, she's lucid!

"What are you doing here?" Blanche asked. "You get fired?"

"No," Anna said with a laugh. "No, I had an interesting afternoon with a young woman and her baby. What are the chances you remember Chad today?"

"Your husband?" Blanche asked. "I've been trying to forget. He can't be in trouble again, being dead and all."

"Wow, you're really on your game today. Do you remember that affair he had when Michael was a baby?"

"Anna, the world remembers. You wouldn't let us forget. You chirped on that for years."

"Well, so did you," she said, but inside she was so thrilled to have her mother to talk to. "It turns out there was a child from that affair and I met her. She's Michael's age and she's married and has a baby. She told me the whole story, what she knew from her mother. Amy didn't know Chad while she was growing up but apparently he did help out with the cost of her education and I suppose other things. I believe he has remembered her in his will, though we haven't gotten around to that yet."

"I thought he was a phony," Blanche said. "Putting on airs like he was some big shot."

"I thought you liked him," Anna said. "You counseled me to stay with him. You said if a husband's affair is the worst thing you go through…"

"I did? Well, at least he has a job."

Anna frowned. "Would you like me to tell you all about it?"

"About what?"

"The young woman," she said. "His daughter."

"By all means. And could you get me a water?"

"Certainly," Anna said. She fetched a glass of water for Blanche and then launched into the story, starting with seeing her at the celebration of life, then seeing her in the park. "She must have been in the area of my office deliberately." She described Amy and her husband and baby, told her a few of the things she learned, though she tried to keep it brief and simple. Blanche nodded a lot and muttered, "Uh-huh."

"And so now I suppose I'll have to tell the kids," Anna said.

"Yes, I guess," Blanche said.

"You must be feeling very well today," Anna said. "You're sharp as a tack."

"As usual," she said. "It's nice talking to you."

"And it's wonderful to talk to you."

"Good! By the way, where is your house?"

Anna felt her stomach clench. "Mill Valley," she said. And she bit her lower lip.

"That's right, now I remember. Listen, if you see my daughter around there, tell her to come by, will you please?"

For a moment Anna was stricken. She couldn't speak. She took a deep breath. "I can do that," she replied, tears in her eyes.

"And that other one," Blanche said. "The boy. He must be grown by now. I really didn't mean to never see him again but that's how things work out sometimes. I thought we'd find each other."

"What boy?" Anna asked.

"You know," she said. "First I had the boy. I couldn't keep him. But when the girl came along I wasn't about to give another one away."

"What was the girl's name?" Anna asked, on the edge of her seat. "Do you remember her name?"

Blanche struggled. "It'll come to me, gimme a minute. I'm so tired right now."

"Try to remember. Do you know who I am?"

Blanche smiled and her old face looked so soft and sweet. "Of course. You're the best nurse here and you're my nurse. I think I should lay down. I need a little help."

"Sure," Anna said, helping her mother stand and then pivot to sit down on her bed. When Blanche laid down, Anna lifted her legs onto the bed. Within seconds, Blanche was snoring and Anna knew all conversation was over for the day.

There were three stages of assisted living and three stages of rehab care, in most cases terminal care. For assisted living there were apartments with galley kitchens, mostly couples occupied them, then efficiency units that had sitting areas and bedrooms, then bedrooms that opened into a nursing round. Then rooms in the nursing home division where residents ate their meals together in a dining room. Then memory care for residents with dementia—that wing required more staff. Then the hospice unit. Those rooms were filled with sick and memory-challenged residents who would not be going home.

Blanche was still in an assisted living room with full-time nursing supervision and full meal service. Blanche was on a waiting list for memory care. Nothing much would change for Blanche except the geography. But these memory lapses were becoming more and more frequent.

Anna sought out the senior nurse, Rebecca, as she had many times before. She described their conversation. "I have heard Blanche speak of the boy. I assumed she was speaking of her grandson."

"She specifically spoke of giving him away. And then 'the girl' came along and she kept her—that would be me. My mother always told me everything, but I've never heard of that. Could this be true? Could this be something she's never talked about before?"

"It's true our Alzheimer's patients remember old memories better than recent memories, so if something that happened fifty years ago comes to mind they talk about it. But it's also true they tell wild tales that no one can make any sense of. Is it possible your mother

had a son before you were born and had him adopted
and never mentioned it to you?"

"I've never heard mention of it before," Anna said.
"She was twenty-eight when I was born. She said the
man she was involved with had been married, had no
intention of leaving his wife or, even if he did, was
not inclined to marry her. Without even thinking twice
about it, she said she was going to have me, raise me,
and we'd be fine one way or another. And we were. But
she never mentioned another child. Never."

"You can chalk it up to dementia," the nurse said.
"Or you can research it. You know where your mother
lived before you were born. You can try one of these
ancestry DNA services. I hear some are very good."

I'm a judge, Anna thought. *I know how to get information.*

But the larger thought she had was how much vital
family information was hanging out there, stuff she
wasn't sure of. Could she have a brother? Did Chad have
any more children? How had he managed to give money
to Amy and her mother without Anna ever knowing?
How many branches were there on her family tree exactly?

Suddenly, her body felt very heavy, as if each step
she took, emotionally and physically, took great energy.

SEVEN

It hit her when she got home. In fact, as Anna pulled into the garage, she felt the emotion welling up inside her like a pressure cooker and she broke down in the car. She pushed the garage door button, lowering the door, leaving her to sit in the car in the semidark. And she came apart like a cheap watch.

Chad had been dead for five months. In that time she'd learned that his long-ago affair had born fruit and the strain of trying to figure out how she was going to tell her kids had been wearing her down. She'd been trying to decide if she hated him for keeping such a thing secret or, more often these days, if she longed for their life back. She struggled with whether she owed it to the kids to tell them she had been the one to bring up the possibility of separation and divorce. Her idea, not Chad's. Their marriage hadn't been perfect, but by comparison to the lives of many of the women she had helped through the legal system, it was heaven. That was small comfort at the moment. Chad left a mess for her to clean up alone.

She realized, not for the first time, that she didn't miss Chad so much as she missed marriage. It had worked for her. It had worked for Chad for that matter. It was convenient; there was always another person to share the weight with even when things in the relationship were stormy. There were times, she had come to realize, that having a close enemy or stranger can be slightly more helpful than having no one at all.

If missing her marriage wasn't challenge enough, she was losing her mother and possibly gaining a brother. All in one day. Just how many people in her life lived in such secrecy? How had her mother, her best friend since birth, never let it slip before? And why hadn't she? She should have known that Anna wouldn't consider it shameful or embarrassing to have a child while not married! Even twice!

She reminded herself that perhaps it was a delusion born of dementia, and that was somehow more painful. And she fell into hard sobs, still sitting in the car. She had cried for her lost husband before now, but most of that had been the self-pity side of grief, missing him and feeling alone, anger with him for leaving her to deal with everything, craving just one more discussion about what was wrong with them now. And of course she wondered if he was planning to come home from his adventure and tell her about Amy and his first grand-child. He had said he wanted to have a serious talk.

Her kids were having a very hard time with Chad's death—Jessie was angry, Michael was devastated and

Bess seemed to have withdrawn even more than usual. Of course, Bess was in law school, a perfect excuse to avoid the whole group dynamic, but Anna worried about what was going on in that head of hers. She was the quietest and perhaps emotionally the most vulnerable.

She moved into the house, sweating from being closed in the steamy garage. She mopped her face and threw a fistful of soggy tissues in the trash can. The tears kept coming with the occasional hiccup or small gasp. Her face was wet and hot and it felt like there was no end in sight and she didn't know where to turn.

She felt she had put all her emotional energy into trying to figure out who she was supposed to be now that she was no longer Chad's wife and these other issues had come up, issues that would complicate what was left of her family even more. Untangling all of this and putting things back together was going to be harder than ever. Her brain was sludge and she couldn't make a bit of sense of anything. *Was I the wife betrayed and left behind or the wife who failed? Was I the sister who never knew it, was I the daughter who never heard the truth about her family? My life was built on so many lies. My mother was devoted to me and I thought she told me everything, no matter how hard the truth was, but apparently that was not the case. And my husband...?*

She couldn't believe the irony. Her birth story mirrored Amy's. Her father was a married man who obviously wasn't committed to either his wife or his mistress, and Chad had done the very same thing. And yet she wondered why? He said he wanted to talk when he returned from his trip and she'd assumed their marriage was over. Why didn't he tell her the truth? She drew in a jagged breath. *Did he ever love me?*

Her phone chimed and she saw that it was Joe. She thought about letting it go to voice mail but instead she answered and blubbered. In her head she was making perfect sense but into the phone she was just tossing out random words like *lost my mother*, and *Chad's secret family*, and *I just don't think I can take much more.* Finally she said, "I'm sorry. I just can't talk about it now. I'm at the end of my rope." She was still crying, sounding a bit out of control.

"Anna, where are you?" Joe asked.

This was personally so humiliating. She never fell apart. She argued emotional and complicated cases all the way to the Supreme Court and never caved into tears. Even Chad had rarely seen her cry and never like this. And it just wouldn't stop.

She disconnected. She would call him back after she got control and could actually speak. She turned off her phone. After about ten frustrating minutes, she stripped and got in the shower, letting the warm water run over her while she cried.

Joe had been visiting his daughter, Melissa, and on his way home when he passed the Mill Valley exit he thought of Anna. It had been almost a week since he had talked to her. He pulled up her number on the dashboard and called. The connection wasn't very good, what with the freeway and engine noise, but even so he could tell she was crying. The gist of what she was saying was that her mother had died and she didn't want to talk because she was at the end of her rope. Then she rang off.

He tried calling her back straightaway but his call went directly to voice mail. He drove probably five miles before he decided to go to her house to make sure she was okay. When he thought of all she'd been through lately, his feeling about that brief exchange was not good. He hadn't ever thought of Anna as depressed or suicidal—she was the most stable and capable woman he knew. But as he drove toward her house, he became more desperate. He hadn't been in touch with her for several days. What if she'd spiraled downward and he missed the signals, having been out of touch.

When he arrived at her house, his fears only intensified. The garage door was closed but he could hear the car engine running inside. He tried banging on the front door, but there was no response. He had to climb over the locked gate into the backyard but was rewarded by finding the kitchen slider unlocked. He opened it and called her name, then went immediately to the garage. He had to step over her discarded shoes and her purse, dropped with the contents spilling out. "Anna!" he yelled.

The car was still running in the garage but there was no one inside so he turned it off and doubled back into the house. He picked up the purse, absently scooping the contents back inside. Once inside, he called out again, "Anna!" And again, "Anna!" He walked through the kitchen, great room, into the hall, calling her name as he went.

"What are you doing?" she said. She stood in her

bedroom doorway, wrapped in a terry-cloth bathrobe, her wet hair dripping onto her shoulders.

"Oh, Anna, thank God," he said. Before he could stop himself, he rushed to her and pulled her into his arms. "Thank God!"

She stood still against him. "Thank God for what?" she asked.

"Thank God you're okay! You scared me to death. You were crying hysterically! You said you were at the end of your rope! I had no idea what you might do."

She pulled back from him slightly. "That I might take a shower must not have come to mind…"

"The car was still running in the garage," he said a bit desperately. "You had sounded so…out of control."

"Yes, that," she said, dropping her gaze. "For a little while I had lost my mind." She shook her head. "Humiliating."

He was still holding her upper arms. "Anna. Your mother? You lost your mother?"

"Well, not in the usual way. Blanche is thoroughly alive, but while I was visiting with her she asked after her daughter. Me. She didn't know it was me."

It took a moment for Joe to digest that. Then he just grabbed her close in his arms again. "Oh, sweetheart, I'm so sorry."

"I should have been prepared," she said. "I knew it was only a matter of time. In fact, we got a lot of time, thanks to a good doctor and the right medication. But somehow I thought it would happen more slowly, not a normal visiting day gone suddenly around the bend. One minute she was asking about the kids and the next asking me if I knew her daughter." She laid her head on Joe's shoulder as if that last statement made her weirdly tired. Her hands rested lightly on his arms and she said, "Joe? Is this my purse?"

He pulled back a bit. "It was on the garage floor and the car was running. I picked it up but I don't know what I was planning to do with it. Give it to you, I guess."

"Whew, I guess I was really out of my head."

"So you decided to take a shower?" he asked.

"It was gut instinct," she said. "The weight of the last several months coupled with all the unknowns and possible new revelations. My head was spinning. I felt so lost. I couldn't stop crying. So I decided to give up and cry and went into the shower to do it."

"And did it work?" he asked.

"I think I was in there a half hour," she said. "I don't think I have a tear left. I'm a little tired…"

"When did you last eat?"

"I don't know. I think a half bagel this morning. But it was a full day."

"If you want to get dressed and dry your hair, I'll poke around the kitchen and see if I can throw something together for dinner. For both of us."

"I think maybe I am a little hungry."

"Now that I've found you safe, I'm suddenly starving," he said. "Take your time." He turned her around so she faced her bedroom doorway. "Here," he said, handing her the purse.

He stood there for a moment as she went into her room and closed the door. He shrugged his shoulders. He wondered if she had any inkling of what might be happening with him right now. Unlikely, given the amount of confusing information she was juggling in her mind.

Joe had always loved her but had never put a romantic spin on it. She was married and not just married to anyone, but to his best friend. Truthfully, he hadn't really noticed those feelings until he had survived his divorce. Then he realized he liked her, appreciated her, felt she wasn't getting the love she deserved from Chad. He kept it tamped down. It never in a million years occurred to him that she would one day be single, even though he knew Chad was not the best of husbands.

He went to the kitchen and began checking out the contents of the refrigerator and pantry, coming up with a nice breakfast for dinner of sausage, eggs, Tater Tots and English muffins. He whipped up some hollandaise just to impress her. He could hear the distant hum of a hair dryer and he set their plates and utensils on the breakfast bar and lit a couple of candles.

He poured himself a glass of wine and waited for her. When she came out, he could feel his eyes warm at the sight of her. She had put on a pair of yoga pants and an oversize shirt, very stay-at-home casual, but to him she looked ravishing. No makeup but Anna didn't really need makeup. She had pulled her shoulder-length hair into a simple bun on top of her head.

"Wow, you went to some trouble," she said, eyeing the place settings and candles.

"It was no trouble at all. I hope you like breakfast."

"It's my favorite meal, even if I don't indulge every morning. I'm usually in a hurry."

"Wine with breakfast?" he asked.

"Why not? Sounds like an adventure. You couldn't have come all the way from your house when you called. Where were you?"

"I was on my way home from Melissa's in Bodega Bay. I try to see her every couple of weeks. It's harder for her to get to me in Palo Alto with the little kids and her husband's work schedule. After you hung up I just took the next exit."

"Thanks, that was really nice of you. I'm sorry I worried you. I was having a bad day."

He pulled a clean dish towel off the serving platter, which was nicely laid out with the meal he had prepared. He pushed the platter toward her and poured her wine. "Was there more than your mother's confusion?"

"Oh, yes," she said, dishing up her plate. "At one point she said, in all innocence, that she had given up the boy but decided to keep the girl. She didn't realize she was talking to me. It sounded like she was saying she had given up a baby before me. I don't know if I'll ever find out. I can't exactly count on her to tell me the truth."

"Then again, she might. Or there are those DNA search firms. If there was a child and he decided to look for his family, it could be even easier."

"I'm trying to figure out why she wouldn't have told me," Anna said. "Me, of all people. She should know better than anyone I wouldn't judge her."

Anna told him what she had learned from Amy that afternoon, which had been more about Amy's childhood than about Chad, and then repeated her visit to the nursing home. Eventually they got around to talking about Chad again.

"Did you know he was unhappy?" she asked Joe.

"Yes and no," Joe said with a shrug.

"I can't wait to hear you explain that answer."

"When Chad was happy, there was no happier guy. When he was unhappy, which was not infrequent, he was dour and depressed. And there was always something nagging at him. I always wondered if he got into psychology because he wanted to fix himself. Because he wanted peace."

"Well, he found it," she said somewhat sadly.

"But what about you?" he said. "Over thirty years with him?"

She laughed ruefully. "Believe me, I knew when he was unhappy. Every time." She got up and walked around the breakfast bar and began to rinse their dishes and slip them into the dishwasher. "That was always the great challenge with Chad. When he was content, he was the best man in the world. He was a perfect partner in almost every way. When he wasn't, he was flailing around looking for where to place blame. Pretty often the blame fell on Max Carmichael, the CEO of their practice. Sometimes it fell on a client who was challenging him. And then of course there was me. I was a frequent whipping post. But I was used to it. I signed up for it, after all."

"What do you mean by that?"

"Over the years we fell into a routine. Chad was mostly supportive—he was definitely committed to his kids, which certainly helped me when they were younger. And if he was struggling, I found a way to prop him up. But as he got older and I became busier, I grew impatient, and I didn't want to put my work on hold while we worked on Chad's latest crisis. I suppose it was very selfish of me, but I was ready to concentrate on my career. Chad was not. He needed a full-time wife and caretaker. I was the one to first suggest a separation. I thought it was time we went in our individual directions. One of our pivotal events was an argument about his rafting trip."

"But, Anna, he loved you. He admired you. More than once he admitted he didn't deserve you."

"He married me because he thought I was strong enough to hold him up. You know the story of how we met. He fell off the pier and thought he was drowning and I was the closest one. So I pulled him out."

"The most attractive love story I've ever heard," Joe said, laughing in spite of himself.

"It's quaint, I'll give you that. But from that moment on he expected me to fix everything. And I did. Eventually I got used to it. I could almost anticipate his mood swings."

"But you loved him."

"I did," she said. "When it was good, it was very good. Just like Chad."

"And when it was bad?" he asked.

"When it was bad, I became an overachiever. The first time I thought my marriage was over, I went to law school. I felt I was doing that out of self-preservation, but the truth is, I owe it to Chad. If I had been more comfortable in my role, in my life, I wouldn't have taken on so much."

"Then there's the bench," he said.

"And not surprisingly, that was about all Chad could take. It wasn't long after I accepted my appointment that Chad, once again, became unhappy. But this time he said he thought we had less in common than ever. That's when he began to move away. We only went to counseling because I insisted."

"You outflanked him," Joe said. "But he was very proud of you."

"He resented me," she said. "He once looked me in the eye and said, 'You think you're so smart.' Now what was I supposed to say to that?"

"What did you say?" Joe asked.

"I said I knew I was smart!"

Joe let out a big gust of laughter and Anna quickly joined him. They carried on like that until tears were running down their cheeks, slowly getting back to control.

"You know what I'm really glad about?" she asked. "I'm glad I'm not dead and you and Chad aren't sitting here talking about what a pain in the ass I was."

"I always thought you were smart," he said.

"Chad apologized for saying that but he couldn't erase the fact that that's how he really felt. As if I was showing off. He was threatened by me. By my position."

"And yet you loved him."

When she nodded, she pursed her lips. "Whatever it was, we didn't get a chance to fix it or make it better. And now we never will."

"You'll have to fix whatever is going on without him. You're a strong woman and amazing mother. It's perfectly all right for you to think about yourself for a while. Guilt free."

"I have to completely reinvent myself and I have an entirely new past to try to build it on. A new set of facts!"

"You had such a crazy day," Joe said. "What was the worst thing?"

"I don't know," she said. "Possibly my mother checking out like she did. And dropping the idea of an older brother existing out there somewhere."

"Then what was the best?"

Her facial features froze for a moment. "Let me think." She drummed her fingers on the counter. Then she smiled sweetly. "I held the baby. Chad's granddaughter. He had never even seen her. She has no real connection to me but I feel like she does. It was also nice that Amy told me, to the best of her knowledge, Chad didn't have an ongoing relationship with her mother. But he was a cad. He should have told me about Amy and made arrangements to help support her. He helped, Amy said, but it sounds like he really didn't do his share."

"I'm pretty sure he was afraid of losing you."

She laughed. "He could have gotten a lot of mileage out of telling me that!"

"I know," Joe said. "Are you planning to tell the kids pretty soon?"

"Yes, of course. Not only do they deserve to know they have a sibling but, selfishly, when I die I'm not going to leave behind a lot of mysteries and questions.

I've always tried to impress on them that the truth is easier and safer. Bess simply can't lie, Mike hates lies but he has figured out how to say very little and Jessie can be brutally honest but with a strong deference to her own feelings and needs. I never told my children about Chad's affair. I didn't think it was pertinent. I thought it was selfish of me to be tempted to tarnish his reputation. But then, I didn't know about Amy."

"Now you know."

"I have one more piece of information to get from her. We didn't talk about Chad's will. Surely she's the ten percent."

"Hopefully he doesn't have more families scattered around," Joe said.

"God help us."

Joe stood and walked around the breakfast bar. He slowly and casually put his hands on her waist and pulled her a bit closer. "I'm going to leave now," he said, and his voice had become a bit gravelly. He lowered his lips to hers and kissed her, short and sweet. He noticed she let her eyes gently close, breathing in, breathing out. He pulled her closer and went in for the kill, covering her mouth in a searing kiss, and her lips opened under his. Joe groaned a little bit against her mouth. Their tongues played; their arms tightened and he was feeling aroused.

"I'm going to go now."

"You don't have to, Joe."

"Yeah, this time I do. The next time I stay over, I'm not likely to stay in Mike's old room and I'm not going to lay beside you after four hours of talking about the mess Chad left behind. Next time, there will be no ghosts in the room with us."

"I don't think I could have gotten through these dark days without your support and understanding. But I'm also ready for the dark days to be over."

"I know that for all his charm Chad hurt you."

"Over and over," she admitted.

"What do you want for the rest of your life?" Joe asked. "What would bring you the ultimate happiness? The Supreme Court? Grandchildren? True love?"

"That all sounds fun, but what I'd really like is for someone to love me as I am. I want someone who thinks I'm beautiful fifteen pounds overweight, who wears earplugs because I snore rather than scolding me for what I can't help or fleeing to another bedroom. I want someone who believes in forgiveness and gives it and asks for it. Asking for it—that's huge. And no matter what you've heard, love does mean you have to say you're sorry. I don't know if it's possible, but I won't have another relationship unless it can be authentic. I don't expect perfection and I don't have it myself but what matters is acceptance and commitment."

He smiled and gave her a squeeze. "You're going to be fine, Anna. What you want is reasonable and should be plentiful."

"It should be," she said. "We'll see."

"If you think there's any way I can help, please let me know. For now, I'll text you when I'm home. Thank you for letting me make us dinner. Thank you for everything."

* * *

Joe's love for Anna was the kind of love that went with close friendship, with great admiration, with pride. He certainly never had a plan in mind, like if Anna was single... But once the worst of his grief and hers had passed, he realized he had always loved her.

Back when his own marriage was falling apart, Chad and Anna struggled through Chad's affair. It was such a messy ordeal and they flirted with the idea of divorce. At that time the very idea of ever marrying again was sour in Joe's mouth; he felt he'd failed at marriage. But he did have a moment or two when he thought if Chad was fool enough to leave Anna, Joe might find himself in a very awkward situation.

But now his marriage had been over for almost twenty years, his kids were grown, one married and the young mother of two small children, one in a post-grad program at Berkeley, and he hadn't even entertained the idea of a second marriage. He'd had a couple of girlfriends over the years, but nothing serious. And now, Anna's marriage was not only over, she had admitted it had been strained for a while.

A whole new world was opening up to Joe.

EIGHT

Jessie waited at the same sidewalk table where she'd had her first date with Patrick. When he asked her where she'd like to have dinner, she asked if they could come here. It was nostalgic and sentimental to her. She'd been seeing him for just a few weeks and she was dead in love. He was already forty-five minutes late.

He was a busy man, she understood that. His time was very valuable. She was getting used to it, at least a little bit. When they were together, when he was focused on her, she was in heaven.

"Another glass of wine, madam?" the waiter asked.

"I'd better stick to water until my date arrives," she said.

"Don't fill up on chips," he advised in good humor.

"I'll try," she said, giving him a smile.

Late, she thought with aggravation. She not only wore her hair down the way he liked it but she'd run by the hair salon and had it blown out, making it full and pretty. She had freshened her makeup and had brought a change of clothes to the office. After a few more minutes she visited the ladies' room and then upon her return to the table she tried to occupy herself with people watching. A few people still wore masks, a holdover from the pandemic from a year before.

It was right at the onset of the pandemic that she and Jason had run into trouble. With businesses and restaurants closed and the hospital so busy, she became horribly lonely and they argued all the time. That led to him breaking up with her. He said she was a cranky old nag and, being a doctor herself, she should have been much more flexible and understanding.

Those had never been her strong suits.

Her cell phone rang and she lifted it from the table. She didn't recognize the number, but she answered.

"Dr. McNichol?"

"Yes."

"This is Cheryl Mattson. I'm a neurosurgery nurse and I work with Dr. Monahan. He asked me to give you a call to tell you he's sorry he's running late. He's seeing a patient."

"He's already almost an hour late," she said a little more hotly than she had intended.

"He was extremely busy and said to tell you that you shouldn't wait for him."

"How much longer will he be?" she asked.

"This is his last patient. He should be out of here in a half hour to forty-five minutes. That's just a guess."

"Tell him I'm waiting," she said. And she hung up without saying thank-you or goodbye.

She looked at her Instagram account and Facebook

page to kill time. Actually, she killed time this way far more often than she would like to admit. It wasn't usually satisfying. In fact, it was often disappointing or frustrating. Like now. Bertie Newsome, one of her colleagues, was engaged and was planning a wedding to her future husband to take place in December; it was a never-ending catalog of photos of everything from the diamond ring and possible wedding cakes to the townhomes they considered buying. Jordan Hillerman, a classmate from med school, was having twins! Priscilla Silver was posting pictures from her honeymoon in Aruba.

The whole world was marching on while her life was agonizingly stagnant and there was no good reason for it. When she listed her attributes in her head, it seemed she had everything. She lived in an upscale community in a luxury town house, she was a doctor in a thriving practice. She was an associate in that practice and would probably make partner in another year. She thought her nose was a little small for her face but she was so often complimented on her beauty that she had decided the nose wasn't a problem. She was smart, self-supporting, an overachiever...and so lonely. Even now in her new relationship with Patrick, even with his attentiveness, she was lonely. They couldn't go out every night or even spend the night together every night, what with their busy schedules, but when they weren't together he would call. It had great promise. She just didn't understand why it didn't feel like quite enough.

It was no doubt her father's death that weighed her down. That left a gaping hole in her heart. After all, her father had been the first man in her life to let her down. She strove all her life to make him proud and he said he was, but it was unconvincing. He clearly enjoyed Michael and Bess more; Mike because he was a boy with similar interests and Bess because she was the baby and Dad had doted on her.

Really, Jessie felt she had always been left behind. Even now, waiting for her date, scrolling through the Instagram lives of her friends and seeing their joy. Why didn't she ever have joy?

Quite by accident, looking at Tina's Facebook page, she saw pictures of a beach gathering. Volleyball, bonfire, laughter at a beach bar, many people some of whom she knew from the hospital. And Jason. With his arm casually draped around Tina's shoulders. Tina was a colleague, a pediatrician. She was very popular, though she wasn't all that pretty. In fact, she was so far from perfect. She was a short, roundish blonde with a smile too wide, large blue eyes and a double chin. But she had a wicked sense of humor that people loved. Jason had always liked her and perhaps these days he was liking her more.

How dare he get on with his life so easily.

"There you are," Patrick said, leaning down and giving her a peck on the cheek. "Sorry to keep you waiting." He sat, looked immediately at the menu. The waiter was instantly at the table. "Ah, Miguel. How are you today?"

"It's a good day, thank you."

"I'll have a cerveza and plate of loaded nachos for a start. Jessie?"

"You can bring me that wine now," she said. Then despite her wish to be more accommodating, she put on a little pout.

Patrick seemed not to notice. He talked about a cervical laminectomy he performed first thing that morning, a meeting he had with a surgeon about a heart-lung transplant that was scheduled and some kind of issue with his assistant and the accounting department about billing.

Then he took a break to drink some of his beer and shovel a few nachos in his mouth. He pushed his plate toward her but she just shook her head. "Are you all right?" he asked.

She shrugged. "You were very late."

"I apologized," he said. "I had Cheryl call you. If you didn't want to wait, you didn't have to."

"Did it occur to you to call me yourself?"

He appeared momentarily frozen. He dabbed his lips with his napkin and leaned back in his chair. "What's wrong?"

"I don't know," she said, shaking her head. "I felt abandoned."

"Though of course you weren't. I was tied up. We got a little behind schedule and there was a patient who had come a long way to see me, so I made sure to see her."

Jessie lifted one brow. "Oh? And what was so important?"

His jaw clenched. "A fifteen-year-old girl, with her parents, came all the way from Reno. She has a glioblastoma, temporal lobe, and I'll be operating on her on Tuesday. She's frightened, as anyone would be. There were a lot of questions. As expected. I wasn't about to cancel or reschedule. Or cut her short."

"Oh," she said, contrite. "Well, I had a hard day, too."

"I didn't have a hard day, Jessie. I was running late." He drank some of his beer. "Do you want to talk about your day?"

"No, I just want to eat," she said. "Maybe it's low blood sugar..."

He granted her a small smile. "Then let's get you fed."

And she thought, *Oh God, I'm doing it again! What is the matter with me?*

She forced herself to be pleasant, to laugh at the right times, to show empathy when it would count, to ask him questions that would get him talking and take the pressure off herself, to have a lovely dinner. She was rewarded for this effort by having him ask if she'd like to come to his place and she said yes, thinking that the pleasure of lovemaking would take some of the pressure off her poor head.

For a while, that seemed the answer, for Patrick was the most wonderful, tender and powerful lover. But after sleeping for a couple of hours, she startled awake, her head pounding.

Jenn called Michael and in her cheery little voice said, "I've made the most wonderful batch of enchiladas and I'd love to share it with you."

"That's so sweet, but I can't really go out tonight. I have to do a little laundry and I have some lesson plans to work on. I've got football practice every day and have no extra time."

"That's all right, Mike. I'll bring the enchiladas to you."

"My apartment is kind of a mess..."

"So I'll help you straighten up while you work on your lessons."

"You're determined, aren't you?" he asked, adding a little laugh, hoping to lighten up the message.

"If you'd rather not have company, just say so," she said.

He thought for a moment. "Enchiladas sound good."

"I'll pack it up and see you soon!"

So then tonight would be the night, he thought with despair and fear. He would break up with her.

Over the enchiladas she made because he loved them? Classy.

Jenn was one of the best girls he'd ever dated and he was crazy about her. She was a beautiful girl with creamy skin and long, soft brown hair. When he looked into her eyes, they reflected the same blue as his, but lighter. She was funny and had a gentle, kind and patient nature. She taught second grade; she would have to be patient. But maybe the most important thing about her was she wasn't given to melodrama. So many young women her age were teetering on the fine ledge of high drama. He wasn't so sure they didn't welcome it!

Not Jenn. She came from a pretty functional family who seemed to laugh through their quirky dysfunctions, kind of like his own family in that way. Jenn had a granny who enjoyed her vodka and she was hilarious when she'd had a couple. Michael had Blanche, who didn't drink much but her crusty demeanor and sailor's mouth made them all laugh and Blanche just enjoyed the heck out of it.

Jenn loved teaching and she wanted to have a family someday. She considered educating to be custom fit to her future plans. She thought she could continue to work while she raised her children. Since Michael loved coaching and teaching, her plans were well suited to his.

And he loved her. She was steadfast and honorable. She was decent and yet the sexiest woman he'd ever been with. She turned him on like mad, though his libido hadn't been working too well since his dad died.

So why break up? It was complicated but he knew what his relationship with Jenn meant he should do. He should ignore his feelings of fear and inadequacy, propose, marry her and they should settle into the life where they had so much in common and have a family together. They would be so happy, teaching and enjoying life in a friendly little northern California town.

But the thought terrified him and he felt frozen. Ever since his father died he was suddenly afraid of being a husband and father. He'd never measure up to the kind of man his father had been. Chad McNichol was always wise, always kind and funny and supportive. And what if, like his father, he brought children into the world and then died? They would feel as bereft and lost as he was feeling and that would be a tragedy. Better to not go there if he couldn't perform. From what he was feeling now, he couldn't hold a candle to the kind of father he'd had.

He heard his front door opening. Jenn used pot holders to carry the hot glass baking dish into his apartment. There was a bag on the ground behind her. She was all smiles, her cheeks a little pink from cooking and her eyes bright in anticipation of seeing him. "Michael, grab that bag, will you please?"

"What's in here?" he asked, grabbing the bag by its handles.

"Sour cream, salsa, chips, avocado, a couple of extra tortillas. Hungry?"

He put the bag on the counter and reached a hand into the soft curling hair that fell over her shoulder. She turned her head and kissed his palm.

"Let's put the enchiladas in the oven to stay warm and have a glass of wine," he said.

"Wonderful." She got the glasses while he got the wine. They were equally comfortable in each other's apartments and spent the night together several times a week. Until Michael's father passed away. Since then it had been less frequent.

They sat at the small, round dining table in front of the window. In Michael's apartment there was actually a view of the courtyard and pool area rather than another building or a parking lot. Jenn had no view whatsoever; she occupied a small one-bedroom with windows that looked straight at a brick wall that belonged to her neighbors. She had suggested a couple of times that they could pool their resources and look for something a little nicer. He had just said, "Maybe."

"Listen, I've been meaning to talk to you about something. Things between us have been pretty strained since my dad died. It's not your fault, but we can't ignore the fact that we're not as good as we were."

She reached for his hand and gave it a squeeze. "I haven't been worried about it, Michael. But it's not your fault, either. You and your dad were so close. I'm sure this has a lot to do with the grieving process."

"I'm screwed up, Jenn. I'm just not sure of anything right now. It's probably because of my dad's death, but it's affecting how I feel about everything."

"Everything? What everything?"

"Mainly my personal life," he said. "We were on this track of moving toward commitment, but it's just not working for me right now. I have to put the brakes on."

"Okay," she said uncertainly. "It's okay if we don't make any more plans until you're feeling more in control."

"That's the thing," he said. "I might not ever feel better."

"I know you don't think so right now," she said. "Don't be too hard on yourself, Michael. There's no hurry. We have lots of time. Maybe you should talk to someone? A counselor?"

He ignored the suggestion because the last thing he wanted to do was see a counselor. His dad had always been his counselor. "We need to break up," he said. "Every time I see you or talk to you, I feel bad. Guilty about not giving you the attention you deserve, about not giving our plans any priority because right now I just can't make plans. I know it's screwed up. But I don't want to have plans."

She looked genuinely confused. "All right," she said. "So, no plans…"

"I have to break this off, Jenn. It's not working for me. I think it's probably my issues but I'm not ready. We need some space. Distance."

"What kind of distance, Michael?"

"We need to break up, Jenn," he said again. And then he hung his head.

"Are we talking about a break?" she asked. "Because you said you loved me."

He shook his head forlornly. "I don't feel love for anyone right now, including myself. It's not how I want to feel. I'm just empty of feelings."

"Except self-pity apparently," she flung back.

"It's not self-pity," he said defensively. "It's something else. Depression or grief or something. I can't help it."

"Have you talked to anyone?" she asked. "A professional? A therapist? What would your dad tell you to do?"

"That's the thing. When your dad is a counselor, it becomes a personal thing. He'd take me out to the golf range or maybe a field and we'd play with a ball and talk about things, and in a little while everything would be clear. But he's gone and there isn't anyone else I want to talk to."

"How about your mother?" she asked. "I know you're very close and you respect her opinion."

"I don't want to put a burden on her now. She's going through her own hard time."

"I bet she wouldn't consider it a burden," she said. "You should talk to her about this."

"I'm sorry, Jenn. I know this isn't fair to you. I just feel lost. And suffocated. It's not your fault."

"We talked about getting married," she said. "You said you wanted a family."

"I'm just so confused right now…"

"So if we were married," she said. "And if you had a son or two and you lost one of your parents, would you just bail? Say, 'Sorry, Jenn, but you and the kids are on your own because I'm hurting'?"

"That's why I have to back away right now," he said. "I'm not sure what I feel. I'm messed up."

"I'll say," she said. "You could talk to me, of course. You said you loved me. You said you thought I was the woman you wanted to be with forever. We've talked till late into the night so often, so why can't we talk now? Is this what happens to you when you hit a rough patch? You quit?"

"It's not just a patch! I lost my best friend, my dad! I'm not quitting," he argued. "I'm having trouble feeling! I took a pretty big hit."

She slowly stood. "I thought I had that job. Best friend."

"Something went wrong," he said.

"I'll say."

"I don't know how to fix it," he said.

"Why don't you think about that for a while," she said. "Because what you're doing isn't going to fix anything." She picked up her purse. She left the bag of groceries on the counter and the enchiladas in the oven.

Her glass of wine was hardly touched. "If you come up with any better solutions, I believe you have my number. You've used it almost every day for two years."

"Wait," he said. "Don't you want to eat?"

"I don't have much of an appetite anymore," she said.

"But your dish…"

"Don't worry about that," she said. "It's the least of what I lost today."

And with that, she turned and let herself out of his apartment.

Michael didn't move. He felt even worse than before. He felt like the biggest failure. He couldn't remember a time in his life before now when he had struggled so hard for judgment and good sense. He'd never felt so lost.

Lunch with Bess was always a melancholy affair for Anna. True to form, Bess had a routine, a very rigid schedule. She had sushi every Saturday at four in Oakland near Berkeley where she lived. It was very rare for her to invite a friend or friends as she was very solitary, but now and then there would be a girlfriend or study partner.

When Anna walked in, the man behind the sushi counter waved a big hello to her and of course Bess was seated at her usual table in the rear of the small sushi bar. One of the reasons she had sushi at four on Saturday was because the bar was not crowded and she could have her favorite table. It wasn't as though Bess became upset if she couldn't have her table, but she did become disgruntled. She was a creature of habit. It gave her comfort.

"Mom!" she said, closing her book and looking up in surprise. "I didn't know you were coming!"

"I hope it's all right that I'm here," Anna said. "I left you a message yesterday. And today."

"I didn't listen, I'm sorry. The only voice mail I ever get is from the insurance company or the health care supervisors trying to convince me I need more attention, but I don't. Once when I answered and talked to one of them, they didn't even know my age or whether I had preexisting issues. Oh, and I get quite a few calls from the car warranty people. Why don't these people get serious jobs?"

"Maybe they tried," Anna said. "What are you having?"

"The Zee roll, half a morning star roll and half a Lee's special roll."

Like always. Bess ordered the same thing every Saturday at four.

"You could get the same thing if you like," Bess said, which was her way of saying she had ordered exactly what she wanted to eat, wouldn't want to share, couldn't change her selections. She was as rigid as a steel rod.

"I'll order something else, thanks," Anna said. "It's nice to see you. You look wonderful."

Bess laughed a little bit. "I never look wonderful, especially not lately. I used to at least try a little makeup but since law school I don't even bother. No one cares how I look, including me."

Anna quickly ordered. Out of habit she ordered more

than she could eat, prepared to share with Bess, knowing Bess wouldn't touch Anna's food. It just wasn't part of her plan. In fact, her dishes were arranged in a clockwise fashion, and it was always the same, just as her closet was color coordinated, her drawers stacked with perfectly folded sweaters, pajamas and undergarments.

It was how Bess managed her life. It was how Bess was in control. She didn't have to make too many choices and nothing was left up for grabs.

"Tell me about your case law," Anna said, just looking for anything they could actually talk about.

"We're working through some tax law right now and it's complex. I like it. No one else does."

Anna laughed at that. "They will become tax attorneys when they find out what the billable fees are. But why do you like it?"

"It's complex but at the end of the day it's really simple. It's mostly just math, except in the case of fraud. The IRS makes the rules and prosecutes if they're broken but their rules are poorly written and ambiguous. It's like mystery multiple choice and one has to figure out what they meant. There are taxes, fees and percentages. It becomes complicated with interest and penalties, which are often discretionary. No one really goes to jail. Well, sometimes, if there's fraud, premeditated fraud. But it's soft time."

Anna was momentarily taken aback. "Soft time?"

"Easy incarceration. White-collar incarceration. Color TV, state-of-the-art gym, internet, catered meals…" She lifted one of her sushi bites to her mouth. Chewed. Swallowed. "Conjugal visits."

Anna laughed. "And what more could a felon want?"

Then Bess rattled off several paragraphs of tax code from memory, most of it involving rather obscure situations like property tax on a chicken coop in one state, sales tax on deodorant in another, "Because antiperspirant is considered an over-the-counter drug." She went from real-estate taxes to capital gains deductions, pausing only for a bite of sushi.

"That memory," Anna said. "Remarkable."

"You have a great memory," Bess said.

"Nothing to yours!"

"I think my memory would be more fun if it wasn't directly tied to the fact that I'm so weird."

"I wouldn't call you weird," Anna said. "You like things a..." She paused a moment. "A certain way. That's all."

"I certainly do. And not many people understand. Martin seems to. I'm not sure why."

"Martin again."

"Martin kind of likes tax law and is willing to drill me on it. But his first love is cybersecurity and identity theft, that sort of thing. Because it's a little harder to untangle. He's like me in that way. The bigger the challenge, the more he likes it."

Anna swallowed. "I think you've mentioned Martin before but I can't remember in what context."

"I study with him," she said. "He's a hopeless nerd, like me. He's just a smart nerd, not on the spectrum. But his memory is even better, if you can imagine."

"Hard to," Anna said.

"And I sleep with him," she said.

Anna nearly choked. "You do?" she asked weakly. Bess just nodded and continued to work away at her sushi. "Are you in love with him?"

"I don't know. Probably. But we have a lot in common and spend a lot of time together. He's a great study partner. He pushes me. I do like him a lot. Of course."

Of course, Anna thought. If Martin was like Bess—brilliant, gifted, almost a photographic memory, low on emotions, high on autonomy—they could marry and produce a flock of adorable robots.

She wanted to scoop Bess up in her arms and cradle her, like a defenseless child. Bess, who could solve major legal and computer problems but didn't know if she loved someone. Beautiful Bess, who didn't bother with makeup but didn't even realize she didn't need it.

"Do you think law school was the right choice?" Anna asked.

"Yes," she said. "But there are other things, too. I'm drawn to science and research and computers. I just have to go to school forever, I guess." Then she smiled brightly.

"No, not exactly," Anna said, also smiling. "Eventually you have to go to work!"

"I look forward to that," she said. "But work worries me. There are times I get a little bored."

"Well, that's always been a problem. So, tell me more about Martin. Is he…kind?"

"He is," she said with a smile. "He helps a lot of people. And not just with law school. He has a five-year-old brother who is special needs and he helps him and his classmates. He's a good person."

It flashed across Anna's mind that that explained a lot—Bess was never labeled special needs or autistic or disabled or anything, but there was no question she was not the average twenty-four-year-old. "He must be sensitive to your needs," Anna suggested.

"I guess so," she said.

"What does he look like?" Anna asked.

"Well, let me think about that," Bess said. "He's six feet tall and has dark hair and dark eyes and big feet. But he's actually good at some sports while I'm only good at chess, bridge and dominoes. He's not clumsy like I am. He's steady. He plays football in the park on weekends. Just a friendly game, he says. But he also likes chess."

"Do you have a picture?"

"Yes," Bess said, grabbing her phone out of her purse and clicking it open to display a picture of a young man in sweats and a tee, holding a basketball against his hip. And of course Bess hadn't volunteered a picture until she was asked.

He was beautiful. Stunningly, John Kennedy Jr. beautiful. "Bess, he's so attractive."

"Is he? I suppose he is. I've never been a good judge of physical beauty."

Anna folded her hands on the table. "What does Martin like best about you?"

"I only know what he says..."

"What has he said?" Anna asked.

"Well, he likes that I'm honest, but I don't know how not to be. He said he admires my focus, but I think that's another thing I can't help. If something takes root in my head, I can't shake it loose. And he likes the way I taste."

Anna felt a flush creep up her neck. "You don't have to tell that. That can be private."

"Okay. Is your sushi okay?" she asked, nodding at Anna's plates.

"I ordered too much, as usual. Are you happy?"

"Of course," Bess said. "I had my usual meal and, as a bonus, I could talk to you."

That was how Bess structured emotional responses— did they fit into her routine, was it uneventful and was there no anxiety related to uncertainty or change. But Anna just said, "That's very nice, thank you."

Being the parent of an adult child like Bess took diligence. Anna had to constantly remember that Bess's idea of pure joy didn't bear any resemblance to her own. To Bess, never being spontaneous was joyful. If she could manage her world by wearing the white blouse every Monday and the black blouse every Friday, by eating at the sushi bar every Saturday at four, ordering the same meal, that was joy. She liked the challenge of her studies; conquering them made her feel strong. And when things were off and uncertain, she became very anxious until she could wrestle her routine back into order.

Bess had lived in a group home for a year during college; getting her there had been one of the biggest arguments Chad and Anna ever had. Anna didn't want her to go away, didn't want her to live away from her. In that, Chad had been right; he had been wise. Bess had learned to function in a world that couldn't accept her peculiarities. Would she ever have a normal life? Not Anna's kind of normal. Not ever. But she could have a comfortable life, a successful life. She could be her own kind of happy. Anna struggled to remember that.

For what felt like the millionth time, Anna was reminded that accepting people as they are is the hardest work there is.

"Tell me something, Bess. What's the very best thing about Martin?"

She didn't hesitate or pause to consider. "He has never once suggested there are things about myself I should change."

Anna smiled. "That is truly a rare thing in a man."

NINE

On Sunday, Anna received a call from Amy. "I know you're very busy but I have something to tell you. Something I believe you want to know, though you haven't brought it up."

"What's that, Amy?" Anna asked.

"Can we meet, or is your day too wildly busy?"

She sighed. She had groceries and dry cleaning to pick up. Michael planned to stop by later, by which she assumed dinnertime. Jessie had left a message for her to call and she had planned on changing the sheets and doing some laundry. "I have a little time. Would you like to meet?"

"That would be ideal," Amy said. "Nikit isn't on call today and he offered to keep Gina. And frankly, I could use a little time away from the baby. I'll come closer to you if you can think of a place."

Anna's first thought was to be disappointed the baby wasn't going to be included, but she kept that to herself. She reminded herself that Amy and the baby weren't really a part of her life, but rather Chad's. And Chad was gone. "There's a little Mediterranean grill in Mill Valley. They're always busy but they have some nice booths in the bar. I'll call and see if I can reserve one."

"Perfect!" she said. Then she asked for directions and promised to meet her in an hour.

For a moment, Anna had the weirdest thought flash through her mind. *What if Chad sees us?* This happened a lot, the urge to text him something before remembering he's gone. Or the urge to check her messages to see if he had called. Just then she wondered what Chad would think of her meeting his daughter behind his back.

Maybe it was the memories. She and Chad used to like to duck into Christos around happy hour to indulge a glass of wine and maybe a Greek salad or stuffed grape leaves, pita and hummus with olives. If they'd been out for some reason, Christos was a favorite stop before going home and they'd take some baklava to go.

"Thank you for meeting me," Amy said when she arrived. Once again Anna was struck by the resemblance to her own daughters, yet another reminder that Chad's genes were relentless. And to think she took one look at her at the celebration of life and suspected her of being a mistress! She thought, *Chad's type!* How crazy that seemed now.

"Of course," Anna said. "It sounds like you have something on your mind."

"Yes. Or something I want to get off my chest. I was completely honest with you about my relationship with my father, but I left out some details about how I found out about him."

"Well, there's time, Amy. Let's order you something to drink. A coffee or other drink?"

"I'd love an iced latte," she said.

Anna ordered for them and also asked the waitress to bring some baklava.

"This is so perfect," Amy said. "I wish I had known about you a long time ago."

"I do, too, although I can't imagine how many things that might have changed!"

"I know," she said. "Please understand, I didn't know this until my mother was sick. Remember I told you I met my father when I was a teenager? I was sixteen. I don't know why I wasn't more specific. I told you he was introduced as a friend of the family. Well, apparently he did tell my mother to get in touch if she ever needed help, and that's what she did. I witnessed a school shooting, the Saint Mary's High School shooting twelve years ago. Six of my classmates were murdered by a senior with his father's automatic weapons. I was a very lucky survivor."

"Oh, Amy! I'm so sorry."

"Thank you," she said. "I think I'm all right, thanks in large part to my father, who I didn't know was my father at the time. My mother called him, told him what had happened, said I wasn't sleeping, explained my anxiety and asked him to help. He asked her to bring me to his office immediately. That's when I met him and learned he was a therapist. We spent some time talking about the event and my PTSD and he arranged for me to see another therapist. He never explained the real reason. He just said there was another therapist who was more of an expert in problems like mine. But he checked on me."

Anna was thankful to be reminded—Chad was a professional. And he was a good man, down deep. She thought she remembered: an Oakland high school, six dead plus the shooter's suicide making it seven. Many were injured. It traumatized the town, the Bay Area. It was 2009, following a terrible recession and unemployment. Tensions were high, gun laws were lax; a young man all screwed up and very angry helped himself to the automatic weapons in his father's unlocked gun cabinet.

"That's when I became aware of him," Amy said. "But it wasn't until my mother was near death that I knew he was my biological father. I didn't know he went to my graduation. High school and college actually. I didn't even know he was there. After high school, he began to help with my tuition."

"I thought you said he helped all along…"

"My mother told me that he sent money occasionally, just a random check now and then. She said she always meant to send it back. She didn't want him to ever claim me or assert his legal rights, but it turns out that was not his plan. Maybe he was feeling guilty."

"I'm so sorry for all you've been through," Anna said.

"Please don't say that. I've had such a good life. My mother had a great job she loved. Even though my mother and stepfather divorced, they had a good relationship and we stay in touch. I have two younger siblings. And I have Nikit and now Gina. I love my work. I'm sorry for all you went through. I must come as quite a shock."

"Oddly, once I thought it through, not much of a shock at all," she said. "I only knew there had been a relationship, but it had ended."

"That's what I was told, as well."

"I've been dealing with marriages gone bad for many years, as a prosecutor, as a defense attorney and as a judge. I have a lot of friends, some of them have relationships I actually envy. For the most part, many of our friends envied us. But I'm sure they didn't see into the viscera of our lives."

"Everyone knows, people have intensely dramatic and secret private lives," Amy said. "I didn't really get to know my father but I thought he was charming and kind."

"He was exactly that!" Anna said. "He must have been so happy to know you, finally."

"I think so, in a way, though he did say he wasn't quite ready to be a grandfather. I think maybe he struggled with that idea. He didn't say so but I think he wondered how that worked with a child you'd never communicated with. Does he get invited to the baptism? To Christmas dinner?"

"Do you tell the family?" Anna added.

"That's why I wanted to see you," Amy said. "I'll tell you whatever I can about my relationship with him. There isn't much to tell, but I'm willing. But the real reason I wanted to talk to you is, it seems there has been some money left to me."

"Ah," Anna said. "You're the anonymous recipient. I thought so."

"You did?"

"Since meeting you," Anna said. "It all began to make sense."

"How is that so?"

"My late husband bequeathed ten percent each to our three children and another ten percent to an unknown recipient. I didn't know about you until we met. You, however, knew about me and my late husband. It fell into place very quickly."

"Do your children know?"

"Not yet."

"Do you plan to tell them?"

"I know I should," Anna said. "What do you think?"

"I think if they know about me and want to meet me, it's their right. But they have to want that. I won't make the decision for them. I have a personal ethic—the truth is always better. In fact, in the end, easier."

"In my case, it's an occupational hazard. I'm dedicated to the truth."

"Of course you are," Amy said, smiling. "Your honor."

"Your last meeting with Chad? What was that like?"

"It was a courtesy call. I invited him to lunch. I introduced him to Nikit. I told him I was expecting. His first grandchild, he said. He got a bit gloomy about it actually. He asked me if I felt he had failed me." She looked down into her coffee and was quiet for a moment. When she looked up again, her eyes glistened with tears. "I told him that I wished a relationship between us could have been handled differently, though I didn't know how that might have worked. I told him yes, there were times I needed a father. And he asked me to forgive him."

That was truly the first time Anna felt sorry for Chad. A child, as beautiful and smart as Amy, must have been hard to keep secret. Anna didn't ask Amy if she forgave him.

"I also told him I was glad to know him now," Amy said.

"I will tell my children about you and your baby," Anna said. "I may take a little time to think it through, trying to come up with a logical and meaningful way of doing so."

"You can tell them also that I haven't spent any of the money he left me. I understand they might feel cheated somehow."

Anna was actually surprised by feeling absolutely no envy of that money. In fact, oddly, she was relieved to know that in the end Chad had done something decent. Admittedly, her life would have been quite different had she known about Amy sooner. "It must have been what Chad wanted or he wouldn't have done it. And though it won't be soon, you will have more college tuitions to finance—best to tuck it away. Thank you for being honest."

Amy nodded and looked around Christos. "This

place is fantastic. Maybe we'll meet here again some-time."

"Whenever we can," Anna said. "We're going to stay in touch."

Anna's court roster was heavy with cases and Phoebe, her best friend and clerk of court, complained bitterly. And that's how her Monday began.

"I'm not trying to rush you or crowd you, I don't want you to take on more than you can handle emo-tionally, but let's make getting these cases on the cal-endar a priority. I'll get you the help you need. But we have to mop up!"

"Absolutely," Anna agreed. When Anna took note of the number of files that made their way to her desk, she knew it was going to be a brutal week, complete with plenty of homework. One of the holdovers from the days of the pandemic was the frequent use of video conferencing for meetings, which cut down on the time factor and helped them get work done in a more effi-cient manner.

It was September; children were back in school and thankfully attending in person and not remotely as had been the case last year. They were booking cases to be heard all the way into November. In addition Anna was signing off on multiple divorces where there was no contest, child custody issues with CPS, search and seizure warrants and other miscellaneous cases. She was able to push many to Family Court. Lunch every day was brought in and eaten with staff members while working. Her secretary, Irene, was riding the law clerks hard. Anna's had always been a busy courtroom. Her briefcase was full when she left the courthouse every evening, and on Saturday there was no rest for the wicked and Anna was back at her desk. Phoebe and a couple of the clerks were also there giving up their weekend to help catch up.

Grueling workweeks were not unusual for Anna, but in the past she might've called Chad and asked him to stop at the grocery store or grab some takeout—a pizza or Chinese. The only work he did on weekends was routinely done at home and he used his days off to golf or get together with friends. She'd been finding over the last six months that these little things—not having someone to grab dinner or run an errand—added up over time.

She called Joe. "How was your week?" she asked.

"Busy, but I bet not as busy as yours. Is your courtroom packed?"

"Standing room only, in person and virtually."

Joe had called a couple of times during the week and all she had done was complain about how busy she was. "I haven't even had time to talk to you and I wanted to tell you something. Amy called me last weekend, we met and some questions were answered." She told him about their discussion over lattes at Christos. "It has weighed on my mind ever since. I'm trying to think of how and when to tell the kids. They need to know they have a sister."

"Have you come up with a plan?" he asked.

"Just a very bad one. Except for holidays and special occasions, we're not usually all together as a family and I want them to hear the news together. I think telling them one at a time could just set up trouble. I could tell Jessie and she would call Michael and give him her version or vice versa. And where Bess is concerned, I don't have any idea what her reaction will be or who she would talk to about it. She has a boyfriend, it seems, but I haven't met him. I want them to know the facts. But I don't want a thirty-year-old indiscretion to tear my family apart."

"It wasn't your indiscretion, Anna," he said. "How could they blame you?"

She actually laughed. Did he know so little about families, about kids? They blamed their parents all the time! Sometimes until they were old and gray. It wasn't uncommon that people blamed their parents after they were long dead. She'd seen it all through her legal career as an attorney and judge and it was impossible to determine if it was justified or not. The only thing she was completely sure of—she had loved her husband and had done her best to be a good wife and mother. But is that what her children thought?

"Sometimes it seems like it's always the mother's fault. In some eyes, anyway. I'm sure I was far from perfect. But I didn't have an affair. Sometimes I wish I had."

"Where did that come from?" Joe asked.

"Well, there were times…" she said, letting her voice trail off. "There were times I was lonely. There were times Chad didn't try very hard. There were times I suspect he blamed me for his unhappiness when any card-carrying therapist knows we're in charge of our own happiness."

Joe was quiet for a moment but she could hear him breathing into his phone. "I remember something that cures you of melancholy. Are you working all weekend?"

"I'm going to go see Blanche at about two this afternoon and I'm taking Sunday off. Why?"

"I think if I bring you Thai takeout, I'll be your hero!" Joe said.

"Well, at least you'll be my good friend," she said.

Anna was thinking about Joe in a way she never had before. Oh, she'd always known him as a man she trusted and respected, a huge success in academia, a man admired by many. But she was married. She thought of him as Joe, her friend. In this new incarnation of their friendship, thoughts of him now stirred deeper emotions.

Joe would bring her Thai food because he remembered that Thai food made her happy. She realized that Joe treated her the way she wished Chad had, as if her happiness mattered.

During her visit with her mother, Blanche recognized her for a little while, then slipped away from her again. She spoke to the nurse once more and the news was no better; she was headed for memory care and hospice and this could well be what she knew of her mother from here on.

She wondered, Did the average person in the world ever realize what a woman, widowed at fifty-seven, with a complicated family had to carry on her back? She was crumbling under the weight of responsibility of a home, family, job that served the people. There was no room for her emotional load. When women came into her courtroom, women who had equal stress on a wait-ress's or teacher's income, she understood them. She not only understood them, she identified with them, and hers was a privileged life.

On that same day, she found herself staring into the bathroom mirror and gently pulling back the skin on her face, tightening it. She thought maybe the last ten years had caused her mouth to droop and jowls appear on her jawline. But her eyes were remarkably wide for a woman her age. She had thought about a facelift; her neck was getting crinkly. But women born and raised in the San Francisco area tended to have great skin, given their lack of exposure to the sun. It could take ten years off a face.

When Joe finally arrived, he was carrying two large sacks of food and the aroma was spectacular. She took one of the bags from him and led the way to the kitchen. "I'm so glad you're here," she said. "I saw Blanche today and she's teetering on the edge, her lucid periods dimin-ishing. At least she's not in any pain, and even though she's not really all there, she doesn't seem to be suffer-ing any great anxiety." She put her bag on the kitchen island and took his bag out of his hands. "Dementia is one mean SOB."

When she turned toward him, she found herself in-stantly scooped up into his arms, his lips on hers, his big hands moving up and down her back. Her breath caught, her eyes widened in surprise, and then slowly she let herself fall into his kiss. It was so odd to her that it felt like something she'd known for a long time when in fact he'd just kissed her for the first time a week or two ago. Her eyes slowly drifted shut, her lips completely relaxed; her arms went around him to embrace him and it was delicious. He pressed her back against the island and held her there with his whole body. He was firm and strong and she immediately felt his desire rising against her, and this time, she knew, he would not say goodbye when this kiss, this long, deep kiss, was complete.

He pulled away from her lips just slightly and whispered, "I had a hard time waiting for this."

She nodded, hoping for more.

"We're alone, aren't we?" he asked.

"We're alone."

His breathing quickened a little and he pulled her closer, kissing her more. Their tongues played and their bodies strained. "Anna, I've been thinking about this moment for days."

"When did this happen to us?"

"I don't know," he said, tenderly brushing her hair back over her ear. "It seemed like a natural progression. We were friends…"

"Good friends…"

"Dealing with our grief and trying to put sense to troubles, and somewhere in the process we became closer. But I've always felt the pull."

"You have?" she said, genuinely surprised.

"Oh, I have. The first time the thought occurred to

me was after Arlene left. I don't know if you realized it but we were both struggling with our marriages at the same time. When I was divorced, I felt so free. The weight of a bad marriage is such an enormous burden, and when it was gone, even though we still had our issues, I felt like I'd shed a hundred pounds. My mind turned to you so naturally, but you were managing to put your marriage back together."

"I was in law school. Trying to save myself, trying to be prepared when he did it again."

"And I stayed away because you were a temptation."

She touched his cheek and smiled. "I noticed you had gone missing but I never thought it had anything to do with me."

He kissed her again. "It had everything to do with you. I found myself wishing Chad was stupid enough to let you go and that could have been bad all around."

Anna thought about that for a moment and in an instant she could see how devastating that might have been, nothing but doubt and hard feelings and suspicion, not to mention the rebound effect. It would not have worked. But would this?

"Is this happening?" she whispered.

"Not in the kitchen, I hope," he said. "The bedroom, then?"

"If you're sure," she said, and was conscious of how weak and uncertain her voice was. It was not a sound she heard often. Anna was, if anything, strong and decisive.

"Oh, honey, I'm sure," he said with a kiss. "I don't want to rush you. Seduce you, absolutely. Not rush you."

"How can I be nervous?"

"Good question. Why are you nervous? I can see you wondering if you're ready for that level of intimacy with me, even though we've known each other forever, but—"

"I've had only one partner," she said. "And we certainly weren't burning up the sheets, especially the last few years."

"No one before Chad, then?"

She shook her head.

"Amazing," he said. "Well, come with me, Anna. I hear it's like riding a bike." He took her hand and led the way. "I think we're going to be just fine."

As they stood in the bedroom beside the bed, he kissed her again and again while he slowly lifted her sweater and peeled off his shirt. They pressed together and somehow her bra disappeared and they were flesh to flesh.

"This is so nice," he whispered.

I never realized how much I wanted this, Anna thought. She had learned to live without this in her life and it was a great loss. She wanted not only to feel loved and desired, she wished to desire again. Life moves a little more slowly when you're older except in this. In this, desire was quickly raging within her and she felt so much younger and more vital. She thought about their ages—fifty-seven and sixty-three—and something she didn't know ten or twenty years ago was that passion could be amazing and crazy even at this age.

Within moments their clothes were gone, the covers were drawn back on the bed and they lay together, naked, holding each other. He had tossed a condom on the bedside table, just his tacit gesture that he would protect whether or not he thought it was necessary. And it brought to mind that she could return the favor. As women of her age often experienced some challenges, she had a few tricks up her sleeve. She rolled away from him long enough to fetch a small vial from the bedside drawer. She held it up. Lubricant. A little help. "Do you think this stuff goes bad if too much time has passed?" she asked.

He laughed and took it from her. "I'm sure it's good. Let me take care of this when it's time."

Anna had been nervous, but not hesitant. Now, in his arms, naked against him, she was amazed at how confident she felt. It's good when a woman feels wanted, feels chosen by the very one she would choose. He murmured against her neck and breast, told her she was beautiful, massaged and stroked every inch of her body. His fingers were soft and deft, soft as a feather sometimes, more firm and insistent other times.

And she touched him. His back was muscled, his arms were strong, his butt was solid and his... She stopped herself before she gasped. She had mentally prepared herself for an older man but Joe was as powerful and erect as a young man. When she filled her hand with him, he moaned and whispered her name.

With fingers and tongue, he worked on her until she was whispering his name, as well, exercising that special place between her legs, driving her mad with longing. Without asking, just knowing, he reached onto the bedside table for the condom and the little vial. Using his fingers as his eyes, he applied the lubricant and just that brought her close to completion.

"Hang on," he whispered. "I'm coming with you."

She welcomed him by spreading her knees, and unlike anything she'd ever experienced before, he filled her with one slow, deep thrust. And then he moved, very slowly, taking his time. She watched his face, his eyelids falling sensually, his jaw tightening, and she rode with him. It wasn't long before she took a trip over the moon and shuddered with satisfaction. He drove her up and up and up; she exploded from within and fell gently to the earth, happy and safe in his arms.

They panted with fulfillment. Things she'd known about him seemed suddenly brand-new. She knew he had a hairy chest, but against her breasts and under her hands, it felt like something she'd never known before. His long legs felt even longer wrapped around her; his lips were unbelievably soft as he nibbled at her neck and ear. He had a most alluring musk, intoxicating as it filled her head; and she couldn't help it, she wanted him again. He turned on his side and cradled her in his arms.

"Okay?" he asked.

"The best," she said.

"You're wonderful. I knew it would be wonderful," he said.

She let her fingers dance through the hair on his chest. "I don't want to ever move," she said.

"That suits me fine, though we might get dehydrated and very thin. In a few minutes we can warm up that Thai dinner. But we can come back here whenever you want to."

"Will you stay?" she asked.

"For as long as you like. This is your space, Anna. You have to tell me when you're ready to have it back to yourself."

Anna asked herself how it was possible that was the best lovemaking of her life. It must have a lot to do with how long it had been for her, how starved she was for a touch, for the give and take of physical love. Chad was hardly lacking in that department, but the last few years had been wanting. He complained that with age his libido was just not what it once was. But he didn't try, either.

What was it with men that their sex drive ruled the world? If they were in the mood, women were expected to accommodate them, but if they didn't feel the driving force of desire, it was off the table. She had asked him, *Can't you at least hold me? Kiss me?* He made a very lame attempt, a kiss, a brief hug, then said, *Sorry, babe, it's just not working for me.*

Joe didn't have any wardrobe choices so he pulled on his jeans and sweater while Anna opted for some soft lounging pajamas. Back in the kitchen, Joe pulled out container after container of Thai takeout.

"It looks like you have one of everything," she said.

"Pad Thai, coconut shrimp, green curry with eggplant, Thai larb with chicken, lettuce wraps, noodles… You shouldn't go hungry unless you're very fussy."

"You know I'm not," she said. "Let's dish up and take our plates to the living room and sit on the floor around the coffee table."

They talked first about the food, which was amazing. Then they talked a little about their kids and spent time talking about Anna's challenge with telling her kids about Amy. "The poor girl never got to have a life with her father."

"You never felt you'd been dealt a bad hand with your single mother and unknown father," Joe said.

"But it was hard and I was only too aware. I was determined not to find myself in the same pickle as Blanche. I played it safe to the end."

The last few years, she said, were difficult. There wasn't much affection in her marriage and she'd begun to think, What's the point?

It was March of 2020 when the coronavirus began to hit hard. It actually crept up slowly, as if no one knew how seriously to take it. Then overnight states recognized how virulent in nature it had become with thousands dying daily around the world. New York had to bring in refrigerated trucks to hold the dead. Many cities attempted to shut down, San Francisco being one. Employees were sent home to work while in quarantine. Shops and restaurants closed their doors, large gatherings from conventions to sporting events were canceled.

Anna and Chad were locked in together, working from home. Many changes were upon the people of the world and San Francisco had a healthy share. Anna worked on video conferencing while plexiglass barriers separating the court staff and the jurors from each other were installed. She tried not to go to the courthouse every day; she had groceries delivered. Everyone donned masks. The election for US president was in full swing along with protests and people were a little crazy.

Not a little. A lot crazy.

Chad stayed home. Chad, for reasons that made perfect sense, had an office in their home. Anna had always used the kitchen or dining room when she worked from home. Chad had to have a door that closed so he could counsel online with complete privacy.

But for Chad, such a social creature, being shut in at home with Anna and no one else took its toll and his mood became darker and darker. He became more miserable by the day. They did not see their kids—Jessie was at the hospital or her practice every day, Michael and his girlfriend saw only each other and taught school remotely, Bess continued in law school, masked up. It was a long, hard, lonely spring and summer, and fall.

"Chad slid into one of his morose periods when the governor appointed me to the vacancy in the Superior Court. And once the vaccine was approved and being shipped, the first thing he did was make a reservation for a rafting trip in Idaho. With a group he didn't know. He was betting travel would be allowed in April 2021. The fact that he didn't swim didn't concern him. 'There will be life preservers,' he said." She shook her head. "I said, 'Swimming is not your strong suit.' And he said, so snottily, 'As you should know.' There were times I thought he was one-upping me. As if he were jealous. Then I would think that was impossible."

"I think it's entirely possible," Joe said. "He was a man, after all. He might have gotten the idea you didn't depend on him."

"Joe, I *couldn't* depend on him! First of all, he was

unfaithful. Once for sure and possibly other times. And he had bouts of melancholy. It was very tiring."

"But you didn't complain?"

"I tried not to, but I got so tired of hearing him complain and whine that life just wasn't giving him enough. I'm afraid the last couple of years were a huge challenge and I'm sure I bitched a lot. I'm very sad about that. By the time he died, we weren't in a good place. That was when I started to realize how ridiculous it was for us to live together if we didn't enjoy each other's company at all! I suggested that when he got home from his trip, we should talk about a separation."

"And what could Chad have done to change that?" Joe asked.

She thought for a moment, taking a leisurely bite of her dinner, chewing thoughtfully. "He could have said he didn't want that," she finally said. "That in itself would have made a huge difference. He might have given some thought to what he was leaving for me to handle alone—like a secret daughter and granddaughter. Just explaining all that to our children is stressful. I don't want them to be angry with him and yet I can't make excuses for him, either. But most of all…" She stopped for a moment and chewed her lip. "It might have been nice if he had ever once appreciated me. I know I was far from perfect but I made a lot of sacrifices for the sake of our marriage and family."

"Gratitude, then?" he asked.

"If he'd shown the least bit of gratitude for anything, it would have made a difference, but what I wanted from him was simpler than that. I wanted him to see me. I longed for him to see who I really am and love me that way. That probably makes no sense."

"It makes perfect sense," he said with a kind smile. "To be accepted as you are."

"He was counseling couples who were struggling with marriage, just unable to make it work, and I always thought it was simple. Respect, acceptance, compromise and commitment. I understand the need to be reminded of those things. I understand the need to work on them every time they seem to slip away. But at the end of the day, those are the things you need to do. Some days it's easier than others." She twirled her fork around in her food a little. "It's very lonely when you think your partner, your spouse, isn't willing to give those simple things to you even when it's difficult."

"And you felt Chad didn't?"

"I felt Chad couldn't. Because he was busy thinking of himself." She looked at him with sad eyes. "I had decided it was time to think of myself, too."

TEN

Jessie hadn't seen Patrick in almost a week. Five days, to be exact. He'd gone to Boston for a neurosurgery conference where he was presenting and he called her a couple of times, but they hadn't talked long. He said he was exhausted, which of course he should be if he had prepared a presentation, delivered it and was thrown off his body clock due to the time difference.

He didn't even want to talk? She was beginning to feel taken for granted, or rather, feeling not quite that important. It was a familiar feeling.

She had everything worked out in her mind. She would be with Patrick forever. They might never marry, that was all right. He was too old, in his mind, to start a family, but she had never really longed for children. As long as she had Patrick, she could be happy. He hadn't quite reached her expectations, but it was still early in their relationship.

She knew he was now back in town. He said he'd be in surgery for several hours on his first day back and he was starting at six a.m. so, regrettably, he might not be able to see her for another day or two. But couldn't he at least let her know he was back, was thinking of her, couldn't wait to see her?

She called him a few times, but was forced to leave a message on his voice mail. She thought even if he was terribly busy he should have time to send her a text. So she sent him a few texts. The first few said, I miss you so much. The seventh said, Are you ignoring me?

She was working all day, of course. She had patients to see, lab work to review, specialists to call, even an office meeting with the other doctors, and yet she had time to text and call. At the end of the day she went to the hospital to check on a couple of patients, though she didn't have to. They were thrilled to have the added attention and she reassured them they were going to be fine. But her real purpose was to see if Patrick's car was in the parking lot.

And it was not!

She drove by their favorite taco shack and his car was there. She parked in the parking lot and walked into the restaurant. She didn't have to go very far—Patrick was seated at *their* table with an attractive woman. Patrick was wearing his scrubs, like he was barely off work, but the woman was dressed richly. She wore a camel-colored pencil skirt, heels—not in-the-clouds high, but three inches, anyway—a lightweight ivory sweater with a cowl neck and a fashionable leather belt over the sweater. Her brown hair was supershort and she wore gold hoop earrings. She had a briefcase and some papers on the table, but Jessie immediately thought that could be a decoy. She walked into the restaurant, to the bar area, and ordered some nachos and tacos to go. While she waited, she watched Patrick. He never looked around to notice her. In fact, he never seemed to notice anything but his nachos, tacos and the woman.

The woman shared his nachos. How sweet.

When Jessie was leaving with her takeout, he finally noticed her. He frowned; she glared. How *dare* he! He didn't have time to even text her? But he could have dinner with a sexy woman?

Her fury grew as she drove back to Mill Valley. This, too, was familiar. She'd been down this exact road with more than one boyfriend. By the time she got home, there was a text from Patrick.

I'll give you a call tomorrow. I've been slammed today and I'm going back into surgery tonight. I won't get home before midnight.

And she responded, Yes, I saw.

He did not text back an explanation or excuse, and although she was melting down from within, she didn't say or do anything more. But she wanted to.

It was nearly seven the next evening by the time her doorbell rang. Having thought ahead a little, she had brought home pizza and wine and beer, knowing exactly what he liked—what type of beer, what toppings, even that he preferred thin crust.

By the look on his face, he wasn't going to be impressed by her thoughtfulness.

"Patrick!" she said.

"We have a problem, you and me."

"What do you mean?"

"I want you to hear something," he said, stepping into her town house. "Let's sit in here," he said, throwing an arm wide, indicating her living room.

"Would you like a beer or glass of wine? I picked us up a pizza…"

He just pressed Play on his phone. *Where the hell are you? You should be back by now! I've called several times and went straight to voice mail. I know you're home by now! You said you had patients but surely there's time in your very busy schedule for a call or a text to at least tell me you're back! I had hoped to at least see you for a little while. If you can fit me in.*

"I was frustrated…by not hearing from you…"

"I told you I was getting in from Boston late, that I had a full surgical roster for the next day and was operating on the east coast time change."

"Did… Didn't you get to rest in Boston?"

"No, Jessie. Boston was not a vacation, it was work. I was in conferences or meetings day and night. Not only was I presenting, I had meetings with colleagues to discuss spinal cord surgical procedures and other professional matters. There are not that many opportunities for one-on-one discussions."

"Sorry. I, ah, was anxious to see you after being apart and—"

"Did you hear your tone? Accusing and reprimanding?"

"I…ah…"

"Seven angry voice mails and fourteen texts and then I see you at the restaurant."

"So," she said, throwing her shoulders back indignantly and lifting her chin. "Let's talk about that! You were too busy for me but you were there with a woman! A very attractive woman!"

"That was Darcy Masters, a sales rep from the Philligan Neurological Institute, talking to me about a new state-of-the-art microsurgical robot. We've had the appointment for months and have had trouble getting together. I kept her waiting for a couple of hours and told her the only time I had was a break between surgeries but I was starving. She offered to buy my dinner if I'd fit her in. I had to go right back to the hospital."

"Oh. Well, I was just getting some dinner on the way home…"

"You're sure you didn't make a special trip?" he asked.

"Of course not," she said, but her cheeks flushed with the lie.

"We have a problem," he said. "Rather, I believe you have a problem and it's affecting me in a very negative way."

"What are you talking about?" she said, giving her hair a toss.

"Seven messages and fourteen texts, getting more sarcastic and angry by the minute, that's what I'm talking about! It's insane."

"Okay, I won't do that again."

"You won't do it to me again," he said. "This is where we say goodbye."

"What? Just because we have a slight difference of opinion? We're just getting to know each other!"

"And in such a short period of time you've managed to make me feel like a caged animal. Like a stalked and captured prey. Listen, I'm going to do you a favor here." He stood and reached into his pocket and pulled out a business card, handing it to her. "Do yourself a favor and give this guy a call. He's very good. He's helped me and a couple of friends. He gets very high marks for taking on big egos and disbelievers."

She looked at the card. She laughed out loud. *Thomas Norton, PhD, Bradford Institute of Psychotherapy. Counselor.* "My father was a psychologist," she flung at him. "Believe me, if there was a problem—"

"And the cobbler's children have no shoes," he said. "Suit yourself. But I think you could benefit from a little assistance."

"If I agree to see this guy, can we try again?"

"Absolutely not," he said. "I know better than to get into a toxic relationship."

"Toxic! How dare you say that to me!"

"Can I make a suggestion?" he asked.

"I don't think so!" she snapped.

"Get together with some of your family and closest friends," he went on, ignoring her. "Ask them if there's been a problem communicating or understanding each other. Feel free to use our relationship as an example— I told you I'd be back in five days but would be tied up for a day or two longer, catching up on work and surgery here. It all worked out exactly that way and yet you somehow felt slighted and ignored. Ask the people you're closest to if they have experienced this kind of disconnect. Get help. You don't have to live like this."

"But, Patrick! You're done with me?"

"Yes, Jess. You're in trouble. You may have a personality disorder. A lot of beautiful young women think it's just part of looking for the right guy, but it's more serious than that. You're demanding and abusive."

"That's not true!"

"Sadly, it's totally accurate."

She felt herself crumbling. "I bought us a pizza," she said, a catch in her voice. "Your favorite kind."

"Think about yourself for a while," he said. "Put yourself first. You don't have to live with disappointment. Nor do you really want a man who is constantly bent to your demands. Believe me, it wouldn't last. Talk to someone. Get help."

"I'm a doctor!" she said, shouting. "I'm a busy doctor! And my father was a therapist! I don't need help!"

"Being a doctor is no pass," he said. "Trust me, I know that from firsthand experience. Doctors are as messed up as anyone. In fact, for some, with the pressure they're under, they're even more vulnerable. And sadly, least likely to ask for help. Do yourself a favor. Don't be that doctor."

"Patrick, I had a bad week! Be fair!"

"This has nothing to do with fairness, Jess. You are one giant red flag. Staying with you now would only make things worse for both of us." He stopped at the door and threw her a wan smile. "Here's to better days for you."

And he left.

* * *

Anna found a renewed source of energy in her nights with Joe. Although her office was flooded with work, she felt somehow better equipped to handle it. She might have been mentally reluctant to move in a new direction, with a new man, but she found talking to Joe almost daily and spending a night or two a week with him gave her a sense of comfort and well-being. And confidence. It was amazing what being intimate did for the nervous system.

But she didn't tell anyone. Not even Phoebe, who she could trust to keep a secret if there was a secret to be kept.

"I'm just a very private person," she told Joe. "I'm used to not talking about my private life."

"You aren't afraid the kids will give you trouble, are you?" he asked.

"The kids love you," she said. "I'm not sure that's the same thing as approving of me sleeping with you. Chad has been gone for six months. That's not a long time."

"Ah," he said. "You're waiting for their approval?"

"No! I think there's a secret widows or divorcées handbook that specifies the length of time that's appropriate. And I think it's longer than six months."

"Is it longer for widows or divorcées?" he asked.

"I don't know. I just know that anything in an elected official's private life can be overscrutinized. But that's the half of it. My kids are a little unstable. I'm not sure where they are in dealing with their father's death. The last time I talked to them Jessie was angry, Mike was brokenhearted and Bess was coping in her own way by not feeling anything. But Bess has a man in her life now and I want to meet him and see if he's right for her. And there's the small matter of finding out if I have a brother. I sent in one of those DNA kits and have signed up online for their search program."

"And have you talked to Amy lately?" he asked.

"Yes," she said softly. "I went by her house one afternoon and held Gina. Amy woke her to lift her into my arms. She's so sweet. Amy goes back to work in a week and there will be a nanny. Not a live-in nanny but a woman in the neighborhood. Amy assures me that I can stop by, with notice, to see Gina, whenever I like."

"You know what you're doing, don't you?" Mike said. "Your family fell apart with Chad's death and now you're trying to reconstruct it."

"And it is completely unrecognizable!" she said. "And I keep looking for you in the family picture and I'm not sure where you are!"

"Why don't we just not worry about that for a while. No one suspects I'm anything but a family friend and there's no worry about making it more at this time. Anna, what you and I have found, it's okay if it's just about us. It's only been a few weeks that our status has changed. Well, except for one thing…"

"What one thing?" she asked.

"I love you," he said. "That's not a big change. I think I've always loved you."

Anna loved him, as well, but she merely smiled in return. She wasn't ready to commit, though she felt in her bones that this was somehow meant to be.

About once a week, Anna would either work from

home and Joe would come to her or she would leave the courthouse a bit early and go to Palo Alto and spend an evening and night with him. They did this without changing their habits as far as their families knew. If Anna got a call from one of her kids, she'd chat for a while, claim evening and early-morning meetings. "We're desperate to catch up on cases that have been postponed over and over so do me a favor and give me some notice if you want to get together. My whole office has been working a crazy schedule." Joe talked to his son, an Oakland firefighter, a lot but saw him only about once or twice a month, and Melissa, his daughter, he tried to visit in Bodega Bay at least once a month.

The rest of the time belonged to Joe and Anna... and their jobs, which were quite demanding. They each traveled back and forth to work and each other's homes with files and laptops and iPads. They learned how to make stacks of work material on each other's dining tables and countertops. Work that usually went ignored as they concentrated on each other.

"Why aren't you using Chad's office?" Joe asked Anna.

"I'm not sure," she said. "I've never been comfortable there, maybe because it was Chad's space and he was so protective of it. And also, he was always so critical of my work-mess, as he called it. Whether I was studying for a law degree or working as a judge, he never quite accepted my work clutter as necessary, even though he had the only work space with a desk, credenza and door that closed. During the pandemic lockdown, I threatened to write a book on how to create efficient piles of work. He wasn't amused, but still didn't offer to share his space."

"It's free now," Joe said.

"I don't know why, but it still isn't mine. I cleaned it out, made sure the counseling office got all his records and packed up our personal records, but it still doesn't feel like mine."

"Then get rid of it and do something else. Flip-flop rooms or something. Get a new desk. Anna, you're a judge. You don't have to work on the kitchen counter anymore."

"But you do," she reminded him.

"I'm different," he said. "I'm a teacher and I have an office on the campus. I bring work home because it's convenient. Detectives don't come to my house late at night for a warrant."

"One thing is settled," she said. "We have too much clutter between us to ever live together."

"We wouldn't if you'd make yourself a home office."

"I'll get right on it," she said. But she was thinking, *One thing at a time.*

The more time she spent with Joe, the more she realized there had been something missing in her marriage. It was especially obvious with the smallest changes— she could turn over in the night and he was immediately there. Chad had not been much of a cuddler and scooted as far away as he could get. With Joe, they had watched movies in bed together and they were always touching. Even the smallest touch was significant. Sometimes only their feet were touching, but it mattered and sent warmth radiating through her. In the morning when she woke, he was usually curling around her. But she enjoyed just as much those mornings when he rose early and had coffee ready for her in the kitchen.

Whatever the circumstances, Anna had the one thing she didn't think she needed. She had love in her life again, and it was rich. She was relaxed and calm at her center. She fed hungrily on the sex, something she hadn't anticipated or longed for until it happened, and the one thing she always thought she had with Chad she now realized was wanting—companionship. Anna and Joe had long conversations about everything from movies and books to politics and religion.

Anna had learned early how to support Chad and he required a lot of support, but she had never been supported. She only realized since being with Joe that even though she'd accomplished so much against so much adversity, Chad had not been proud of her. Oh, he said so, but it just didn't ring true. There was a slight pullback, a slight curl of the lip as he said, "Oh, Anna is the accomplished one in the family." Chad considered himself the steady one in the marriage, yet Chad was the one who had a crisis about every four years, a crisis of, "Is this all there is?" Then he would work through it and emerge both satisfied and grateful. But the six or so months it took him to come to terms with his personal crises were hard on Anna.

One early morning when Joe and Anna had to rise and go to their jobs, she turned into Joe's arms and said, "I didn't realize until now—I was lonely in my marriage."

"I'm not surprised," Joe said. "I loved Chad and he

was a good friend, but he was also selfish. Focused on himself. Yet he was well-known as a great counselor because he was smart and objective. I never figured out how he managed that, but it's true. In work he was supportive of women, in his personal life, he wanted to be catered to by his woman."

"Huh," she said. "Women loved Chad. Too many of them, in fact."

"He was what we call a mother-man," Joe said. "He wants to be the leader, the protector. He wants a soft woman who needs him, who depends on him, who just couldn't make it without him. But that sort of woman is a lot of work so he opts for someone strong, someone who can take care of him. He once told me you were the smartest, most capable woman he'd ever known."

"He told me that, too. I'm trying to remember if his lip curled when he said it. I know that when he said he was proud of me for being appointed to the bench he had a slightly sour look on his face."

"It was easy for Chad, a therapist, to give lip service to wanting his partner to be his equal," Joe said. "He was probably sincere, as long as you didn't stray a quarter inch ahead of him in accomplishments. Anna, sooner or later you'll see, you were the glue in the family. You always have been."

"Chad was as involved a father as I was a mother..."

"Still, you were the binding force," Joe insisted. "He depended on you for everything."

And I was lonely, she remembered. *And didn't really know it until Joe became my friend and lover.*

"I can't put off telling the kids any longer," she said.

"If I wait any longer, who knows how much I'll have to lay on them at one time! It started out with a secret sibling, now it's a sibling with a child and their father's old friend has become their mother's boyfriend. Oh, and there's a hint of a missing uncle out there somewhere. I don't dare wait another month."

"The leaves are changing," Joe said. "On Saturday, let's take a long drive north. We can talk about it in the car and stop for seafood. If you want support, I can shore you up when you tell them."

She rubbed her temples. "It gives me a headache just imagining it."

"Stress is no one's friend," he said. "Can you sneak away this weekend?"

"I'll check with Phoebe, but I think I can. I really need this over with."

The early October sun was bright and warm on Saturday. Joe got up early to make the drive to Mill Valley to pick up Anna. The afternoon before he bought a few snack items and drinks at the grocery store and assembled them in a basket and cooler for the road.

He called her from the car. "I realize I'm a little early and I don't want to rush you. Just let me know when you're ready."

"I'm ready!" she said. "I can't wait."

And Joe realized they'd never spent a whole day together since they had attained this new status. When she opened the door for him, the bright shine of happiness on her face just melted his heart and he grabbed her in an embrace and kissed her till she laughed against his lips.

"I looked forward to this all week," he admitted.

"Should we put together a little something to snack on while we drive or if we should stop?"

"I've already done that," he said, grinning like a boy.

"What a guy. Then let me get my purse and let's head into the hills."

They chose to drive through the coastal towns north of San Francisco and into Sonoma where there were plenty of vineyards and restaurants because eventually they'd want to stop for a meal. The scenery was amazing on this bright fall day and they encountered dozens of groups of cyclists enjoying the cool fall air. The hillsides to the east of them were starting to color beautifully.

But the best part of the drive was being together in the car. When they crossed over some road construction, they had a conversation about infrastructure and what it might entail in California. When they saw a group of about a hundred cyclists gathered in a park as a resting stop, they talked about what they might have in common when it came to outdoor exercise. When they were driving through Sonoma, they talked about vineyards and wine and even stopped at a winery to buy a few bottles for later.

They talked about their parents, their kids, their jobs. They even spent a few minutes discussing catalytic converters on cars. They pulled into a rest stop but passed the picnic tables and opted for a grassy spot under a big tree.

"I feel like I'm getting to know you all over again," Joe said.

"After we've been on the phone for an hour or spent an evening together, I wonder if there will come a time when we have nothing to talk about. It doesn't seem so today."

"There will never be a time we have nothing to say to each other, but I look forward to the time we can be quiet together. I read all the time and so do you—you can't talk while you're reading. But you can be together just the same. I've been divorced for a long time, since my kids were little, but that's something I never had with my wife. We never had companionable silence."

Anna laughed. "Nor did Chad and I. Chad always had a lot to say."

"Didn't he play the counselor card and ask you how you felt about things?"

"Very rarely," Anna said with a laugh. "Chad always wanted to make sure I understood how he was feeling."

"Yeah, that was Chad," Joe agreed.

"But he did know empathy well. There were times I needed him and he could comfort like a pro."

"Which is what he was," Joe reminded her. "Let me ask you something. If you could wave a magic wand and have anything you want, what would it be?"

"Ah, you might have found my fatal flaw," she said. "Not that I would wish for too much, but that I want too little. All I ever wanted was someone to be tender with. Someone to trust and love and believe in. I learned early on that my husband wasn't perfect, but then neither was I so why would I judge? I had always hoped that if I could be thrilled with the love of a simple, honest, dependable man, that he would therefore be grateful for me. Even with the rough patch we were traveling through, I still believed it was possible. But now he's gone and I'll never know."

Joe leaned toward her and kissed her. "It's still possible, Anna," he said. "I'd like to apply for the job."

ELEVEN

Michael called his mother at about ten in the morning, respectful of the fact that it was Saturday and she had been working late every day. "I thought I'd swing by the house and make sure everything is handled—like trash collected, yard and pool clean and serviced, you know. Things Dad would have done." Though even Michael knew that Chad wasn't that great with household chores.

"Oh, Michael, that's not necessary, really. I called the yard and pool people and they're on top of it. And I'm not going to be home today. I'm driving up to the wine country with a friend."

"A friend? Who?"

"Someone I've known for years. From work. I don't plan to be home until early evening. Do you need me, honey?"

"No," he said. "No, of course not. I just wanted to help out."

"That's so thoughtful," Anna said. "Don't you have a practice or game or something?"

"No, we had a game last night. We won."

"Congratulations! I'm sorry I missed it! I'll make it a point to see the next one. Why don't you take a day off. That's what I'm doing. The last few weeks have been so intense."

"Good idea," he said. "But if you need anything done, you'll let me know?"

"Of course, sweetheart. I'll talk to you later. Maybe tomorrow?"

"Perfect," he said.

But Michael's life was anything but perfect. He was miserable. If it wasn't bad enough he was grieving the loss of his dad, he had broken off with Jenn and she had disappeared. Michael tried to remember what he thought the result of breaking up would be and it was nothing like what had actually happened. He thought he had been doing the difficult but noble thing by breaking up, setting them both on a path of starting over, but that wasn't what happened. Jenn was angry and out of patience, which he now realized was just what he deserved. He'd been an idiot, letting a woman he cared so deeply about get away.

He parked his SUV in front of his mother's house, thinking about what to do next. After a long mental study of his emotions, he got out of the car and opened up the garage. It looked pretty good, since he'd done a serious cleaning and trash hauling just a couple of weeks ago. He let himself into the house; everything was tidy and in order—no dishes in the sink, the bed made, his mother's briefcase and laptop and some files on the breakfast bar, a sight he'd grown accustomed to.

He peeked in his dad's office. It was stripped. The desk dominated the room, there were still books on the shelves, but it was apparent it was no longer in use. He pulled out a couple of built-in file drawers and saw that they had been cleaned out except for those that belonged to Anna—her retirement, her insurance, her bank statements. Everything for Chad McNichol or Chad and Anna seemed to be gone. For the first time he asked himself why his mother's work files and laptop were still in the kitchen when there was a beautiful office available.

His first thought was, *My mom has it all under control.* His next thought was, *She sure adjusted quickly to Dad being dead.*

He sat on the couch and called Jenn. His call went to voice mail. Again. "Hey, Jenn, are we ever going to actually talk? Because I don't like the way we left things. I'd like to talk about a few things. I think I'm even more messed up than before and maybe this is all a big mistake. I think I have a few things to explain. I don't think we're done with this yet. Maybe I was premature and there are things to work out, but if you won't even take my calls how can we ever work anything out? So, how about you call me back this time? Or maybe text me or something? Or maybe you were just ready to break up and this is this easy way?"

Of course he immediately regretted it. It was entirely his fault and he knew it. He had been panicked, worried that he could never be the kind of awesome family man his dad had been and was afraid to commit. Because what if he had kids who loved and needed him and he

died? Who would take care of them then? He wasn't a
PhD and Jenn wasn't a judge! Money was tight between
them. What if he had a couple of adorable little kids, a
gorgeous sexy wife and went skiing and bam! Hit a tree!

The chime on his phone rang. He had a text.

You want to talk?

Yes! I know I messed up but I really miss you.

Do you want to come over for dinner? To talk?

Oh, he really did. He texted her back that that would
be good and she told him to be at her condo at seven.
He arrived early and sat in the parking lot until the appointed time, but when he got to her door, he had lost
all his cool. He realized he should have stopped to buy
her flowers, but he hadn't. When she opened the door,
he snatched her up in his arms and devoured her with
a kiss so hot and hungry there was no time for talking.
He was so overcome he could barely get in and close
the door.

This was one of the things that ate at him—that they
were so right for each other. As he held her face in his
hands he was overwhelmed by passion. From the sounds
she made, she was just as gone. He could vaguely smell
the aroma of something Italian and noticed a long ba-
guette on the counter, but couldn't stop from hugging
her, kissing her, pulling at her clothes and walking her
backward toward her bedroom. "God, I missed you…"
he mumbled.

"Missed me? Or missed this?" she asked.

"It's all the same," he said. "I can't have this with anyone but you!"

"Michael…" she said in a breath. And she pulled his shirt free of his jeans.

For several blissful minutes they worked at freeing each other from their clothes without ever breaking their kisses, then fell onto the bed and rolled around, filling their hands and mouths with every essence of their bodies. They strained together, wanting each other madly. They whispered of missing each other as they came together frantically, their passion powerful and demanding.

And fast. Bam. He hadn't waited for her because he'd been so desperate and needy, so he tried to slow down long enough to at least give her some pleasure. Thankfully she was in as bad a state as he was and he felt those spasms he knew so well.

"Ahhh, there you go," he said very softly, covering her face with tender kisses.

They collapsed in each other's arms. Her head lay upon his chest and she ran her fingers through the hair on his chest; he loved it when she did that. "I think we managed to last all of five minutes," he said.

She looked up at him. "I guess you haven't been seeing anyone else."

"Of course not," he said. Then as if he surprised himself, "You haven't, have you?"

"No, but I was getting ready to. Or put it this way, if you were gone, I wasn't going to sulk and whimper. I wasn't going to wait and see if you ever came back."

"Jenn, I was just screwed up. Depressed, I think. And stupid."

"And are you back now?"

"I guess. But I'm still messed up and unsure about our future."

She wrestled free of his embrace and grabbed her T-shirt off the floor and pulled it over her head. She sat on the bed beside him; he was stretched out long and lean, his hands behind his head. He was completely naked and her overlong T-shirt covered her nudity. She sat cross-legged.

"Listen, if we had just been dating casually and you hit this period of confusion and depression and needed a break to figure things out after your dad's death, I'd just say okay, good luck, and back away quietly. But we were different. We were past all that. We were committed, looking for a larger condo so we could move in together and we were planning to get engaged. We picked out rings and were saving to pay for them. We said we loved each other, that we trusted each other, that we were going to have a family together."

"That we were taking it slow," he reminded her.

"Because of our budget. Two teachers can't afford to leap into a fast marriage before they can pay the bills."

"We were going to get married in about two years," he said. "Lately I've been doubting everything."

"I didn't sense doubt just now."

"You know what I mean. I just need a little break! Some time alone to get my head together."

"For an unspecified length of time?" she asked. "You wanted to shut it down. Until you wanted sex! I think you overlooked the part about being together in good times and bad. You came over to talk and had me naked in sixty seconds."

"You didn't fight that," he pointed out.

"So now are you going to go away for a month until you get horny again? And then tell me you might've made a mistake until you get laid again? Michael, I'm sorry for your loss and I'm more than willing to do whatever I can to help you get through it but you have to decide—are you in or out? I don't want to be your booty call!"

"You're more than a booty call," he said defensively. "I think of you as my very good… My only best… The only girl I'm… You know."

"The only woman you're currently having sex with?"

"That, for sure," he said. "Here's what might work. Let's go back to just dating. Seeing each other, for lack of a better term. Let's scrap the plans, the rings, the bigger condo, all that, and just be with each other. Maybe we'll get back to all the other stuff later."

"Later? Like in six months?" she asked.

"I don't know," he said. "We'll play it by ear. We'll start over! A new beginning."

"Except in this beginning, before we say I love you or I want to be with you forever, we'll go ahead and have sex. Like whenever you feel the need."

"Or *you* feel the need," he said gamely.

"So instead of honoring our commitment and taking it from there, like maybe going to counseling to help you with your issues, we'll just wipe out the plans and promises and jump right into being intimate with no strings?"

"You make it sound kind of heartless, but yeah—no strings. But of course I wouldn't date anyone but you."

She gave a sarcastic laugh. "That's awful giving of you, Michael. Sounds a little like a man negotiating a divorce and saying, 'I hope we can be friends.' And 'friends with benefits wouldn't hurt.'"

"You're being very cold," he said. "I do love you, you know."

"Oops," she cautioned. "If you want to start over, you can't say that yet. Have you by any chance talked to a professional about this problem you've had since your dad's accident? You must know a ton of therapists."

"Jenn, I just need a little space…"

"And just what do you intend to do with this space since you've done nothing so far?"

He propped himself up on his elbows. He crossed his long legs at the ankles. "I think you're being deliberately difficult."

She laughed, but not for long. "I'm going to take a shower. A long one. When I get out, be gone. And don't take my lasagna. I'm not looking for a good friend and occasional sex. I'm looking for a man who keeps his word and would go to any lengths to work out anything we, as a couple, might face. Oh, and also a man who is at least as concerned about what I might be going through, being dumped twice in one month. Believe it or not, I had to sweep up the pieces of my heart the last time you said, 'Let's forget all our plans and promises until maybe never.'" She got up and walked with dignity wearing only her T-shirt. She went into the bathroom and closed the door, locking it.

This didn't go at all the way Michael had hoped it would. He thought he would carefully explain what he needed, how he wanted their relationship to be for right now, and she would take care of it. Deliver. Give him what he needed. Make the peace between them so he could feel better.

I must not have explained it well, he thought.

Annoyed that she was acting so stubborn, he pulled on his clothes and left. And he was starving, yet he couldn't think of eating.

Jessie had taken the only available Saturday appointment with Dr. Thomas Norton. He practiced in the city on the bottom floor of a Victorian that had been turned into apartments. Presumably the counselor lived on the second and third floors of said Victorian. It was in the pricy area near Nob Hill; Dr. Norton must be doing all right.

The ground floor was divided into a waiting area, receptionist counter, rooms for meeting clients, and she could see a kitchen down the hall in the back of the house. The receptionist asked her to take a seat and fill out the customary paperwork and provide ID and insurance information. The wait was not long once her paperwork was complete. She was shown into a small office paneled in stained oak with bookshelves and tasteful art. The room was dominated by a desk but in addition there was a small round table and three chairs. It was only moments before a sixtysomething man came into the room. Her first impression of him from his average looks and half smile that played along his lips was that he appeared safe. Then she realized that was probably a look he had worked at and perfected. He had thick dark hair streaked with gray, quite a lot of it, bushy dark eyebrows, a stocky frame and the most engaging blue eyes. They twinkled.

He sat at the table and invited her to join him by patting the place across from him. "Dr. Jessie McNichol, is it?" he asked.

"Just Jessie is fine," she said. "I don't know why I'm here."

He chuckled softly. "I've never heard that before."

"No, really. My father was a therapist. He died recently. Dr. Chad McNichol."

He looked momentarily stunned. He pulled off his glasses, held them away from his face, closed his eyes softly. "I'm so sorry, Jessie. I met your father on several occasions. I'm sorry to say we never spent much time getting to know each other, but I always heard good things about him."

"Thank you," she said.

"Perhaps that has something to do with you being here?"

"Not really," she said with a shrug. "I'm told I have a personality disorder."

"I see," he said. He put his phone on the table between them. He had a notebook in front of him, the pen casually resting atop it. He wasn't writing. Yet. "I'm recording our session because my brain resembles a colander these days. I'll transcribe from the recording and then delete it. I may take a few notes just to keep me on track. So, who is it that diagnosed you with a personality disorder?"

"My boyfriend," she said. "Ex-boyfriend."

He actually laughed, though respectfully. "I hope you benched him when he offered his diagnosis?"

"No, he benched me. Dr. Patrick Monahan."

He was quiet a moment and then said, "Just the two of us here and yet a room full of doctors."

"You know Patrick. He said you helped him."

"That was kind of him," Dr. Norton said. "Yes, I do know him. A gifted neurosurgeon. And what did you think of his diagnosis? Or would that be better termed disposition."

"He's probably right," she said. "I'm hard to please. I'm easily irritated. I don't mean to be. I don't want to be. But I am. There you have it."

"Is this something you feel like working on?"

"What if I said no?" she asked.

"Then I'm sure we could find something to take up the time. Most of us have multiple issues that could use polish. You would be amazed."

"No, I wouldn't be surprised," she said. "My father, remember?"

"Of course. So if you could talk about anything today, what would you choose? It's your hour and I want to be of service."

"Well, there is one thing I have no one to talk to about. I'm an internist. A good one, some people say. But the thing is, I don't like being a physician. I haven't in forever."

"Hmm. That's a dilemma, isn't it? Why did you choose it?"

"I wanted to excel. I wanted to be the best at something. I wanted my father, a PhD, to be proud of me. And yet he was always proudest of my younger brother, who barely got through college."

"That must be annoying," Dr. Norton said. "Have you any idea why?"

"I'd be guessing, but because he's the only boy? And also, he's so likable—never angry, never irritable…"

"There it is again," the doctor said.

"Funny how that keeps coming up," she said dryly.

"Do you mind if I ask—when was the first time you remember being easily irritated and angry?"

"As a child I had tantrums," she said. "My mother called me her cranky baby. She said she worried about having another baby because I was a lot of work. So I don't know if this is a problem I've always had or something I've always been accused of."

"Tell me something, Jessie. When are you happiest?"

She thought for a moment. "I'm not sure. I think it's when I believe I'm achieving something, when I expect to be praised."

"Yet you're praised for your work as a physician, you told me so. But you're not happy in your work."

"Sometimes I am," she said. "When I can actually make a difference in a life. It's usually simple and routine—prescribing the right drugs or changing a diagnosis through medical intervention. It's just that… Well, it seems so simple and brief. Catching an A-fib, for example, prescribing a blood thinner, getting them to the cardiologist, a follow-up, and with the right aftercare, the prognosis is excellent. I do like the feeling of that even if it is routine."

"Let's take a different path. When are you happiest and not associated with work?"

She chewed her lip for a moment. "Recently, when I was dating Patrick. More to the point, when Patrick was courting me. When he was calling me all the time. Sometimes it was only a quick call or text to ask me for a special date or to clarify where and when. Or when we were together to do something low-key, like cuddling on the sofa, watching a movie. Or those few times I cooked for us and we ate in, just the two of us. I had only been going out with him for a couple of weeks when I began to have fantasies of being together and doing something quiet. Forever. It wasn't necessarily marriage, but rather some certainty. A feeling of belonging. Safety." She laughed lightly. "Patrick has a sailboat he loves. That is not a quiet pastime. Believe me, it's work."

"What are your hobbies?"

"I don't really have any," she said with a shrug.

"Do you hike? Jog? Knit? Work out? I know about sailing and I get the impression you find it to be something of a chore."

"I read," she said. "I like movies. I like to cook but at the end of a long day I don't usually have the energy it takes to create something labor-intensive. But when I have time I love to slice, chop, measure, sauté… It's relaxing and calming."

"If you wanted to spend the afternoon doing something you find relaxing and enjoyable, what might it be?"

"An art gallery or museum," she said. "God knows there are plenty to choose from in San Francisco. And this is very nerdy, but I could spend hours in the library or in a bookstore. You'd think, after all my years studying in libraries that wouldn't appeal to me much, but it's never grown old."

"Art museums or libraries, alone or with friends?" he asked.

"I don't mind going alone but I would go with a friend, but—I don't have many friends who find that fun. Most people I know like parties. I'm not much for parties. My last boyfriend and I took a lot of trips together with a group and really…" She shrugged.

"Does being with a lot of people make you tired?" he asked.

She grew impatient. "I don't see what this has to do with me being irritable," she said, conscious of the fact that she was acting irritable. "Yes, large groups of people make me tired. See, I'm not fun."

"Who says you're not fun?"

"I don't like the same things other people like. I don't like big gatherings or parties or big groups of people. I'd rather watch sports on TV than go to a stadium and have some fan spill his beer down my back. And the sailboat—it's so lovely, but you have to work hard before you get to rest in the sun with a book! Hasn't he ever heard of a hammock!"

Dr. Norton laughed heartily at that. "You make a very fine point. It may take us a while to find the problem, if there is one. Would you mind telling me about your family?"

With a heavy sigh, she started with her mother, clearly the overachiever in the family. Then she described Michael, who was Mr. Personality, tireless, active in every and any sport. And finally Bess, the brilliant oddball and youngest of them all. Then she told him about the will and the fact that they all had different opinions of it. She was the only one who was angry that they'd never been told, annoyed because it hadn't been explained by her father ahead of time so they could all adjust to the news.

They talked for another forty minutes and she mainly answered questions that seemed to revolve around describing herself. She grew exhausted.

"I have a couple of preliminary ideas and I don't think they'll surprise you. You're an introvert. A card-carrying introvert. You are exhausted being around groups of people, particularly active people. Introverts are known for having to take a nap after a day of meetings and they almost always go home early from loud parties. You're not in the least shy and you don't dislike people, but you like them in small doses. And you have a bit of a temper. That's not something I've seen in you but something you have reported. It's possible you haven't managed your expectations of others, which can lead to disappointment. Those two things—temper and expectations—are very easily managed and even changed through modified behavior exercise. Given your discipline, you could probably do it without supervision if you really wanted to change it. Or I'd be happy to see you for a few weeks and guide you through it, if it's important to you."

"How long would it take?" she asked.

"Did you ever ask your father how long someone would have to be in therapy to achieve certain results?"

"I never had to ask," she said. "He sometimes described certain nameless patients and their problems and some of them were going to see him for years!"

"Well, that is not the case with you. I can't say this with absolute certainty without thorough testing, but I don't believe you suffer from any sort of mental disorder that would require long-term therapy and even drug therapy. You have a few personality quirks that I suspect are more force of habit than anything. Some guidance and tweaking might benefit your overall sense of well-being."

"Will it make me happy?" she asked.

"I don't know," he answered. "I'm often surprised by where people find happiness. Some poor souls find it in horrible and dangerous places, but you aren't one of those people. I usually caution my clients to be very careful in looking for happiness because it can be elusive, sneaky, even diabolical and tricky. But if I help you find a sense of well-being and confidence you may blink once and think, That felt like happiness. Most people are about as happy as they make up their minds to be—a quote most often attributed to Abraham Lincoln."

"Well, let me ask you this," she said. "Are you happy?"

"Oh, I'm tremendously happy. Every day. My wife says I'd be happy in a ditch with bombs falling on my head. I don't think that's entirely true. I suffered through a hemorrhoidectomy very unhappily and I was very grumpy. But I had heart bypass surgery and it was difficult but I was very happy to be alive and was praised as the best patient in ICU."

She made a face and crossed her arms over her chest. "I think I'm being had," she said.

"Would you like to appraise again in, say, six weeks?" he asked.

"Is that what you recommend?" Jessie asked.

"Here's what I think, Jessie. I think, given your intelligence, discipline and determination to excel, you will have a very good life with or without me. But if you also want joy, I might know a shortcut or two."

"Does that line always work?"

"Most of the time," he said. "Life's surprises can get in the way or delay progress, you know how it is. But you're sitting in a nice spot right now. I predict good results for you. What do you say?"

She thought for a moment. Although she was tired from talking about herself, tired from digging into her emotions, she had rather enjoyed the hour. "What have I got to lose? Let's see where we are in four weeks."

"Excellent. Listen, do you like cats?"

"I don't know. Why?"

"I just had a thought. You might like having one. They're very independent, answer to no one, usually self-sufficient, sometimes affectionate, more often not, but… But they're company. There's something about being owned by one that fills the lonely space with a presence. And hair. Tons of hair. I have a cat. And a robo vac." There was the sound of a door closing in the hall. "I have a group starting shortly. When would you like to come back?" He pulled his iPad from his desk, opened it and said, "I have Tuesdays at five for the next several weeks, if you're interested."

She took it. And as she was leaving his building, she felt oddly relieved.

For three years and change Anna had looked forward to going to work in the morning. Even during the pandemic when they kept going to the courthouse at a minimum for safety reasons, and when they did work there, they were few and wore masks. The plastic shields and face guards were still up in the courtroom.

On this Monday morning, Anna went in a bit early even though she wished to be somewhere else. Her weekend with Joe had been so wonderful. They had a beautiful Saturday road trip and stopped at several vineyards, then had dinner at an oceanfront bistro in Bodega Bay, the same town Joe's daughter, Melissa, lived in. "That's how I know the best spots." Then home to Anna's house and Joe spent the night.

After a long, slow Sunday morning with Joe, Anna had gone to see her mother in the afternoon. Blanche gave only a slight expression of recognition before she began asking for things.

"Can I have a glass of juice?

"Reach for that throw at the end of the bed—my knees are cold.

"Where is that other nurse, the one whose name I always forget?

"Are we playing mah-jongg today?

"When is dinner? Have we had dinner?"

Anna could coax her to talk a little bit, asking her questions about what she'd been doing or, better still, asking her questions about long ago. Her short-term memory was shot but her long-term memory was still pretty functional. So she asked, "Remember that apartment in Oakland with the dumbwaiter? It used to be a house and had a fantastic attic."

"I think I left a few things there," she said. "I have to put my feet up."

"Your feet are up, Mom. Let me cover them with the throw."

"Mom? Are you my mom?"

"No," Anna said with a laugh. "You're my mom."

"I don't think so," she said. "That's so unlikely."

"That's right, you said you had a son and gave him up. Do I have that right?"

"I said that?" she asked. "Can you tuck in this throw? My knees just stay cold."

"Sure, of course," Anna said. "Yes, you said that. You said there was a boy that you had to give away but you kept the girl."

"I guess that's right, then. I think I need another throw over my legs."

Anna just patted the throw that was already there, as though she'd covered her anew. "Who was his father, then?"

"He wasn't important, when you get down to it. I was young and as stupid as all young girls. He was older. He's dead by now, I'm sure."

"And who was the girl's father?" she asked.

Blanche was quiet for a long time. She never did answer the question. An hour later when Blanche had started to doze and Anna was leaving, Blanche said, "It was hard then, you know. Having a baby without a husband. The hardest thing I ever did. I always wonder how I got into that mess."

"Tell me about it," Anna said.

She was answered by a soft snore.

The next day in her office, checking emails and looking through her calendar, she came across an email from the Family Tree Agency, which she had used to check her DNA, and they sent her a long list of names of people who were looking at their possible family connections, names of people who wished to be contacted if there was any kind of match. Most were expecting to find ancestral connections.

There was a man, a sixty-three-year-old white male, born in Modesto, California, with no information about his biological parents except that his mother put him up for adoption when he was a newborn and she never registered with any of the internet agencies giving her permission to be located. And according to the DNA ladder in the agency where Anna had sent her specimen, there was a possible partial match. A strong possible match.

His name was Phillip Winston and he was, of all things, an attorney. He lived in Rhode Island. She couldn't use state or county money to investigate this man before contacting him, but she knew of many resources through the DA's office of investigators who could work on the project for her, and if it looked legitimate, she would then contact this man.

TWELVE

Jessie was surprised to find how much she enjoyed going to therapy. She'd been cynical to start, but it certainly was true comfort. In just two more weeks of counseling and behavior modification, learning ways to keep herself from caving in to feelings of inadequacy, she was noticing an increase in her level of confidence. Most of that came directly from talking through situations that threatened to make her angry or leave her feeling as though she just wasn't getting enough attention.

What struck her as so odd was that her sessions with Dr. Norton were not emphasizing that she change so much as reinforcing that her instincts were appropriate, though at times her responses were not. For example, expecting a man one is sleeping with to at least communicate was not wrong, but berating him in a temper was not going to get the desired response. Her tone could be harsh. Angry.

Rather than working on stopping the anger, she was

learning to channel it into more positive encouragement to get her point across.

"Isn't that manipulative?" she asked, aware that even her question held that edge of anger.

"You could look at it that way," Dr. Norton said. "But I'm here to tell you, if your goal is to change the way you're treated you will have to learn to speak as you wish to be spoken to."

He gave her homework to do—sentences recited and repeated that softened and emphasized her kinder, gentler side without de-emphasizing her need to be treated a certain way. "It's achingly simple. Rather than, 'You never even bothered to call me!' you might try, 'It would feel so good if you could just give me a quick call to say you're back in town and let me know your schedule.' Just take the accusation out and replace it with a gentle request. And remember, there will be times the response could be that he's very sorry but he's all tied up. Then you have to think about whether your request is unreasonable. Be fair. People don't respond well to being told what to do, especially angrily."

"Why does it at times feel like a foreign language?"

"Who knows how we actually learn our communications?" he said. "It's not always a simple matter of repeating what we've heard our parents say. Sometimes rooted into our words are competitive feelings, a need to fight for our space, a need to defend ourselves. It's just a matter of being able to do that clearly, with confidence and without creating more conflict. And sometimes we have to push back. Just not all the time."

It was a bit frustrating for her to think she needed

help communicating when she was a highly educated physician!

"But you don't always need help," Dr. Norton reminded her. "You apparently communicate with your patients in an authoritative and empathetic way, something you no doubt learned in medical training."

She had, and when pushed she had to admit it had not come easily. It was in fact an older and experienced nurse who had coached her, reducing the lessons to a simple, You'll catch more flies with honey.

This was somehow harder.

"I'm going to be in therapy forever," she complained to Dr. Norton.

"You'll be in therapy as long as you are impatient," he had countered. "If you think about it, you have a lot less work to do than a client who is battling early childhood abuse or addiction or some other difficult situation."

While Dr. Norton was exceptionally kind to her, very encouraging and hopeful, he did not mince words. Being selfish and given to angry outbursts was a disorder. Perhaps not the worst imaginable disorder, but still… And behaving in a way that was jealous and entitled? Disorder, also. It was completely survivable, he assured her, as long as she was in the driver's seat and wanted to make a change.

"Let's be clear," she said. "I just want to make a change so that in the end I get my way and don't feel hurt and abandoned anymore."

"I suspect that's one of the best motivations there is," he said.

He seemed to still want to talk a great deal about her family and her childhood, though she couldn't imagine what that had to do with anything. The fact was, she'd had a very nice childhood. She had loved her mom and dad very much, and when her baby brother came along, she loved him. She couldn't remember ever not loving them.

Little by little she began to remember very small things from when she was four, five or six years old. She remembered that she had to sit on her mama's lap because her brother was sitting on Daddy's lap. For a while her daddy slept in her brother's room and didn't sleep in her room because there wasn't as much room for that extra bed. Her mom and dad both worked and she remembered that she was in a program at school and her grandmother went to her program while her dad went to Michael's. It seemed like a Christmas program.

"My mother wasn't very patient," she said. "I probably get it from her. And when Bess was born I thought, *Yay, another girl.* I took care of her all the time, watched over her, fed her, changed her. I was so relieved not to have to contend with another boy."

But then Bess turned out to be different from other children and didn't adjust to preschool or day care. She had trouble being touched, had difficulty around large groups of children. She needed lots of special education and sometimes medication to relax her compulsions and help her focus.

"I'm going to go out on a limb here and suggest that, as the firstborn, you got a lot of attention and praise and affection. And then a baby came along who required the same, and that left your cup a little empty, sharing all that adulation. And then a third baby came to the family and this one turned out to really be special needs and you lost more of your position."

"But I loved them!" she said. "And I helped, I really helped."

"Of course you did, but you also suffered a little loss and maybe unintentional neglect."

"Because they had to read to two or three children instead of just one? Even I am not that ridiculous and selfish!"

"Of course you're not, Jessie. But you are vulnerable," he said. And there was something about the gentle way he said it that made her heart melt. "And who knows what was going on with your parents at the time. You weren't the only living being in that house with a life. A complicated, sometimes difficult life."

She learned that sometimes it was possible to experience loss as a child and not spontaneously get over it. There were times it set up a pattern of always expecting to be left out. Hurt. A sense of longing that is difficult to satisfy. Dr. Norton asked her to examine relationships that were meaningful to her and how she had been affected.

She thought about boyfriends, right up to Jason, who left her because she was always mad. Her brother was seldom in touch and they disagreed with each other about everything and he accused her of always being mad.

Jessie cried a lot with the remembering. She thought a lot about her father and how much he praised her, how much attention he gave her, but the second he shifted his focus to Michael, she felt slighted. She cried because of how immature that seemed. She cried because she wished she could take back some years and do them better. With all the love and support she'd gotten from her parents, why couldn't she have been a better, more grateful daughter?

She reported to Dr. Norton that she'd been feeling terrible regret and emotionalism and he said, "Sometimes just taking a closer look at things gives us a chance to purge. Are you feeling more in control now or are you in need of help? I can get you a prescription if you're struggling."

"I'm just feeling hyperaware," she said. "And like I owe the world an apology."

"Not at all, Jessie," he said. "You've actually done the world a great service. You've taken care of dozens if not hundreds of sick patients, you love your family and you're looking for ways to better communicate with them and you're learning more about yourself every day."

"You could have warned me," she said. "I didn't realize it would be this difficult and painful."

"Growth has its price," he said. "But not growing has a higher price."

It had been a difficult year for Anna but the last couple of months had brightened her outlook on just about everything and that was primarily because she had Joe in her life. His love and support had meant so much to her. She hadn't realized that her life had been lacking in love and romance until Joe filled up that space inside her.

Joe didn't mind at all that many of his intense discussions with Anna were on the subject of Chad. Not even when Anna was grieving Chad, missing him. After all, Joe missed him, too. They'd been friends for a very long time, and while Joe still held a few confidences for Chad, the one really major secret Chad had never confessed. Joe did not know Chad had a child outside of his marriage.

What he did know and would never share was that Anna was correct—Chad wanted his wife to be smart, accomplished and, as he had said more than once, the most competent woman he'd ever known. He had confided long ago that he chose Anna to be his wife for that specific reason. He wanted a partner whose intelligence and abilities he could rely on so he could concentrate on becoming a success in his field. He had said so more than once. He didn't want a woman who couldn't balance a checkbook or perform CPR or make critical decisions about managing a home and family, plus earn a living. Chad had been well aware that his particular field was a tough one to break into and tougher still to become successful in. Counselors were a dime a dozen in California and certainly in San Francisco. Making a good deal of money at it went with reputation earned through accomplishment. And the competition was fierce.

"I knew Anna would be the best right hand a man could have in a marriage," he had once told Joe. But years later he had said, "Do you have any idea what a toll it's taking on our family for her to be in law school? I don't know what the hell she's trying to prove."

She was undoubtedly trying to prove she could take care of her family without a devoted husband, which Chad had established he might not be. He had established that very well with an affair. A rather long-term affair that had lasted many months. Chad had admitted he had lied about his marital status, thus giving the other woman reason to think he was available.

Anna was correct, it was a good marriage. Because it was more of a business arrangement for Chad than a love match. Since Joe's own marriage had gone so wrong, Joe often wondered if maybe Chad had the right idea. But there was that one thing Anna didn't know. Chad confided to Joe, "I've never been in love, not really."

Joe was in love. He wondered just how blissful life with Anna could be if he gave her everything she'd been lacking. He was filled with pride just considering her accomplishments, but more than that, he admired her moral core. She was an exemplary jurist because she could easily combine her knowledge of the law with her strong moral compass. If he were lucky enough to be her partner, he would make sure she knew he embraced her achievements.

He would enjoy loving Anna. Together, maybe they would make up for lost time. Maybe the best was yet to come.

There was a fierce, wet cold in early November and Joe was spending Saturday night in Mill Valley. The wind blew outside and he wasn't aware it was morning until he looked at his cell phone on the bedside table. He rolled over, scooped Anna into his arms and pressed himself against her back, spooning her.

"Well, good morning," she said with a light laugh.

He kissed her neck, nuzzling her for good measure. "It's eight o'clock," he whispered. "I slept like the dead. Because sleeping with you is always an adventure."

"Is that because I make so much noise in my sleep? Snoring and talking."

"You were either very quiet last night or I was very tired. I'm not sure I even rolled over." He pulled her closer. "Let's not get up."

She laughed appreciatively. It was deliciously obvious he was in the mood. She hadn't thought of herself as a woman in need of good sex but she found she was definitely appreciating it with Joe. Anna was delightfully surprised and happy to learn that feeling great passion was a little like riding a bike. She was not too old for it, after all. "I'll make us some coffee," she said.

She pulled a Danish breakfast roll out of the freezer, stripped the paper off and put it in a pan to warm in the oven. She rinsed off some dishes from the evening before, put them in the dishwasher and got out cups.

Then she heard the sound of the garage door rising and she froze. Within moments Michael walked into kitchen, a nonplussed look on his face. "Whose car is that?" he asked.

"Good morning, Mike," she said. "What a nice surprise."

"Mom, do you have company?"

"As a matter of fact, yes. Joe and I went out last night and he stayed over. I told him to just park in the garage. I'm making coffee."

"Mom? Joe?"

"It would have been easier had you called to let me know you were coming by but I guess it doesn't really matter. I was planning to tell you, anyway. I guess you could say we're dating, me and Joe."

"Dating? Dating?"

"For lack of a better word. We've always been good friends and since your father passed away we seem to have gotten closer. Perfectly understandable, I guess."

"But wait," he said. "What about Dad?"

"Oh, I think your dad would approve, though whether or not he did was not the first thing on my mind. He's gone, after all."

"But does this mean… Are you over him? Dad?"

"That's not really an issue, Mike. I had no plans to be dating anyone, but Joe and I shared a loss, did a lot of talking, mutually supporting each other in those difficult days following your father's death, one thing led to another and…"

"Good morning, Mike," Joe said, coming into the kitchen. Thank God he was fully dressed, shirt, shoes and all.

"You and my mother are dating?" he asked.

"Exactly," Joe said easily. "It's not as though we had to get to know each other first. We began supporting each other in grief, which was the natural thing to do. It's like dating an old and dear friend. I hope you don't mind because we're having fun. And fun has been in short supply lately."

"This is a little awkward, made more so by the fact that I'm in my pajamas and robe. Will you excuse me a moment?" Anna said.

When she got to her bedroom she noted that Joe had made the bed as well as gotten dressed. Hiding the evidence? Well, it had to come out and this was not a moment too soon. She was glad that it was Michael first; of all her children he was the one she was most comfortable with.

She dressed in her closet, hanging her robe on the hook and selecting a soft velour sweat suit. She slid on her black Skechers and quickly ran a brush through her hair. Just for the heck of it, she put on some lip gloss and thought, there, she didn't look half-bad for someone who had had a very active night and rather shocking morning.

Her cell phone was chiming. It sat on the bedside table and she crossed her fingers, hoping it wasn't some work-related emergency. She thought she was going to be unlucky since she didn't recognize the name on the screen. M. Vanderoot. Probably someone from the DA's office looking for a judge to sign off on a warrant. "Hello," she said.

"Judge McNichol? My name is Martin Vanderoot and I'm a friend of your daughter, Elizabeth. I'm calling you because Bess seems to be having some kind of… I don't know what to call it…"

"What's happening?" she said. "Just tell me what's happening?"

"Right now she's quiet but she was flipping the wall switch on and off, counting. Then she seemed to be hiding in the closet and didn't want to come out. Then she was turning the water on and off in the sink, then the closet again, then the light switch, and nearly crying. She's rubbing her arms like they itch. I have no idea what's—"

"She's having an anxiety attack," Anna said. "It's been a very long time since she's had that problem. Please ask her if she has taken her medication."

Anna could hear the young man asking Bess the question but she couldn't hear or make out the answer.

"She said she doesn't know. How can she not know?"

"Do you have a car? Can you bring her to me? I could come there but it might be better if she comes here. Tell her to bring any medication she might have. I might want to take her to the doctor, but for now, I just want her to feel safe. Can you put her on the phone?"

She heard him call Bess to the phone. Bess didn't say hello, she merely made a sound into the phone. "Bess, are you not feeling well? I asked Martin to bring you home. He'll bring you here to me. Put whatever medication you have in your purse, please. Can you do that, Bess?" Again, she just made a sound into the phone.

Anna went into the kitchen and she found Joe and Mike sitting at the counter with coffee. "I just had a call from a young man Bess is seeing. It sounds like she's having an anxiety attack along with a little OCD. I asked him to bring her here."

"We could go to her apartment," Michael said.

"I thought about that but I think it could take a while to calm her down and we might have to see the doctor, if we can even get in on a Sunday. She'll be safe here and I can manage. Michael, will you stay until she gets here? I feel like my family is falling apart right now."

"I'll stay," he said. "I can help with Bess, if you need it."

"Would you like me to go now?" Joe asked. "Tell me what you need, Anna."

She was torn. She didn't want Joe to be burdened with whatever stuff her family was going through, but she didn't want him to leave, either. "Can you stay until Bess gets here?"

"Sure."

"There's no traffic on Sunday morning. It shouldn't take too long."

Anna fixed herself a cup of coffee and pulled the Danish out of the oven. She talked to Michael while getting out plates and forks. "Are you here to see if there are any chores that need your attention? Because I really don't need your help with anything. And the weather is so cold, gloomy and overcast—no yardwork, that's for sure."

"I'd be happy to help you with anything you need but I came for another reason. I guess this isn't a good time, but I was looking for advice. I think I made a big mistake with Jenn."

Anna looked at Joe and lifted both eyebrows.

"I'll stay out of your business unless you ask me to butt in," Joe said, holding up his hands.

"I think my girlfriend issues have to wait until we resolve my sister issues. I wonder what threw Bess into a tizzy."

"It's been a long time since she's had to deal with these side effects. Maybe the pressure of law school is greater than she has let on." Again Anna's cell chirped. This time the name and number were well-known to her. "Jessie, my love. What timing. Our family is in a state."

"Is something going on?" she asked.

"Michael stopped by to see if I needed any help around the house and yard and I just got a call from a young man who is with Bess. Apparently she's having an anxiety attack and is freezing up. He's bringing her here."

"And I was just calling to see if you felt like a Sunday brunch," Jessie said. "I'll come over to make sure Bess is okay. See you in twenty minutes."

Anna sat at the breakfast bar and gently rubbed her temples.

"That's all we need," Michael said. "Bess freaking out and Jessie on her way to boss everyone around."

"I'm counting on you to stay calm," Anna said. "This would be a very bad time to antagonize your sister."

"I should be going..." Joe said, standing.

"No you don't," Anna said. "Please stay. It's the worst possible time, but once Bess is calmed down, we have to have a little family meeting and, like it or not, you're part of the family. If you run now, I won't have an ally anywhere."

"Michael?" Joe asked.

"Yeah, stay, Uncle Joe. Jessie might go easy if you're here."

Anna knew it was not Joe who would keep Jessie from throwing her weight around, but Bess. Jessie always pampered Bess. Jessie arrived close on the tail of Bess and was armed with a small vial of Xanax, with which she dosed her sister. In her childhood home and in the presence of her family, Bess calmed down visibly and immediately.

The story came out. Bess was preparing a presentation for one of her law classes in which she would have to play the part of a litigator in front of a great many law students. Bess did fine as part of the class, always seated in the rear of the room in case she needed to make a fast getaway, but arguing in front of fifty people was just more than she could bear. It was not uncommon for people on the spectrum to have great anxiety in large groups, even high-functioning autistic people like Bess. She'd spent years in manageable groups learning modified behavioral techniques to help with such a reaction and she also had antianxiety drugs to take when needed. She'd been doing so well she hadn't taken her medication in a long time. She was completely unprepared for her meltdown.

Jessie responded very favorably to finding Joe was present. *They're dating, or whatever you call it*, Michael whispered in Jessie's ear. And Jessie said she couldn't have planned that better herself.

Martin gave Bess a little kiss on the cheek, asked her

to phone him later when she was feeling better, and he left her with her family.

"Martin seems like a very nice young man, Bess," Anna said.

"Of course he's nice," Bess said.

"Good, she's back," Jessie said. "Bess, would you like a nice cup of tea?"

"As opposed to a mean cup of tea?" Bess asked. Then she smiled, though the smile was tremulous. "Thank you, Dr. McNichol."

"Well, now," Anna said. "This is the last thing I thought would happen, but I was wondering when I would get the three of you together. I have some things to tell you." She took a deep breath and said, with her usual confidence, "Bamber swinpool faletter as pump-dill clamperdose runkerplum balleroon piddle horse peling quader pell…"

And Jessie said, "Oh, shit!"

THIRTEEN

"Mom! Don't panic. Just stay calm. Joe, get my medical bag from my car—it's in the back. Michael, call an ambulance and tell them to hurry. She's having a stroke."

Garbled words spilled from Anna's lips and she began to argue in a language no one but Anna could understand.

"I want you to listen to me," Jessie said. "You're having a stroke but I'm here. We're going to get you help, and everything is going to be all right."

"Would it be faster to just take her?" Joe asked when he returned with the bag.

"Bad idea. The paramedics have life-saving drugs and equipment in the ambulance. Get me a glass of water. Quickly." Jessie pulled an aspirin bottle out of her bag and shook one out. "Mom, open up." But instead of opening her mouth she began to babble again. Jessie pushed in the aspirin and put the glass of water to her lips. "Come on, swallow it."

"Isn't that for a heart attack?" Joe asked.

"For clots. If she has had an ischemic stroke, which is the case eighty-five percent of the time, the aspirin can prevent a second stroke caused by blood clots. If it's a hemorrhage, not a good idea. We're going with the numbers. Her symptoms indicate a stroke, hopefully a transient attack that we're catching in time." She dug around in her purse for her cell phone, calling up a number. She held her mother's hand while she waited impatiently.

"Patrick, thank you for taking my call. I'm with my mother, she's had a stroke. I gave her an aspirin and will ride in the ambulance with her. Are you available? I want her with the best."

"Take her to Mercy. I'm on my way."

"Thank you! Thank you!"

Jessie smiled at her mother and gently smoothed back her hair. "You're in the best hands in the city." Anna responded with her blather. Jessie just said, "It's okay, this will pass, I promise." And then Jessie did something she rarely did. She prayed.

She looked at Bess, who was crying, rocking and biting her fingers. Not her fingernails, her fingers. Jessie reached over to her and pulled her hands from her mouth. "It's okay, she's going to be okay. Michael will stay with you and I'm taking Mama to the hospital. I will come back to you when I can but first I want to take care of Mama. Bess, stop biting, we'll be okay."

"Jessie, what can I do?" Joe asked. "Can I go with?"

"She's going to ICU, possibly to surgery. They aren't going to let you in but if you make sure Michael has your number, I'll be in touch with him and he can let you know what's happening. We caught it right away. Her odds of surviving this with a drug as opposed to surgery—excellent. I won't leave her. I promise."

The sound of sirens could be heard and it was only moments until two paramedics brought a gurney, following Michael down the hall and into the family room. Jessie stood and told them she was a doctor, had given an aspirin and called Dr. Monahan, who was meeting them at Mercy Hospital in San Francisco.

"Michael, you've got Bess and I'll call you as soon as possible." She gave his hand a squeeze. "It's going to be all right. Don't leave Bess."

"I won't. Call me, Jess."

It was a very long day of tests and examinations for Anna and Jessie never left her side. An IV had been started in the ambulance, and when it had been established that a clot or clots had caused the stroke, a drug had been administered via IV to bust apart the clot. It was successful but the amount of damage caused by the interruption of blood flow remained in question.

While Anna was going through tests and exams, Jessie made a few phone calls. To her brother, of course, who would pass information on to Bess and Joe. Then she called Phoebe, the clerk of court, who would notify everyone in the judge's office and arrange to have Anna's cases passed on to another judge. She called the memory care unit where Blanche was housed, even though it was questionable whether Blanche would even be able to make sense of the news. She called her aunt and uncle, Chad's brother and sister, and asked them to notify other family on that side. And she called her office and two of her partners to explain that she'd be taking some time off to oversee her mother's care and make sure she was settled.

Then she took her place at Anna's bedside. Anna was still babbling but every so often she caught a real word and that alone gave her hope.

Jessie had seen Patrick on and off through the day. They spoke only briefly and only about Anna's condition. Patrick was very hopeful that the damage caused by the stroke had been minor and that Anna would make a full recovery. Then at nine that night, Patrick came to Anna's room with a large latte in a paper cup and a breakfast croissant in a bag.

"Have you eaten at all today?" he asked her.

"Cookies," she said. "I don't have much of an appetite. I don't know how I'll ever thank you for what you did for me today."

"You would have done as much for me," he said. "And aside from helping you find the best neurological team, I wasn't needed. Eat a little of this if you can. You have to keep your strength up." He glanced at Anna. She looked peaceful enough, as though she was resting, but her lips were moving, and when Patrick leaned close, Anna was softly reciting numbers. Not counting, just running numbers. "Don't be surprised if that goes on through the night."

"Isn't it the weirdest thing?"

"What's weird is that it's all making perfect sense to her. Tomorrow she'll be a little more alert. Her blood pressure is stable, and when she's coherent, we'll have her evaluated and order some therapy. We won't know how much will be necessary for a few days. But she'll recover."

"Will she be back to her normal self?" Jessie asked.

He shrugged. "The potential is there, Jessie. I don't detect any left-sided weakness or paralysis. It's perfectly safe for you to go home."

"I intend to be here when she wakes up."

"You came in the ambulance. Where is your car?"

"I was at my mom's when she stroked. My car is there. After she's awake and at least knows where she is and what has happened, I'll Uber to her house to pick up my car, maybe get a change of clothes."

"I'm leaving now. I can take you to your mother's if you like. I have patients in the morning and won't be able to leave once the day starts."

"I understand completely," she said. "Lord knows you've done enough for one day and night. I promise, I don't expect anything more."

"Expectations aside, don't hesitate to call. I mean it, Jessie."

"That's very sweet, Patrick, thank you." Given their history, she was amazed he'd even answered the phone when he saw it was her number. "By the way, I've been keeping company with an old friend of yours, Dr. Norton."

His eyebrows shot up in surprise. "Are you, now? How do you like him?"

"I think he's wonderful actually. Thank you for that."

"Glad to help. I switched your mother over to the

neurology team—they're outstanding. They'll oversee her recovery. My work here is just about done—glad there was no surgery involved. I'll keep tabs on her progress, of course."

"My mother had the three of us together, just by accidental chance, and she said there was something she wanted to tell us. I got the impression it was something important, then right at that moment she checked out and began babbling."

"If it was important, it'll come back to her."

"The way that worked out, the three of us together, I'm glad it went that way." She got a little misty. "This could have been so much worse. After just losing my dad, I don't know what I'd do without my mom."

He put a hand on her shoulder. "You didn't lose her, Jessie. In large part due to your quick thinking and experience. Try to get some rest tonight. And call me if you need me."

"That's very kind of you, Patrick. I don't know how I'll ever repay you."

"Not necessary, Jess. Just take care of yourself."

Anna was confused and restless. She couldn't remember any details from the day before. They said she had a stroke but all she could remember was that no one understood what she was saying, though it all made perfect sense to her. She felt impossibly tired but she was afraid to sleep. She kept dropping off and would awaken with a start, afraid she might wake in another strange place.

She saw the bag and tubing running from her arm

upward but she couldn't remember what it was called. She wondered how much of her brain was left; she felt like a stranger in a strange land.

To her surprise, Jessie was sitting in the chair beside her bed, holding her hand on and off. Something about this was odd but she couldn't determine what. Thankfully she knew who Jessie was. Then she was suddenly aware that she had a cell phone and believed, for a moment, that the number was forever lost. Every time one of these passing thoughts occurred to her she'd try to sit up or get out of the bed. She'd thrash about until someone gently pushed her shoulders back onto the bed.

Then she opened her eyes, noticed that the room was darkened; there was a night-light casting a dim glow into the room and Jessie seemed to have a light blanket draped around her shoulders. Anna laid very still, appreciated the sight of her daughter resting in the chair. She thought maybe Jessie had been with her a full day but the last thing she remembered was being home. She'd been with someone. Was it Chad? No, Chad was not with them anymore.

Jessie opened her eyes, looked at Anna but didn't move. "I am a judge," Anna said calmly and with only a very slight slur.

"That you are," Jessie said. "How do you feel?"

"Very sleepy. What happened?"

"You had a stroke but the super-clot-buster drug was administered in time and I think you're going to be fine. Aside from a lot of confusion, it appears you survived it without much consequence. I don't see any paralysis or drooping."

"I don't remember," she said.

"Do you remember the ambulance?" Jessie asked.

Anna didn't trust her speech quite yet so she just shook her head.

"It may or may not come back to you. You might never recall the event but other things will come back. You'll be evaluated by the neurologist to see if there was any damage. I imagine there will be a CT scan. For right now, you can take a rest."

"I have a phone," she said.

"Yes," Jessie said. "When you're more alert, I'll give it to you."

"I was at home," Anna said.

"Yes, I was with you. I brought you to the hospital in the ambulance."

"And you've been here?"

"Yes. This is our second day. You've been sleepy and confused but I do think the confusion is lifting and the fog is clearing."

"Have I eaten?" Anna asked.

Jessie smiled. "No, just fluids. Are you hungry?"

"I think so," she said. "Can I get up now?"

"Let me help you sit up, but please don't get out of bed yet. One thing at a time. I'll see you get something to eat." Jessie helped her sit up, did some magic to make the back of the bed raise, and a woman wearing scrubs appeared. "My mother is starting to talk now. Can you let the doctor know? And can we get her something to eat? Maybe toast or gelatin or something like that."

"I hate gelatin," Anna said. "I read that it's made from the toe-jam of horses…"

Jessie laughed. "I don't think horses have toes," Jessie said. And to the woman she said, "Maybe we should make that ice cream."

"And coffee. With cream and sugar," Anna said.

Jessie frowned. "You don't take cream and sugar."

"I do today. How long have you been here?" she asked, not realizing she was repeating herself.

"This is my second day here with you. It takes a while after a blood clot for the brain to untangle but it doesn't appear you've had much, if any, damage. Your speech is quite clear now."

"It wasn't before?"

Jessie shook her head. "It was another language entirely, though not a known language. Scrambled. Very typical, Mom."

When the ice cream and coffee arrived, Jessie asked the nurse to stay with Anna so she could step out of the room and make a couple of calls. And suddenly something came to Anna and she said, "Jessie! Are you calling Michael?"

"Of course," she said. "He'll be so thrilled to hear you're sitting up and talking."

"Jessie, Michael needs something. He's in trouble or something! I can't remember what but I think it's urgent!"

"We'll take care of it, Mom. Don't worry. Michael is fine. Just worried about you."

"But what's wrong?"

"We'll go over all of that a little later. Try out that ice cream."

A parade of people followed the ice cream—nurses,

therapists, doctors—all checking on Anna's progress, asking her questions and patiently telling her what to expect in the coming days. The important information she got out of the long stream of visitors was that she would be evaluated for possible damage caused by the stroke and registered for physical, speech and occupational therapy as needed for as long as necessary.

She wanted to go home but was repeatedly told it would be another day or two until more information about her condition could be gathered.

Jessie was finally persuaded to leave, though she promised Anna she'd be back after picking up her car and getting a change of clothes.

A man in scrubs came into the room. Anna was gripping her phone in her hand and she thought she recognized the man, but she just shook her head.

"I'm Patrick Monahan. I know Jessie and she called me when you were having a stroke. I've been here several times but you've been a little confused and sleepy. That's predictable, by the way."

"I have a cell phone," she said, then thought how stupid that sounded.

He smiled, put his hands in his pant pockets and rocked back on his heels. She briefly thought how handsome he was. "Good," he said.

"How does it work?" she asked.

"Give yourself another few hours, don't worry about it or think about it, and it will begin to work."

"Why are you here?"

"Jessie is a friend and I've known her awhile now.

She called me when you were in crisis and I promised to follow your progress, which has been great, by the way."

Suddenly she recalled Judge William Andrews, the man who medically retired, leaving a vacancy in the Superior Court that she filled. The memory and the fact that she recalled it when she still wasn't sure how to operate her phone startled her. And Judge Andrews had had a stroke, was confined to a wheelchair, could not walk and could barely speak. He was older, but how could that be determined to be good news? She was only fifty-seven and did not want to end her career nor her active life just yet.

"Why did I have a stroke?"

"I don't know," he said. "The neurologists will look into the possibilities. Your blood pressure wasn't high that anyone knew of. Perhaps a genetic predisposition? We may not find a definitive answer but the real challenge now is to be sure a second stroke is prevented. With the right medication and regular exams, your prognosis is excellent." He smiled and took her hand. "I think you're going to be fine, Anna. Is it all right that I call you Anna?"

"Yes, of course. It's just that I have so much left to do."

"I think that's a good thing. We're here to make sure you have the time to do it."

Those should have been comforting words and Anna was glad he had stopped by to try to reassure her, but she just could not get Judge Andrews off her mind. She had visited him in a nursing home after his stroke and he was in terrible shape without much hope of getting

better, and that was three years ago! The fact that Judge
Andrews was a good thirty years older than Anna did
not give her much comfort. In fact, in some ways it
was harder. The thought of having another stroke and
being unable to work or even enjoy life for decades
was terrifying.

Worst of all, Anna, the most capable woman, had
pride that bit at her and she couldn't fathom being a
burden to her family.

The nurses got her up and walking, using the rest-
room; she had a little dinner and while she was oddly
off balance, weak and everything felt awkward, at least
she was out of bed. All she could think about was her
fear of a debilitating stroke, one that left her helpless
and crippled.

And then toward the end of the day, while she sat up
in her bed trying to remember how to use her phone,
reading through the many old text messages, Joe walked
into her room. She looked up at him, instantly remembered their last time together and held out her arms.

"Joe!" she said.

He went to her, sat on the edge of her bed and embraced her. She put her head on his shoulder and began
to cry softly.

"Am I going to be okay?" she asked.

"Yes, Anna. It appears they got to it in time and the
drug—TPA—successfully broke up the clot. You'll have
some therapy but you're very lucky. Thanks to Jessie's
quick thinking, I believe."

"I can go back to work?" she asked. "I've forgot-
ten things."

"Things that will either come back or you can re-learn."

"We were together," she said.

"Yes," he confirmed. "The night before. And your kids all dropped in unexpectedly so the cat's out of the bag on us."

"Was it Sunday morning?" she asked.

He nodded. "Bess had some kind of breakdown, an anxiety attack over school. Michael has been with her at your house ever since. Jessie has been checking in on them by phone, making sure Bess is okay and filling them in on your progress. I wanted to be here with you sooner, but I was told you weren't allowed visitors until your condition was properly evaluated. You've been in very good hands, I take it."

"But Jessie has to go to work!" Anna said.

"I think everyone is taking time off right now," he said. "You're a priority."

"I could have been paralyzed! In a wheelchair for the rest of my life!"

"Shows you how little control we actually have," he said, holding her close. "If you'd been alone, this could have gone badly."

"Where is Jessie?" Anna asked.

"She's in the hall. I passed her on my way into your room. I think she's giving us a few minutes alone. And we need a lot more than a few minutes. When you get through the next days or weeks or whatever, when you're feeling better and more secure, we'll take a vacation."

"Are you crazy?" she asked. "I can't remember my

cell phone number! Well, I couldn't, then Jessie told me... My brain has been a mess! How am I going to go back to work?" She was thinking, desperately, *I'm only fifty-seven and just survived a life-threatening stroke!*

"It's going to be all right," Joe said. "But don't worry about making plans. You're going to have to get through this, get acclimated at home and work, and soon life will seem normal again."

"I hope so," she said.

Leaving the hospital was almost as traumatic as waking up in the hospital. Anna was really depleted in the confidence department. Armed with a treatment plan that included regular visits with a neurology team, medication for her blood pressure and blood thinners and regular appointments with speech and physical therapists, not to mention her very own internist, she was released. Regular checkups and scans would reveal any new clotting issues but her doctor was very optimistic.

To err on the side of caution, she wasn't going to be driving herself for a month at least. If she went into the city for appointments, Jessie would take her or she'd grab an Uber. Her legs were weak, unsteady, and she went home with a walker. She wouldn't be going back to work until she felt confident about her cognitive skills and her memory and judgment, but Phoebe was willing to bring work home to her and even work with her.

"And what about Joe?" Jessie asked as she drove Anna back to Mill Valley.

"What about him?"

"I hadn't wanted to pry, but are you serious?"

"No," Anna said quickly. "I mean, yes. I mean, no. Oh, dear, I don't know. I've always loved Joe but never thought of it in romantic terms, and really, we were literally propping each other up after your father's death when the idea of a romance presented itself. And now… Now the idea is almost terrifying. It is to me, anyway. And it should be to Joe."

"But why?" Jessie asked. "He was so worried about you! He plans to come over tonight!"

"I don't want to get serious about a man and stick him with a woman who can't walk or talk or tie her own shoes!"

"I know you're worried about another stroke, but the odds are good that with the right follow-up treatment, you're safe from that. Mom, you're still young. You have a lot of very functional years left if you take care of yourself and I mean to help you do that."

"Jess, you have to get back to your practice!"

"I will, but not until I'm comfortable that you're capable of taking care of yourself!"

Her instincts told her to argue that she was perfectly capable, but she was suffering a lack of bravado. "Thank you," she said in a voice even she didn't recognize. It was not the strong voice she usually used. "The truth is, that whole thing scared me."

"Of course it did."

"Oh God, there is so much to do. So much to talk about!"

"I gathered that," Jessie said. "Something about a baby…"

"Where did you get that?" Anna asked.

"You did a lot of babbling, most of it nonsensical. I wasn't sure if it had any real meaning or not. You recited numbers all through the night."

She had to talk to her kids. She had to call Amy, fill her in. But first the business at hand. "Is Michael all right? And Bess?"

"I'm going to be straight with you and I hope you can handle it. Bess needs some follow-up, maybe a program and regular meds. Your stroke really threw her and she hasn't left your house since it happened. That's okay, she can get beyond this, but a great deal of pressure isn't good for someone as mentally delicate as Bess. On the one hand, she's an intellectual giant, and on the other, a little girl with little impulse control. I'm looking into the right program for her and she's taking a leave from law school for now.

"As for Michael, he'll be fine. He just has a few challenges in the love department. He was all set to settle down with Jenn, then Dad died and Michael lost his mind a little bit. He broke up with her, regrets it hugely, tried to slap it back together and just made it worse. Jenn wasn't having it. She was very disappointed he bailed on her when things got tough." Jessie looked over at Anna. "You should have told me, Mama. Men are weak."

Anna sighed heavily. "Not all men," Anna said. And she thought, *Just some of the men we've relied on.*

It was the very next day that Anna called Joe. He was delighted to hear her voice even though he said, "I'm just between classes so can we talk later?"

"Of course," she said. "I'm home now and struggling with fatigue and still there's some confusion. I want to explain something quickly, while I can think. I live in constant worry of another stroke, and if there is one, it could go so badly. So please know that I appreciate you and love you as I always have, but I can't even think about a serious relationship until I'm fully recovered and there's no danger of me being a crippled woman for decades."

Joe actually chuckled. "But of course we can talk on the phone while you're busy controlling the future."

"You make fun of me now, but you might thank me some day."

"Whatever makes you comfortable, Anna. I'd like to see you."

"My kids are staying with me now," she said.

"I've always been welcome in your house in the past," he said. "I'm sure I can behave honorably in front of the kids. I've known them since they were born."

"I just don't want you to have any expectations!"

"God forbid!" he said, but he laughed.

Anna sat at Chad's desk, facing the computer monitor. She never liked using his office for any reason. For so many years it was off-limits because his counseling work was strictly confidential. She faced the man's face for the video conference.

"I suppose I should thank you for seeing me this way," Anna said to the man. "It saves me a trip into the city. But I'm not sure this is necessary."

"It's nice to meet you, your honor," he said, offering a warm smile. "We meet at the suggestion of your daughter. I'm Dr. Tom Norton."

"How do you know my daughter?" Anna asked.

"Didn't Jessie tell you how we met?"

"I'm very forgetful these days," Anna said, though truthfully she had recovered most of her memory. Just the few days surrounding the stroke were still blank and might always be so.

"I met Jessie a couple of months ago and she called me and asked me if I'd have a session with you via video. She wondered if talking about your medical emergency would help in your adjustment. What do you think?"

"We'll see," Anna said. "Are you planning to 'shrink' me? I was married to a therapist for over thirty years so I'm quite up-to-date on the buzz words."

"I was thinking maybe we'd have a short conversation about anything you like," Dr. Norton said in a very good-natured tone of voice. "Is there anything you'd like to talk about?"

"My daughter, who is your patient…"

"So you do remember how it is I know Jessie," he said almost teasingly.

"She has strapped herself to my side and it's time for her to go. She has important work to do. She has patients to tend to."

"Don't you think she's capable of making that decision for herself?" Dr. Norton asked.

"She doesn't need to worry about me," Anna said.

"Ah. Well, my experience is that worry and need are usually mutually exclusive. People never worry because they need to. They worry when they can't seem to stop themselves. You're the one who has had a significant medical event. Are you worried about anything?"

"I'm worried about everything," Anna said. "But mainly I'm worried that I'm the only parent left to my children and they're not quite ready to be abandoned. They have always depended on me. And I'm not at my best. I wonder if I ever will be again. I'm walking a tightrope now. I've had a stroke! There is a danger of another, and one more debilitating."

"You feel vulnerable," the doctor said.

"Extremely!"

"And am I correct in believing you are not used to the feeling? It doesn't come along often?"

"When it has, I knew exactly what to do," she said. "This time it's beyond my control."

"I don't usually correct people when they explain their feelings, but this is not beyond your control. You have excellent medical supervision and are following the doctors' orders. And your health has been described as excellent."

"It could happen again just the same," Anna said. "I want to face it head-on, plow through the uncertainty, go back to work, get my children back on track, and I'm too distracted. And I tire so easily."

"Have you talked to your doctors about the lack of focus and the tiredness?" he asked.

She nodded. "They say it's normal and I should be patient. And maybe walk a mile a day. With a walker!" Then she snorted derisively.

Dr. Norton smiled. "Sounds easier said than done.

The walking shouldn't be a problem. May I suggest something else?"

"You can always suggest…"

"It's not uncommon for people recovering from a major medical event to struggle with depression. I wonder if—"

"Do I look depressed?" she snapped.

"Depression is not often diagnosed through appearance, but it does hide itself in impatience, confusion, exhaustion and uncertainty. If you'd like, I can confer with your doctor, your neurologist, about a mild antidepressant that works with your other medications. Tell me something, are you struggling with feelings of hopelessness or thoughts of dying?"

"I'm afraid to tell you anything," she said. "It sounds like you're going to recommend more drugs! And I've never before taken so many drugs!"

"Let me explain, your honor—"

"For God's sake, call me Anna!"

He smiled. "And please, you can call me Tom. Everything you're feeling is normal. Okay, *normal* is a bad choice of word. It's typical. That's better. You've had a bad experience and there are some lingering side effects that will diminish in time. We might be able to speed up the process with a few sessions and perhaps an antidepressant or antianxiety medication. But it's your choice."

"First, I should talk to my children," she said.

He lifted his eyebrows. "Do you think they'll have an opinion about your medical treatment?"

"Without a doubt," she said. "But what I need to talk

to them about is a family affair. Their father left a bit of a complication for me to tidy up. He was famous for doing that. It turns out my children have a sibling they don't know about."

He looked only a little surprised. "I can see how that could be stressful."

FOURTEEN

One thing that worked out conveniently, and was purely circumstantial, was Anna having all of her children under one roof even if it was because of her health. Michael went to work every day but stayed every night in the home where he was raised just in case he was needed. On the upside, he left early and came home late, thanks to his coaching duties. Bess was improving thanks to her medication and a new day group she was participating in for counseling and a little modified behavior therapy. But she needed the support of her family while she was attacking that anxiety she had neglected for a while.

And Jessie had not left her mother since the stroke. It wasn't even two weeks yet since that event and she had not gone back to work. Instead, she was riding herd on her family in much the same way her mother always had. Only Dr. Norton knew part of Jessie's motivation came from the fact that she wasn't anxious to go back to work.

But Jessie was so busy, making sure Bess was delivered to her group sessions and Anna to any doctors' or therapy sessions. Thankfully Anna seemed to be doing better all the time, growing in confidence. Her doctors were happy with the results of another CT scan and her blood work and blood pressure were all satisfactory.

Just seeing Anna getting her confidence back was enough for Jessie. And Bess was definitely benefitting from her new medication and group therapy. As for Jessie, herself, she was feeling stronger and more relaxed all the time, but it went without saying that a leave of absence from her practice was a contributing factor.

Anna spent a couple of hours in the kitchen on this particular Sunday afternoon putting together a dinner for her kids—homemade pizza, salad and garlic breadsticks. Michael was planning on going back to his apartment for the week so she was unsure when the next time they would all have dinner together might be.

"There's something I've been meaning to talk to you about," Anna said. "Get yourselves dished up and be prepared for another paradigm shift in our family order."

"This should be good," Michael said.

"It's about that ten percent of your father's will that goes to an anonymous recipient. She is not anonymous anymore. I've known who she is for months now. Sometime around the time Michael was born your father was romantically involved with a woman. I didn't know her and I don't think I will ever know the detailed circumstances surrounding their relationship, but your father did confess to the affair. As you can well imagine, it was a very tenuous time in our marriage. We almost separated. We talked about divorce. But we were young, broke, had two small children and our options were very limited."

"Dad?" Michael said, shocked. He dropped his slice of pizza on his plate and pushed away from the table a little bit.

Jessie couldn't believe her ears. "Not Dad!"

"It was a very difficult time," Anna said. "I didn't think we'd make it."

"He told you?" Jessie said.

"I guessed," Anna explained. "There were a lot of unexplained phone calls and your dad seemed to be out a lot. I accused and poked at him until he admitted he'd been seeing another woman. He said it was a stupid mistake on his part, he had no idea what compelled him to do such a thing and he begged to be forgiven. He said it had been a very brief relationship. I don't know exactly how long they were involved, but he insisted he loved me and of course loved you. The forgiveness part took a while, believe me. I was very angry and it was hard to trust him after that. As far as I know, that was the only time."

"Is it the woman?" Jessie asked. "Is that where the ten percent went?"

"No, that would be simple to explain. The thing I didn't know until after he died was there was a child. I might never have mentioned this to you otherwise. She's about six months younger than Michael and I didn't know she existed until I met her after your father's death. The reason she wanted me to know about her is because of you three. She is your sister."

"Well, that's interesting," Bess said dryly. "Someone was thinking below the waist."

Anna actually laughed at that. "Leave it to you, Bess, to boil it down to the bare facts. Yes, your father made a mistake that was probably driven by hormones, a mistake I never would have shared. Except for the outcome, which is your right to know."

"Does she want to meet us or something?" Jessie asked.

"She revealed herself to me and told me a couple of important things. One—that it is entirely up to you if you want to meet. And two—that she hasn't spent the money he left her."

"Did he know about her the entire time? Her whole life?" Mike asked.

"I believe so," Anna said. "Her name is Amy, and as she tells it, her mother explained she was involved with a married man, though she didn't know at the time he was married. When she realized she was pregnant, she never even considered termination. She decided she was having her child and would raise her as best she could. She married a few years later, had a couple of other kids and sadly passed away six years ago."

"Are you furious?" Jessie wanted to know.

"Now?" She gave a short laugh. "I'm furious with him for going on that damn rafting trip. And I wish he had told me, though I'm sure our marriage wouldn't have survived that information. We nearly divorced over his brainless fling!"

"Do you suppose there were many others?" Jessie asked.

"I have no idea, but I wasn't concerned. I didn't spend my entire marriage being suspicious. I was alert but not suspicious. We had our ups and downs, but honestly, no more than most married couples. I had an epiphany recently. In the last year, your father thought we were growing apart. I think it was something else altogether. About six months before his death, Amy contacted him to let him know he was going to be a grandfather. Amy thought he should know. I think your dad was restless for any number of reasons—growing older, having made mistakes in his past, not achieving all he had hoped for and, not the least, having a child no one knew about. I have wondered some things I'll never have answers for—like, was he planning to come clean about his secret child? There was one thing I know about your dad. He was always one to unburden himself. He liked to admit his errors, wipe the slate clean, apologize and suggest a fresh start."

"Is that where I got it?" Michael grumbled.

"I say this from experience, Michael. It's easier in the long run not to do things for which you have to beg for forgiveness."

"And I bet infidelity is a real game changer," Jessie said. "How'd you manage to forgive him?"

"Instead of deciding whether or not I could forgive him, I worked on strengthening myself. I worked on my own confidence, which was sadly lacking. I went to law school. I worked on me. I thought it was my only choice because I couldn't support myself and two children on a secretary's salary and at that time in our young lives your father didn't earn enough to support two households. At the time we stayed together because it was the most practical thing to do. Over the years I realized how hard your dad was trying to make amends and how much time and energy he was putting into being a good father. Eventually I got tired of being angry and was too busy to spend my energy that way. It took a lot of self-talk but I traded my anger for gratitude."

"And you fell in love again?" Jessie asked.

"More importantly, I grew to like my husband. To respect him. His blunder might have been a big one, but at the end of the day, he came through for us."

"I think you came through, too," Jessie said very softly.

"Thank you, Jess. That's so kind of you to say."

"Can you tell us about this woman? Amy?"

She began to tell them what she knew, almost all limited to Amy lately—that she was married to a doctor, worked as a nurse practitioner, had been very close to her mother and was now a new mother herself. "How ironic that Amy's situation and mine are so similar. Grandma Blanche was involved with a man who turned out to be married and she chose to have and raise me alone. Just like Amy's mom."

"It sounds as if you like her," Michael said, and he had a bit of a bitter tone when he said it.

"As a matter of fact, I do. I haven't seen her in a while but I did call her and tell her about the stroke and how overwhelmed I've been since it happened. But yes, I like her. And the baby is precious. But there's no reason you have to make a unanimous decision about whether or not you want to know her. It's perfectly acceptable for you to each make your own choice. As for that money—"

"It's not about the money," Jessie said.

"I don't want her money," Michael said.

"How much money?" Bess asked.

Anna laughed. The kids were so different in disposition but she had grown to really appreciate each of them. "The same amount as each of you, Bess. Can I just give my opinion about that? Amy told me that your father…her father…contributed to her education when she was in college. He did so without drawing any attention to himself but her mother later told her he had helped. In what amount, I have no idea. But he helped with school. I'm so happy to know that—it was his obligation, in my mind. And he left her a little something. I'm happy about that, as well."

"You're not jealous?" Jessie asked.

"I went through that stage thirty years ago. Now I'm just glad he did the right thing. Here's what I'm going to do. I'm going to write down Amy's number for each of you. Take your time in thinking about contacting her and it's all right if you don't. When I speak to her next, I'll tell her you're informed and she may hear from any one of you." They all nodded, looking around the table and making eye contact with each other. "Good, then let's kill this pizza," Anna said.

Later that night, Anna was sitting in her bed with her TV on and a book in her lap when Jessie tapped lightly at the door. Anna called for her to come in and was secretly glad for the company. She'd been thinking about calling Joe but she'd rather not. She feared she was using Joe as some kind of crutch or distraction, and holding him at arm's length was so exhausting. She really wanted to collapse into his arms and feel the ease and comfort of having a treasured friend, a new lover, care about her.

"You're still up?" Jessie asked.

"It's not that late," Anna said. "What's keeping you awake?"

"The idea that my father was a scoundrel," she said. "What he did!"

Anna put an arm around the daughter who was taller than her, pulling her close. They both leaned back against the pillows. "He was a fallible human being, that's all. As we all are. And his mistake was one of the most common. I was very disappointed. I wanted his love for me to outweigh all temptation, but apparently that wasn't the case."

"It really pisses me off," Jessie said.

"I know," she said. "But it's not our burden to carry and I think he paid for it in guilt and regret."

"Michael is furious about it," Jessie said. "Why is he so furious? He usually runs away from conflict and won't argue for anything."

"That's easy," Anna said. "Michael is afraid he's exactly like his dad. That was a good thing when he thought of Chad as perfect, though he had some trouble with that, worried that he couldn't live up to his dad's excellent reputation. Michael was a college grad, teacher, coach, while Chad had a PhD and was a pretty well-known therapist. Confronting his dad's imperfections—that would be hard for the son who worshipped him."

"I thought he was pretty perfect, too," Jessie admitted. "It kills me to think of what he did to you. You were just a young woman! Your heart must have been broken!"

"Sure," Anna said. "Jess, my heart's been broken a hundred times. That's the thing about life."

"Who broke your heart, Mama?" she asked, sounding like such a little girl.

Anna chuckled. "Going back to the fifth grade, Jennifer Cranston and her gang of six made fun of me and bullied me every day and I was reduced to tears so often my teacher thought I had the worst case of hay fever she'd ever seen. A couple of those mean girls moved away and it just faded into nothing. Then in the way life has of giving us breaks now and then, Jennifer came to me looking for a lawyer when she had no money to speak of and needed help because her husband was leaving her and screwing her out of alimony and child support."

"It must have given you some satisfaction to tell her to take a hike," Jessie said.

"Nah, I helped her. Got her set up pretty decently, too. But the way of the world is that some things never change, some good deeds never go unpunished. She was ungrateful and kind of snotty about it. But I made a deal with myself a long time ago—I'm not going to let the bad behavior of others turn me into a bad person. I have to look at myself in the mirror every morning."

"You've always been the brave one," Jessie said.

"Me? Oh, hell, Jessie, most of the time I'm worried about everything. But I learned how to look like I've got it handled. You'll never win a case in court if it's obvious you're in doubt. You don't get to sit on the bench if you're quivering in your boots."

"And you like it on that bench!" Jessie said.

"Honestly, it wasn't something I even dared hope for. I'm not about to give it up just because it scares me."

"Are you worried now?" she asked.

"I don't know if you remember this, the judge who vacated the seat in Superior Court had a stroke. A bad one. He's been wheelchair dependent ever since. He's never going to fully recover. He's almost ninety, but still…"

"Oh, Mom," she said, snuggling closer.

"Incentive to get better. Better than ever, if I can. I'm not going down without a fight."

Jessie put her head on Anna's shoulder. "I think I've taken you for granted. I'm so proud of you."

"And I was just thinking the same thing about you."

"I need to apologize for something. I need your forgiveness if you can." She sat up straight so she could look in her mother's eyes. "I always made you the bad guy."

"Did you?"

She nodded. "I accused you of nagging Daddy, of always telling him what to do. You were always in his business."

"That's true. I did nag. Not all the time, but I was guilty of it. The thing about nagging is that it's not nagging if you ask a person once. It only becomes nagging when you're asking for the fortieth time. Your dad had a tendency to ignore me. Not just saying no, or sorry I'm too busy. Ignore. Then asking again and again becomes nagging. I was guilty of that, sure."

"And you were not the bad guy."

"Well, thank you, sweetheart."

"And I watched him just try to get on your last nerve by complaining about everything from kids to work to the state of the lawns in the neighborhood or how unhappy he was, just in general. You had twice as much to do and you hardly ever complained."

Anna smiled. She'd only waited thirty years to have a little appreciation from Jessie. "I used to tell your father there was an antidote to unhappiness. It's called gratitude. If you're busy giving thanks for what you have it's very hard to think of what's not quite good enough."

"Hmm. I guess you've said that to me before..."

"Probably."

"I'm going to give up men," Jessie said.

Anna's eyes grew wide and she mockingly looked around. "It must be working. There hasn't been a man in sight around here, except your brother."

"I'm serious. I've been trying to get a man since sixth grade and none stick. I quit."

"Jessie, you've had a lot of boyfriends!" Anna argued.

"That's right, when all I ever wanted was one good one! The new Jessie is a single woman who answers to no one!"

Anna laughed. "I thought you never did!"

"I was faking it. This time it's going to be on purpose. They always dump me. I must be impossible as a girlfriend, so I'm going to quit being that."

Anna hugged her close. "Whatever you want. You will always have me. For as long as I last."

"Tell me what's going on with Jenn?" Anna asked Mike.

It was just the two of them, sitting at the kitchen table with coffee on a Sunday morning. And for once Jessie and Bess were not around.

"Well, all my feelings were flat," Mike said. "I had been struggling with losing Dad and I thought there was no room in my head or my heart for Jenn. So I suggested we break it off—at least for a while. Biggest mistake I ever made."

"But why?" Anna asked.

"I just wasn't feeling in love anymore," he said. "I wasn't feeling anything except the grief of losing someone I loved. So when I tried to pick up the pieces, Jenn was mad and not very forgiving. She's still mad."

"What exactly is she mad about?"

"She said I'm immature. That I don't have the determination to stick around when things get tough. Now that I look back, I see her point. But I was suddenly afraid I'd never be as great a father and husband as my dad. And now I find out my dad wasn't that great."

"Oh, Michael…"

"Well, he did some pretty awful things we never knew about."

"He did some pretty human things," Anna said.

"Don't get the idea I think what he did was okay, but there's hardly a person alive who is without flaws. Your dad needed a lot of love and support. More than I did, when you get down to it. You're a lot like him."

"That would have been a compliment six months ago," Michael said.

"It's still a compliment," she said. "He was a good man who did good things. He was a good father, except he may have failed Amy. What's most important to me is that you don't make some of the same bad choices."

"Like what?"

"Well, like thinking you have to be filled with feelings of being in love all the damn time. No one is in love every minute. But once we make a commitment we stick around, and when those days aren't perfect, act like they are. Show your partner love and respect, anyway. Worry about her for once. It's not all about you and your special little feelings."

"Is that what Dad did?"

"Look, ninety percent of the time he was a loving, giving, supportive guy. But ten percent of the time he was not in love and he moped around like he was walking to the gallows, looking for someone to make him feel better. Someone to prop him up and rescue him. No one wants that job. Jenn was telling you that she was glad to be patient and kind and help you through your grief if she could, but if you're just going to abandon her when times get hard, who signs up for that?"

"I didn't really mean—"

"Yes, you really meant that," she said. "Your feelings were a little off so you thought if you abandoned her, you'd somehow get it together. But it didn't work. It takes compromise and sacrifice to make a partnership work. From both people, not just the girl."

"Is that what I did?"

"Sounds like it. Michael, sometimes a good partner puts his needs and desires last, making sure to nurture his woman's needs and desires. And you know what? I bet you'd feel better faster."

"I might be too late," he said. "And now I'm screwed because I really do love her."

"Then find a way to throw yourself on her mercy. Apologize. Tell her you lost your head and made a mistake. And while you're at it, promise you won't do that again and mean it. You know there's a real trick to making a good relationship last."

"What's that?"

"Keep your promises," she said. "And stay. Never run out. Stay."

FIFTEEN

Jessie went into the city alone. She stopped by her practice to check in with the staff. Her assistant, Heather, hugged her. "You look so well rested!" Heather exclaimed.

"I don't know how that's possible. I've been even busier than as a working physician!"

"How's your mom doing?"

"She's doing great actually. There was no paralysis. But of course she isn't driving yet. She's still in PT, to which I drive her, and uses a walker about half the time because she can get unsteady. Her neurologist is monitoring her, and until he's convinced she's stable, she's going to be a passenger. Her clerk is bringing some work to the house, slowly building up the amount of time she puts in, but honestly, you'd never know she had a close call. Her memory is back to as good as ever, though she has no memory at all of the stroke, the ambulance, the thirty-six or so hours that her brain was scrambled in ICU. And she looks better than ever. Probably from the extra rest, though the fatigue irritates her."

"And how are you doing? Because you look great," Heather said.

"I have a million things to keep up with. My younger sister has been with us the last couple of weeks while attending some group therapy but she's planning on going back to her apartment in Berkeley this week. She has a boyfriend and it cramps their style to have the constant crowd of family around. But he's so nice and so crazy about her, not the least intimidated by her rather unique personality. So I've been getting both my mom and my sister to doctors' appointments, running errands, cooking, shopping, everything necessary to keep my mom from doing too much too soon. She's still napping so much. I'd say I should do that for a couple more weeks and hope to come back to work. Part-time at first, just so I'm available. I'm going to continue to stay with my mom for a while, until I'm convinced she doesn't have a health risk."

"Isn't the only risk a second stroke?" Heather asked.

"Yes, and with the blood thinners and blood pressure medicine, I want to be sure she doesn't have any side effects or other issues before I leave her on her own. The TPA worked like a miracle, but if she'd been alone..." She grimaced and shook her head. "It could have been a tragedy."

"Well, we really miss you around here."

"That's nice to hear," she said. And she thought that, strangely enough, she kind of missed being around.

She said hello to the partners, the other physicians

if they were in the office, and repeated nearly all the same conversations. Then she dashed across town to Dr. Norton's office. She could have taken her session virtually, but was going to be in the city, anyway, and really looked forward to seeing Dr. Norton in person.

She waited in his office and he came in, his glasses on his nose, that warm smile on his lips, a folder of papers in his hand. He beamed when he saw her sitting at the table. "Look at you! Your mother must be doing so well—you look fantastic."

"A woman never gets tired of hearing that," she said, grinning at him.

"What's going on?"

She went through the litany of chores and responsibilities she shouldered every day and mentioned that she had just visited the staff at her office, promising them she'd be back part-time in just a couple of weeks.

"How do you feel about that?"

"I think I'm actually looking forward to it. Maybe part-time is the answer for me. I know I don't dread it and that surprises me more than you!" And she laughed. "There have been a few developments since I talked to you last. On the most significant side, my mom revealed to us that we have a sibling we've never met. She told us the story when we were all together." And Jessie relayed the details to her counselor.

"How interesting," he said. "Were you surprised?"

"Oh, shocked, really. We all were. No one had a clue, including my mom. But my mom met the girl, woman now, and her husband and baby, and despite the fact that it must have stunned her, she got to know them and thinks a lot of them. I plan to meet them all as soon as I can. I'll phone first or something. Make a date. But shame on my dad for having that secret all those years."

"Would you have changed it in any way?"

"It would have been best if he'd never done it, I suppose. And then he lied about it so he wouldn't lose his marriage and family, so I understand. I don't approve, but I understand. I don't think I realized until now just how many issues my father had."

"How do those issues impact you?" he asked.

"I have another sister," she said with a slight shrug. "I think, when you get down to it, my father must have gotten in over his head. He obviously caved in to a flirtation and look what happened. He had a child he couldn't acknowledge without putting his wife and other children at risk."

"Not all that uncommon a situation, I think."

"You hear a lot of that sort of thing?"

"Sure," he said. "Don't you?"

"Hmm," she hummed, thinking. "Well, I was going to say patients, but then I remembered a couple of our staff have been in similar situations. Our receptionist is a single mom, never married, but I don't know the circumstances."

"If you don't mind me saying so, you look untroubled," the counselor said.

"First of all, my father is gone. I'm still sad about that. Second, getting mad about it is useless—it's too late for him to apologize. And I want to hear this woman's story. This half sister of mine. Because I think it's pretty obvious I have daddy issues. I think I have for a long time, like since my little brother came home from the hospital, which coincidentally is about the same time my father was having a secret child with another woman."

"Daddy issues?" he asked.

"To be honest, there were things I knew even if I couldn't admit them. Like the fact that I wanted to be his favorite when clearly Michael had that honor. But I always knew Michael wasn't his favorite so much as he was the only son and got more of our dad's attention. I was jealous. Most older children are when the new baby comes along—they write books on it. And now look what I've just learned—that he was in a very delicate situation at the time, had admitted to his wife that he'd been having an affair, their marriage was rocky, they were fighting and unhappy—and for a little three-year-old, that must have been upsetting and confusing. I suppose I must have translated that as disappointment. Or as I got a little older, maybe I felt let down. I do remember thinking I just could never get enough praise from my father."

Dr. Norton was quiet for a moment. He smiled slightly. "I think that's a very enormous thing to resolve."

"I couldn't have without my mother revealing the story," she said. Then she laughed. "It was the last thing I expected to hear."

"And look at you," he said. "You appear to have a new strength. A new confidence. In fact, I haven't seen you look so good since I met you."

"You said that already."

"It's completely true, but I'm sorry to go on and on."

"Well, my mom is doing very well. I'm still very wary and cautious but I think she's out of the woods. And while I'm very busy helping her and staying at her house rather than my own condo, I think I'm getting more rest. It's a different kind of busy than seeing patients. Maybe that was the answer all along. A little break from work, less pressure and a change of scenery."

"Let me ask you something," he said. "This issue of feeling angry and unappreciated, can you trace that back to your father? Or the demands of your job? Or a need for more vacation time?"

"I'll have to think about that," she said. "Because maybe. But maybe not."

"Do think about it and let's pursue it. In fact, there's a wonderful book about the psychology of happiness that asks the question about what works for one person and not for another. For example, there must be busy internists who feel better when they're working than when they're not. There are lots of studies on how retirement and too much leisure is unhealthy just as there are studies of how overwork is unhealthy."

"Of course," she said. "That could depend on what drives you."

"Or it could depend on where the real source of happiness is. Is it external or is it internal? Is it something you can locate and build on or is it something that is hidden until you take the right steps to find it? Do you get it from work or the absence of work?"

"Do you get it from successful relationships or from

learning to live free of them, avoiding toxic relation-ships?" she countered.

"I would be very interested in what you think has improved your peace of mind so much in the short time we've been working together," he said.

"It's probably very simple," she said. "My mom is going to be just fine after a real serious medical scare. And in taking care of her, I got some much needed time off from work."

"Perhaps. But can I ask a favor? Could you please do a little journaling between now and next week? Pro-pose the question, the simple question, of When do I feel best? And write about it."

"Sure. Easy-peasy."

He laughed. "You're so accommodating. That request is usually answered with a very loud groan from clients. Oh, no, not journaling! But just a page or two a day, asking and answering the question. Of course, you can tear it up and throw it away afterward if you want to."

It was her turn to laugh. "Why, thank you."

"Would you like to come to the office next week or meet on video chat?"

"I think I'll come into the city. It's a nice change and my mom is getting so independent she can use the time alone."

"I'll look forward to it. Headed back to Mill Val-ley?" he asked.

"Yes," she said. "My mom is working with her clerk at the house so I'm going to grab a bite to eat. Maybe I'll take something home for them."

"Hey, by the way," he said. "Did you by any chance get a cat?"

She laughed at that, her face brightening. "I did not, but I went to a pet store and the woman there was so mean! She said if there was no way I could take care of a cat, there was no reason to get one. I might have gone on and on about long hours and living alone and all that. But I did see this adorable puppy. She was black and white and brown with a squashed little face and the biggest eyes. I almost took her home just from the cuteness, but I didn't want the poor animal to suffer. She was some kind of spaniel. Adorable."

"It's possible you've been bitten by the bug," he said.

"And what bug is that?" she asked.

"Animals are good for the heart. And blood pressure. They make us feel loved, but more, they make sure we know we're needed. They really don't do well without our care. And we don't do that well without their unconditional love."

"You have seventeen cats, don't you?" she asked with a laugh.

"I have only the one and he's mean as a snake, but I know deep inside he loves me. I pet him when he demands it and I leave him completely alone when he hisses at me. It's a love match made in heaven."

"What's his name?" she asked.

"Gretchen."

"But you said 'he.'"

"I named him before we could determine the gender. Believe me, he doesn't know the difference."

* * *

Jessie so enjoyed being out of the house and back in the city she found herself walking around the shops along the pier, winding her way through the tourists. She decided to stop in at her favorite Mexican restaurant for a little lunch, and on her way there, she passed a free clinic. There was a line out the door, a few men, twice as many women and children. How had she never noticed this before? It was a storefront operation and the waiting room was full.

She squeezed in ahead of people and they let her pass, probably only because she managed to look as if she belonged. She couldn't get near the counter, but standing a bit off to the side, she watched as a receptionist chatted with a Latina woman who was obviously very pregnant. In crisp, beautiful Spanish the receptionist said to the woman, "How many months and how much bleeding."

The woman answered, "I'm ready to give birth and I'm having the pain, but blood comes."

"Do you have a doctor? Have you had prenatal care?"

And just as the question came, the woman fainted.

Out of pure instinct, Jessie found herself kneeling beside the woman, one hand on her abdomen and one on the woman's carotid artery, taking a pulse. In very unpracticed and choppy Spanish, she asked, "How long have you had the pains?"

"Seven hours."

"And now?"

"Constant," the woman said.

Her uterus was as hard as a rock. The stain on the crotch of her pants spread.

Jessie hardly noticed the commotion behind the reception desk and then there was a young woman kneeling across the patient. "Are you with this woman?" she asked Jessie.

"No, I just came in to ask about the clinic," she said in English, which given the condition of her high school Spanish was safer. "She fainted, but she's awake. Final stages of labor, I'm guessing. Water broke. Oh, I'm a doctor. Can I help you get her to an exam room? Or at least out of the waiting room?"

"That would be so helpful!" the young woman said. "Señora, can you walk a little bit?"

"*Sí,*" the woman answered. "If you help me *poquito*."

Together, Jessie and the other woman helped her to her feet, and though she was bent over her big belly, she took the necessary steps. At the first door they came to, they shuffled the patient inside. It was a very cramped exam room. They helped the woman onto the table, pulled out the extender, and the young doctor called for a nurse. Then she shook out a sheet, pulled on some gloves and began to pull on the patient's trousers. "We never cut them off in here if we can help it," she explained. "They're hard to replace. Grab some gloves."

"Sure," Jessie said. She tossed her purse in the corner of the room and grabbed gloves from where the doctor had gotten hers.

Together they covered the patient, pulled her pants down and off. The nurse entered and there wasn't room for one more human being in the room. "Salena, we need an incubator and call 911. Tell them we have a new-born and a postpartum patient." Then she deftly pulled apart the patient's knees and said, "Holy Mother. Can you rustle me up a clean towel? Cabinet behind you."

Sure enough, one glance said the little baby was crowning.

Jessie stood ready with a clean towel and watched in absolute admiration as the little doctor, smiling sweetly, one hand on the crowning head and one hand on the woman's brow, gently said, "The baby comes now. One little push and we have it. It's okay. One little push. *Gracias*, Madonna." Then she slid her hands to the birth canal and, with very little help from the mother, a good-looking baby boy was delivered right into her hands. "Wonderful!"

The nurse pushed the incubator on wheels into the room, left it at the end of the table and squeezed around the doctor, opening a cupboard and pulling out some supplies. She handed the doctor the clamps to tie off the cord and the baby was passed into Jessie's hands.

She held the baby while the doctor clamped and cut the cord. "Please dry him off and swaddle him and pass him to his mama. She'll want to look him over before the ambulance comes. By the way, I'm Cassie Forrest. Family medicine. I run this clinic."

"Jessie McNichol," she said. "I'm an internist. I'm part of a practice in the city. Rigby and Wright, Internal Medicine."

"What are you doing here?" Cassie asked.

"I was just passing by and saw the clinic and, for

no reason, wanted to check it out. I've never noticed it before."

"We've only been open six months, which was long enough to have standing room only every day even though there are a lot of free clinics throughout the city. This is certainly one of the smallest."

"You do have to be comfortable in tight quarters to work here."

Cassie laughed. Then she pulled her stethoscope from around her neck and listened to the baby's heartbeat. Jessie passed the baby into his mother's arms and then there was a flurry of rapid-fire Spanish between the patient and doctor. Jessie only picked up a bit of it. Mama wanted to know if the baby was all right—was he big enough, did he cry enough? The doctor assured her he was large enough, that he came easily and appeared to be healthy, but they would have to go to the hospital. Mama said she had no money for the hospital and the doctor said it was just for emergency care and so it would be covered. The doctor asked if the woman's family could be called and she said her husband would come when he was done working.

His baby was being born, but he had to work. He's working but has no medical coverage. Well, thus the free clinic. Duh.

"Hey, Cassie," said a loud male voice. The door opened, and a paramedic in a uniform pushed in a gurney. "If you miss me, you can just call me, anytime. You don't have to get all dramatic."

Cassie squeezed around the exam table to make room for the paramedics and their equipment.

The paramedic was very handsome. Jessie felt a little unsteady just looking at him.

"*Buenos dias, Mamasita.* Did you bring us a new little *bambino*? Oh, he is a handsome boy. We're going for a little ride to the hospital. The doctor is going to check you over and make sure you and the baby are okay."

Cassie translated and the new mama, tears on her cheeks, thanked them all profusely. She even grasped Jessie's hands, thanking her. On the way out of the tight-fitting exam room, the nurse plopped a bag on the mama's gurney. Her pants.

When the room was clear, Cassie started cleaning up. Of course, in an operation like this, everyone pitched in. The doctor was not waited on like in snazzier, more expensive clinics. She tore off the soiled paper, began to wash down the table, filled the sink with water and antiseptic. "It was nice of you to stop by," she said with a laugh. "How can I help you?"

"Do you need some help?"

"Nah, I got this. Just tell me what I can do for you?"

"I think… I mean, maybe I can help out here. As a volunteer or something?"

"Seriously?"

"It's kind of exciting," Jessie said. "And I think you have your hands full."

"Well, no shit. I mean, no kidding. I have a hiring process even for volunteers—I have to document you, check your credentials and licenses, and you should probably have an introduction to the facility and staff, though that won't take long. I have to completely vet you. But I'm too busy today. It'll have to be another day, probably when the clinic is closed."

"That's fine," Jessie said. "I'll give you my card and you can email a list of everything you need and I'll bring it all at the appointed time."

Cassie stopped scrubbing. "I can't pay you. But you would be a godsend."

Jessie handed her a business card. "Email me soon. I'm on leave right now, taking care of my mother who is recovering from a stroke and she's doing great. I was thinking of going back part-time, anyway. I think this might be what I'm looking for. And the sooner, the better."

Anna had spent all morning with her clerk, looking through some cases and deciding whether to postpone, send to another court or adjudicate them. This clerk who had worked in her office for just a few months was Cameron. There were a few cases that could be decided without scheduling court—some property settlements, lawsuits, a couple of assault cases. Then they began to resettle her into what had been Chad's office.

"You're going to work in here now?" he asked. "You said you wouldn't."

"I thought I'd have to redo it, switch the furniture, but I changed my mind. I'm not spending a nickel on this space just to indulge my petty anger that it was off-limits to me for so many years. It's mine now, like it or not. I'm not planning to work from home all that often. I have a fantastic office in the city and I like it there. This is my backup office."

"Whatever you say," Cameron said.

"So I'll work in here, but I ordered a new chair that should be here tomorrow. I have a new tower and monitor for the desktop and I need you to set it up."

"I can do that," he said.

"Of course you can. I'm going to take a meeting on my laptop in my bedroom while you bring that large stack of books from the garage and put them onto the shelves. Please make a list of things I need from pens to tablets to Post-it notes and I'll order them."

"I'll order the office supplies, have them delivered here," he said.

"You do that," she said. "Don't overdo. This isn't going to be my go-to office. I'm planning to work in the city most of the time. Now get on it while I have my meeting."

"Yes, ma'am," he said.

Anna went to her room, got comfortable in a chair in the corner and clicked on the conference program for her meeting with Dr. Norton. She had to wait a few minutes for him to come on-screen. "Hello!" he said. "How goes it?"

"Very well. You?"

"It's a good day. Tell me about your plans for Thanksgiving."

Anna told him about her plans to cook for Thanksgiving, making lists, having the kids all at home and feeling so comfortable in her surroundings finally. Her panic of another stroke diminished by the day.

The doctor touched his own face under his nose and

she looked at the screen. She jumped in surprise and grabbed a tissue from the box on the table.

"I'm sorry," she said. She dabbed at the blood running from her nose. "This is new. I had a bloody nose this morning and this is the second one today. I might have to put you on hold awhile. Unless you want to just watch me bleed."

"Have you told the doctor?"

"The occasional bloody nose is not unusual. The bruises…"

"Was that an answer?" he asked.

"Of course I mentioned it to Jessie."

"And you mentioned your two bloody noses in one day? And quite a few bruises?"

"She's gone into the city today."

"Are you alone?" he asked.

"There's a clerk here," she said. "Oh, hold on. This is getting ugly." She put aside her laptop and grabbed more tissues and was mopping up her face, getting blood on her hands. Finally she headed for the bathroom and got a hand towel, pressing that over her face. With a blood-stained towel pressing over her nose, she headed for the kitchen. She found an ice pack and pressed it over the bridge of her nose.

Forgetting about the videoconference call on her computer, she went to the sofa and reclined. Her face was frozen before long, the ice was so cold. She wasn't sure how long she'd been there, trying to stop the bleeding, when young Cameron came into the living room, took one look at her and screamed, "Holy shit, your honor!"

"It's a bloody nose," she said.

"It looks more like a bus accident!" He ran to the kitchen and loaded up on paper towels, wetting some of them. "Try pinching the bridge of your nose."

"I have. It'll stop soon."

Together they concentrated on getting the bloody nose to stop but for the next fifteen minutes all they did was collect bloody towels, tossing them on the coffee table. Anna began to choke and cough, gagging on the blood that was running down the back of her throat.

The door from the garage opened and slammed shut and Jessie walked into the family room to find a young male clerk bent over Anna, a large pile of bloody paper towels on the coffee table beside them. She calmly walked over to them and said, "Oh, dear. Stay right here."

Jessie opened her doctor's bag on the kitchen counter. She pulled something out, cut it with her scissors and came back to the sofa. She stuffed some thick cotton up Anna's nose.

"Lay back on these pillows and breathe through your mouth."

"Did you just stuff tampons up my nose?" Anna asked.

"Sort of," Jessie said. "I think your blood thinner needs to be adjusted."

"We used tampons in wrestling," Cameron said. "It works."

Anna laid there for a while, the strings of two tampons trailing across her cheeks. "This is becoming concerning," was all she could think of to say.

Though it took quite some time, with Jessie's help, they finally managed to stop the nosebleed. Jessie cleaned up her mother's face, discarded the wet towels and put in a call to Anna's doctor. A changed prescription was called into the pharmacy.

"This is getting to be a lot of trouble," Anna said.

"Patience," Jessie advised. "We're getting there."

SIXTEEN

It was the night before Thanksgiving and Michael sat in his apartment alone, slowly nursing a beer. He had thought about going out with some of his buddies, but before he had even completed the thought, he lost interest. He could have gone to his mother's house, but Jessie and Bess were both there, staying the night, helping with the preparations for Thanksgiving dinner. He just didn't feel like all that fake happy-family bullshit. They weren't a happy family anymore. He felt they'd lost it all when his father died and then lost it all again when they found out their father had betrayed them. Betrayed them all, when you got down to it.

His thoughts were distracted by the ringing of the phone and he smiled to see it was Jenn calling. If there was an upside to all the crap he'd been dealing with it was Jenn. He had called her to tell her his mother had had a stroke and that was all it took to get them talking again. She couldn't tell him to go jump off a bridge when his mother could be dying.

He might've played up that stroke a bit, making it sound far worse than it had been for sympathy, and he felt no shame at all. Jenn, empathetic and kind, had been willing to chat, encourage him, offer any kind of assistance he might need. What he needed was Jenn. He didn't deserve her but he needed her.

"Hello there!" he said. "Happy Thanksgiving, a little early."

"Same to you! How is your mom doing?"

"Better, though there was some drama last week. Apparently she got a nosebleed that was really tough to stop. Once things calmed down and got under control there were a lot of laughs—I guess Jess walked in on her clerk trying to help Mom and Jessie stuffed a couple of tampons up her honor's nose. She got a picture. It's hilarious."

"Poor Anna," Jenn said, but she chuckled.

"I guess they're going to wind down the blood thinners a little bit. This is not a good time for my mother to be in a car accident!"

"Like it's ever a good time! Will you be having dinner there tomorrow?"

"Sure," he said. "Where else? How about you?"

"Here, with my folks and sisters. Julie, Beau and the kids are already here. They flew in earlier today. Tommy and Susanne are driving from Sacramento and coming tomorrow morning but of course they're staying over."

Jenn was the youngest of three girls and the girls were close. Like best friends. "And you'll stay over, too?" he asked.

"Actually, this is my home now," she said. "I gave up my apartment. I'm going to live with my parents for a while and save some money. Maybe in a year or two I'll be able to afford a small house. That's my goal, anyway."

He could now afford a small house. Thanks to his father. The liar and cheat. "Not a lot of privacy for you in that plan."

"I don't need a lot of privacy but I could sure use a more permanent investment and one that doesn't look out at a brick wall or a parking lot. My fifth year in the school district is coming up, too. That's a nice pay increase. And I've been thinking about taking on a part-time job."

"You're really serious about this savings program."

"I am," she said. "There's a private school that provides after-hours care. They have after-school care till ten p.m. for working parents. They pay decently and you know me and kids. It would be like getting paid to play."

"You aren't going to have much time for yourself," he said. "For, you know, grown-up fun."

"I'll manage," she said. "Is your mom going to be able to go back to work any time soon?"

"She's been working from home a lot, but she still gets wobbly and tired. She's improving with physical therapy and I've noticed the walker isn't being used anymore, but I also noticed she shuffles a little when she walks."

"She might be a little nervous," Jenn said. "Maybe she's worried about falling."

"Could be," he said. "She does seem to be taking things slow. And then Jessie won't let her do too much."

"So, is it just the four of you for dinner tomorrow?"

"Bess has a boyfriend and he's going to stop by for a little while. And our friend Joe is spending the day at his daughter's house in Bodega Bay, so on his way back to his house, he's stopping by. That's it."

"How about that new sibling?" she asked. "If you don't want to talk about it, that's okay."

"There's nothing to talk about. But no, she's not coming. Really, that wouldn't be cool. I mean, it's not my mom's long-lost daughter. It's my dad's secret illegitimate daughter."

"I really think it's amazing that your mom has met her, befriended her, gotten to know her..."

"My mom's really liberal."

"I was thinking she's very forgiving and loving."

"She thinks the baby is cute," he said. "But it's not her grandchild, it's my dad's grandchild... Not cool."

"Do you ever get tired of being so judgmental? Stuff like this has been happening for centuries! Kings and queens have been sired out of wedlock. Sometimes these scandals have started wars and sometimes they've created new dynasties."

"This isn't that."

"But it isn't your half sister's fault. And it sure isn't her new baby's fault. Your niece, by the way."

"And it's not my fault," he said.

"Don't be juvenile, of course it's not your fault. But you have a blood relative you've never met and you should meet her. Just meet her. You don't have to support her or be best friends or anything. Just say hello. If you want to really be an above-average human being, you might ask her if there's anything she'd like to know about her father."

"Why would I want to do that?"

"Because you loved and admired your father," she said patiently. "By all accounts he was a very neat guy. I barely knew him and I really liked him. You have great parents. And he was crazy proud of you! The fact that he slipped up has nothing to do with you."

"Jenn, you don't know how it feels…"

"It sounds very spoiled," she said. "But it's your life. If you want to punish your dad by being angry and refusing to acknowledge your half sister, knock yourself out. I think the only loser in that equation will be you. I better go help with the pies."

"Listen, don't go yet. It's the holiday season. Maybe we should get together—"

"No more booty calls, Michael. Sorry."

"Not a booty call!" he insisted. "But maybe we could have coffee? Or ice cream? Or just talk?"

"We're talking…"

"How about face-to-face talking."

"I think we were arguing," she said. "I'm sorry about that. I'm too opinionated sometimes. What you do with your new family scenario is your deal, not mine. I just can't help but think your dad… Well, what do I know. Seemed like your mom was a bigger person. Always trying to do the right thing. You know?"

"And you think getting to know Amy is the right thing?" he asked.

"I didn't say that—I think introducing yourself, telling her who you are, I think meeting her, is the right thing. Maybe you do that and find you have nothing more to talk about. But withdrawing and being angry about it, about her? That's for sure the wrong thing. That makes it all about you. There are other people in this drama, after all."

"There are," he said. "Tell me about your sisters. Tell me what the kids are up to. Tell me what your Thanksgiving dinner is."

She laughed. "You're so good at changing the subject."

But that wasn't his intention, to just change the subject. He didn't want her to say goodbye.

The next morning he called Jessie. He asked her about the details of their family dinner, the time, was he expected to bring anything. To which she laughed and said, "Hardly, Michael. But you might be called upon to help with cleanup."

"I can do that," he said.

Then he got busy on his computer, and with only a name and phone number to work with, he located this mysterious sister on Alameda Island. He knew what little his mother had shared, that she was a nurse practitioner married to a physician and they both worked in the city. Hospitals were not closed on holidays and they could be working, but he couldn't bring himself to call ahead. Instead, he stopped at a roadside stand, bought a floral arrangement and drove to the island and got out of the car. He rapped lightly on the front door.

A beautiful woman about his age opened the door. Seeing the flowers she said, "Oh!"

"I'm sorry to bother you on a holiday," he said. "My name is Michael McNichol."

She put her hand over her mouth and her eyes welled with tears. "Oh, God," she said. "You look like him!"

"I should have called," he fumbled.

"Come in," she said emotionally. "Come in!"

"Amy!" a man's voice shouted from within. "I'm going to be late! Can you come and get this—"

A handsome man stood in the foyer, balancing a baby on his hip. He was wearing scrubs and tennis shoes.

"Nikit, this is Michael McNichol. Michael, this is my husband, Nikit Singh, and our baby, Gina."

The baby shyly buried her head in her father's shoulder while Nikit stretched out a hand. "How do you do! I'm so sorry, but I have to get to work. Amy, you're okay?" he asked, passing her the baby.

"Of course, Nikit. I'll see you later."

"I should have called," Michael said again. "It's a holiday and everything…"

"Not at all, we're glad to meet you. I'm sorry I can't stay. Amy will have to fill me in later." He gave his wife a kiss on the lips and gave a quick wave before going out the back door.

"He's on call in the emergency room today," she said. "Come to the kitchen." She struggled with the baby and flowers and he followed. She put the flowers in the sink and put the baby in a high chair. She sprinkled some Cheerios on the tray. "How about a cup of coffee?"

"It looks like you're in the middle of cooking and I don't want to—"

"It's nothing, really. Just my contribution to the dinner. We're getting together with some of the neighbors later. I have all day to make my dish."

"This was very spur-of-the-moment," he said. "I didn't give it much thought. My mother gave me your name and number. She gave it to all of us. I'm going over to her house a little later. I just thought—"

"I'm glad you came by." Without asking him again, she fixed him a cup of coffee. "How is Anna? I've talked to her on the phone a few times and she's sounding good—strong and coherent. But I haven't seen her."

"She had a bad bloody nose," he said.

"Those damn blood thinners," she said. "Cream and sugar?"

"No, thank you. She seems to be doing fine now."

She served him his coffee, made herself a cup, and while it brewed she fixed the baby some milk in a sippy cup. "It's lucky for you all that you have a doctor in the family. I'm sure your sister is taking very good care of your mom. Michael, I'm so curious about your teaching job. Tell me about it. Please!"

He described his typical day, teaching health in the classroom, filling in for other teachers from time to time, taking on the occasional gym class, coaching football in the fall and baseball in the spring and summer. "Next year I'm helping out with wrestling in the winter. That's just to be sure I never get an afternoon off."

"But you have summers, right?"

He nodded. "I almost always get a summer job. I've

been working at Costco the last few years, when they have an opening for me."

He asked her about her work and she explained that she was a nurse practitioner in women's health, working at the same hospital as her husband, and that Nikit was a vascular surgeon. They met when he was in his residency at the same hospital. "We've been married almost four years now."

"You married young," Michael observed.

"I was head over heels," she said. "Nikit is the most wonderful man and doctor. Who could say no?"

They talked for a while about the Bay Area, their families, their plans for the future. Gina was nodding off in her high chair, content on Cheerios and milk. "You should know, in the little bit of time I was able to spend with your father, he talked about his children with great pride."

And Michael surprised himself by saying, "Our father."

Jessie had been in the kitchen all day but for her it was like a day of rest. She texted her brother four times; he was asked to make a grocery stop on his way to dinner for butter, half-and-half cream, dinner rolls and large pimento-stuffed green olives. The butter was for the rolls and vegetables, the cream for the coffee, the rolls for rolls and the olives because after cooking all day Jessie favored a martini.

"Thank you!" she gushed when he came in the door. "You are the best brother."

She had prepared the traditional Thanksgiving dinner just as her parents usually did. She often helped in the kitchen but never took charge in her mother's kitchen, even if her mother or father weren't half the cook Jessie was. Truth be told, she hadn't had such a fun day in ages. In fact, the last week or so had been crazy fun.

The turkey would come out in thirty minutes. While it sat, before carving, she'd whip the potatoes, warm the rolls, butter the vegetables and dish up the stuffing. The gravy was the only thing she cheated on, and not because she had trouble with gravy. Her gravy was perfection. It was a time thing. She wanted everything hot when she served it. So she got premade turkey gravy from the deli and warmed it.

She put out a fancy platter of cheese, crackers and fruit and poured a little wine for everyone. Just a little. The McNichol family was a walking pharmacy these days. Well, Anna and Bess, anyway.

The table was beautiful, thanks to Bess. It helps to have the person with a touch of OCD prepare the table. Jessie thought if she measured she'd find the exact same distance between flatware and plates at every setting.

For the first time, Blanche would not be with them for Thanksgiving dinner. She was no longer leaving the memory care unit; her legs were weak and bloated, she was often incontinent and could become terribly confused. Anna and the girls planned to visit her on Saturday afternoon.

Jessie put the cheese platter and wine on the coffee table for her family while she put the finishing touches on dinner. She got it all on the table and then made herself that martini and it was as crisp and icy and dirty as if a professional had done it.

"Come to the table, please," she called. And she put her drink and herself across from her brother and sister.

"Martini?" Michael asked as he took his seat.

"I've earned it. Want one?"

"I think I'll stick with the wine, but thanks."

There were many exclamations of praise as the dishes were passed around and Jessie glowed in the wake of their appreciation.

"Excellent, Jessie!"

"You are gifted!"

"The best ever."

It wasn't until the meal was almost finished that Jessie said, "I never took over the kitchen before. I wish Dad was here."

"He would have been proud," Anna said.

"Jess, do you have a new man in your life?" Michael asked.

"No, why?"

"You've been in a good mood for, like, weeks!"

Jessie just laughed at him. "No man. However, I am changing up a few things. I should probably tell you. Starting with—I'm getting a dog."

"We haven't had a dog in the family since Bruce," Anna said. Bruce was the dog the kids grew up with and conveniently passed away when Bess was getting ready to go to college. "What kind of dog?"

"The cutest little King Charles spaniel. He's four years old and needs a home. I'm going to pick him up tomorrow. I've been visiting shelters online and in person for the last couple of weeks and I met this very nice volunteer who promised to keep an eye out for a good rescue for me. Well, along comes Wriggly, an adorable little guy. His owner is moving into an extended care home and can no longer take care of him. Her kids and grandkids are not nearby and are too busy for Wriggly and she's looking for someone who is willing to bring the pup to visit his previous owner sometimes." She shrugged. "Easy-peasy. I'm happy to do that. I met them and Wriggly liked me. And Mrs. Sinclair hates to part with him but… I'm afraid there's no other solution."

"How are you going to manage that with your schedule?" Anna asked.

"First of all, he's very polite and housebroken, though he hasn't been alone that much, given his owner is eighty-six. And second, I've already checked out a doggy day care in the area. He's all signed up." She smiled and her face lit up. "I'm very excited."

"Will you bring him here?" Anna asked.

"Is that a problem?" Jessie asked. "I'll look after him. I won't expect you to take care of him. But I'll take him to day care when I work. He should have the company of other dogs."

"Is this what's put you in such a good mood?" Anna asked. "Taking on a pet?"

"Possibly, but there's another thing. I've started helping out at a free clinic. It's the Bayside Free Clinic in the northwest end of the city. I stopped in there one day just to ask about the operation and helped deliver a baby."

"And you never mentioned it?" Anna asked, shock

in her voice. "That seems like a momentous event to not even talk about it!"

"I know," Jessie said. "OB was never my favorite rotation, but when a woman gave birth right in the clinic, I sprang into action, remembered everything and was able to work with the staff. I was so impressed with the doctor and staff in this little storefront clinic that I offered to volunteer. I was waiting to get approval. I had to be fully vetted and accepted. The project is headed by a very serious board of directors."

"But your practice?"

"Yeah, they're not paying you at the free clinic, are they?" Michael asked.

"No, but I'm going to work it out with my office to reduce my hours there. Between Mr. Wriggly and the clinic, it should make for a very full schedule. But don't worry, Mom. You are my absolute priority. I do think you'll be kicking me to the curb very soon."

"I'm going back to the courthouse part-time next week. Until Christmas. I can Uber into the city. I'll still work at home some of the time if I haven't scared my clerk off with my bloody nose. It's time for me to move forward."

"It's starting to feel almost normal here," Jessie said. "Except for the empty chair. I do miss him. Some days more than others."

"I have some news, too," Michael said. "I visited our sister today. She's very nice."

SEVENTEEN

Jessie didn't think her life could change so much in such a short period of time. The day after Thanksgiving she went to Mrs. Sinclair's house to pick up Mr. Wriggly and brought him home to her mother's house. He had such a sweet face that Anna immediately fell in love. Wriggly had a nice soft bed, a padded pet carrier, bowls and toys. But that night when they went to bed and Wriggly put his little paws up on Jessie's bed, she gave him a small boost up and he curled up beside her. She felt him burrow into her bed a few times and in the morning his head was on her pillow.

On Monday she took him to doggy day care but only for half a day and she thought about him the whole time. She picked him up at noon.

"Everyone loves Mr. Wriggly," one of the women who watched the dogs said. "He's very friendly, very socialized and made many new friends. He's so well-behaved."

Anna went to PT on Tuesday and Thursday and to

the courthouse on Wednesday and Friday, and Jessie insisted on driving her and taking her home again. When they were having a quiet dinner on Saturday night, Anna laid down some new rules. "I think I can manage on my own now. It's been six weeks since the stroke. I'm cleared to drive again, my blood work is good and I'm not worried about marathon nosebleeds."

"I don't mind staying here and helping out," she said. "At least I'm sure you're eating and sleeping and getting around without being unsteady."

"If I have a problem I'll call you. And I think I want my house back."

"All right, then. I'll relocate myself and Wriggly back to my condo."

And, Jessie thought, it was time to begin looking for a small house with a yard for Wriggly. She was so thoroughly in love; she didn't think she could love a pet this much.

When she was growing up, they had a yellow Lab named Bruce and of course the whole family loved him. He lived to be fifteen; large dogs just didn't last as long as little ones like Wriggly. He passed away when Bess was beginning college. None of the kids, then on their own, even considered getting a dog. Not yet, anyway; they were all busy and working all the time.

But this timing was perfect.

Jessie fell into a very good routine. She worked in her practice three and a half days a week, and if Cassie could use her help, which she always could, she would give her another day or two every week. Sometimes if the clinic opened evening hours, she would go there for a few hours. Then she would rush home to Wriggly and they would take a short walk or maybe just watch a movie together.

Christmas was fast approaching and Jessie told her therapist, "Despite the fact that my dad has only been gone nine months, I'd like to do what I can to make it the best Christmas ever."

"How does the rest of the family feel about that?" Dr. Norton asked.

"Well, Bess can be convinced, although she'll probably make a list of requirements and a spreadsheet of events and a timetable. That's her usual way of handling things. Michael will probably go along with that idea. He's pretty much a pleaser. Mom would be relieved to have the pressure taken off her. She spends all of her time worrying that we're all adjusting to the changes in our lives."

"It appears you are," he said.

"I hate to say this but Mom's stroke was a gift to us, in a way. We were all so freaked out at the idea of losing her, too, that we pulled together in ways we hadn't in years. Michael and I were always so competitive, vying for Dad's love and approval. I tried to do it through overachieving and Michael did it through being Dad's favorite playmate. Neither of us feels that pressure anymore. Both of us miss him in different ways."

"Tell me some of the ways your life has changed in the past six months, Jessie," he prompted.

"You know all the ways!" she said. "I'm in here every week and every week there seems to be something new to report. I don't have a minute to spare, but early in the new year, I'm going to start looking at houses. Wriggly and I need a little more space. Maybe a yard."

"That sounds promising. Though I don't know when you'll find the time."

"Sunday afternoons. And I can take Wriggly with me to look at houses. There isn't a lot in my price range in Sausalito, but Mill Valley, near my mom, might have some possibilities."

"You're having a very good time with Mr. Wriggly, aren't you?"

"He's a dream," she said. "I've never been loved by anyone the way I'm loved by him. I'd marry him if I could."

"I certainly don't feel that way about Gretchen, though I will confess to being very fond of him. How have your feelings changed in the past few months?"

"I'm not sure," she said.

"Are you still journaling?" he asked.

"Yes, and from what I can see when I read it, I have a boring life."

"But you don't," he said. "You have a demanding and, I dare say, fulfilling life. You have a new family member, a new avocation in your little clinic, your family seems to be on their feet—and you contributed mightily to that. And at the risk of appearing condescending, you are not at all cranky."

She laughed at him. "I'm probably too busy to be cranky."

"That's not it," he said. "You're on a road to personal discovery. This week, journal about how you feel and how your feelings have changed. That's an assignment."

"Can't you just tell me? Because something tells me you think you know a bit about it."

He grinned boyishly. "Nice try, Doctor," he said. "You have been doing things differently than you were when you came in for your first session and I suggest to you that it has led to changes in how you feel."

"Possibly," she said. "But none of it was by my intention. Except Wriggly—he was on purpose and he has changed my feelings. I'm deep in love."

He wrote something down on a piece of paper and handed it to her. *Whether by circumstance, intention or accident, how have different actions related to different feelings?*

"Okay," she said. "I'll make a list."

"And may I see some pictures of Wriggly? Because I know you have some."

"Of course," she said, beaming. And she went through her phone, showing him a lot of pictures.

"You're right, Jessie," he said. "He is a beautiful, sweet-looking pup."

Because she was nearby, she went to her favorite Mexican restaurant. She went directly to the bar and was greeted by a smiling waitress. "*Hola*, Dr. Jessie," she said, pronouncing Jessie as Yessie.

"*Hola*, Marcita. How are you?"

"Excellent. Today do I get you a table?"

"No, thank you. I just want three tacos to go."

"*Sí. Uno momento.*"

She climbed on a stool to wait and decided she would report to her journal notebook that, for whatever reason, waiters and waitresses appeared to be friendlier these days, but it could be all about the holidays. The restaurant was decorated as were so many of the little shops. In fact, Cassie and her husband had spent last weekend putting up some decorations in the clinic. It caused Jessie to be reminded that her mom and dad had always decorated quite a lot and this year it would be Anna alone and she was still in recovery. Jessie would stop her before she started and make sure she had help with the decorating. She would call Michael and go over and help. They'd have to get it done right away before Anna dug into the decorations.

She collected her tacos, left a nice tip and wished the waitress a merry Christmas. As she was leaving, someone called her name. She turned and saw Patrick, sitting at his favorite table, now kept warm on the patio by space heaters. He had not been there when she came in. She would have noticed. It had become habit for her to look at that particular table.

She walked toward him. "Hello, Patrick. How are you?"

"Great, but how are you? And how is your mother? Won't you sit for a minute?"

She thought about it briefly, then slid into the chair across from him. "Just for a minute. My mom is doing great. She's coming back into the city, to her office and the court, at least a couple of days a week. There are still a few adjustments—getting that blood thinner right, for one thing. But you should see her—she looks great. And she's determined. She moved me out and sent me back to my condo—said she's ready to have her house back. If you want my opinion, she's a rock star."

"That's outstanding," he said. "How about you?"

"Great, thanks. I just stopped off for some tacos to go."

"Are you in a great hurry? I'd love to buy you a glass of wine."

She lifted her bag. "I don't know. I have a young gentleman waiting for me."

He grinned. "And who might that be?"

She put down her take-out order and fished in her purse for her phone, scrolling through the pictures of Mr. Wriggly.

"And who is this?" he asked.

"It's the craziest thing. I thought I should have a cat. You know, something warm and fuzzy and counting on me to come home and feed him, but I fell in love with a little spaniel. Of course, the first one I saw was sold but a nice lady at a rescue told me about Wriggly, whose owner was going into a nursing home and had to give up her dog. Wriggly and I have promised to go visit her once in a while. I never thought about that before—what happens to the pets when their owners get sick or even die. But I'm crazy about this little guy."

"I bet you have a lot of people counting on you these days," he said.

The same waitress who had given Jessie her takeout brought Patrick his nachos, his usual order.

"Jessie, let's get you a glass of wine. Have your takeout put on a plate and you can help me with my nachos. We have some catching up to do."

"I don't want to keep you," she said. "You're probably going back to the hospital…"

"I'm done for the day," he said. "I'm having a beer. I'd like to hear about the rest of the family. Any other new additions?"

The waitress took the bag from Jessie and quickly disappeared. In record time she returned with the tacos on a plate and the only kind of wine Jessie ever ordered in hand, all as if the waitress knew what she would like. She just smiled. "No other additions, unless you count Bess's boyfriend, who she's been keeping a secret from us for a year. But that's certainly not devious or even secretive for Bess. It's her minimal-literal mental capacity. She didn't mention him and no one asked her if she had a boyfriend. Oh, and I guess there are more additions. After we—" She stopped herself before she said *broke up.* "I very recently found out that my father had a child he kept secret. My mother found out first. A woman who happens to be a nurse practitioner married to a doctor."

"What doctor?" he asked, his interest piqued.

"Nikit Singh. A vascular surgeon."

"Only the best!" Patrick said. "I've known him a few years now! He's amazing. His wife is your sister?"

"I haven't met her yet, but I'm planning to. My mother and brother have met the Singhs and have nothing but good things to say. It's a very confusing situation—we didn't know until after my father's death that there was a secret sibling. My mother knew there was a relationship, but—" She shrugged. "It's certainly not Amy's fault."

"Nor any of yours," he added. He pushed the plate

of nachos closer to Jessie. "Every family has issues and dark family secrets. Some more than others."

"I'm learning that."

"You really do have a lot going on, don't you?"

"And then there's the clinic," she said. "That was a complete accident. I saw the clinic, stopped in out of curiosity and helped deliver a baby. Now I volunteer there. Not that often—I do have to work. But it's the most amazing little place with a dedicated staff that works miracles on a daily basis."

It turned out Patrick had volunteered in one of the city's free clinics earlier in his career before he became so busy. But he seemed mesmerized by Jessie's experience and asked lots of questions.

Then he tried to order her a second glass of wine.

"No, thanks. It was really great seeing you, especially when I didn't have a family member's health on the line! I have to get going."

"Let me drive you over the bridge," he said, speaking of the Golden Gate to Sausalito.

"That's very nice of you, but I drove in today since I have parking at the clinic. And I have to stop and pick up Wriggly at day care."

"Day care?" he asked with a bold laugh.

"Yes," she said. "I don't want him to be alone all the time and he now has friends at day care. He's a very social little guy."

"You're doing a lot of giving these days."

"I'm very happy," she said. Then she was startled. Could that be it? Could that be the change and was the result happiness? "It's good to be needed," she said. Indeed, everyone needed her. Like never before.

Patrick covered her hand with his. "I'd like to see you again, Jess. I've missed you."

She was a little startled by that. "Really? You said I was a red flag!"

"We had a situation. Not a good one. I was not in a position to invest—how can I say this?—a great deal of time in someone who was unhappy and angry."

She tidily packed up that last taco. It was for Wriggly, after all. "I believe you said that just fine. Thanks so much for the glass of wine. It was lovely seeing you and I'm glad you're looking so well."

He stood. "Jessie. Will you have dinner with me sometime?"

She put her purse strap over her shoulder. "No. Take care." She turned and walked away. Her first thought was, *How does he dare?* But her second thought was, *I bet my darling little Wriggly will love this taco.*

Michael and Jenn both taught in Richmond, right across the bay from Mill Valley. They were in different schools, of course. He taught and coached high school and Jenn was an elementary school teacher. But he'd been exhaustively searching the area for houses. Jenn wanted a house. He thought it might be the only advantage he had.

It was a Sunday afternoon when he went to her parents' house. For once it was sunny, a condition they didn't see that much of in the Bay Area. It was a beautiful, though cold, pre-Christmas day.

Just to be safe, he had talked to Jenn that morning and asked her how she was spending her day and she said she was going to do a little baking while watching her annual viewing of *An Affair to Remember* followed by *Holiday Inn*. So, he didn't feel too badly about interrupting her day. Those movies could be viewed later. She might even invite him to join her.

He rang the bell and she answered. She was so beautiful. He couldn't stop thinking about her. She was way under his skin. "Hi. Are you too busy for a treat?"

"What kind of treat?" she asked.

"I'd like to show you something," he said. "I'm not going to tell you what it is. I just want to show you. It'll take about an hour."

"I was just getting all my baking stuff out. I was about to start measuring. Can it wait till later?"

"Actually, no. There's a time limit on it. How about you get a jacket and let's do it."

"I hate surprises," she said, standing firm.

"You just hate them when they don't work out. Sometimes you love them. I think you're going to like this one."

"I think you're up to something," she said.

He grinned at her. "Of course I am. Otherwise, it wouldn't be a surprise. Come on, be a sport."

"All right," she said. "But this better not be a trick!"

"It's not a trick, Jenn. It's a surprise. Those are two entirely different things."

She grabbed a jean jacket and hollered into the house that she was going with Michael to see something and would be home in about an hour. She hauled herself up into his SUV and buckled up. "How's everyone at your house?" she asked.

"They all seem to be good. My mom is just about back to normal. Bess is as weird as ever but she's doing fine. Jess is not around as much, a good thing, but she seems like a whole new person since she got her dog. Wriggly is quite the guy. For a little dog he's not yappy or annoying—he's pretty cool."

"I can't wait to meet him."

"I see your dad has the Christmas lights up," he said.

"Oh, yeah, he's all over it. They're going to bring the tree in later today and start getting out some of the decorations. My mom has been shopping like crazy, getting ready to shock and awe the grands. Since my brother-in-law's parents live kind of close, we'll have everyone here for most of the time. Christmas morning, for sure. We'll have to share the kids a little bit. And the in-laws are coming to a big dinner one night. We have lots of lists going, getting ready."

"You haven't gotten yourself that second job yet, have you?" he asked.

"No, I'm waiting till after the holidays. A lot of high school and college kids pick up part-time work while they're on break. There's no need to compete with that."

"How's it going, living with your folks?" he asked.

"Surprisingly well, considering I'm the youngest and they don't let me forget it for one second. I'm surprised I don't have a curfew."

"Oh? Does that mean you're going out a lot?"

She threw him a look. "I've had a couple of wine breaks with the girls but I haven't gone out with any guys, if that's what you're trying so clumsily not to ask me."

"That was it."

"Where are we going?"

"You'll know when we get there."

"Are we going wine tasting? Are we going to vine-yards?"

"No. How's your grandma doing?"

"She's fine. She'll be with us for Christmas. How about your grandma?"

"Blanche isn't doing that well," he said. "She's really deteriorating. She doesn't make sense a lot of the time, poor old girl. But I think she's getting along okay at the nursing home. She has always had a gift for making friends. Even if she can't remember them or their names an hour later."

"Where are we going?" she asked a bit more forcefully.

"Just up the road. Not very far. San Rafael. Have you been there? It's really close but I think I only drove through it or past it before. It's not a bad-looking little town. Good roads, lots of older neighborhoods with real nice yards. Have you? Been there?"

"I don't think so," she said. "What's in San Rafael that you want to show me?"

"Just give me five minutes, Jenn."

"I don't know why you don't just tell me."

"Okay, look. You gave me an idea and I started looking at houses. I got a Realtor and gave her the parameters—has to be fairly close to work, has to be at least three bedrooms, solid, not run-down. I said I could do a few things, cosmetic things, but I'm not a builder and I can't do anything major like electrical or plumbing or putting on a new roof. I've looked at a few houses." He whistled. "They're pricey. But my dad left me some money, and my mom told me when they originally wrote their wills they wanted to help us afford a house. Because it's so hard to buy a house in California. So, I had a little money, I have a great job, I looked around. And I found this sweet little house in a nice neighborhood. The houses are kind of old but the owners aren't—most of the neighborhood is young."

"You've been looking at houses?"

"This is the block. Look how nice it looks and it's the beginning of winter. The lawns are so neat, the gardens meticulous. Most of the houses have freestanding garages in the back. I know, there are a lot of cars parked on the streets. That's the one."

There was a mission-style house, a woman in a suit and heels standing in front on the sidewalk.

"Oh my God, it's *pink*!"

"Yeah, that's a downside," he said. "Come and see the inside…"

"It's pink! Not slightly pink. Pepto-Bismol pink!"

"I know, but come on. The inside is amazing."

He introduced Jenn to Maura Cummings. "Thanks for taking time on a Sunday to show me this house again. I really want Jenn's opinion before I make a decision."

"Perfectly reasonable," Maura said.

"It's really pink," Jenn said.

Maura laughed and said, "It sure is. That can go away in a few hours. We can even make it a condition of sale."

The front door was beautiful, had an arched doorway in the Spanish influence. The foyer was large, the living room and dining room generous, and you could see through the house to a cozy covered patio. The rooms were tiled in burnt-orange Spanish tiles with thick, soft area rugs throughout. The kitchen countertops were off-white quartz. The kitchen was big—work island, breakfast bar and all. It looked as though it had been recently remodeled. To the right of the kitchen was a large bedroom and bath with shower, to the left of the living room, a main bedroom with a large bath containing both tub and shower. There was a third bedroom next to it.

"Three bedrooms, two baths, almost sixteen hundred square feet, recently remodeled kitchen and main bath. The owners had it inspected and it's in excellent condition."

"Wow, it really is nice inside," Jenn said.

Maura walked over to the dining room sliders and opened them. "Take a look out here. The owners enjoyed entertaining outside and went to a lot of trouble to make sure it was attractive and inviting. They will, of course, leave that wonderful gas grill, if you want them to."

The backyard was lush and expertly trimmed with trees mature enough to block their house from the neighbors'.

"Come look at this," Mike said, taking Jenn's hand. He pulled her to the side of the house and showed her a walkway on that side, edged by mature plants, a couple of plum trees and a tall wooden gate.

"And look at the trees. Plum, lemon, lime and peach. And that's the garage."

"It's kind of small," she said.

"I know. I think it will only take one small car, if that. And it can't be enlarged." He turned back to the Realtor. "Let us poke around a little bit and talk. I promise we won't open any drawers or closets."

"I'll wait out front, but please, check out the closets and kitchen cabinets. There's a remarkable amount of space for a little house."

"It's not that little," Michael said. "My apartment is about seven or eight hundred square feet. One bedroom. Galley kitchen."

"I didn't know you even knew what that was," Jenn said. "Listen to you, the seasoned home shopper. How much are they asking?"

He showed her the flyer and she grabbed her heart and choked. He laughed. "Pretty steep, right? My folks bought their first house in Oakland for fifty thousand. But look at the kitchen—she's right, there's a lot of space. There's even a pantry. And most houses this old don't have an actual laundry room, but this one does. I think maybe it was an afterthought. I think that bedroom, bathroom and laundry room were added on. This is a pretty nice house," he said, standing a bit taller.

He heard the sound of the front door closing behind Maura. He stood in the center of the living room, watching in appreciation while Jenn poked around in the kitchen. She oohed and aahed over shelves that slid out, custom drawers with wooden dividers, lazy Susan storage in the pantry.

"Lemons, limes, peaches and plums?" she said. "This kitchen? Amazing. It really is nice, even if it is pink on the outside."

"I told Maura to find a house for someone who loves to cook," he said.

"Why would you do that?" she asked a bit hesitantly.

"Because, Jenn, you love to cook. And I love you," he said. "And I am only interested in buying this house if you'll live in it with me."

She took a step back and put her hands behind her back. "No, Michael. I'm not going to be your roommate or co-owner or live with you. I'm happy for you that you can buy a house like this, but I'm looking for more security than—"

He reached into his jeans pocket, pulled out a small box and dropped to one knee. He was shaking. He was terrified. He wouldn't blame her if she told him no.

"I know I fucked up. I even know how I fucked up and I also know it might not be the last time because I'm an idiot, which is why I have to find someone really smart to marry. Jenn, I've figured a few things out about why I fell apart. Okay, my mom helped me figure it out and set some new goals. Believe me, if anyone knows relationships..." He flipped open the lid of the ring box and a very respectable diamond ring twinkled inside. "I love you with all my heart, Jenn. Feeling that caught me off guard. I've never felt this way before. I'd do anything for you. All I need is for you to give me a chance to prove I can be a better, stronger man. Well, and marry me, because we both know I can't make it without you."

"Oh, Michael, I don't know." She brought her hands out from behind her back and twisted them. "We haven't actually even made up since that booty call incident."

"Sure we have! I apologized, you chastised me, I groveled, you said it will never happen again, et cetera. Makeup complete."

"I'm not sure…"

"I'll get you a contract—if I flake out again you can have a million dollars!"

She put her hands on her hips. "There you go again, promising things you don't have and won't have. Unless…" She put her hand over her mouth. "Did your father leave you a million dollars?"

"Of course not. He left me a very nice down payment on a house in San Rafael that I'll be spending my first weekend in painting. Jenn, baby, my knee hurts. I love you so much. I'm sorry I was an idiot. This ring needs to be on your finger!"

She looked at him, down there on one knee. "It is very pretty."

"It's very pretty, but if you want to exchange it, I'm good with that."

"Here's what I'm going to do. I'm going to say yes, but I'm not walking down the aisle until we've had a very long talk and some premarital counseling."

"I can do that," he said.

"And I'm staying with my parents until we resolve a few things."

"Okay. I hope we resolve them quickly."

He reached for her hand and slid the ring on her finger. Then he struggled to get to his feet. He rubbed his knee and thought, *Very romantic, Mike*. He lifted her chin, kissed her hungrily and said, "Well? Do we make an offer?"

"How else are we going to save this neighborhood from the Pepto-Bismol house?"

Anna was feeling pleased with the way things were shaping up at her house. Jessie and Mike had been over on Sunday evening; they ate pizza and decorated the house. With Mike carrying the boxes in from the garage and Jessie pointing and ordering placement and Mr. Wriggly running around in circles, occasionally stealing a decoration, it took only a few hours. There was still pizza left when Joe showed up. Anna's children put the boxes in the garage and left as soon as possible.

How grown-up and discreet Jessie and Mike were, Anna thought.

Anna had done the whole DNA search and had received almost a catalog of connections in return, but she honestly hadn't given it much hope. All she really cared about learning was if she had an actual brother she'd never been told about. Wouldn't it be ironic if her husband had kept a child secret from her and her mother had done the very same thing. But when her chart of ancestral heritage came along, she began to lose all faith in the project. Her DNA was supposedly French, Bulgarian, Irish, Portuguese and a large part Chinese. The Chinese just threw her. Oh, there was a smidgen of Native American and it seemed that everyone with any experience in this kind of search reported the same sort of thing.

The catalog of possible familial links didn't seem to offer anyone who could possibly match with her.

But then Phillip Winston contacted her. He'd been looking for family members because he'd been adopted and had never known any biological family. As an attorney, he specialized in estates—wills, inheritances, trusts, foundations, that sort of thing. And he'd spent nearly his entire life on the east coast. His adoption records, which had been sealed and were anonymous, had originated in Modesto, California, which was the only real plausible connection Anna and Phillip had to each other. He shared only a couple of the ancestral origins—a little French and Irish. But he did want to explore all possibilities and he asked her to please resubmit her sample and he said he would do the same.

"Haven't you been curious?" he asked her in a phone call. "I know you had your mother and could ask her questions, but didn't you wonder about extended family?"

"For no reason I can explain, it was never that important to me, until recently when my mother, who suffers from dementia, remarked on having given away 'the boy.' By the way, that came into the same conversation when she told me if I saw her daughter to please ask her to come and visit."

"I'm so sorry, Anna," he said. "That must be so difficult."

"It's very hard at times, but she was a wonderful

mother," she said. "She had a hard life but she was fearless."

She did absolutely like Phillip on the phone. He was a very nice man; he asked all the right questions and welcomed her questions, as well. They got off the subject now and then and discussed a little politics and other things. He was widowed but had three grown children and a couple of grandchildren, and had only lost his parents a couple of years before.

Their second DNA submissions came back. His was the same as before but hers showed more French, Irish, Portuguese, a small amount of Native American ancestry, the Chinese connection was miniscule and it triggered an even stronger connection to Phillip Winston.

"It's possible I'm your half brother," he said.

Blanche had lived in Oakland when she was born, but it was possible she had once lived in Modesto or maybe gone to Modesto for medical treatment.

"Have you tried asking your mother if she had a son?" he wanted to know.

"Yes, but after that one mention she didn't seem to recognize me or the question. Sadly, I don't know how much longer Blanche will be with us. She sleeps much more than she's awake lately."

"I know it's very close to the holidays and I probably couldn't ask for a more inconvenient favor, but I'd like to take a chance on seeing her. In case, you know. In case I learn that she's my mother. Would you allow it if I promise not to get underfoot? I'll get a hotel and rent a car."

"I understand your desire to do that and I won't ask

you not to, but given my position in the court, first I'm going to have to ask my clerk to vet you."

"Of course. I'll email you my information. I'm very easy to find and research. I've lived in the same house for twenty years, I have no criminal record and am in good standing with the bar."

"I'm just afraid you could be disappointed," she said.

But he felt he had to try.

Anna mentioned this to Phoebe and Phoebe offered to get a little research done on Phillip Winston Esq. of Rhode Island. Then she mentioned it to Jessie and Michael and she would tell Bess the next time they were together.

Mike said, "Are you shitting me?"

Jessie said, "All right, I hereby order you to stop coming up with any more missing or secret family members."

She had already decided she wasn't going to make a big deal out of this. Just because some guy who was looking for his family had decided they might be related did not mean she had to hold a family dinner and provide entertainment. She asked Joe if he would accompany them to the nursing home and that was going to be the end of it. Just because Phillip Winston thought he might've found a sister did not obligate her and her family to a celebration.

However, Anna went to see her mother the day before Phillip would arrive. Blanche was in a very cranky mood. Her legs were terribly swollen; she'd been in bed with her legs elevated, had been given diuretics and pain meds, so she was mean and loopy.

"Hi, Mom," Anna said, kissing her forehead.

"Is it time for you to visit?" she asked tersely.

Well, at least Blanche knew who she was. "I was in the neighborhood."

"It's not a good time," Blanche said. "I'm dying."

"I hope not," Anna said. "I heard your legs are particularly bad today."

"That's what happens when you waitress for fifty years."

She was relatively lucid, which could last seconds or more than an hour. Anna jumped on it. "Mom, I have been wanting to ask you something important. Do I have a brother?"

Blanche gasped. "What?"

"Did you have a baby boy before I was born? A baby you had to put up for adoption?"

Blanche looked at her in disgust. "Just because marijuana is now legal doesn't mean you should be smoking a lot of it! You've lost your mind."

"Well, I had to ask. You said something…"

"With all the shit they give me in here, I imagine I say a lot of things!"

"Sure. So tell me about what's going on with your legs," Anna said.

"They hurt and ache and won't hold me up. They're big as elephant legs and just as useless."

"Can I get you some juice or something?" Anna asked.

"You can get me out of this hellhole," she said.

"Why don't I read to you," Anna said. "Maybe you'll be able to close your eyes for a while."

Blanche didn't say okay or thank-you or anything. She rolled onto her side and Anna picked up a book from the bedside table. It was a large-print, illustrated copy of *Watership Down* that Jessie had given her for Christmas. Blanche could no longer enjoy reading, but she had pictures and if someone read to her it sometimes soothed her.

Anna might've been disappointed for Phillip; he had not found his mother. But it was what she had expected. And she had a grudging respect for Phillip coming all the way to San Francisco in hopes of finding his roots.

Joe came over the evening before, after Anna had seen Blanche. They cooked a light dinner of chicken and vegetables, had a glass of wine, and she told him about her visit with Blanche. "I do wonder why I have so little interest in lost or missing family," she said.

"Maybe you're just fine with what you have," he suggested.

"And yet they keep turning up all over the place. First Amy and her family, then my mother in her delirium suggesting another child somewhere, now this man flying all the way from the east coast. I'll tell you what, it could be a lot of trouble if he turned out to be a relative."

"How so?" Joe asked.

"Think about adding one more and his family to this group," she said. "I only have a twelve-place setting of china!"

The next day Anna and Joe met Phillip at a small restaurant not far from the nursing home. They had a nice, if perhaps slightly nervous, lunch and Anna explained that she had tried, once again, to ask about a possible brother. And it had made Blanche angry and uncooperative.

"I tell you this so you'll check your expectations at the door," she said.

"Understood," Phillip said. "It's not my intention to upset anyone."

"And I want to make certain you're not completely disappointed."

They walked into Blanche's very small space in a three-bed room. Anna was smiling. Blanche was sitting up in her chair, looking a little better than she had the day before.

"Hi, Mom," Anna said. "I've brought someone who—"

Blanche went completely pale. She wiped a hand over her face. "Rick," she said. "Rick!"

"Mom?" Anna asked.

Blanche looked up at Anna. "Where did you find him? How did you find him?"

"Who, Mom? Do you know this man?"

Blanche held out her hands to Phillip Winston. "Did someone tell you? I called your mother but she said she hadn't heard from you. If she did, she would give you a message. Did you get the message? Did you?"

Phillip came forward, taking both her hands in his. He sat on the side of her bed and looked into her old rheumy eyes. "I didn't get a message," he said.

"I thought so," she said. "I thought you'd find a way to get in touch if you had. That's what I thought."

"Where did you think I'd gone?" he asked.

"The army. That's what you said."

"Mom, do you know this man?"

"Of course," she said. "It's Richard Allston." She looked back at his face. "You don't look a day older. I knew you'd age well. Not all of us did."

"Do you remember what year it was?" he asked her.

"I'm not sure but… I was eighteen. It was a boy. What happened to him? I was eighteen. You should not have left like you did."

"Eighteen," Anna said. "Nineteen fifty-four."

"Did you give him up?" Phillip asked.

"What else could I do? I thought you'd come back and we could start over. Are you mad? Because I was eighteen."

Anna and Joe stood helplessly in the room, Phillip sitting on the bed, feeding Blanche careful questions, asking her for names and dates and other information, but it wasn't long before her mind wandered off. She stopped remembering or answering, one or the other. Anna knew for elderly people with dementia that it wasn't unusual for them to have vivid memories of things that happened fifty, sixty or even seventy years before, sometimes things they'd never spoken about, sometimes things they wished they could forget, while events that happened the day before were long gone.

After just a few minutes, when it appeared Blanche was losing her focus, Joe went to the car to get Anna's briefcase. She spent a few minutes helping Phillip find his ancestry account, pulled up the names that had been sent to him as people with whom he shared DNA, people who might be relatives, both living and departed. There was a Richard Allston Jr. who was registered.

He was sixty-three, four years younger than Phillip. His picture was posted and the resemblance was astonishing.

There was a picture of Richard Allston Sr. in an army uniform and it could have been a younger Phillip, the resemblance was so strong.

"I'll be damned," Anna said.

Phillip Winston stayed for a week. For two nights following the recognition that Blanche was his mother, he stayed in the hotel, researching on his laptop and visiting Blanche during the day. She was able to repeat the same things over and over again—it was 1954, she was eighteen, she had a baby and gave him up—but she really couldn't elaborate. She had other very old stories—there was a girl named Carol who had lied to her and stolen money out of her purse, there was an incident at a dance club when the police rounded up a lot of young people, there were protest marches going on in San Francisco. There was a baby, this time a girl who she couldn't give up, and she did not know the baby's father's name. It could be she couldn't remember or it could be she never knew.

Phillip discovered that Richard Allston Sr. had died at the age of fifty-five. Heart failure was named the cause but there had been no autopsy. However, Richard Allston Jr. was alive and well, so another reunion would soon be in the works.

Phillip was invited to Anna's house to stay a few more days and given Michael's room. Joe stayed, too. Just because Phillip was a long-lost brother and had been carefully researched by Anna and her clerk didn't mean he was beyond any possible suspicion. They talked and talked and talked, drawing for each other life histories and sewing the details together.

After a week it was time for Phillip to get back to his family, his kids and grandkids. His parting was bittersweet; he had found his mother but he was unlikely to see her again. He'd plan another trip for the early spring, but Blanche was failing.

As for Blanche, she seemed to have come alive a little with Phillip's visit. For a while she believed her long-lost lover had come back to her. Her health seemed greatly improved, though it was a brief improvement.

The family was both elated and quite tired by the time Christmas was upon them. Anna planned a dinner to include Michael's new fiancée, Jenn; Martin and Bess; Amy, Nikit and Gina; Jessie and Mr. Wriggly. Joe helped with the cooking and more family stories were told until they could tell no more.

"No one is to look up or research any more missing or secret relatives until I've had a chance to get to know the ones we already know about," Anna said. "I think my head might explode."

EPILOGUE

It had been just over a year since Chad McNichol's untimely death; a year since his family had celebrated his life, grieved his loss, began to retrieve his secrets and make peace with the highs and lows of any human life. They may have had an official celebration of his life, but it had been too soon.

Now, a year after his passing, it was time to put it all in perspective and truly appreciate the ways in which they had grown and thrived and how much of that had to do with Chad, directly or indirectly. It was Anna's suggestion that they all come together, not for a ceremony, but for fun and community. She reserved a bunch of picnic tables in a park near her home and Bess was all too happy to make a list of everything that was needed, from wine and burgers to covered dishes. And it was a perfect list.

Anna had long since stopped being in any way angry with Chad for his mood swings or his very inconvenient death and instead offered up gratitude for the amazing family he had sired. All of them. She was remembering good days and years of laughter and affection.

Jessie brought Mr. Wriggly to the picnic as well as what could only be described as gourmet potato salad and appetizers. Michael brought a soccer ball, goal nets, a cornhole game and a Jenga hardwood puzzle that stood five feet tall. Amy brought a giant pot of beans, Jenn brought a rich, messy dessert and Anna provided the meat. Uncle Phil did the barbecuing and was helped by Joe.

Patrick and Nikit kicked the soccer ball around waiting for Joe and Michael to join them and have a proper game. The women huddled near the warm grills because, although it was April, the weather was still quite cool. Baby Gina, whose favorite place was Anna's lap, was bundled up nicely. Martin and Bess played Jenga, a game guaranteed to drive anyone with even a little OCD completely mad.

This, then, was the first official McNichol family reunion and all the players were present. Patrick and Jessie had resumed dating, more successfully this time. So far. It was looking good since Jessie, who was loath to give up either her newfound happiness or her counselor, was a new woman. And she was spending less time in her practice and more time at the clinic, taking on a management role and serving as a community liaison in San Francisco. She was talking about pursuing another degree in public health, but it was still just talk. There was hardly a spare hour left in her day.

Jenn and Michael lived together in a house that had gone from pink to white and they were planning a summer wedding. They were trying to keep it small, but the guest list was growing every day.

Blanche didn't see Phillip again after his pre-Christmas visit and, even then, she never understood that he was her son. It gave Anna some comfort that Blanche thought she was being reunited with her one true love. Anna arranged for the three of them to have official blood tests to establish that they were, indeed, related. Of course it was impossible to establish what had really happened surrounding Phillip's birth, but it sounded as though Rick's mother did not want her son mixed up with Blanche and never mentioned her to Rick. Rick apparently never knew Blanche was trying to find him.

Blanche passed away quietly just a few weeks ago.

They ate, they played, they told stories. The sun was setting and no one seemed to want to go home so they finally packed up the picnic and retired to Anna's house, where they kept the party going until very late. Uncle Phil retired to his guest room after nodding off during conversation in the great room. It was almost midnight when Anna stood on her front walk and waved goodbye to everyone. Joe dropped an arm across her shoulders and pulled her close. "You should be very pleased with that crowd. After all the upheaval of the last year, don't they just look like the most sane family you've ever seen?"

"I was thinking that," she said. "A year ago I didn't know how we'd get through it. Everyone had a different set of problems. It was a tangled mess."

"You were always the glue that held your family together," he said.

"No. Chad was the therapist," she reminded him.

"But he knew you were the glue. He told me that," Joe said. "He said Anna is the head of this family."

"He said that? I mean, he told me I was capable but frankly I thought that was just his way of getting out of difficult situations and letting me handle them."

Joe shook his head. "You were better at it. He knew that. He genuinely loved the kids and he was a trained therapist, but you knew instinctively what to do."

She was quiet for a moment. "Sure would've been nice if I'd known it," she muttered. "I lost a lot of sleep worrying about what to do next with all these wacky kids and their problems."

"I think you're going to get a break from worry—they're all in a good place." He laughed and walked her back into the house. "No telling what will come up next so don't turn your back."

"Oh, believe me, I won't," she said.

"Just know I plan to have your back till the end."

Anna leaned against him. "A partner who has my back. That's all I've ever really wanted."

* * * * *

*Please turn the page to enjoy an excerpt from
Robyn Carr's novel* Sunrise on Half Moon Bay
available now at your local bookseller.

ONE

Adele Descaro's mother passed away right before Christmas. While she missed her mother, Adele was relieved to know she was no longer held prisoner in a body that refused to serve her. It had been four years since the stroke that left her crippled, nonverbal and able to communicate only with her eyes and facial expressions. Adele had been her primary caretaker for those four years and now, with Elaine at rest, she could get back to her own life. If she could remember what it was.

She was thirty-two and had actually spent the last eight years mostly as a caretaker. *Mostly* because Adele had also helped to care for her disabled father for four years. Her mother had done much of the work and then, within just a few months of his death, she had suffered her debilitating stroke. Devastated by this cruel turn of events, Adele resigned from the part-time job she'd taken as a bookkeeper at a local inn and dedicated herself to Elaine's care full-time. There had been help from a visiting nursing service and from Justine, her much older sister. Justine was, in fact, twenty years older, now fifty-two.

Adele was happy she had made her mother's care her priority, but was aware that in doing so, she had allowed herself to hide from her own life, to put off her own growth and keep her dreams and desires just out of reach. Now her opportunity was at hand. She lived in the comfort of the home she'd grown up in, had friends in her little town and the time to pursue whatever her heart desired.

Justine, a successful corporate attorney in Silicon Valley and the mother of two teenage girls, hadn't been able to pitch in much time so she contributed to the cost of Elaine's care and provided a modest income for Adele. She had made it a point to stay with Elaine every other Sunday so Adele could have at least a little freedom.

The truth was that for the past four years, or actually eight if you really thought about it, Adele had been fantasizing about how she would reinvent herself when the time came. Now that it was here, in the cold rainy months of a typical Pacific winter, she realized she had yet to come up with a plan.

Adele had left her graduate studies in English Literature at Berkeley to return home when her father was released from the hospital. "To help out," she'd told her mother. Her father, Lenny, had been a maintenance supervisor for the Half Moon Bay school district and had taken a bad fall while trying to fix a heating vent in the ceiling of an auditorium. He was in a body cast for months, had several spinal surgeries and spent years either in traction or a wheelchair. But the worst of it was his pain, and he became dependent on powerful pain medications.

Adele's mother needed her help, that was true. But she might still have continued her graduate studies. But Adele had another problem. She fell in love and got pregnant—accidentally. The father of her baby didn't want the child, so in addition to her pregnancy, she suffered a broken heart. She'd intended to raise the child on her own but she'd suffered complications; her baby was stillborn and her already broken heart was completely shattered. The safety of her home was her refuge, even with her disabled father's condition casting a pall over life there.

Then, as if to drive home the fact that she was not quite ready to get on with her life, her mother had her stroke.

And now, here she was, still with no plan whatsoever. She gazed out the kitchen window. It was early March in Half Moon Bay, and fog sat on the beach every day until noon. It was like living in a heavy cloud. Adele had no motivation whatsoever. She found herself eating a cardboard container of lentil soup from the deli while standing over the kitchen sink, alone. She was wearing a lavender chenille robe and had slopped some soup on the front. She was not ready for bed early; she hadn't bothered to get dressed today. She could have spent the day reading great literature or better still, drafting a life plan. Instead, she'd watched a full day of *M*A*S*H* reruns while lying on the couch.

She'd been sleeping on the couch for months. She and

the couch were as one. She had often slept there in her mother's final days so she could hear her in the night. Adele's bedroom had been little more than a changing room.

The doorbell rang, and she looked down at the mess on her robe. "Great," she said. She took another spoonful of soup, then went to the door. She peeped out. It was Jake Bronski, probably her closest friend. He held up a white bag so she could see he brought something for her. She opened the door.

"Hi, Jake. Sorry, but I'm just on my way out..."

"Right," he said, pushing his way in. "You were invited to a pajama party, I suppose?"

"Yes, as it happens," she said meekly.

"Well, you look stunning, as usual. Why don't you slip into something a little *less* comfortable while I set the table."

"I will if you promise not to clean the kitchen," she said. "It annoys me when you do that."

"Someone has to do it," he said. Then he smiled at her. "Go on, then."

"All right, but eventually this has to stop," she said, even though she had no desire for it to stop.

She went to her room. It had been her parents' room until they each got sick and they converted the only bedroom downstairs, which had an adjoining bath, into a sick room. They were fortunate that her father had remodeled the house a bit before his accident since these old homes didn't usually have large spacious main floor bathrooms.

Maybe that was why she had trouble sleeping in her

bed—it was her parents' when they had been healthy and happy.

She stripped and got into the shower. Jake deserved that much. She blew out her curly hair and rummaged around for a pair of clean jeans. Of course she came from that ilk of women who gained rather than lost weight in their grief. How was it you could barely swallow any food and yet gain weight? She sighed as she squeezed into the uncomfortably tight jeans and added some lip gloss.

When she returned, she found the kitchen had been cleaned and the table was set for two with place mats, good dishes, wine and water glasses. Jake had even put his offerings in serving dishes—tri-tip on a platter, Caesar salad, green beans sprinkled with pieces of bacon. On the counter were a couple of generous slices of cheesecake with berries on top. A bottle of wine had been opened and was breathing.

"Your mother isn't coming?" Adele asked.

"*Dancing with the Stars* is on," he said, by way of explanation. "What did you do today?"

"Not too much," she said.

He held her chair for her. "Addie, have you given any thought to talking to someone? A professional? I think you might be depressed."

"You think someone can talk me out of it?" she asked facetiously.

"What if you need medication?"

"Jake, my mother just died!"

"I realize that," he said. "But for the last few years

we talked about the things you wanted to do when you weren't tied down anymore."

"That's true, but I didn't want her to die! And I think my grief is normal, under these circumstances."

"I couldn't agree more, but you're turning into a shut-in. You are free to live for yourself. You can finally get together with friends, get out, do things."

"Enjoy this wet, cold weather, you mean? Maybe when the sun comes out, I'll feel more motivated."

"You had a long list of things you were going to do. I can't even remember everything…"

She remembered. "I was going to remodel or at least give this house a face-lift so I could put it on the market, find myself a chic little apartment with a view, finish my graduate studies, date Bradley Cooper—"

He smiled. "I can help with the house," he said. "Anything I can't do, I can find you the right person. Have you seen Justine lately?"

"I don't see too much of her now that I don't need her to help with Mom," Adele said. "She brought the girls down a couple of times after Christmas."

"She should do better than that," Jake said, frowning.

"I could just as easily go to San Jose and see her. She's not the only one in this relationship."

"I don't think she realizes how much you need her," he said.

"Well, we're not close. We're family. We'd never be friends if we weren't family. We're nothing alike."

"Lots of siblings say that about each other. I'm not close to Marty. If he weren't in constant need of money, I'd never hear from him."

The two of them did have that in common, Adele thought, but for very different reasons. Marty, short for Martin, was Jake's younger brother. He'd been twice married, had three kids from those two wives, presently had a girlfriend he was living with, and was not doing very well at supporting his extended family.

For Adele and Justine, the twenty-year age difference was just the beginning. They had never really lived in the same house. Justine was in college when Adele was born. Elaine had been in her forties when surprised by a second pregnancy. Then, probably because of her age and experience, Elaine made Adele the center of her universe in a way Justine had never been. Adele had been dreadfully spoiled, her parents doting on her every moment.

It wasn't as though Justine had been pushed to one side, but she certainly didn't get as much attention. Many times Justine had told Adele the story of her asking their mother to make her wedding gown, Elaine having been a gifted seamstress. But, according to Justine, Elaine had said, "How could I find the time? I have a small child!" When Justine pointed out that the small child was now in school, Elaine had said, "But I have myself and Adele to get ready for the wedding!" So how could she find time to make a complicated gown for the bride?

It had ever been thus as far as Justine could see. Adele was the chosen one and Justine was expected to understand, step aside and worship her darling baby sister. Justine's great accomplishments, and there were many, were taken in stride while Adele's merest babble was praised to the skies. Justine used to claim, "If Adele put a turd in the punch bowl, Mother would say, 'Look what Addie made! Isn't she brilliant?'"

As Adele remembered too well, her parents didn't exactly respond that way when she came home from college pregnant, refusing to name the father. Her own father reacted like he'd been shot in the gut, and her mother cried and cried, wondering what miscreant had knocked up her pure and precious daughter.

When her baby boy had been born dead, Adele's father pronounced that now she could start over while her mother had called it a blessing. It was only Justine who had offered true and genuine support. "Having children of my own, I can't imagine what you must be going through. Anything I can do, Addie. Anything. Just tell me what you need."

That was probably the closest Adele and Justine had ever been. It was brief, bittersweet but meaningful. There would always be at least that bond.

"I think tomorrow night we should go to a movie," Jake said. "We haven't done that in years."

"Not years," she argued. "Maybe almost one."

"Let's get out," he said. "Not that I don't like our dinners in, but how about a movie. I'll sit and quietly eat popcorn while you ogle Bradley Cooper."

"You know the first time you rescued me I was about four years old."

"More like ten," he corrected. "Headfirst into the pool and you sank like a rock." Jake had been a lifeguard at the community pool. He was eight years her senior and like a big brother to her. After that incident he taught her to swim. Now she could swim like a competitor when she got the chance. They had almost a lifetime of history. Their families lived a block apart in an older residential section of Half Moon Bay, California. Mr. Bronski used to walk to his market every day, Mrs. Bronski often visited with Addie's mother and they both volunteered at the schools. Beverly Bronski remained Elaine Descaro's most frequent visitor until her death.

They'd remained close through so many monumental events. Thirteen years ago, Jake had married Mary Ellen Rathgate and within two years she'd left him for another man, breaking his heart. Ten years ago, Max Bronski died of a heart attack. Eight years ago, Addie's father broke his back on the job and was disabled for the remainder of his life. He had barely left the bonds of earth when Addie's mother suffered her severe stroke. Since neither was close to their siblings, Jake and Addie had only each other to lean on for a long time now.

They cleaned up the dishes together and even though Adele had a dishwasher, Jake washed and she dried. They talked about the neighborhood, the people they knew in common, their families. Adele said Justine worked all the time. Jake's younger brother, Marty, didn't have the same history with the market that Jake had and only worked there when he was between jobs. "I think it's high time he grew up," Jake said, not for the first time.

When Jake was leaving, he told her to plan on a seven o'clock movie the next night. Dinner might be popcorn, and if they were still hungry afterward, they could get a bite to eat. He put a big hand on her shoulder, gave it a squeeze and said, "It was nice to spend some time with you, Addie."

"It was. Thank you, Jake. See you tomorrow."

He gave her a gentle kiss on the forehead before leaving.

Jake had had a thing for Adele for years, but it seemed the timing was never right. When he first saw her as something more than just a kid, when she was blossoming before his very eyes, she was still a teenager and he was a man in his early twenties. Then she went to college, and he fell in love with Mary Ellen and married her in short order. By the time Mary Ellen had dumped him, leaving him shattered and lonely, Addie was involved with someone at Berkeley so he put her from his mind.

But every time she was home in Half Moon Bay for holidays or just to spend a weekend with her parents, she became bigger than life and he was aware of a bothersome desire. Yet, she was involved with someone. Then he heard through her mother that her romance had failed, so he lectured himself on patience and gentlemanly distance.

When she enrolled in graduate studies, he was blown away by her brilliance. He loved talking with her when she was in Half Moon Bay because she was fascinating; he believed she knew a little bit about everything. He could sit in a mesmerized trance just listening to her talk for as long as she'd go on.

Then she confessed she was involved with someone.

She didn't want to say too much about the new relationship. "But are you in love?" he asked her.

"Oh, I'm just a goner," she said. "But I'm playing it as cool as I can so I don't scare him away. This time I plan to take my time, not like the last time when I dove in headfirst and almost drowned."

He couldn't help but think about how he'd been with Mary Ellen. She had been so beautiful, so sexy, it took him about five minutes to want her desperately, and once he claimed the prize, he found there was very little substance there. Mary Ellen, God bless her, was shallow as a birdbath. She cheated on him almost immediately.

He gave Addie a lot of credit for taking it slow.

Then she returned home. Not for a visit, but to stay. She said it was because her father was injured and facing surgeries, but Jake had known Addie for a long time and he could tell there was more to the story. Then he watched her grow before his very eyes and knew what the something more was. She was pregnant. And she did not have the love and support of the baby's father. She was alone.

Jake made sure he checked on her often, at least a few times a week. If the moment presented itself, he just might tell her that he was willing to be that man. He had come to realize how much he wanted to be with her. But he never found the appropriate time.

There was once a moment of affection that he thought might lead to intimacy. They had a conversation about everything she'd been through losing her baby, and it was intense.

It filled Jake with joy that she felt comfortable confiding in him until she started sobbing. Jake did the only thing he knew to do—he comforted her. He wrapped his arms around her and kissed her forehead before he found his lips on hers. They kissed, clumsily, and then she'd pulled away. She'd been through so much and apparently was ill prepared to deal with anything more.

He had been waiting five years for her to decide she had a little more to give. And he gave as much as he dared.

She wasn't the only one with fragile feelings.

A nice dinner with Jake the previous night and an invitation out for the evening had put Adele in a more positive frame of mind. But who better than her older sister to knock her off that perch. Justine called to say she was coming by because there was something she needed to talk to Adele about. It was Saturday, and she wasn't going to her office.

Justine was Adele's opposite, in appearance and almost everything else. She was a tall, slim blonde while Adele was a shorter, rounder brunette. They used to joke that they weren't from the same family. But Justine's hair was colored and she wore blue contact lenses, making her look more Scandanavian than Italian. And she was chic, but then Justine lived in a professional, high-income world and was expected to be chic. Adele, on the other hand, always thought she'd be a natural as an English professor, one who wore oversize sweaters and flat black shoes. And she usually pulled her hair back in a clip or pinned it in a boring bun.

They had very little in common, yet another reason they weren't close.

When Justine arrived, Adele eyed her stylish haircut. "How much does that supershort blond coif cost?" Adele asked. "Because I've been thinking about making a change…"

"It's pretty expensive, actually," Justine said, giving Adele a brief hug. "I'm thinking of letting it grow out… Scott isn't crazy about short hair."

"So what if he isn't? It's your head, right? And I think it's wonderful. Would you like coffee?"

"I suppose it's too early for wine," Justine said. "How are you getting along since the funeral? Are things beginning to fall into place?"

"I suppose," Adele lied. "Not nearly as quickly or neatly as I hoped. All those things I'd been looking forward to, like having the time and energy to lose some weight and get in shape, or maybe at least look at a university program catalog, go back to my studies… Day after day goes by and I haven't done anything. I suppose I'm a little depressed."

"There's a lot of that going around," Justine said dourly. "Listen, I have to tell you some things. It's difficult."

Adele didn't like the sound of that, yet she couldn't imagine what might be coming. Justine lived a charmed life. "Where do you want to sit to have this difficult conversation?" she asked.

Before she even finished the sentence, Justine had taken herself to the living room and sat on the edge of a wingback chair. That sight alone, her tall, lithe and lovely sister perched, stiff and tense, in the old chair, emphasized to Adele that she hadn't even started her re-decorating-remodeling project. Justine's house, though she was terribly busy, was breathtakingly decorated and picture-perfect. This old house was not only dated, it was threadbare. And her usually poised sister was very uptight.

"Let me cut right to it. Something has happened," Justine said. "There have been some changes in the company. My company. Serious downsizing and out-sourcing. My job hasn't been eliminated yet, but there's no question there's going to be a major change. One that will involve an income adjustment."

"Oh no! Why is this happening?" Adele asked.

"A lot of complicated reasons that all boil down to profits and losses. We've merged with other software manufacturers twice, laid off employees and tacked a not very subtle For Sale sign on the door. They're par-ing down corporate officers to combine them since the latest merger. When two companies become one, there's no point in two VPs of Operation, two presidents, two general counsels. I've already been asked if I'm inter-ested in taking over Human Resources since I have ex-perience in dealing with many of their legal issues. I'm thinking about it, but it comes at a significant pay cut. It has forced me to think about other things."

Could one of them be asking your husband to get a real job? Adele thought. She kept her mouth shut about that. Instead, she asked, "Like what?" Wondering what any of this had to do with her.

"I'm planning to see a headhunter, look for another

firm that's in need of general counsel. Since I'm experienced in corporate law, I could join a law firm but I'd be on the bottom rung. Or... I've even given some thought to private practice. My experience in Human Resources lends to a number of specialties. I have an open mind. I might be qualified to work for the state. Whatever, I have to be thinking now. I have a feeling, a strong feeling, my income is going to be severely impacted. Soon." And she wondered how Justine's husband was handling this news.

Justine started dating Scott in college, right around the time Addie was born. He was undeniably smart, though not a great student and not really motivated, except maybe on the golf course. Based on what little information Justine had shared over the years, Scott had never leaned toward ambition, but he was a steady, good man and devoted father. He got his degree in business, started out in sales for a big sporting goods manufacturer. He did pretty well, and while he was doing that, Justine took the LSAT and killed it. She went to law school—Stanford. Scott was very supportive of the idea. *Just make me a stay-at-home dad with a set of clubs*, he had said.

Since Scott traveled all the time in his first job, they settled in San Jose in a small town house. It was convenient for him as a base of operations and close enough to Stanford for Justine to commute. That was such a long time ago. Adele remembered that town house. She'd been there quite a few times as a little girl.

She remembered Justine had said Scott was excited that his wife was going to be a successful lawyer.

"That's all we want," he had said. "She'll knock 'em dead in the legal world, and I'll take care of all the domestic details."

That transition had been gradual, but eventually it led them to where they were now—Justine, a self-made woman with a high-paying corporate job and Scott, a stay-at-home dad and husband who worked part-time in a sporting goods outlet. He had been a volunteer EMT, played a lot of sports, loved hiking, kayaking, scuba diving, boating.

"What does Scott say about this?" Adele asked.

Justine shrugged. Then she said, "He'll support my decision." She straightened. "I wonder how difficult it would be to find a small family law practice looking for someone like me. Or to start my own practice—a one-woman practice."

"Has it ever occurred to Scott to get a serious job?" Adele asked. "I mean, forgive me, since I haven't had a serious job in my life."

Justine smiled patiently. "Your jobs have all been serious, and without you we'd have been lost. If you hadn't dedicated yourself to Mom's care, it would have cost our whole family a fortune. We're indebted to you. And I agree it would help if Scott worked more than part-time, but I think that ship sailed years ago. He's only worked part-time since Amber and Olivia came along."

Adele adored her nieces, ages sixteen and seventeen. She was much closer to them than she was to Justine.

"I'm sorry you're going through this," Adele said. "I wish there was something I could do."

"Well, the thing is, the future is looking very uncertain. I might need your help," Justine said.

"What could I do?" she asked.

"Adele, I don't like to push you, but you have to get it together. We have to make some decisions about what you're going to do, what we'll do with the house. I realize what I've given you for your hard work hasn't been much, but I don't know how long I can keep it up— paying for the maintenance on this house, the taxes, a modest income for you… I don't want to panic prematurely," Justine said. "Maybe I'll be able to work everything out without too much hassle, but if I run into trouble… Money could get very tight, Addie. All those promises I made—that I'd help financially while you fix up the house, that I'd give you my half of the proceeds when and if you sold it… I might not be able to come through. I know, I know, I promised you it would be yours after all of your sacrifice, but you wouldn't want me to ignore the girls' tuition or not be able to make the mortgage…"

"But Justine!" Adele said. "That's all I have! And I was considering finishing school myself!" Though if she was honest, she had no plans of any kind.

Justine reached out to her, squeezing her hand. "We're a long way from me needing money. I just felt it was only fair to tell you what's going on. If we're in this together, we can both make it. I swear, I will make this all work out. I'll make it right."

But as Adele knew, they had never really been "in it together" in the past, and they wouldn't be for very long in the future. Addie's dedication to their parents allowed Justine to devote herself to her career. For that matter, it should be Justine and Scott shoring each other up. At least until Justine had a better idea. But where was Scott today? Golfing? Biking? Bowling?

Adele realized she had some difficult realities to face. When she dropped out of school to help her mother care for her father, she wasn't being completely altruistic. She'd needed a place to run away to, hiding an unplanned pregnancy and covering her tattered heart. She'd never told her family that her married lover—her psychology professor—had broken down in tears when he explained he couldn't leave his wife to marry Adele, that the college would probably fire him for having an affair with a student. For her, going home was the only option.

At the time Justine and Scott had been riding the big wave and didn't lust after the small, old house in Half Moon Bay. That house was chump change to them. So, they worked out a deal. Adele had become her mother's guardian with a power of attorney. But the will had never been adjusted to reflect just one beneficiary rather than two. In the case of the death of both parents, Adele and Justine would inherit equal equity in the eighty-year-old house and anything left of the life insurance. At the time, of course, neither Adele nor Justine had ever considered the idea that Adele would be needed for very long. But before Adele knew it, eight years had been gobbled up. She was thirty-two and had been caring for her parents since she was twenty-four.

Adele, as guardian, could have escaped by turning over the house, pension, social security to a care facility for her mother and gone out on her own, finding herself a better job and her own place to live. She wasn't sure if it was her conscience or just inertia that held her in place for so long.

"I just wanted to make sure you understood the circumstances before anything more happens," Justine said. "And since you don't have any immediate plans, please don't list the house for sale or anything. Give me a chance to figure out what's next. I have children. I'll do whatever I can to protect them and you. They're your nieces! They love you so much. I'm sure you want them to get a good education as much as I do."

Does anyone want me to have a real chance to start over? Adele asked herself. This conversation sounded like Justine was pulling out of their deal.

"I'll think about this, but Scott has responsibilities, too," she pointed out.

"He's been out of the full-time workforce for so long…" Justine said.

"Just the same, we all have to live up to our adult commitments and responsibilities. And you've had a highfalutin job for a long time. You've made a lot of money. You can recover. I haven't even begun."

"I need your help, Addie," Justine said. "You need to come up with a plan, something we can put in motion. Make plans for your next step, put a little energy into this old house, make suggestions of what we should do with it, everything. Let's figure out what to do before I find myself short and unable to help. I'm sorry, but we have to move forward."

TWO

Justine's visit and her ominous predictions created a pretty dark day for Adele. Her head ached from her brow being furrowed all day. She hadn't even begun to figure out what she wanted to do next before Justine threw a wrench into everything. Addie was lost in deep thought; she took a couple of hours with a calculator, looking over the numbers. They were pretty bleak. It had been a consideration to get a home equity loan to improve the property before selling it, but if Justine couldn't swing it, how was Addie supposed to? She was pretty sure one had to have a job before being approved for a loan.

Addie had no money, no income, just what Justine provided. There was a little saved from the insurance, but without money from Justine, she was going to run out soon. How could her sister do this to her now? While Addie cared for their mother, Justine and her family had been to France and Italy and Scotland, not to mention many long weekend trips here and there. They had all the sports equipment under the sun and lived in a very nice house. And now, after Adele had put in eight years, Justine was warning her that she might pull the rug out from under her? How could she?

She tried to remember that Justine hadn't had it as easy as it all looked. Law school was a struggle for her, though in the end she graduated with honors. Then she worked long hours while Scott started to work shorter and shorter weeks. When Justine wanted a baby and didn't conceive, she saw infertility specialists and was thirty-five before being blessed with the birth of her daughter Amber. Then, like so many infertile women, she ignored birth control after Amber was born, thinking she just couldn't get pregnant. Olivia came eleven months after Amber.

Adele couldn't really remember all the details of Justine and Scott's early years together, but by the time her nieces were born when she was in high school, it was obvious that Scott made sure the girls got what they needed but he didn't go much further. Justine stopped at the store for groceries on her way home from work, sometimes at ten at night. She spent her days off doing laundry, and if she couldn't stay up until midnight working on briefs, she'd get up at four in the morning to work. And then Scott would criticize her for not working out and complain about the toll her long hours took on the family. But he somehow justified an expensive country club membership. Scott did most of the cooking, but it wasn't much of an effort. He didn't like labor-intensive meals after a rugged day of playing golf.

Adele witnessed a lot of those squabbles because she was a frequent babysitter when her nieces were little.

But none of that was Adele's fault! Now she feared Justine would go back on her promises and take advantage of her again.

She thought about canceling the movie date with Jake because she knew she wouldn't be good company, but she didn't have the heart after he'd been so sweet to offer. So she got dressed and was ready when he picked her up. "What are we going to see?" she asked when she got in the car.

"Anything you want. There are plenty of sexy leading men for you to choose from," he said. Then he grinned.

"Anything is fine."

So they chose the latest hit movie, bought popcorn and drinks, and she stared at the screen blankly. He asked her three times what was wrong, and three times she said she just had things on her mind. The movie was over before she'd really let herself enjoy it. Jake grabbed her hand and said, "Come on." He pulled her up and out of their row, out of the theater into the dimly lit hall that led to the lobby. "We're going to Maggio's. We'll get a dark booth in the back and talk. Whatever it is, it's better to get it out."

"What makes you say that? I'm a little moody, that's all. You've seen me—"

He was shaking his head. "You're not just moody," he said. "Any time you don't stare with big cow eyes at Bradley Cooper, the man you hope to marry, we've got us a problem. So, we'll go have a little wine. Maybe some pasta or pizza but wine for sure."

She raised a brow. "You think you're going to get me loose and talking?"

He nodded. "As only a good friend could."

They drove to Maggio's, a little hole-in-the-wall Italian pizzeria. It was one of his favorite places. Jake pulled his truck into a small parking lot behind the restaurant. They did a huge take-out business, but there was a small dining room with only eight booths. It was compact, each booth could hold six people so the maximum they could serve wasn't even fifty, and in all the years Adele had known about the restaurant, it had never been full. The front of the store, where people picked up their meals or pizzas, was always hopping, and there were a couple of tables on the wide sidewalk where people could sit outside in nice weather.

Adele and Jake entered through the back door because Jake knew the owners and most of the staff. People hollered "Hey, Jake" or waved a hand in their direction. They slipped into the restaurant and found a booth near the back. Adele loved that it was dimly lit and decorated with plastic grapes. They slid into the booth and sat across from each other.

"Hey, Jake," the waitress said, slapping down a couple of napkins. "Haven't seen you in a long time."

"It hasn't been that long, has it?" he returned. "You know my friend Adele, don't you?"

"Yeah, sure, how you doin'? And what can I start you off with?"

"A glass of cabernet for me," Addie said.

"Same," Jake said. "And we'll look at the menu for a while."

"I bet you know it by heart, Jake," she said, smiling prettily into his eyes. "I'll be right back."

"All the women in town like you," Adele said. "Why don't you ever take any of them out?"

"They don't all like me," he said. "And Bonnie, there, I think she's been married a bunch of times."

"Really?" Adele asked.

"Well, at least twice. Been there, done that."

Adele remembered too well—it was a scandal in the neighborhood at the time. Jake was in his midtwenties, Adele still in high school, when he married Mary Ellen. It didn't go well. Jake's mother complained to Adele's mother that there was a lot of bickering, and in no time Mary Ellen had become Jake's unhappy wife. Though she never missed a word of their mothers' gossip, the only thing she actually *saw* was that her friend Jake was suddenly alone, miserable, brokenhearted and inconsolable. Mary Ellen left him after a year, and they were divorced by two years. She had now passed her third divorce, been with numerous men she hadn't married and was said to be keeping company with a much older guy who left his wife of almost forty years for her.

"Yeah, I'd love to know what happened there, if only to understand it," Adele said. Jake was handsome, sweet natured, smart and most importantly, kind. His market was like the cornerstone of the older section of Half Moon Bay. He'd served on the city council for a couple of years and was greatly respected. By comparison, Mary Ellen was attractive but not very smart. But she must have some serious skills—she certainly had no trouble getting a guy though she did have a short attention span. Adele suspected an abundance of phero-mones. She also seemed to be cunning.

"Maybe when I understand what happened, I'll share," Jake said.

Their drinks came, they ordered a pizza to share and Jake went in for the kill. "How about if you tell me why you didn't drool over Bradley," Jake said.

She told him Justine had come by for a brief visit, complaining about having some job and therefore financial issues, and that she might not be helping out as much as Adele had expected. "It emphasized all the things I haven't done," she said. "I was going to change my life, you know—starting with a makeover of myself and the house. Neither has had much attention for the past few years. I was waiting for the inspiration to kick in."

"We've been over this," Jake said. "You have plenty of time for all that. And *you* don't need a makeover. The house could use a little paint, but other than that…"

"I haven't even made a list," she said. "I kept thinking I was making plans but they were just fantasies. Plans require at least a list. Not to mention the purchase of a bucket of paint…"

"Well then, let's talk about what you'd like to do and you can go home and make a list, but Addie, stuff like this doesn't usually cause you to ignore a good movie. Or—" The pizza arrived just as he finished his thought. "Or ignore your best guy, Bradley." He peeled off a piece of pizza and gestured toward her plate. "I can help with this, you know. I remodeled my mother's house, and I've done a lot of my own work in my house."

"You're so busy," she said, chomping off a mouthful of pizza.

"Even if I'm not available to pound nails or paint trim, I know a lot of contractors, who to call, where to find them, and if you ever run into a problem—I know how to talk to them. You never saw my mother's house after I did the kitchen and both bathrooms. Damn good for a grocer, if you ask me."

"I'm sorry, Jake. I should have gone to your mom's to see your work. I'll be sure to go now. She always came to see my mom, to read to her."

"You know she enjoyed that," he said. "Sometimes she spends an hour at the store, visiting, talking to shoppers. I'd see one thing in her cart, but just couldn't get her to leave. I told her I could bring her what she needs, but walking to the store is good for her. I won't complain until she starts coming in five times a day, and then—"

His voice faded to a low buzz as something caught Adele's eye. The couple in the front left booth, sitting together so they faced the front door, backs to Adele, leaned their heads together for a deep kiss. The man's reddish-brown hair curled around his collar, just a little long. The woman's short white-blond hair was teased up all spiky in a slightly dated style.

Then Adele's brain started to play tricks on her. It looked like Scott, her brother-in-law, his tongue down the woman's throat, his hand cupping the back of her head. They broke apart, laughed into each other's open mouths and she stroked his cheek briefly, saying something that made him kiss her open mouth again. It *was* Scott. He must think that even though Adele lived in

Half Moon Bay, she would never be out on a Saturday night, having a pizza. It was a good bet, since that was a very rare occurrence. Adele would have pizza delivered. And a date? Forget about it.

Then Scott and the unknown woman became other people as a very old and painful memory rose to the surface. Hadley and his wife materialized in their place. Hadley, her psychology professor, with whom she'd had a steamy affair. She'd taken the class because he was so hot. Hadley, the father of her baby. He had told her it was impossible for him to leave the wife he claimed to hate, to marry Adele. He told her the university might fire him for falling in love with a student. They decided she would terminate the pregnancy. He would then divorce his wife, they'd have a fresh start, begin to date as if the affair and the baby had never happened. They'd marry and eventually have a family. Everything would be fine and they'd live happily-ever-after. And she'd been naive enough to believe him.

She did what many a woman her age would do—she drove by Hadley's house a dozen times a week. Then one morning she saw what she should have known she would see. He stood in the doorway with his beautiful blonde wife, an arm around her waist. She still wore a robe or dressing gown. There was a small blond child holding on to his leg. The child was also beautiful. Angelic. Hadley's wife had a small baby bump. Hadley pulled her against him and covered her lips in a loving kiss. A deep and long kiss. One of his hands cradled her head while the other ran smoothly over the bump.

Hadley wasn't kissing his wife as though he was planning on getting a divorce.

Adele was supposed to have an abortion while Hadley got the gears moving on his separation and divorce. He said he'd try to scrape up some money for the procedure, but he couldn't be obvious about it or his wife wouldn't let him go. They would have to be discreet.

Eight years later, she still couldn't believe she'd bought those lies. She didn't go through with the abortion but her baby slipped away, stillborn. And Hadley never came looking for her. While she cared for her parents and mourned the loss of her son, she'd heard he was suspected of other affairs with students.

Scott and the woman he was with materialized again. The bastard was stepping out on her sister. She briefly thought about rushing over to them and pouring something over their heads, like a pitcher of beer. Luckily, she didn't have anything like that on hand.

She noticed out of the corner of her eye that Jake looked at her, looked in the direction of her stare, looked back at her. Her mouth was open and gaping, and a large piece of pizza drooped limply in her hand.

"Addie?" he asked.

"Shit," she muttered. She closed her mouth and looked at him. "Jake, I need a favor. Can we get a box for the pizza and leave? Right now? I can explain when we're in the truck."

"Something happened," he said. "What happened?"

"Shh," she said, hushing him. "Can you go back to the kitchen, ask for a box, pay the bill and get me out of here? Quietly?" she whispered. "The guy in the front booth with the blonde—that's my brother-in-law. And that is not my sister he's making out with."

Jake couldn't resist. He looked again. "Whoa," he said, probably recognizing Scott at last. Then he slid out of the booth and made tracks to the kitchen. He was back with a box very quickly, and they transferred the pizza into it.

"I hope everything was okay," Bonnie said as they were leaving.

"Oh, it was fine, I just remembered I left the stove on," Adele said with a smile. By the time she got to Jake's truck, she felt weak. When he got in and closed his door, she was shaking. "That bastard!"

"What's he doing here?" Jake asked. "He lives in San Jose, right?"

She held out her hands, examining her trembling fingers. "He probably thinks no one knows him here, which except for me, maybe no one does. And he probably thinks I'd never be out for the evening, because what are the odds? While my sister is home worrying about her job, her husband is out deep kissing some woman—"

"Cat," Jake said.

"Huh?"

"Cat Brooks. She owns that kayak and snorkel shop on the beach. Cat's Place. It should make a killing, but it's been through three or four owners in the last dozen years. I think she owns it with her brother or something."

"Well, that makes sense," Adele said. "Scott works part-time at a sporting goods store in San Jose where he gets a discount on all the gear he can stuff into his car. That's what he does—plays. He loves to kayak. And golf and scuba dive and play ball and you name it. I bet his salary doesn't even cover the cost of his toys. Justine works such long hours, he complains that she works so much and this is what he does instead."

Jake put his truck in Reverse and backed out of the lot.

"And I'll have to tell her," Adele said.

"You have to?" he asked. "Why do you have to?"

"Come on!" she said. "I can't let Justine get caught unaware! Telling her now might not even help. Clearly he's into something serious, and he can't support himself and his fun times. Justine has been the primary breadwinner for at least twenty of their twenty-eight-year marriage! And he has the nerve to complain about her hours. As if the income would just materialize while she took time off to entertain him. Oh! I want to kill him right now!"

"Addie, don't do anything too soon here," Jake said. "I've seen it before. She might hate you for telling her."

"Now why would she do that?" Adele asked.

He took a breath. "It was Marty who told me Mary Ellen was cheating. I hit him in the face."

"Because you didn't believe him?"

"No. Because he ruined the illusion I had that I could make it work in the end. It was like a knife to the heart. It was in that instant I knew it was over. And it was going to get ugly."

"I'll tell you what's going to get ugly—me driving to San Jose."

* * *

Justine felt confident she'd made an impression on Adele. Surely her younger sister would finally get serious about getting her life on track so that Justine wouldn't feel obligated to support her forever. Just from looking at the comparable sales in the area, she judged the house to be worth roughly six hundred thousand, and it was paid off, free and clear. If she could get her own Realtor and decorator involved in cleaning up and staging the property, it could be worth more. She'd worry about how to scrape up the money to help in that effort later.

Adele would probably have to put off going back to school for a little while. She had to get a job. Justine was determined to make it up to her. Somehow. Eventually.

It was true that her company was struggling right now, downsizing here and there, and the stress was overwhelming. But she was hoping she could repair her real problem before she talked to anyone about it.

Scott had informed her that he didn't love her anymore. He was sorry but he couldn't help it. He didn't have much hope for the marriage; he thought it might be best if they broke up. He wanted to cash out. She was holding him back, expecting too much from him.

She was completely caught off guard. She had been asking him to apply himself a little more to what she thought had been a pretty satisfactory partnership. Their relationship was hardly perfect, but then whose was?

They'd been seeing a marriage counselor for three months, and she had no grasp of how that was working out. Some days Scott would say, *I think we're making progress here—I know I'm feeling better about things.* Other days he'd grumble that she wasn't really involved in the marriage, or their family life for that matter. He told her she was "emotionally unavailable" too often. "When was the last time you watched me play ball?" he asked. "When was the last time we went to a movie?"

Her work was very difficult and demanding, what more could she say? If she wanted to keep her job, she had to be on top of it. She worked sixty hours a week and brought work home, as well.

It was when he started saying things like, "I feel like I have a hole in my heart," and "I'm not really living, just existing," she began to suspect there was another woman. Those were women's words. Scott didn't say things like that. In fact, he had trouble sitting through a chick flick with dialogue like that. It made him roll his eyes. Now he was saying those things to her with a straight face.

In their thirty years together, two dating and twenty-eight married, she had suspected there were other women now and then, but there was never any clear evidence. Just a name that came up too frequently, that faraway look in his eye, a very unreliable schedule. He'd go MIA for a while. During their first decade of marriage, he traveled all the time while he was in sales. She'd had trouble getting pregnant and blamed his travel schedule. When she passed the bar, he was more than happy to take a less demanding, less lucrative job to improve their odds at reproduction. Seventeen years ago she had Amber and eleven months later, Olivia. He was a stay-at-home dad and she was so happy;

her baby daughters were everything to her. She was a successful businesswoman with a supportive husband and two beautiful daughters. She didn't have a jealous bone in her body.

But she had to work. She was the bread and butter of the family. Getting home to her husband and babies was her reward for every hard penny she earned. She was successful, Scott urging her on every day while he stayed home and planned their vacations. In more recent years when he had so much time on his hands because the girls were self-sufficient and he only worked part-time, she never wondered where he was—he was busy every minute. They texted and spoke several times every day.

Maybe she should have worried sooner. Now she didn't know what to do. She had asked him about other women and he'd said, "Don't be ridiculous." That wasn't a real answer, was it? Should she get a detective? It was a thought. She didn't know what she would do, how she would live. What would the girls say? Do? Would Scott try to take them from her? They adored him. Would they want to be with her, when she worked sixty-hour weeks?

At first she thought she couldn't let him leave. She didn't know how she'd get by. It never once occurred to her that her life might be slightly less tense without him constantly keeping score on her hours and familial contributions.

Now that she thought about it, Scott had always been a lot of emotional work. It wasn't easy trying to get a law degree while making sure she was always a good wife. True, she couldn't do all the wifely chores and work as an attorney, but a good balance was that she made enough money for a weekly cleaning lady. What she did do was never mention she was the breadwinner, never minimize his contributions. She took time to praise his every effort, compliment his mind and frequently mention how stimulating she found him, scream with joy during mediocre sex. It wasn't until he said he no longer loved her that she realized the enormous emotional weight of that effort.

Scott ran the house and made sure the girls got to school and every extracurricular activity, lesson or practice. Now that Amber was driving, he had even more free time. It took him roughly two hours a day to do his chores—she still did the laundry, stopped for groceries on the way home, cleaned the kitchen after dinner. The hours left over—some six or more a day—he could devote to biking, kayaking, working out, running, hiking, swimming or various sports training. He was a member of two bowling leagues and one baseball team. He watched hours of sports on TV, most of it recorded for later. He worked part-time at the sporting goods outlet off and on, never more than twenty hours in a week.

How dare he not love me, she thought angrily. *If anything, I shouldn't love him!*

There was a time Adele was an adventurous soul, like back in college and grad school. But for the past six to eight years, she'd done little driving, staying close to home, rarely leaving Half Moon Bay.

This was an old town, originally called Spanishtown

and settled before the gold rush, officially becoming Half Moon Bay in the late 1800s. The history of the town was carefully preserved. It was a sweet town on the ocean that attracted tourists. This part of San Mateo County was known for farming of vegetables and flowers, surfing and other water sports, a quaint and quiet getaway filled with and surrounded by beautiful state parks, redwoods and wonderful beaches. It got its name from the crescent-shaped harbor just north of the city.

Addie thought of it as calm, sometimes too calm. Maybe a little old-fashioned and stifling. When she was young, she couldn't wait to knock the dust from that little old town off her shoes, to get out and enjoy the freedom of college in a bigger city. Now that she'd been held hostage there for eight years, she was nearly phobic about leaving.

But leave she would, if only for the day. She wasn't going to let Justine down, even though it appeared Justine would let her down. They might not be the closest of sisters but if Adele had one shining trait, she was fiercely loyal. She thought she was more loyal to Justine than Justine was to her, but that was okay. She believed that what goes around comes around and she'd invest now, hope for good things to follow.

Plus there was Amber and Olivia, and Addie loved them.

Adele called Justine first thing in the morning. "I know we just talked yesterday but I need to see you, in person, alone, as soon as possible. I'll drive to San Jose if necessary, but it would be better if you came here. I don't want to try to talk to you with the girls or Scott around. It's a very private matter."

"What's bothering you, Addie?" Justine asked.

Of course Justine would think it was Adele who had the problem, that it was something she was embarrassed to share or have anyone overhear. "We have to talk. It's urgent. Please decide where we should do it."

Justine sighed into the phone. It was clear she couldn't imagine Addie having a truly urgent issue of any kind.

"I have a lot to do today. Are you sure this can't wait?"

"I'm afraid it can't. Do you want to meet somewhere or what?"

"Can you come to me? Scott's playing golf and won't be home until after two. Amber and Olivia are both busy with friends, and I expect they'll be gone all day. If you come to me, at least I can get a few things done in the time I would have spent driving."

"Okay," Adele said in a shaky breath. She hated the freeway. And left turns. And other cars. She hadn't driven to San Jose, forty miles away, in years and she recalled it as traumatic. In fact, she hadn't driven out of Half Moon Bay in a couple of years. She was used to getting teased about it.

"Wow," Justine said. "This must be important."

"It is."

Adele thought about the one time Justine had really come through for her—when she was brokenhearted, pregnant and alone. Justine was supportive and non-judgmental.

"These things happen, kiddo," she'd said. "But you're doing the right thing. Adoption is a good option."

"If I can make myself go through with it," Adele had said. "I feel him moving and I want to hold him."

"Of course you do. And women do raise their children without fathers all the time. But if you're serious about that, there are legal ways to make the father responsible. He can pay support. Just think about it. I can help."

But that option had been taken away from her when the baby didn't survive. It was Justine who showered her with sympathy, paid for the mortuary and cemetery costs, held her while she cried and encouraged her to grieve, get counseling and try to move on. For that compassion, Adele would be forever grateful.

She did love and admire Justine. She was also quite jealous, an emotion she fought constantly. It was just that until she saw Scott misbehaving, she thought Justine had everything, beautiful home, perfect daughters, happy marriage, great career. She had been so lost in thought that she was almost surprised when she pulled up to her older sister's house. She had managed the drive without incident.

She looked up and admired the place. It wasn't an estate or anything, but it was so much larger than the house they grew up in, plus it was relatively new—about fifteen years old. The kitchen was spacious, the great room was grand and welcoming and overlooked a small but beautiful pool and meticulously groomed yard. There were five bedrooms and as many baths, and the third port in the garage was stacked with sporting gear—skis, paddleboards, kayaks, golf clubs, et cetera. Justine and the girls also had skis and bikes and paddleboards, but the gear was by and large Scott's.

Now she wasn't sure what Justine was up against. Did Justine know her husband was unfaithful?

Justine opened the front door to greet her with a frown. "Oh jeez, you're pale. Come in. You know, now that you're officially off the caretaking job, you might want to broaden your territory. Do more driving, go farther, get your confidence back, put yourself out there."

"I will," Adele said, as she had been saying to herself for more than a couple of months.

"Let's go sit on the patio," Justine said. "I made a fresh pot of coffee and I have some cookies."

"I was going to give up cookies," Adele said. "Maybe I'll start tomorrow."

Adele sat at the patio table and let Justine serve the coffee, which seemed like the last thing she needed. She was jittery enough, and not from the drive on the crowded California freeway. Even on Sunday morning it was like bumper cars, but she'd managed it just fine.

"You going to spit it out?" Justine asked. "So we can spend what time we have figuring it out, whatever it is?"

"Scott is cheating on you," Addie blurted. "I saw him."

Justine jerked in dubious surprise, her chin lowering as did her brow. She frowned. "You saw him having sex?"

"No. I—"

"You'd better be specific. And very sure of what you're saying because this is serious."

"Oh, I know it is. I went for a pizza with Jake Bronski last night. Maggio's. Do you even remember it?"

Justine nodded gravely.

"Eight booths in the dining room. We went in the back door because Jake knows everyone there. We had just gotten a glass of wine when I noticed the couple two booths ahead and to the left. They were sitting side by side facing the front, maybe watching the front entry. They probably thought they were alone since we snuck in the back. They were kissing. Kissing like they couldn't stop. Like they really needed a room."

Justine was quiet for a long moment. "Kissing?"

"Powerful, desperate, crazy kissing. Like in the movies kissing. Mouths open, devour—"

Justine held up a hand to stop her. "Was there any evidence of an affair? Or was it just kissing?"

"Seriously? *Just?*" Addie laughed, though not in humor. "I never thought to follow them. You have a provision for movie-star kissing in the marriage contract?"

"Okay, thanks for telling me," Justine said, as if she couldn't bear to hear any more. "I can take it from here. And if you think of anything else…"

"I know who she is. Well, Jake knows who she is. The woman who owns that kayak rental shack near the ocean, down the bike path past the beach bar. Her name is Cat Brooks. She's not very pretty."

Justine seemed to wince ever so slightly. "Thanks."

"What are you going to do?"

"I don't know. But I know how this will turn out. Scott is caught kissing outside of our marriage and we're going to fight about it, quietly so the girls don't hear, then he's going to grovel, beg for forgiveness, make a lot of promises about his perfect future behavior, then things will be tense for a while and he'll invest a lot in flowers and maybe a little jewelry and then it will be over. It will pass."

"It sounds like you've been down this road before…"

"Except for the getting caught part. He's never been caught before, but we've had the discussion…"

"Why? He must have done something if you talked about it?"

"There were a few times I wondered if he was lying to me about where he'd been. You know—the timing was just off or his story would change. And he couldn't be reached… Didn't answer his phone. There was some texting with this woman or that—but I didn't see anything real damning. Still… It's not like I have a lot of time to chase him around, but if the girls can't reach him and call me… Don't worry about this. We'll get it straightened out."

"Do you think he's having an affair?" Addie asked, grabbing one of the cookies and taking a big bite.

"I suppose it's possible, but honestly I doubt it. Scott is very critical of men who step out on their wives. But believe me, I'll conduct a thorough interview. It's one of my particular skills." Then she smiled. Weakly.

"Where was he supposed to be last night?"

"A bowling tournament. He's in two leagues. I guess there's been some lying. I will find out how much."

Adele wasn't buying that smile. "You can talk to me, you know."

"Thank you, honey. That's very sweet. I'm sure we'll

work this out quickly. And I won't tell him where I got the information."

Justine spoke as if Adele couldn't possibly be experienced enough to help her through this, to be a confidante.

"I suspect he was in Half Moon Bay because she lives there and he never thought he'd see me," Adele said. "I hardly leave the house."

"You're going to have to change that, Addie. It's not good for you."

"Yeah," she said, noting how quickly the subject changed to her. "I'll get right on that."